# Praise for Patricia Gaffney and her novels

"Patricia Gaffney writes with power and passion. . . . She is one of the finest writers to come along in years."—*Romantic Times*

## Forever and Ever

"Powerful. . . . Her superb writing and character psychology is much in evidence here. This is a strong novel, with an affecting situation, compelling characters and fine writing."
—The Romance Reader

"An exquisitely moving and beautifully rendered love story . . . as magical and glorious as a reader could desire. The stunning intensity of this love [story] will hold you captive from first page to last, and *Forever and Ever* will linger in your heart."
—*Romantic Times*

"The third and final of Ms. Gaffney's books set in the imaginary village of Wyckerley in Victorian times is surely her best, and that is saying something as the other two are excellent—keeping her firmly in the top echelon of romance writers."     —*Rendezvous*

"This touching story, filled with sensual tension, runs the emotional gamut, culminating with love winning over pride and ambition."          —*Publishers Weekly*

"Simply glorious."                    —Nora Roberts

"Lovely writing and a story that is honestly and passionately told."
—*Romance Forever*

continued . . .

### To Love and To Cherish

"Magnificent! Powerful, beautifully written, and as deeply moving as it is richly romantic . . . destined to become a classic."
—Mary Jo Putney

"A beautiful story that tugs at the heartstrings. A powerful tale of love and faith." —*Romantic Times*

### To Have and To Hold

"Compelling and sophisticated." —Virginia Henley

"Patricia Gaffney writes with power and passion."
—*Romantic Times*

### The Saving Graces

"Anyone who's ever raised a glass to toast her woman friends will love this book—its raw emotion, its rueful humor, its life lessons." —*The New Orleans Times-Picayune*

"This ode to the friendships between women could easily become the northern version of *Divine Secrets of the Ya-Ya Sisterhood*." —*Booklist*

"A jewel of a book and every facet sparkles." —Nora Roberts

"Rich, lovely . . . an intimate portrayal of friendships through the eyes of four unforgettable women. I hated to put it down!"
—Michael Lee West

*continued . . .*

### Sweet Everlasting

"A romance of immense beauty and emotional power . . . exquisite!"
—*Romantic Times*

"A beautiful, tender love story, evoking your senses and stirring your emotions. It will renew your faith in unselfish love."
—*Rendezvous*

### Crooked Hearts

"With a lyrical voice and keen wit, Patricia Gaffney weaves compelling stories that echo in the human heart." —Nora Roberts

"Absolutely marvelous . . . it's been a long time since I read a book this wonderful. I loved it." —Joan Johnston

### Outlaw in Paradise

"Sophisticated, humorous . . . a delightful, mature romance that brings readers a unique look at the Wild West."
—*Romantic Times*

"Lively [and] exceptionally well-written." —*Library Journal*

### Wild at Heart

"Delightfully different . . . *Wild at Heart* brims with laughter and passion." —*The Literary Times*

"Wonderful and enlightening. . . . Ms. Gaffney once more stretches the boundaries of the genre as only a premier writer can do." —*Romantic Times*

# Forever and Ever

Patricia Gaffney

NEW AMERICAN LIBRARY

*For James Holmes Gaffney,*
*the world's greatest dad*

NEW AMERICAN LIBRARY
Published by New American Library, a division of
Penguin Putnam Inc., 375 Hudson Street,
New York, New York 10014, U.S.A.
Penguin Books Ltd, 80 Strand,
London WC2R 0RL, England
Penguin Books Australia Ltd, 250 Camberwell Road,
Camberwell, Victoria 3124, Australia
Penguin Books Canada Ltd, 10 Alcorn Avenue,
Toronto, Ontario, Canada M4V 3B2
Penguin Books (N.Z.) Ltd, Cnr Rosedale and Airborne Roads,
Albany, Auckland 1310, New Zealand

Penguin Books Ltd, Registered Offices:
Harmondsworth, Middlesex, England

First published by New American Library, a division of Penguin Putnam Inc.
Previously published in a Topaz edition.

First New American Library Trade Paperback Printing, April 2003
10 9 8 7 6 5 4 3 2 1

Set in Fairfield Light

Printed in the United States of America

# I

The tower clock on All Saints Church struck the quarter hour with a resonating thud. Connor Pendarvis, who had been leaning against the stone ledge of a bridge and staring down at the River Wyck, straightened impatiently. Jack was late. Again. He ought to be used to it by now—and he was, but that didn't make his brother's habitual tardiness any less aggravating.

At least he didn't have to wait for Jack in the rain. In typical South Devon fashion, the afternoon had gone from gray to fair in a matter of minutes, and now the glitter of sunlight on the little river's sturdy current was blinding. It was June, and the clean air smelled like honeysuckle. Birds sang, bees buzzed, irises in brilliant yellow clumps bloomed along the riverbank. The cottages lining the High Street sported fresh coats of daub in whimsical pastel shades, and every garden was a riot of summer flowers.

The Rhadamanthus Society's report on Wyckerley had said it was a poky, undistinguished hamlet in a poor parish, but Connor disagreed. He thought the authors of the report must have an odd idea of what constituted poverty—either that or they'd never been to Trewythiel, the village in Cornwall where *he'd* grown up. Wyckerley was friendly, pretty, neat as a pin—Trewythiel's opposite in every way. Connor had been born there, and one by one he'd watched his family die there. Before he was twenty, he'd buried all of them.

All except Jack. And here he came, swaggering a little. Even from here Connor could see the telltale glitter in his eyes; it meant he'd recently downed a pint or two or three in Wyckerley's one and only alehouse, the George and Dragon. But his thinness and the gaunt gray concavity of his cheeks stifled anything reproachful Connor might have said, and instead he felt that squeeze of pain in his chest that overtook him at odd times. Jack wasn't even thirty yet, but he looked at least ten years older. The doctor in Redruth had said his illness was under control, so worrying about him made no sense. Connor told himself that every day, but it didn't do any good. Fear for his brother was as dark and constant as his own shadow.

"Don't be glaring at me," Jack commanded from twenty feet away. "I've brought yer ruddy letter, and there'm money in it, I can tell. Which makes me the bearer o' glad tidings." Producing an envelope from the pocket of his scruffy coat, he handed it over with a flourish. "Now, where's my thanks?"

"I'd say you've already drunk it." But he said it with a smile, because Jack could charm the red from a rose—and because he was right about the envelope; it had a nice, solid heft that said the Pendarvis boys wouldn't go hungry tonight in Wyckerley.

"Open it up yonder, Con. Under the trees. Cooler."

"Are you tired, Jack?"

"Naw. What I am is *hot*."

Connor said no more, and they ambled toward a clump of oak trees at the edge of the village green, opposite the old Norman church. But it was warm in the afternoon sun, not hot, and he knew it was the support of the iron bench under the oaks Jack wanted, not the cool shade.

"The George is a rare friendly place," he remarked as they went.

"Is it, now."

"Oh, indeed. The ale's fine, and there'm a gel who serves it called Rose. I think she fancies me."

Connor rolled his eyes. "Jack, we've been in the town for two hours. You can't have made a conquest already."

"Can't I?" He flashed a wicked grin. Only a year ago the white of his teeth would have lit up his healthy, ruddy-cheeked face, and the twinkle in his eyes could have compromised a nun. Now the skin stretched tight over the bones of his jaw, and his smile looked skeletal. Cadaverous. "She fancies me, see if she don't. I telled 'er I'd come back tonight wi' my little brother, and she could pick between us."

"Hah."

"Hah! Oh, 'tis a fine enough place even for you, yer honor. The mugs're clean, and nobody spits on the floor. I'll tell the men they must watch their coarse language, for there'm a barrister among 'em."

Connor snorted. Once he'd had dreams of becoming a lawyer, but they had died a long time ago. He would laugh when Jack called him "your worship" or "your honor" for a joke, but under the careless pose lay a regret so deep, he had stopped thinking about it.

Under the trees, sunlight played on the grass in dappled patterns, shifting with the breeze. Connor stretched his long legs out, watching Jack do the same. Jack was taller, older, and until he'd gotten sick, a good deal stronger. When they were boys, he'd always been the leader, the caretaker. Now their roles had reversed, and they both hated it. Couldn't speak of it. Ironic that, for the last few months, they'd even changed names.

"So," said Jack, spreading his arms out across the back of the bench, "how much have the Rhads coughed up this time?"

The plain envelope bore no return address. Connor opened it and thumbed through the banknotes inside the folded, one-page letter. "Enough to cover the note of deposit I've just signed for our new lodgings."

"Well, that's a relief for you, counselor. Now you won't get pinched for false misrepresentation o' personal fiduciary stature." Jack chortled at his own humor; he never got tired of making up names for laws and statutes, the sillier sounding the better.

Connor said, "I had to pay the agent for the lease of six months. Forty-six shillings." It wasn't Connor's money, but it still seemed a waste, since they wouldn't be in Wyckerley past two months at the most.

"What's our new place like, then?"

"Better than the last. We've half of a workingmen's cottage only a mile from the mine. We'll share a kitchen with two other miners, and there's a girl who comes in the afternoons to cook a meal. And praise the Lord, we've each got a room this time, so I won't have to listen to you snore the glazing out of the windows."

Jack cackled, going along with the joke. There were times when he kept Connor awake, but it was because of his cough and the drenching night sweats that robbed him of rest, not his snoring. "What do they say about the mine?"

"Not much. It's called Guelder. A woman owns it. It's been fairly—"

"A *woman*." Jack's eyes went wide with amazement, then narrowed in scorn. "A woman," he muttered, shaking his head. "Well, ee've got yer work cut out right and proper, then, 'aven't ee? The radical Rhads'll be aquiver wi' joy when they read yer report this time."

Connor grunted. "The woman's name is Deene. She inherited the mine from her father about two years ago, and she owns it outright, without shareholders. They say her uncle owns another mine in the district. His name's Vanstone, and he happens to be the mayor of Wyckerley."

"Why'nt they send you to that un? The uncle's, I mean. 'Tis bound to be far better run."

"Probably, and there's your answer. The society hasn't employed me to investigate clean, safe, well-managed copper mines." No, but the selection process was still fair, Connor believed, if only because conditions in most Cornish and Devonian copper mines were so deplorable, there was no need to doctor reports or tinker with findings. Or pick a woman's mine over a man's in hopes of finding more deficiencies.

He put the envelope in his pocket and clasped his hands behind his head, blinking up at the sky. He'd have no more afternoons to loll away on a bench in the sunshine after today—he hoped; even this brief hour of idleness was making him restless. If Jack weren't here, he'd be settled into the new cottage by now, unpacked, outlining his report or scouting the neighborhood, maybe planning an article he had in mind for the Rhadamanthus Society's monthly broadsheet. "Slow down," Jack was always telling him, "stop and look about you every onct in a while. Sleep late, Con, have a drink. Take a woman."

Fine advice if a man had nothing better to do, or if he could look around at the wicked world and honestly say he wouldn't change anything. But Connor wasn't that man. Too much was expected of him—he expected too much of himself. Slowing down never crossed his mind unless Jack made an issue of it, and then it always took him by surprise. What a foolish way to squander your one short life.

But the June afternoon was lazily spectacular, and he couldn't deny that it was pleasant to sit in the shade while butterflies flickered in and out of sun rays slanting down through the tree leaves. In a rare mellow mood, he watched two children burst from a side door in the church across the way and run toward the green. A second later, out came three more, then four, then another giggling pair. Shouting, laughing, they skipped and ran in circles and tumbled on the grass, giddy as March hares. He'd have thought Sunday school had just let out, except it was Saturday. The children's high spirits were contagious—more than one passerby paused in the cobbled street long enough to smile at their frolicking.

Half a minute later, a young woman came out the same door in the church and hurried across the lane toward the green. The schoolteacher? Tall, slim, dressed in white, she had blond hair tied up in a knot on top of her head. Connor tried to guess her age, but it was hard to tell from this distance; she had the lithe body of a girl, but the confident, self-assured manner of a woman. He wasn't a bit surprised when she clapped her hands, and every shrieking, skipping child immediately ran to her. What surprised him was the gay sound of her own laughter mingling with theirs.

The smallest child, a girl of five or six, leaned against the teacher's hip familiarly; the woman patted her curly head while she gave the others some soft-voiced command. The children formed a half circle around her. She bent down to the little girl's level to say something in her ear, her hand lightly resting on the child's shoulder.

"Look at that, now, Con. That's a winsome sight, isn't it?" said Jack in a low, appreciative voice. "Isn't that just how a lady oughter look?"

Where women were concerned, Jack was the least discriminating man Connor had ever known: he liked *all* of them. But this time he'd spoken no more than the truth. This woman's ivory gown, her willowy figure, the sunny gold in her hair—they made a most beguiling picture. And yet he thought Jack meant something more . . . something about the long, graceful curve of her back as she bent toward the child, the solicitousness of her posture, the *kindness* in it that took the simple picture out of the ordinary and made it unforgettable. When Connor glanced at his brother, he saw the same soft, stricken smile he could feel on his own face, and he knew they'd been moved equally, just for a moment, by the perfection of the picture.

She straightened then, and the little girl skipped away to a place in the middle of the semicircle. The spell was broken, but the picture lingered, and the image still shimmered in his mind's eye.

She took something from the pocket of her dress—a pitch pipe. She brought it to her lips and blew a soft, thin note. The children hummed obediently, then burst into song.

> Do you know how many children
> Rise each morning blithe and gay?
> Can you count their jolly voices,

Singing sweetly day by day?
God hears all the happy voices,
In their merry songs rejoices.
And he loves them, every one.

Smiling encouragement, her face animated, the music teacher moved her hands in time to the melody, and every child beamed back at her, eager to please, all wide eyes and happy faces. It was like a scene in a storybook, or a sentimental play about good children and perfectly kind teachers, too good to be true—yet it was happening here, now, on the little green in the village of Wyckerley, St. Giles' parish. Mesmerized, Connor sat back to watch what would happen next.

The choir sang another song, and afterward the teacher made them sing it again. He wasn't surprised; smitten as he was, even he could tell it hadn't been their finest effort. Then, sensing her charges were growing restless, she set them free after some gentle admonition—which fell on deaf ears, because the shouting and gamboling recommenced almost immediately.

"Looks like a litter o' new puppies," Jack chuckled, and Connor nodded, smiling at the antics of two little towheaded boys, twins, vying with each other to see who could press more dandelions into the hands of their pretty teacher. Heedless of the damp grass, she dropped to her knees and sniffed the straggly bouquets with exaggerated admiration. Her way of keeping their rambunctious spirits within bounds was to ask them questions, then listen to the answers with complete absorption.

Just then the curly-haired little girl, clutching her own flower, made a running leap and landed on the teacher's back with a squeal of delight. The woman bore the impact sturdily, even when the youngster wound her arms around her neck and hung on tight, convulsed with mirth. But gradually the laughter tapered off.

"She'm caught," Jack murmured when some of the children crept closer, looking uncertain. "The lady's hair, looks like." Connor was already on his feet. "Con? Wait, now. Ho, Con! You shouldn't oughter—"

He didn't hear the rest. Impulsiveness was one of his most dangerous failings, but this—this was too much like the answer to a prayer he'd been too distracted to say. He took off across the green at a sprint.

No doubt about it, the teacher was caught. "It's all right, Birdie," she was saying, reaching back to try to disentangle her hair from something on the little girl's dress. "Don't wriggle for a second. No, it's all right, just don't move."

Birdie was near tears. "I'm sorry, Miss Sophie," she kept saying, worried but unable to stop squirming. The music teacher winced—then laughed, pretending it was a joke.

The other children eyed Connor in amazement when he squatted down beside the entangled pair. Birdie's mouth dropped open, and she finally went still. The teacher—Miss Sophie—could only see him from the corner of her eye; if she turned her head, she'd yank the long strand of hair that was wound tight around Birdie's shirtwaist button.

"Well, now, what have we here?" he said, softening his voice to keep Birdie calm. He shifted until he was kneeling in front of the teacher, and reached over her bent head to untangle the snarl.

"It got stuck! Now I can't move or I'll hurt Miss Sophie!"

Around them the children had gathered in a quiet circle, curious as cows. And protective of their teacher, Connor fancied. "That's right," he agreed, "so you must hold very, very still while I undo this knot. Pretend you're a statue."

"Yes, sir. What's a statue?"

A breathy laugh came from the music teacher. He could see only her profile and the smooth angle of her neck. She had cream white skin, the cheeks flushed a little from exertion or embarrassment. Her eyes were downcast; he couldn't be sure what color they were. "The stone cross at the edge of the green, Birdie," she said, amusement in her low voice. "That's a sort of statue, because it never moves."

"Oh."

The snarl was stubborn, and Connor was as anxious as Birdie not to pull Miss Sophie's hair. "Almost got it," he muttered; "two more seconds." Her pretty hair was soft and slippery, and it smelled like roses. Or was that the sun-warmed linen of her dress?

"There are scissors in the rectory," she said, speaking to the ground. "Tommy Wooten, are you here? Would you go and ask—"

"Out of the question. I'd sooner cut off my hand than a single strand of this beautiful hair." And if that wasn't the most fatuous thing Connor had ever said in his life, he wanted to know what was.

She sent him a twinkling sideways glance, and he saw the color of her eyes. Blue. Definitely blue. "Actually, I was thinking you might cut off the button."

"Ah, the button. A much better idea."

"Shall I go, Miss Sophie?" asked a reedy voice behind Connor's shoulder.

"Yes, Tommy."

"No, Tommy," Connor corrected as the last strand in the tangle finally came loose. "Miss Sophie is free."

She sat back on her heels and smiled, first at him, then at the children gathered around; some of them were clapping, as if a performance had just concluded. Her laughing face was flushed, her hair awry—and she was so stunningly lovely, he felt blinded, too dazzled to take it all in. He remembered to take off his hat, but before he could say anything, she turned away to give Birdie a strong, reassuring hug.

"Did it hurt?" the little girl asked her, patting her cheek worriedly.

"No, not one bit."

She heaved a gusty sigh of relief. "Look, Miss Sophie, here's what I was giving you." She held out one bent daisy, the stem wilted, the white petals smashed.

Sophie drew in her breath. "Oh, *lovely*," she declared, holding

9

the flower to her nose and sniffing deeply. "Thank you, Birdie. I'll wear it in my buttonhole." The child blushed with pleasure. Then she was off, eager to tell her friends about her adventure.

Now that the drama was over, the other children began to wander away, too. Connor was still on his knees beside the teacher. "Thank you," she said in her musical voice, and he said, "It was very much my pleasure." They both looked away, then back. He put out his hand. She hesitated, then took it, and he helped her to her feet.

She wasn't as tall as he'd thought; it must be her fine, proud carriage that gave the illusion of height. That and her slimness. Disheveled after Birdie's mauling, she busied herself with pinning up her hair, and the long sleeves of her gown fell back, baring her forearms. The angle of her bent neck intrigued him again, the sheer elegance of it. Watching her now seemed more intimate somehow than touching her had a moment ago.

He ought to say something. "Your choir sounds like a band of angels," he offered—a reckless exaggeration.

She laughed, and the sweet, lilting sound made him laugh with her. "How kind of you, sir. We're hoping that by the twenty-fourth of June, they'll at least sound like human beings. Midsummer Day," she explained when he looked blank. "Two *very* short weeks away." Her clear blue eyes looked directly into his, interested, not coy. "Well," she said softly, and started to turn.

"I'm new to the village," he said, to keep her.

"Yes, I know."

"Do you live here?" Idiotic question; of course she lived here.

"Oh, yes. All my life." Just then one of the towheaded twins barreled into her. She staggered slightly, slipping an arm around his shoulders. The little boy leaned against her in a comfortable way and stared up at Connor curiously.

"Shall I like Wyckerley, do you think?" he asked.

"I'm not sure," she answered after a thoughtful pause. "I suppose it depends on what you're looking for."

"So far, I like what I've seen very much."

She smiled her ravishing smile, but it was impossible to tell if they were flirting or not. He was, but behind her friendly manners and guileless blue gaze might be simple courtesy. While he was thinking of something else to say, something to keep her from remembering that she was conversing with a total stranger in the middle of the village green, someone called her name.

A man. Tall, good-looking, dressed in black, moving toward them from the direction of the church rectory with a long, vigorous stride. In his arms he held a blond-haired infant, wrapped in a blanket.

Connor's smile stiffened. He felt his face going numb.

"Sophie," the man called again, jiggling the baby playfully as he came. "Mrs. Mayhew's here." He came to a stop before them and gave Connor a friendly glance. The baby saw the music teacher and held out its pudgy hands, gurgling with happiness.

Sophie turned to Connor. "Mrs. Mayhew is our organist." A pause. "Well," she said again. She appeared slightly at a loss.

The tall man shifted the baby to one side and put out his hand. "Good afternoon. I'm Christian Morrell—I'm the vicar of All Saints Church."

Connor shook. "Con—" He covered the mistake with a cough. "Jack Pendarvis."

"Glad to meet you."

"Glad to meet you," he echoed, without a word of truth. He felt bleak inside, and absurdly let down. Cheated, as if he'd been declared ineligible for a spectacular prize he'd set his heart on. But if lovely Sophie had to be married, it was good, he supposed, that it was to this friendly, forthright minister; and if she had to have a child, he was glad it was this healthy, happy, golden-haired infant.

She was clapping her hands and calling the children, telling them it was time to go inside the church for the last rehearsal. Connor put his hat on and started to back away. Before he'd gone a foot, Reverend Morrell said amiably, "My wife's gone off to Tavistock to buy a baby carriage. But did she take the baby with her? Oh, no, she left her with her inept and overworked papa, who's been trying for three hours to write a sermon on the virtue of patience."

Connor's laugh was much longer and heartier than the modest quip warranted. "She's a beautiful child," he said—truthfully this time. And the vicar was a fine fellow, and it was a fine day all around.

"Isn't she?" Reverend Morrell planted a kiss on his daughter's apple cheek. "She's perfect, isn't she?"

He seemed to mean the question seriously. Connor laughed again and agreed with him.

The children had started to troop off toward the church. Birdie had Miss Sophie's hand; the teacher had time to say, "Good day to you, Mr. Pendarvis. I hope you'll like our village. Thank you again—for saving me—!" before the little girl pulled her away.

He lifted his hat and watched her hurry up the church steps. In the dark doorway she paused, her ivory dress gleaming like an opal against the blackness behind her. She glanced back at him over her shoulder—and if he hadn't known it before, he knew it now: they *were* flirting. Then, with a bewitching half smile, she was gone.

A long, long moment went by before he realized Reverend Morrell was watching him. The vicar had a look of resigned amusement on his face that seemed to say this had all happened before. "Sorry—should I have introduced you?" he wondered dryly.

Connor looked away, abashed. But why pretend? "Reverend," he said candidly, "I very much wish that you had."

The minister smiled. "Will you be stopping here for long, Mr. Pendarvis?"

He made a vague gesture. "I'm not really sure."

"Well, in any case, Wyckerley's a small place; you'll likely be seeing Miss Deene again."

"Yes, I—" He stopped short. "Miss Deene?"

He nodded, shifting the squirming baby to his hip. "Miss Sophie Deene."

Connor battled a sinking feeling. "By any chance, does her mother own Guelder mine?"

"Sophie's mother? Oh, no; Mrs. Deene passed away many years ago."

Thank God for that, he thought irreverently. Another relative, then. "Her aunt," he guessed, "or an older sister—"

"No, no, *Sophie* owns Guelder."

"Sophie—Miss Deene—*owns the mine?*"

"Owns it, runs it, does everything but go down in it with the miners. We're very proud of our Sophie."

Connor murmured something, tried to put some life into his sickly smile. Past the vicar's shoulder, he gazed across the green at the dark church door. A minute ago he'd thought an angel had passed through it. Oh, bloody, bloody hell. In the blink of an eye, the girl of his dreams had turned into the enemy.

# II

*Do you know how many children rise each morning blithe and gay?*

Sophie shook her head, trying to get the song out of it. Her pony's plodding hoofbeats kept time to the childish melody, and the voice in her brain wouldn't stop singing it.

That was what she got for letting Christy talk her into being children's choir precentor for the third year in a row. She ought to have told him no, she couldn't do it again because she didn't have time. But of course she'd said yes, and of course it wasn't the vicar's fault. She'd agreed because she loved doing it. Loved everything about it, especially the children. Her life might be getting more cluttered and hectic every day, but somehow she'd always find time for the children.

*Do you know how many children—*

"Oh, stop it," she told herself, inadvertently slapping the reins across Valentine's rump. The pony veered right, bumping the gig over the ruts in the old Tavistock toll road. "Whoa, Val," she called, steering him gently back to the center.

Her shoulders ached; she sagged back against the seat, yawning. How lovely to be going home early for a change. One advantage of being choir precentor was that she had to leave Saturday afternoons free, for practice, which always ended by five o'clock. No point in going back to the mine that late; there was no second core on Saturdays, and she could as easily do her paperwork at home. But tonight she wasn't going to do anything. Nothing. She might even go straight to bed, eat dinner there, and read herself to sleep. Ah, lovely.

But first she'd have to have a sit-down talk with Mrs. Bolton about housekeeping matters for the week, meals and so on. And the garden needed attention badly . . . but that would be pleasant, not really work at all. Her pile of mending kept getting higher—she ought to do *that* in bed instead of reading. Or maybe she should write letters; she was so behind in her correspondence, it was a wonder any of her old school friends kept in touch with her at all anymore.

Then she remembered: she'd promised Mrs. Nineways, the churchwarden's wife, that she'd come up with a plan by church tomorrow to insure that the annual rummage sale on Midsummer Day was a success this year—unlike last summer's embarrassing failure, when the parish ladies had grossed a piddling two and a half pounds for a whole year of church programs.

*Do you know how many children—*

"Judas!" she swore—but kept the pony on the track this time. They were trotting past the turnoff to the lane that led to Guelder, and in the distance she could see the chimney stacks, high and black against the twilight sky, belching clouds of white steam into the air. Her father had named the mine Guelder after the roses his wife loved to grow. Sophie loved the name, and the flower, because they were all she had left of the mother she'd never known. And even though it was the cause of her fatigue and the root of all her serious problems, she loved the mine as well, because it had been her father's last gift.

He'd given it to her on the night he died. Almost two years had passed since then, but her satisfaction in the faith he'd shown in her with that last loving act was still as strong and sweet as ever. When she was lonely, tired, overwhelmed by the weight of responsibility for so many people's lives and livelihoods on her twenty-three-year-old shoulders, her father's faith kept her going.

"You're as smart as any woman I ever met, Sophie, and almost any man," he had told her regularly; told her so often, in fact, that eventually she'd come to believe it. Take it for granted. Some might call that conceit, but Sophie preferred to think of it as pride. Her cousin Honoria said she was *too* proud. "Pride is a sin, Sophia, and don't forget, it goeth before a fall," she was fond of warning, with her lips pursed like two prunes. But Honoria's sourness came from discontent with her own life, which to Sophie seemed empty and pointless beyond bearing, so she tried not to hold it against her.

Sometimes it was hard to believe they were related at all, so different did Sophie think—or *hope*—she was from her cousin. Uncle Eustace Vanstone owned Salem mine, but the thought of Honoria having anything to do with Salem, much less managing it in her father's stead, was ridiculous. She'd consider it beneath her, not to mention undignified and unladylike. Eustace was the mayor of Wyckerley, not all that exalted a position in the grand scheme of things, but Honoria took it seriously, almost as seriously as she took her role as daughter of the mayor. She considered herself, except for Lady Moreton at Lynton Great Hall, the highest-ranking female in the district. Sophie could have argued that Reverend Morrell's wife outranked her, Anne having been a viscountess before her marriage to Christy. For that matter, Sophie could even argue (if she cared about such things, which of course she didn't) that she herself preceded Honoria, because her father, when he'd lived, had been older, better educated, richer, and more of a gentleman (in her opinion) than Uncle Eustace would ever be. Truth to tell, the only thing Honoria had on Sophie was age, and since they were both still spinsters, that wasn't exactly a distinction.

Not that Sophie gave such things a second thought.

Instead she thought about the man on the green this afternoon. Memories of him had been drifting back with almost the same frequency as "Do you know how many children." Jack Pendarvis. A Cornish name, and she'd caught more than a trace of Cornwall in his accent. Was he visiting someone here? She didn't know of any Pendarvises in the parish. She wished she'd been able to think of a way to ask him his business. But she hadn't been very articulate. Neither had he.

Smiling, unconsciously touching her hair, she remembered how he'd touched it, so gently, and how he'd stared at her. His eyes were an interesting shade of gray, and the dark pupils gave them a fierce look, intense and a little unsettling. But his mouth when he smiled was beautiful, and he hadn't even tried to hide his admiration. Sophie was used to men admiring her; it didn't embarrass her unless they went too far, said idiotic things or behaved like donkeys. Jack Pendarvis . . . she couldn't imagine him saying or doing anything silly. Telling her he'd rather cut off his hand than a single strand of her hair . . . that was gallant, she decided, not silly. How handsome he was, with his jet-black hair and lean, clean-shaven face. Who could he be? Strangers in Wyckerley were almost unheard of. He spoke like a gentleman, but his clothes had looked a trifle rough. Perhaps he'd been traveling. Yes, of course; obviously. "Do you think I'll like it here?" he'd asked—which must mean he was staying. So she'd see him again.

Lovely.

She slowed the pony for the tight turn between the pitted granite gateposts flanking the carriageway to Stone House. The gravel drive needed tending; the edges were blurred and weeds were shooting up in the center of the wheel tracks. Thomas did his best, but the hard jobs were too much for him; nowadays the grounds and the stable were all he could manage. She wasn't poor—exactly; she could have hired an odd-job man to pull weeds out of the driveway or paint the shutters, trim back the China roses before they ate up the whole house. But she never seemed to have time. And she was turning every penny Guelder earned back into deeper excavations.

It was a risky strategy, one her uncle strongly advised her against. But Eustace's conservative approach didn't suit her. Sophie thought of herself as her father's child: she valued boldness over caution, action over speculation. If she failed . . . oh, but why think about failure? There were degrees of success, but for Tolliver Deene's intrepid daughter there could never be failure. She really believed it.

She was tired, so she halted Valentine at the bottom of the steps rather than taking him around to the stable. Sometimes she put him up herself, especially if Thomas was having one of his bad lumbago days. Tonight, though, she couldn't work up the energy.

Maris waved to her from the open doorway while Sophie was tying the reins to the post. "I'll go an' fetch 'im!" she called. Sophie nodded, and Maris turned and disappeared to find Thomas in his lair over the carriage house and tell him his mistress was home.

Inside, Sophie stripped off her gloves and threw them on the hall table. Standing before the speckled mirror while she re-pinned her untidy hair, she tried to see herself as a stranger might see her. A stranger like Jack Pendarvis. But it was useless; all she could see was her own face, to which she was certainly no stranger. She heard Mrs. Bolton's heavy tread climbing the stairs from the kitchen. "It's only a cold salad tonight unless you want to wait," the housekeeper announced, after a perfunctory greet-ing. "I can make a chop, but it'll be late; I've only just got back from Gerald's."

Gerald was her unmarried son; she visited him every week, Friday night until dinner on Saturday, and cleaned his house and made most of his meals for the coming week. She always came back exhausted and irritable, and Sophie had learned to stay out of her way until Sunday at the earliest.

"Oh, a salad sounds just right," she assured her. "I'm too tired for a big meal anyway." Mrs. Bolton said, "Hmph," and Sophie lost the heart to ask if she could have it in her room. "I'll go and change, then come back down and help you."

"Hmph. See you've got grass stains on that white skirt. They'll never come out, you might as well start cutting it up for ribbons right now."

"I can get 'em out," Maris claimed, clumping toward them from the back of the house, all five feet, eleven inches of her. "Skim milk and starch powder, nothing to it."

Mrs. Bolton scowled at her. "We'll see," she said darkly, and headed for the kitchen.

Maris grinned, showing her crooked teeth. She was carrying a glass. "Here, whyn't you take this outside and watch the sun go down. Take yer shoes off and just set. I can bring supper out in the garden if you want."

"Oh, Maris." She'd made her a glass of cold orange tea and honey; it tasted like heaven. Maris was the day maid; she went home to her family every night. Mrs. Bolton was the one who slept in, in a room off the kitchen in the basement. Sophie frequently wished it was the other way around. "Well, maybe I will," she decided. "I can be snapping the dead heads off the rhododendrons."

"Hmph," said Maris, mimicking Mrs. Bolton. "I was pretty sure you wasn't going to stick yer feet up and do what I told you to do—nothing."

They rolled their eyes at each other and parted.

Sophie's mother's garden was lovely for over half the year-round, but it was never more beautiful than at the warm twilight end of an early June day, when thousands and thousands of roses bloomed in a mad riot of color, climbing the old apple trees and covering the hedgerows, creeping past the borders and overtopping the roof of the garden house. A dozen other flower species were at their peak now, too, but the roses ruled supreme by virtue of exuberance and sheer numbers and their overpowering perfume. Half swooning from the fragrance and the beauty, Sophie sat down on the painted wooden chaise by the garden house and swatted away a bee that wanted a taste of her orange tea. "Hullo, Dash," she said, and the black cat curled up on the sun-warmed flags roused himself to twitch an ear at her. The lightest of breezes shook down a cloud of loose florets from the acacia bush; they landed on Dash's neck, startling white against glossy black, but he didn't even notice. "Should've named you Dashless," she told him, lying back on the chaise and closing her eyes. "Dash-free. Undash."

Mine problems closed in on her as soon as she allowed her thoughts to drift. Copper prices had dropped again at Thursday's ticketing, as they had been doing for months. Overspeculation and the war in the Crimea had put an end to the days, five years ago or so, of fabulous profits. Guelder was a small mine compared to the Devon or Fowey Consols, and one of the few in the county owned wholly by an individual, without shareholders. Well, except for Lord Moreton, who had made a modest investment when she'd needed cash badly. The handwriting was on the wall, though; Sophie didn't need Uncle Eustace telling her it was time to advertise for adventurers—moneyed speculators. Since his alternative was unthinkable—that she sell Guelder to him and take up the infinitely more feminine pursuit of husband-hunting—she was going to have to come up with a workable plan for a stock offer soon. How much should a share cost and how many should she sell? She had two lawyers, and each was telling her something different.

Eyes closed, she put her glass down on the flagstones and folded her arms across her middle. The worst would be having to give up her independence, her sovereignty, she thought, yawning. She'd have to answer to others. Guelder had been her father's mine, nobody else's. *He'd* never sold pieces of it to strangers. Even in the leanest times, he'd held on one way or another, by abandoning risky pitches or laying off miners until the copper standard rose and prices improved. Dickon Penney, her mine agent, was forever telling her to sell off shares; but he wasn't the one who would have to deal with the consequences, was he? Meetings every month at the coinage in Tavistock. Relinquishing shares and declaring dividends . . . a quarterly settling of the mine's accounts, maybe even bimonthly . . .

She heard footsteps on the stone terrace and sat up, amazed to realize she'd been dozing, actually sleeping in her chair. Maris would be pleased. She turned around to tell her—and saw her uncle coming across the terrace, taking the two steps to the grass in one bound. A few months ago he'd hurt his knee in a riding accident, and he still carried a gold-handled cane; but since his knee was healed, it was only an affectation now. He thought the cane made him look more mayoral. Sophie stood up, brushing white petals from her skirts, and smiled a greeting.

He didn't smile back. "You've forgotten, haven't you?"

"Forgotten what?"

His sleek, handsome face was so severe, it looked carved out of marble. He was one of the local magistrates, and she'd seen him make prisoners tremble in the dock with that face. "Dinner," he said shortly. "Tonight. Robert Croddy is coming."

"Oh, *bother*. You're right, I did forget. I'm sorry." There went her quiet evening alone. She hoped Uncle Eustace was interpreting the disappointment she couldn't hide as regret that now she'd be late to his dinner party.

He stood with his legs spread, holding the cane in both hands behind his back, exactly like a London bobby. "I'm not surprised; I thought you might. It's why I stopped here before going home." Salem mine was a few miles north on the Tavistock toll road; Uncle Eustace lived in Wyckerley—as befitted the mayor—and Sophie's house was on his way home.

"I don't know how it could've slipped my mind. I—I've been looking forward to it all week." She thought his shrewd eyes looked skeptical. "You go along. Tell Honoria I'll be there in one hour."

"Ha. Three is more like it."

"No," she said with a smile, "you're mixing me up with your daughter." Honoria could easily take three hours to dress for a simple family dinner. "An hour, I promise, and I'll have Thomas drive me in the carriage." This was a concession: she'd much prefer to drive herself in the gig, but Eustace hated it when she went "haring about" alone, especially after dark.

He nodded grudgingly. "But you'll still need longer than an hour. *Robert Croddy* is coming."

"Yes, you mentioned that." She sent him a humorous look, but he wouldn't smile back. Slipping her arm through his, she began to walk with him around the path to the front of the house, where he'd tied his big bay horse. "Why don't you try to marry Honoria off to Robert instead of me?" she teased.

She felt him stiffen. "Don't be ridiculous."

"Well, you might have better luck. Or doesn't she think he's rich enough?" He wouldn't respond, but she thought that was very likely it. Robert had an interest in Uncle Eustace's mine; he was eligible and unattached, fairly sophisticated—being from Devonport, a metropolis compared to Wyckerley—and comfortably off, a successful brewer's son. But that was probably his fatal flaw for Honoria: she couldn't see herself married to the son of a beer maker.

There was nothing really wrong with Robert Croddy; when her uncle threw them together, Sophie always found his company agreeable enough. But Eustace wanted her to *marry* Robert, and that was an entirely different thing. Sophie didn't want to marry anyone, not for a long, long time. Her life was much too interesting just now to throw away for the dubious reward of a husband.

"Try to arrive by eight," Uncle Eustace said sternly as he untied his horse.

"I will." She gave his hard cheek a kiss, and he finally eked out a smile for her. She had a thought. "Are you still looking for a mine agent to take William Ball's place?"

"I am," he answered, seating himself on his horse, drawing on his riding gloves.

"So you haven't hired anyone yet?"

"Not yet. Why?"

"Nothing, I only wondered. I saw someone in the village today, a stranger. I thought he might be your new man."

"No, couldn't be. I've not even advertised for the post yet."

"Oh." She backed up so he could turn his horse.

"Eight o'clock," he reminded her, settling his hat on his head. It was a tall, citified hat; he'd bought it last year in Exeter, and he was inordinately fond of it. She always thought it looked out of place in the country, especially when he wore it on horseback.

"Eight," she echoed. "I'm really looking forward to it."

Her shoulders dropped once he was out of sight. Dejected, she went inside to change. So she could go out again.

# III

On Monday morning Connor walked the mile and a half from Wyckerley to Guelder mine and applied for work. A man named Andrewson, the captain-at-grass, asked him a few questions—where he'd worked last, whether he wanted tribute or tutwork—and told him to wait in the countinghouse until Miss Deene came. Connor sat in the mine office's tiny anteroom for twenty minutes, staring at ore samples on shelves against the wall, staring at the closed door to the inner office, drumming his fingers, thinking Miss Deene didn't put herself out much getting to work on time. After five minutes more, he got up and walked outside.

Guelder looked typical of the majority of small, mines he'd observed lately, no worse than most, better than a few. It was situated on a denuded upland, the ground barren all around, with grass sprouting through mud and rumble and a half century of mineral waste brought up from the bowels of the earth and left where it lay. The entrance was small and undramatic, just a ladder sticking up from a hole in the middle of the attle-strewn clearing, covered with an open trapdoor and a makeshift roof to keep the rain out. Twin chimney stacks towered over the engine house, from which the sound of the machines pumping out water from fathoms below was low, monotonous, and never-ending. Chains, pulleys, bell cranks, and winding machines littered the ground, and stacks of timber and enormous coils of rope on wooden platforms. The dressing area was partially under-roof, and from here he could see the children and "bal girls"—women, most of them miners' wives—cleaning and dressing the ores. The first core began at eight o'clock, so there were no miners about now, only grass workers and machinery men, and the drivers of mule-drawn carts full of rock and metal and the crude implements used to unearth them.

Over the crest of the hill that wound down to the toll road, a different sort of vehicle came into view, a jaunty, yellow-wheeled cart pulled by a pretty gray pony. A bright red feather waved from the driver's dashing straw hat. Watching the cart draw near, Connor leaned back against the mine office's clapboard side and jammed his hands in his pockets, trying not to be seduced by the beguiling frivolity of the sight, the charming unlikeliness of it in such homely surroundings. But it wasn't easy. He'd been thinking about Miss Sophie Deene for a day and a half. This morning he thought he'd finally banished the last outlaw impression of her as an attractive woman rather than as the owner of one of the copper mines he'd committed himself to investigate. Now here she was, handing the pony cart's reins to Andrewson and jumping gracefully down to the ground in the muddy mine yard, and it was impossible to think anything at all except that she was beautiful.

She didn't wear white today, but she was just as fresh and fetching in a stylish tartan skirt, green blouse, and red kid boots. Connor tried to feel sullen, tried to sneer mentally at the impracticality of those little boots, the silly feather in the girlish, oversize hat. But no luck again; one look around at the men nodding or lifting their caps to her in the yard told him he was exactly the same as all of them: bewitched.

Andrewson was saying something to her, gesturing in Connor's direction. She threw him a brief glance and went back to her conversation. Hadn't she recognized him? Pushing away from the shadowed wall of the countinghouse, he moved toward her.

The wide brim of her hat hid him until he was nearly beside her. When she looked up, she started slightly, and then her lovely face lit up in a smile only a blind man wouldn't know was glad. "Why, it's Mr. Pendarvis," she said wonderingly, while pretty pink color stole into her cheeks. It tantalized him to see that she was flustered. He almost offered her his hand before he remembered himself. He pulled off his own hat, a heavy felt miner's helmet, and said, "Good morning." It was hard not to smile back, hard to bear in mind that everything had changed since the afternoon he'd untangled her hair from Birdie's button. They weren't enemies—not yet—but they would certainly be adversaries, she unwittingly, and so he'd damn well better keep his head.

Andrewson scratched his chin, puzzled. "Didn't know you knew him," he said to his employer. "He never said." She looked at the grass captain in perplexity. "This is the one I just told you about, Miss Deene. He's here wanting work in the mine."

She turned her head on her long neck by slow, subtly incredulous degrees. The pleased smile faltered, lost its charming self-consciousness. If disillusionment had a color, it was the shade of slate-blue her eyes turned behind her thick lashes, like a cloud-shadow moving across a clear, deep pool. "Mr. Pendarvis, you . . . you're a miner?"

Connor felt hot blood rush to his cheeks, at the same time he became exquisitely aware of his loose-fitting pants and dirty gray smock frock, his heavy, mud-caked boots, his graceless hat. There was no mistaking her tone or her look, and her disappointment was as sharp and clear as a slap in the face. "Yes, I'm a miner," he said through his teeth. With enough disbelief in his voice to insult, he said, "Don't tell me *you're* the owner of Guelder mine."

It was her turn to blush. Her posture, already finishing-school perfect, stiffened, and she grew an inch. Her chin went up; she had to reach for the brim of her hat to keep it on. "Yes, I am," she said, and it was a shock to hear chilliness in the warm, melodic voice that had been haunting him since Saturday. "Would working for a woman pose a problem for you, Mr. Pendarvis?"

"Not necessarily, Miss Deene." He let his eyes travel down her elegant body and slowly, deliberately, back to her face. "I expect it depends on the woman." Tension held their gazes, stretching, pulling tighter—until Andrewson cleared his throat and muttered, "Well, now."

Then they both looked away, and Connor told himself to calm down. What the hell did he care what Miss Sophie Deene thought of him? She was pretty; once they'd flirted with each other. That was all. He'd better relax, because interests much more vital than his almighty dignity were at stake. But pride, Connor had been told a hundred times, was his biggest weakness, and she'd made the mistake of wounding it. When that happened, his most natural defense was aggression.

At least he'd made her angry, too—a childish but satisfying consolation. "Will you come into my office, please?" she said, regal as a queen, and his only regret was that she turned and sailed away before she could see his carefully careless smile.

Her cramped office was dominated by an enormous battered oak desk piled high with papers, books, and little bags of copper ore assays. Shelves on every wall bulged with more papers and files, books, maps, boxes, and sacks. There was no rug on the plank floor, no curtain at the one dusty window; the only feminine touch he could see was a jar of wilting wildflowers on a small table, under a pen-and-ink drawing of a white-haired man with a mustache. The late Mr. Deene?

She took her hat off and hung it on a hook on the back of the door, then went behind the desk and sat down in a huge, squeaky leather armchair on wheels. She looked so dwarfed and out of place in her aggressively masculine surroundings, Connor grinned at her. Up came the chin. She folded her hands on the desktop and stared at him down the short length of her perfect nose. "Have a seat," she offered with studied politeness, and even though it was more of a command than an invitation, he sat down in the room's only other chair, a shabby ladder-back with an uneven leg, directly in front of her desk. "So you would like a job. Is it tribute or tutwork you're seeking, Mr. Pendarvis?"

"Which are you offering, Miss Deene?"

"Neither, until I'm satisfied with your qualifications. What experience do you have?"

"I've told all of this to the captain."

Her nostrils flared ever so slightly. "Well, now you can tell it to me."

He had to stop baiting her; Christ, he *wanted* a job. He dropped an ankle over one knee and folded his arms, sliding down a little in the chair. "I worked for the Fowey Consols at Lanescot for seven years, four years at Wheal Lady in Redruth, and at Carn Barra for another four."

He could see her adding it up. "You've been a copper miner for fifteen years?" She kept the dismay out of her voice this time, but he thought he could still see it in her eyes.

"Copper or tin; I've worked both since I was twelve. Oh, and lead once at Portreath, back in 'fifty-three. Forgot to mention that." Although this was Jack's history, not his, he found it surprisingly easy to lie to Miss Sophie Deene. It felt like evening the score.

"When did you leave Carn Barra?"

"Six months ago."

"And since then?"

"I've not worked at all."

This was the tricky part, since he didn't look like a sick man. Staring her straight in the eye, he said steadily, "I left because of ill health."

Her guarded look lifted. "I'm sorry." She said it as if she meant it. "Do you mind if I ask the nature of your illness? Only because—"

"It was my lungs, an infectious fever. The doctors thought it might turn consumptive, and told me not to work underground for half a year."

Compassion softened the corners of her mouth; just for a moment he saw again the sweet-faced girl on the village green. "I'm sorry," she repeated.

"No need to be. As you can see, I'm fine now. Fit and able-bodied, Miss Deene, and ready to work."

He was, but Jack wasn't. Jack's lung fever was indeed tubercular, and the last doctor had said he'd kill himself if he went down in a mine again. Even with that, his chances of reaching middle age were barely even. It was a cruel and bitter sentence, but Jack had come to terms with it. It was Connor who couldn't.

"As is happens," Sophie said carefully, "there's to be a setting next week for pitwork in a new excavation. I'm aware that one of the gangs could use an extra man. That is, if tribute work interests you, Mr. Pendarvis."

A setting was an auction, when miners bid for the pitches they wanted to work, and instead of a wage they earned a percentage of the value of the ore they dug. It was a subterranean lottery, riskier than tutwork—which was merely driving shafts and sinking levels, clearing the way for the tributers—but sometimes it could be much more lucrative. A man could strike a lucky pitch and do pretty well for himself. Or he could lose his shirt. Usually he just eked out a living, and a hard one at that.

But it was nice of her to offer. Connor hadn't expected it. But ore extraction was a complicated skill requiring years of experience—experience like Jack's—and Connor's entire underground experience consisted of four months of tutwork in all of two Cornish copper mines. If he tried to bluff, he'd likely be found out for the novice he was in about two days.

"I appreciate it," he said truthfully. "But I haven't the money to lay out for my share of the grinding and dressing."

"The mine could lend it to you in advance of your earnings."

He smiled thinly. He was familiar with that ruse. "At what percent, Miss Deene?"

She narrowed her eyes at him. "At zero percent, Mr. Pendarvis. It's a free loan with a three-month term, payable in full."

Unusual. Most owners were only too glad to advance capital to miners in need, at prodigious rates that kept them beholden to the company indefinitely.

"Thanks," he said, "but I'll stick with tutwork. It's what I do best." Slow, plodding, molelike labor; it took some skill, a lot of sweat, and no imagination. He loathed it. As she watched him speculatively, he found himself almost wishing she didn't believe him—that she was thinking he *didn't* look like a man who would cheerfully spend his whole life burrowing holes in the ground so people like her could grow rich on his sweat and blood.

"Very well," she said slowly. "Tutwork, then. What tools do you have?"

"Pick, shovel, wedges."

"Blasting tools?"

"Sledge, borer, claying box. Cartridges and fuses."

"Can you buy your candles?"

"I'd need a subsist," he lied. "Two pounds would see me through until payday." Candles were a miner's biggest expense, running to roughly a tenth of his earnings.

She nodded. "One of my tutmen lost his partner and has been working alone for the past two weeks. I should think you could team up with him. I pay five pounds for a fathom, and I pay my men every—"

"*Five?* I've never worked for that. I earned six guineas at Carn Barra."

*Then you should've stayed there,* she wanted to say, he could tell by her eyes; it was fascinating to watch her trying to hold on to her temper. She sat back in the squeaky chair, deliberately relaxing her stiff fingers over the leather-covered arms. "Carn Barra is four times the size of Guelder, Mr. Pendarvis. It's owned by a consortium. Until a year and a half ago, it brought up ore that sold at the coinage for three, sometimes four times the price of my copper. If I could pay my men more, I would, but as it is . . ." She trailed off, giving her head a little shake, as if thinking, *Why am I telling him this?*

She stood. "Five pounds per fathom, that's my wage, and if I hire you, you'll have to subscribe to a list of mine regulations. Once you sign, there's a twenty-shilling penalty for nonfulfillment of your contract. I don't know what the practice is at Carn Barra, but here—"

"Carn Barra has contracts," he said pacifically, getting up, too. "With penalty clauses. Only it's thirty shillings for nonfulfillment, not twenty." Jack had coached him well.

Slightly mollified, she went to a bookcase beside the window and took a sheet of paper out of a box on one of the shelves. Using the window ledge for a table, she bent over the paper and began to scribble on it with a fountain pen. Connor went closer, watching dusty sun shafts light up the copper strands in her blond hair. Her fragrance was roses again, subtle as a whisper, barely there. He liked her flounced skirt; it had a bustle in back, a silly little bulge, charmingly useless. Her green blouse had long, loose sleeves, and she kept pushing the right one up so she wouldn't get ink on it. He noticed the tiny hairs on her forearm were golden, like the hair on her head. He wanted to see if his hands could fit around her trim little waist.

She straightened, turned—and started; she hadn't known he was so near. She held the piece of paper up to her bosom, like a shield. "I've decided to employ you," she said briskly, "on a conditional basis. If you agree to the terms of the labor contract, you can start immediately."

"Conditional? Based on what?"

"Based on what your last employer has to say about your work." She tapped the form against her chest with one fingernail, but when he followed the gesture with his eyes, she dropped her hand to her side. "You've no objection to my writing to the mine captain at Carn Barra, have you?"

"Why? Don't you believe me?" Neither of his last two short-term employers had bothered to check his—Jack's—references.

"It's not a question of believing you."

"Isn't it?" She was singling him out, he was sure of it. She'd hire any man who looked able-bodied, who would sign her labor contract and take five pounds for every backbreaking fathom he dug for her. He went a step closer, and although she didn't give ground, everything about her seemed to shrink from him. Two days ago she'd twinkled her eyes at him, smiled up into his face like an angel. Today she acted as if his miner's garb had a bad smell. "Isn't it?" he repeated, moving even closer, closer than was allowed, not only by courtesy but by everything she believed ought to keep them apart, the wide, gaping social void she was sure separated them. "Are ee sartin it isn't only that ee wants t' put me in my place, Miss Sophie?" he asked softly, nastily.

During the endless minute they glared at each other, he had time to notice that the top of her head came up to the bridge of his nose, and that the clear blue of her irises turned smoke gray when she was angry. And that he could make her blush by looking at her mouth.

"It's customary," she said, enunciating carefully, never taking her eyes from his.

He could imagine them standing by the sunny window all morning, each waiting for the other to back down. He lifted his hand toward her. She didn't move, but her face froze—until he pinched between his thumb and forefinger the paper she was still holding to her breast. He took it from her, then held out his other hand. Another second crawled by. She laid the fountain pen on his flat palm, taking pains not to touch him.

She'd made notations on the form, filling in his name and the date, the wage she was offering, the term of their agreement—two months. He used the windowsill, as she had; without reading the fine print, he signed the contract at the bottom: John Lawrence Pendarvis.

"I want a copy," he said as he handed it back.

She nodded coolly. "Stop in after the first core, and I'll see that it's waiting for you."

"Thanks."

She was glad to put some distance between them, but she made a point of not hurrying back behind her desk. She found a key inside the little netted purse she'd earlier thrown on the desktop, and used it to open the kneehole drawer. From it she took another key, and used that one to unlock a large steel safe behind her chair. Distracted again by the bustle, Connor didn't notice what she was rummaging around in the safe for until she turned and held out two one-pound notes to him.

When she smiled at him with her mouth but not her eyes, he knew she'd seen what he should've hidden: that he hated this, that even though it was part of the game, he could hardly bring himself to reach out for the money she was offering him across her desk.

But he took it, his advance or "subsist," and stuffed it in his pocket without looking at it. "You'll want a receipt," he said tonelessly.

"That's not necessary."

"You trust me to repay you?"

"I wouldn't say that." The humorless smile widened. "I'll keep it back from your first month's wage."

He probably deserved that. He stuck his miner's hat on his head and started to leave.

"Find Mr. Andrewson and tell him I've hired you," she instructed, absently running one hand along the top of her leather chair. "The tutman you'll be working with is Tranter Fox. I think he's at the seventy level today; the mine captain will take you down to him."

"Yes." He'd be damned if he'd call her *ma'am*.

After a pause, she said in a softer voice, "Tranter's a Cornishman, like you. Everyone likes him. I hope you'll—I should think you'd—I don't know why you wouldn't get along."

It was the first kind thing she'd said to him. A hint of a smile hovered at the corners of her lips. She was backing off a bit from the hostility with which they'd begun—wishing him well. He ought to smile back, meet her halfway. That would be practical. Expedient.

But pride was still his downfall, and he was still smarting from the insult of her disillusionment. The dismay in her voice when she'd said, "You're a *miner*?" Two days ago he'd been a man, and she'd treated him like one; today he was a *miner*, and so far beneath her she didn't want to stand next to him.

Instead of smiling, he touched his helmet in an insolent salute and walked out.

Clinging to the sides of a clay-caked ladder, sweating, eyes smarting, descending and descending and descending, Connor remembered why he hated mines. It wasn't the heat, oppressive at thirty fathoms, nearly intolerable at seventy. It wasn't the constant dampness or the dirt and mud and rubble, or the pitch-blackness, or the confinement for hours a day in places no roomier than a coffin. It wasn't even the relentless, body-breaking labor that progressed so slowly and yielded so little.

What he hated about mining was the shameful waste it made of a man's life. Over his head, the whole world "at grass" went about the business of fighting wars or making children, selling shoes, harvesting fields, painting pictures, reading newspapers, dancing, debating, laughing, weeping—and always oblivious to the subterranean sweatshop underfoot, the ceaseless industry of men picking and hammering, breaking and blasting, tutworking and tributing, and dying young so that there could be pennies and teakettles and trinkets for the vital, unaware souls above.

It was no life for a man, no life even for an animal. Looking around at the murky blackness, diffused only by the pale glimmer of candles miners stuck to their hats with bits of clay, Connor thought they might as well be worms—glowworms, glowing yellow instead of green, burrowing holes in the stone and slag at the rate of an inch a day, crawling and winding, throwing away their short turn on the earth by choosing to labor in the darkness. His body despised it and his spirit recoiled from it; the only reason he could bear it even for these few short months was because of the possibility of reform at the end of his servitude as an impostor. That was the slim hope that kept him going.

At Wheal Looe and at Tregurtha, the mines where he'd worked in the spring, he'd learned early that reticence was his best defense against revealing how truly ignorant he was about the craft of mining. Almost anyone can flail away at a granite wall

all day with a pickax, but only a seasoned copper miner can speak knowledgeably to his mates on the subjects of killas and elvans, adits and winzes, flucans, sollars, and slickensides. So Connor had gotten into the habit of shutting up while he labored under the ground, thereby earning himself the reputation of a man of very few words.

But at Guelder, it was clear within five minutes of meeting his new partner that he wouldn't have to feign taciturnity. Even if he'd been chatty as a magpie, it wouldn't have mattered—because Tranter Fox wouldn't let him get a word in edgewise.

"Pendarvis, eh? Now there'm a name to sing out wi' pride. And from Trewythiel, you say! My blessed saints, that's only bird spit from Tregony, where yers truly were born and reared. Did ee ever work at Wheal Albert? No? Bless yerself, Jack, for there'm a cesspool o' bleakness and blighted hope if ever I saw it. Squandered half a year there onct, back when I were tender and green, thinkin' I'd get rich tributing. Judas! Never set foot in Tyward parish, boy, there'm my advice to you. Hand me that mallet whilst ee're only setting there. Think there'm any point in sinking this winze further? They'll be comin' up on it from the gallery below; mayhap we can let Moony and 'is mates hook up to us, and catch our croust early, what say? Have ee met Moony yet? Oh, he'm a right smart lad, like you, but sink me if I don't cadge 'im every time into doing half my work for me. He never suspicions a thing! Haw! Yer candle's blinkerin', take this un quick. No, no, we'll settle up later. So what was it you was askin' me? Oh, how I lost Martin Burr, my last partner. He'm startin' to get about now, I seen him at the George last night, but still on 'is crutch, you know, and 'is daughter had to come and get 'im when he fell over the stoop. That were the bitters he'd drank, though, not 'is broke legs. How'd he do it? Fell off a ladder at the thirty level and breaked 'em both. William Stark said he heared 'em go, crack, crack, and him two galleries down at the time. William might be having us on. But every man could hear Martin bleatin' and carryin' on after, that's sartin. Never heared such howling this side o' hell, and never wish to again. Nobody could get him up till Miss Deene said to send the kibble bucket down for 'im, so that's what we done. Should've ought to've seed 'im, Jack, all on his back, nothing but two breaked legs sticking up over the bucket top, slow rising fathom after fathom, like he were on 'is way up to heaven. But howling all the way, mind; I were clear ashamed of 'im, carrying on like a mewly girl."

Like a high mountain waterfall that never dries up, not even in the hottest months of summer, Tranter Fox never stopped talking. It was a double advantage: Connor could keep his inexperience to himself unobtrusively, and find out all about Guelder mine without asking a single question.

By lunchtime, he'd learned that the mine had been doing well since Miss Deene had inherited it from her father nearly three years ago, a circumstance that had come as a surprise to almost everyone. Not that she weren't known for having a corking good head on 'er shoulders, Tranter assured him. It was just that she was a woman, and she was young, and she'd been sent away to school from the time she was twelve until she turned eighteen, and that "furrin" experience had naturally distanced her from the small, tightly knit community of her birth.

"Now, some o' the miners squirm under her rule, so to say, because she'm a lady and not a man. Others'll defend 'er to their death on account o' their wages have went up since she took over. Me, I like 'er. She treats me square, she don't ask fer what I can't give, and she works as hard at grass as any man I know. And plus she'm a sight easier on the eyes."

Tranter said this with a sooty, gap-toothed grin and a twinkle in his own small black eyes. He was a tiny Cornishman, barely five feet tall, but tough and strong, agile as a monkey. He called Connor "son" and "young fellow," although he himself was barely thirty. Jack's age. He'd been underground for twenty years, he claimed—his first job was hauling water to Wheal Virgin tin miners at the age of nine—and Connor found himself involuntarily listening for the whistle of tubercular lungs or the soft wheeze of incipient pneumonia. But the little miner seemed healthy, and when he wasn't talking, he was singing. Hymns, mainly—"Abide With Me" was one of his favorites—interspersed with profane drinking songs. He was a tiring but likable companion, and by the time they slacked off and climbed down to the eighty level to eat lunch with Moony Donne and his crew of tributers, Connor had decided that, as mining partners went, he could have done much worse.

Lunch, which the miners called their "croust," was a hasty, haphazard meal taken in the coolest, driest place at hand, sitting on gunpowder kegs or the odd bits of plank they toted around with them. Connor hadn't brought any food, so the others shared their bread, cheese, and bacon with him; Tranter Fox even gave him dessert—half an apple and a piece of toffee. Over the clang of the stamping mill and the noisy rhythm of steam engines endlessly pumping water out of the bowels of the mine, the conversation was typical miners' talk, about the richness of the lodes they'd dug or wished they were digging, how much money they hoped to earn at week's end when their ore was dressed and weighed, which man was tireder, which was stronger, which worked the longest hours. Not suprisingly, Sophie Deene was a favorite topic, a subject of great fascination, and Connor heard plenty of lewd wishful thinking—although not as much as he might have expected. Whether they liked her or not, to a man they seemed to respect her, and the only reason he heard for their dislike was that she was a woman.

At eighty fathoms the air was hot, thick, and unhealthy; a sickly vapor composed of candle smoke, gunpowder fumes, and stale oxygen floated damp and sluggish, visible in the candlelit dimness. One of Moony Donne's men swallowed a piece of bread wrong and went into a coughing fit. It reminded Tranter—"Miss Deene's contractin' fer a new ventilator," he announced for Connor's benefit, and the others nodded, muttering, "Aye," and "She is that," sounding proud of it, proud of her. " 'Tis naught but a six-foot cylinder, a pipe, and a valve," Tranter went on, "but onct it's up, they say it'll suck out a couple hundred gallons of air in a minute."

"Is that a fact?" Connor marveled. He would make a note of the improvement in his report to the Rhadamanthus Society, but his cynical side wasn't impressed. Studies had begun to come out in the trade press lately associating air quality and miner efficiency; a man named Mackworth had written an article claiming that by reducing the temperature in deep mines through improved ventilation, owners could save twelve pounds per fathom in labor costs. Miss Deene might very well be trying to clean up the air at Guelder, but Connor doubted if her motives had very much to do with the health of her miners' lungs.

The afternoon passed in a blur of tedium and fatigue. When his core ended, he climbed the endless series of long, nearly perpendicular ladders to the surface, feeling as if his feet were encased in lead. There was nowhere to stop, nowhere to rest; at seventy fathoms, there were four hundred and twenty vertical feet of ladder to climb in bad air, and thirty miners climbing doggedly behind him, all wanting out, anxious for a breath of clean air and a mouthful of hot tea or cold beer. It was exactly like a treadmill, and nearly as pointless and punitive, although the men condemned to climb it had committed no crime. Except poverty, and an absence of choices, and a social system that sentenced them to low pay and a lifetime of drudgery.

Declining Tranter's invitation to join him for a wee drop at the George and Dragon, Connor tramped back to the small, thatched-roof workingmen's cottage he and Jack were leasing. There was a scullery off the kitchen where the miner tenants washed and changed after work. Stripping off his mud- and tallow-stained work clothes, he scrubbed himself in cold water and soap over the shallow basin, rubbing the new bruises on his ribs gingerly, thinking it was lucky he wouldn't be here in the winter or he'd freeze to death trying to keep clean. Dripping, nude, he padded down the short passage to his bedroom and put on clean trousers and shirt, socks, shoes, his waistcoat. Jack's room was on the other side of the thin wall beside his bed, and once he stopped, listening, thinking he'd heard a laugh. But the sound didn't come again; it had probably been Jack coughing.

His stomach growled; he was starving, and the girl didn't come until six o'clock to cook their meal. His lumpy, narrow bed looked tempting; he considered lying down for a nap. But his exhaustion was too deep: if he slept now, he probably wouldn't wake up until morning. He'd go talk to Jack, then.

The door was closed. But Jack hardly ever slept—insomnia was one of the scourges of his disease—and so, after two quick knocks, Connor walked in.

And backed out instantly, face flaming, too shocked to mutter anything but an inaudible "Excuse me," and ducked back into his own room.

He went to the one small window that overlooked a weedy kitchen garden and cranked the casement open. He peered out, but he wasn't seeing the drooping, unkempt plants or the dilapidated birdhouse hanging lopsided on the trunk of a seedy locust tree. All he could see was a woman's enormous white rump rising and falling energetically over his brother's hairy thighs, the two of them seated in a chair, she straddling him, Jack's hands trying to cover her great heaving breasts.

Jack had women all the time, they were like a hobby to him—but Connor had never before observed him with one in flagrante *delicto*. He liked to think of himself as reasonably worldly, but—he was shocked. It wasn't an everyday sight. Nor one easily forgotten. The girl hadn't even been pretty, but he couldn't get out of his mind the image of her dimpled, thrusting buttocks or her blinding white bosom. And Jack . . . that intent, considerate, watchful look on his face, the gentleness of his hands on the woman's breasts, the attentive half smile that froze when he saw Connor in the doorway. It was too exquisitely private, and Connor felt guilty not only for disturbing their lusty tryst, but for being aroused by it. Definitely aroused by it.

Some time later, he heard the door open and close, and the

sound of footsteps hurrying away. A few minutes passed. Jack's door opened again, and a second later there was a knock at Connor's. "Come in." Jack came in.

He was fully dressed, overdressed, really, with his jacket on over his old wool waistcoat and a tie knotted in haste around the frayed collar of his shirt. But he'd forgotten to comb his hair. That one small omission ruined his attempt to look innocent, or at least nonchalant, for whoever his afternoon lover had been had combed his hair straight up with her ardent fingers. He looked exactly like the rooster he was trying so hard not to resemble.

Connor started it by smiling. Jack grinned back, embarrassed but tickled, and pretty soon they were both laughing, reveling in the knowing, infectious sound, egging each other on with it. Jack collapsed on the bed, holding his sides. A coughing fit brought his hilarity to an abrupt end, and afterward he lay on his back, alternately wheezing and chuckling, wiping tears from his temples.

"Who was she?" Connor said. "If I may ask."

"Why, she'm the gel I told you about, the one who serves at the George. Rose, 'er name is, although I calls 'er . . . ah, well."

"Ah, well," Connor agreed. "Next time I'll be more careful before I walk into your room. In broad daylight on a Monday afternoon," he added pointedly.

Jack grinned, sheepish. "You do that. So," he said, to change the subject. "Tell me how yer day went, counselor. Ee're looking a bit fagged. I'm startin' to despair o' us turning you into a real miner, Con. Sad t' say, ee just may not have the stuff."

Connor dropped down in the room's only chair, too tired to joke back. "Guess who owns the mine, Jack."

"Who? Some woman, you said."

"Sophie Deene."

Jack's mouth fell open. "No."

"Yes."

"No! That girl? On the green, the one wi' the children?"

"That girl." He rubbed his eyes. "And she doesn't just own it, she *runs* it. She's the bleeding *manager,* she comes in to her bloody office every day and sits down behind her great bleeding *desk.*"

Jack sat up on his elbows, and gradually his face changed from amazement to amusement. "Uh-oh," he said knowingly.

"Stow it, just—"

"Uh-oh, uh-oh. Now what're ee going to do? You fell in love wi' her on Saturday, and now—"

"Don't be an ass."

"—Now ee've got t' go behind 'er back, pickin' out all the flaws in 'er mine, rattin' on 'er to the Rhads, and her the gel ee'd most like to—"

"Jack, would you just sod that?"

Startled by the anger Connor couldn't hide, Jack held up his hands. "Right you are," he said placatingly. "It's a pickle, I can see that. Oh, I forgot to give you this."

"What?"

"Letter from the Rhads, I expect. Another one o' the blank envelopes, lest yer dark ties to their socialist coven be found out."

Connor chuckled in spite of himself, and reached for the envelope Jack had taken out of his pocket. Inside was a letter, short and to the point. "Good," he muttered when he'd read it. "Fine with me."

"What?"

He looked up. "They say the reform bill may be brought in sooner than they'd expected. Now their man Shavers wants all of my reports by the end of this month or he might lose his chance to offer the bill in the Commons this session. It means we won't have to go to the mine in Buckfastleigh after I'm through here."

"Shavers," Jack muttered, not bothering to hide his disgust. "That flamin' fomenter. Why you care to hook up wi' a lawless jack-rag the likes o' him is a myst'ry to me."

"I haven't hooked up with him. I've never even met him."

"Well, I heard 'im speak onct—"

"And he incited a crowd of tin miners in Redruth to walk out on strike. I know, you've told me a hundred times. What I can't understand is why that makes him the devil incarnate as far as you're concerned. If anybody—oh, hell." *If anybody ought to be in favor of mining reform,* he almost said, *it's you.* But he and Jack had had this argument too many times, and the irony of their reversed positions on the subject no longer entertained them. "Anyway," he finished tiredly, "it seems we won't be in Wyckerley for as long as I thought."

"Which is fine wi' you. On account o' that lady who'm now yer boss."

Connor started to deny it, then didn't. "You ought to see her, Jack, sitting behind this huge desk, looking—well, you know what she looks like—issuing orders right and left, like a . . ."

"Like a man. Bloody right. Puts yer back up, don't it?"

"No. No, that's not it. I don't care that she's the boss." He could even concede, from the little he'd seen, that she was probably good at it.

"Well, what, then?"

"I won't be able to say much good about her mine in my report."

"What's wrong wi' it?"

"The same things that are wrong with all of them—low wages, bad air, unsafe conditions, no contingencies for underground emergencies. Today I heard Jenks, the mine captain, talking about the loss of two or three miners a year as 'natural wastage.' "

Jack sighed. "And so it is."

"Now *that's* the attitude I can't abide. That's the *very* — "

"Oh, Con," Jack said, getting to his feet laboriously, "let's not do this one again, eh? Not just now, anyways, whilst I'm this thirsty and in need of a sip. Come, let's go and have our supper at the George."

"The George? But Maura's coming in twenty minutes to fix our meal. Why—"

"Yes, but she'm ugly as a hedgehog. Last night she spoilt my dinner just by lookin' at it."

Connor snorted. "She's not ugly, you randy old goat. All that's wrong with her is she keeps her legs together. So far. Not like *Rose.*"

"All? You can say *all*? Oh, my boy, ee've been working too hard and too long. Come wi' me now," he urged with mock solicitousness, "let ol' Jack show you how to 'ave a good time."

But Connor shrugged away. "Leave off, I'm not going with you."

"Why not?"

"Because I'm tired, because we're paying this girl two shillings a week to cook for us, and because I've got work to do."

"Rhad work, is it?" Connor nodded, and Jack let go of his arm. "Con, Con, I'm that worried. What ee needs is a woman, in the very worst way. If ee had a warm body in bed of a night, ee wouldn't be ruinin' yer health by readin' books and writin' dull tracts for yer maniac socialist cronies."

Connor managed to laugh at that. But after his brother had gone, he couldn't help thinking that he wrote his "dull tracts" for people exactly like Jack, working men and women throwing away their youth and health just to stay alive, while their labors swelled the profits of adventurers and speculators who wouldn't know a copper mine from a colliery.

Still, Jack had a point: there was something to be said for a warm body in bed of a night. What irritated him was that the picture that instantly sprang to mind at the phrase was the warm body of Miss Sophie Deene.

# IV
---

It took time, but eventually nine hours of battling solid rock and bad air every day no longer reduced Connor to utter exhaustion. On the Friday, when Jack issued his nightly invitation to step over to the tavern with him, he said yes.

One of the draws of the George and Dragon, besides a supper prepared by someone other than the spectacularly incompetent Maura, was a chance for Connor to see Rose again, although with her clothes on this time. She was a big-breasted, black-haired girl of twenty or so, with a cast in one eye and a great, booming voice. She was fond of smacking customers on the back and laughing raucously at their jokes, or hers. But he noticed that when she spoke to Jack, she softened her tone and touched him with great gentleness.

Although they'd been in the village for less than a week, Jack had already made friends with most of the regulars at the George. Many were miners at Guelder and Salem, but others were tenant farmers for Lynton Great Hall, Wyckerley's manor house and the seat of its most exalted residents, Lord and Lady Moreton. The atmosphere was friendly and warm at the George, and even though the Pendarvis brothers, being newly arrived in a village that rarely saw new arrivals, were an object of much interest and speculation, no one pried into their personal histories or held them at a wary distance because they were strangers. In Connor's experience, the local squire and the minister were the two individuals most responsible for setting a tone of welcome—or otherwise—in small, provincial villages. In the case of Wyckerley, those two were Sebastian Verlaine, the Earl of Moreton, and Christian Morrell, the vicar of All Saints Church, the man Connor had mistaken last week for Sophie Deene's husband. He heard the names of the vicar and the earl mentioned frequently among the drinkers at the George, and always in affectionate and approving terms.

"Oh, yes, the vicar am a fine, fine fellow," Tranter Fox opined, and launched into a recitation of the time he'd gotten pinned under a piece of fallen machinery at the seventy level and been given up for a lost cause. Connor, who had heard it six times already, had to listen again to the story of how Reverend Morrell was the only man brave enough to go near Tranter, and how he'd prayed and sung hymns with him until the gallery in which they were trapped collapsed on top of their heads. "Bleedin' *miracle* when the roof caved in on the stamp rod and I were set free. Bloody blinkin' *miracle*." All the men gathered around the cold hearth in the smoky, low-ceilinged public room nodded and muttered in tired agreement, and Connor suspected they'd heard the story even more often than he had.

"Say, Tranter, why aren't you at the penny reading this evening?" asked Charles Oldene, one of the tributers at Guelder. "You know who's reading tonight, don't you?"

General laughter; Connor was surprised when the little Cornishman ducked his head and stuck his nose in his mug of bittered ale to hide a blush.

"What's a penny reading?" Jack asked.

"They have 'em at the vicarage on Fridays," Oldene answered. " 'Twas the vicar's idea, or maybe his wife's, I forget. Every week somebody reads from a book out loud to those who've come to hear."

"What kind of a book?"

"Oh, any kind. Onct Mrs. Morrell read out one about a fellow stuck in a dungeon for years and years."

"*The Count o' Monte Cristo*," supplied Tranter. "Say, weren't that a corker?"

"A right cracker," agreed Oldene, signaling Rose for more ale.

"So who'm reading tonight?" Jack wanted to know.

" 'Tis none other than our own Miss Sophie," said Moony Donne, trying to nudge Tranter in the ribs with his elbow. The miner squirmed away and swore at him, which only made the men laugh again.

"Now, Tranter, don't go on being bashful. We all know you've got your heart set on Miss Deene."

"I 'ave not. Shut up, Charles, by Jakes, ee're a bleedin' nitwit."

Oldene chortled with glee. "She's readin' right now, right this very minute, in that low, soft voice o' hers. Sends shivers down your arms, don't it? Eh, don't it? Why'nt you go and hear 'er, Tranter?"

"Because I don't care to," he answered with stiff dignity. " 'Tisn't my kind o' book, if ee must know. 'Tis all about *faymels*; I heard some faymel even writed it."

That made sense; the men nodded and puffed on their pipes, in sympathy with Tranter's decision.

Connor had caught glimpses of Sophie Deene during the week, quick sightings early or late in the day, always from a distance, and with no sign from her that she'd seen him. Except once, when he'd caught her eye and she'd had no choice but to acknowledge him with a brief nod. The memory of that instant of awareness and interest in her face, gone in a second and replaced by studied indifference, had nettled him ever since.

He stood up.

"Not leaving, are you, Jack?" said Jack. The bitter he'd drunk had put color in his sallow cheeks; he looked deceptively healthy.

"Yes, I'm off. Don't stay much longer," Connor said lightly, touching his shoulder. "The smoke's not good for you."

"Too right. I'll just have this last and be away," he promised—and Connor knew he would still be here when the barman locked the door.

"Where're you bound for so blinkin' early?" Tranter wanted to know.

Connor laid a shilling on the white-ringed table. "I find I'm in the mood for a good book."

Jack snorted. "Might've knowed it. Ee can't set still and do nothin' for even one night. Ee're worse off than I thought! Ee'll ruin yer eyes!"

Connor turned back in the doorway. "I guess it's a chance I'll have to take," he said with a straight face, and walked out into the night.

" 'If I loved you less, I might be able to talk about it more. But you know what I am. You hear nothing but truth from me. I have blamed you, and lectured you, and you have borne it as no other woman in England would have borne it. Bear with the truths I would tell you now, dearest Emma, as well as you have borne with them. The manner, perhaps, may have as little to recommend them. God knows, I have been a very indifferent lover. But you understand me. Yes, you see, you understand my feelings— and will return them if you can. At present, I ask only to hear— once to hear your voice.' "

Sophie looked up from the book to see twelve ladies smiling back at her. No words were necessary; after hundreds of pages read on seven consecutive Friday evenings, they had finally come to it, the perfect moment, the consummation (figuratively speaking only, of course) of the tender attachment of two most beloved characters: Emma Woodhouse and Mr. Knightley. The women seated on long Sunday school benches in the vicarage meeting hall were all misty-eyed, and as enchanted with the love scene as Sophie could wish. It was a relief, for although *Emma* was one of her favorite novels, she had worried a little in the beginning that the ladies of Wyckerley might not altogether approve of its proud, rather willful heroine.

She resumed. " 'Her way was clear, though not quite smooth. She spoke then, on being so entreated. What did she say? Just what she ought, of course. A lady always does. She said enough to show there need not be despair—and to invite him to say more himself.' "

A soft noise from the back of the room distracted her. She

looked up to see all heads turned and every eye focused on the man who was muttering, "Excuse me, beg your pardon," as he tried to climb over Susan Hatch's knees to an empty place in the middle of the last bench.

"Mr. Pendarvis," Sophie exclaimed after a shocked second. "Are you—did you—do you know that we—"

"Isn't this the penny reading?" His face was all polite interest.

"Yes, but—we're reading Jane Austen's *Emma*," she explained, acutely aware that she was blushing. "In fact, we've only a few pages left."

"*Emma*! What a coincidence—it's one of my favorites. Especially the last few pages."

"Is that so." Ignoring the titters, Sophie narrowed her eyes in suspicion. "How does it end?"

Mr. Pendarvis looked disconcerted, but only for a second. He help up one finger. "They live happily ever after."

Cora Swan, the blacksmith's daughter, muffled a laugh into her handkerchief; her sister Chloe echoed it. Mr. Pendarvis sent them a ravishing grin that had them huddling against each other, giggling uncontrollably. Seated now, he folded his arms and looked blandly back into Sophie's scowl, his eyebrows raised expectantly.

Rattled, she glanced around. The women were looking interestedly back and forth between Mr. Pendarvis and her. What she longed to do was order him from the room; but if she did that, the ladies' curiosity would instantly turn to speculation.

Trapped.

Clearing her throat, she found her place and took up the story again. But now her pleasure in the sweet, elegant ending was completely gone, replaced by self-consciousness. What was worse, she heard herself stumble over words, lose her place, skip whole lines—she who was *famous* at the penny readings for her fine, smooth delivery! By the time she turned the final page and read the last eloquent paragraph, she felt as tightly wound as a top.

But another survey of her audience—dreamy-eyed again, half

smiling, utterly satisfied—helped to restore her composure. "Well," she said, closing the book with a quiet snap and laying it on the desk at her back. "How did you like it?" She leaned against the desk casually, to signal the start of the informal discussion period that always followed the readings, especially when a book was finally finished.

"Oh," said Cora Swan, "I loved it."

"Oh, yes, it was *sooo* nice," echoed Chloe. "Do let's read it again right now."

The ladies laughed gently at that, while a few nodded in wry agreement.

"What did you think of Emma?" Sophie prodded.

"Well, I liked 'er so much," said Susan Hatch. "She was so handsome and clever, and smart as any of the men, except for Mr. Knightley." Susan was a parlor maid at Lynton Hall, but she had hopes of one day being the housekeeper; she appreciated smart heroines.

Mrs. Ludd, the Morrells' housekeeper at the vicarage, said, "I thought she got just what she deserved—a handsome husband and all that money."

"I was glad when she decided to stay with her father until he passed on," offered Mrs. Nineways, the churchwarden's wife. "Whatever else, she always did her duty by her father."

"That's true," said Mrs. Thoroughgood. "She was a very dutiful daughter."

"I suppose she made some mistakes," Susan acknowledged, "but it all come out right in the end."

"That's right." "Yes, indeed." "Right in the end."

"She was a snob."

Heads craned; breaths were drawn in. Everyone in the room looked at Mr. Pendarvis in amazement, as if he'd just called Emma Woodhouse a prostitute.

He softened the piercing, gray-eyed stare he'd locked on Sophie and smiled at the ladies, suddenly boyish and self-effacing—and almost immediately they smiled back at him, charmed. She noticed he had on the same dark coat and trousers he'd worn the day they'd met, with a clean white shirt and no necktie. And she could feel herself falling under the same spell as before, responding to the same potent male energy he radiated with such effortlessness. If she hadn't known otherwise, she'd have made the mistake of thinking he was a gentleman, engaged in a gentleman's profession. Which certainly proved the wisdom of the adage about judging books by their covers.

"Are we to assume from that remark," she asked coolly, "that you truly are familiar with *Emma*? With something more than the last ten pages, I mean," she added with false sweetness.

"Well . . . no, ma'am," he admitted, and his candor, she saw, had the effect of endearing him to the ladies even more. "I got the gist of it, though, and I'd say the lady's a snob. And a busybody."

"Oh?" Sophie pushed away from the desk. "And why is that?"

"Well, take this Harriet character, for instance. Isn't she supposed to be a friend of Emma's?"

"Yes, but she—"

"Then why did Emma talk her out of marrying what's-his-name, the farmer who was in love with her?"

"Robert Martin," she said tightly, hiding her annoyance behind a patient expression. "Because she didn't think he was the right man for Harriet."

"Because he was a farmer?"

"A yeoman, yes, and although Harriet was illegitimate, Emma believed her father was of noble birth—mistakenly, as it turns out, but—"

"So *then* it was all right for her to marry a farmer? Because her father turned out not to be a lord?"

"She—yes—but the point is—"

"What business is it of Emma's anyway?" he pursued, still in the smiling, courteous, self-deprecating style that hid, she was sure, a world of antagonism. He'd drawn one boot up on the bench and was clasping his knee, seeming completely at ease. The more relaxed he looked, the tighter her nerves stretched.

"She's a bit of a meddler, isn't she, Miss Deene? Horning in on other people's affairs?"

"She did cause a lot of trouble," Mrs. Thoroughgood admitted thoughtfully. "And she wasn't very nice to Jane Fairfax."

"She was jealous of her," Susan Hatch realized. "She didn't want anybody in the village being more important than her."

The ladies were looking at Sophie expectantly and—she fancied—a trifle worriedly, as if their rock-solid faith in her judgment had been given a slight nudge.

She held out her hand, imploring their understanding. "Yes, she did meddle, but she always meant well. She fancied herself a matchmaker, and it's true she wasn't very good at it, but she *reformed*. Once she realized she'd blundered, she swallowed her pride and set out to make things right."

"That's right," said Mrs. Nineways, "she did," and Miss Pine said, "True."

Sophie said, "And after she pokes fun at poor old Miss Bates at the Box Hill picnic—"

Mr. Pendarvis dropped his boot to the floor. "She makes fun of an *old lady*?"

"*Gentle* fun, unintentionally, and she's ashamed of herself afterward, and apologizes sincerely—"

"I should think so."

She gritted her teeth. Emma Woodhouse was her favorite heroine in all of fiction; she would not stand by while this—this—*miner* defamed her. "The point is," she said again, louder, "she learns from her mistakes. It's true that she's not a perfect heroine, but that only makes her more interesting and human. Her flaws are forgivable because she has a good heart. She can be foolish and misguided, yes, but when she interferes in other people's lives it's because she really believes she's helping them. And in the end everyone—Emma, Harriet, Jane Fairfax, even Mrs. Elton—each marries *exactly* the right person, not only according to their hearts and their temperaments, but their stations, too. All the couples—"

"Their stations? So Harriet could only marry a farmer because—that's what she was *born for*?" No boyishness now; his pale gray eyes speared her, intense and unwavering.

Sophie considered the question and answered it honestly. "Yes."

But she wasn't prepared for the loaded silence that followed, or the uneasy feeling that accompanied her reply—although she believed it was correct. For the first time she saw uncertainty, perhaps even mistrust in the faces of her friends and neighbors. The look on Mr. Pendarvis's face was subtler and better hidden, but she interpreted it easily. It was contempt.

With the keenest relief, she heard the church clock strike nine, the unvarying hour when penny readings concluded, and somehow the sound seemed to dissipate the vague tension that had crept into the room; the bustle and murmuring of the ladies as they gathered their belongings sounded relaxed and close to normal.

"Don't forget, Captain Carnock will begin reading *The Compleat Angler* next Friday," she reminded them. "Tell your husbands, ladies, that it's a marvelous book about fishing. Among other things."

The room began to empty. Margaret Mareton, the Sunday school teacher, had a word with Sophie about the children's play she was directing for Midsummer Day; they spoke for a few minutes, and Sophie agreed to teach the seven-year-olds a song Miss Mareton had written especially for the occasion. All the while, she kept her gaze fixed deliberately on Margaret's face, fighting the urge to look and see if Mr. Pendarvis was still there. But when Miss Mareton thanked her and walked away, she couldn't hold out any longer.

He was gone.

Anne Morrell was leaning in the doorway, holding Elizabeth, her seven-month-old daughter. Anne attended almost all the readings—she was the vicar's wife; it was expected of her—but Sophie hadn't seen her tonight until now. "How's Lizzy?" she asked worriedly. "Not sick, I hope."

"Oh, no," Anne assured her, jiggling the smiling, wide-eyed baby in her arms. "Unless you call insomnia a sickness. I'm beginning to think of it as a penance, although I'm not clear on exactly what sin I've committed to deserve it."

Sophie laughed. "None, I'm sure. You look tired, though." But she didn't worry about Anne, because under the surface fatigue lay a soft, radiant happiness that never left her, and made her look beautiful no matter how weary she was. "I wish I could take Lizzy for a few days, to give you a rest."

"Well, that's nice of you."

"No, it isn't." Sophie cupped her hand behind the baby's soft, spindly neck and gave her a kiss on her sweet-smelling cheek. "It's pure selfishness."

Lizzy's mother smiled fondly. "But you still love your work at the mine, don't you, Sophie?"

"Oh, yes—but I didn't mean I don't have *time* to take Lizzy. It's just that I'd be missing a certain, how shall I say, prerequisite."

"Oh," Anne said, laughing. "Yes, well, Mrs. Ludd keeps telling me I ought to hire a wet nurse, but I don't want to. If I did, I'd only have more time to myself, which would mean I'd have to pay more duty calls on needy parishioners. And let's face it, no one would like *that*." Sophie pretended to be shocked, but she was used to Anne's irreverent humor by now. "Besides, as much as she wears me out, I can't bear to let this little monkey out of my sight for more than a few hours at a time." She made a moony face at her daughter, who returned it with a sleepy smile.

"Tell me, Sophie," she said as they went up the stairs together, "who was that man at the reading tonight? I didn't recognize him."

"His name is Mr. Pendarvis."

"Pendarvis? He must be a Methodist; I'm sure I've never seen him before."

Anne was new to Wyckerley, only three years or so. "No one's ever seen him," Sophie explained. "He's only just arrived."

"Really? How exciting. He's awfully good-looking, isn't he? I used to think black-haired men were handsomer than fair-haired—before Christy, of course. What brings him to our little village?"

"I've given him a job at Guelder. He's a miner."

"Is he?"

"He doesn't look it, does he?" Sophie said quickly.

"Oh, I wouldn't know." She laughed lightly. "After all, what does a miner look like?"

Sophie frowned; it wasn't the answer she'd wanted. "I meant to say, he doesn't *speak* like a miner." Even in her own ears she sounded defensive.

"What do you suppose made him come to hear the last bit of *Emma*?" Anne wondered as she rocked Lizzy, who had begun to fret.

"I'm sure I can't imagine." *He came to provoke me, of course,* she thought in silence. They had arrived at the front door of the vicarage. "Where's Christy tonight?" she asked, throwing her shawl over her shoulders.

"He had to go to Mare's Head for a christening."

"Whose baby is it?"

Anne hesitated a fraction of a second. "Sarah Burney's."

"Oh."

The two women exchanged looks. Sarah Burney was the scandal of the neighborhood. Educated, respectable, the daughter of a lieutenant in the Royal Navy, Sarah had fallen in love with a petty officer under her father's command. Before they could marry, he'd been killed in the British bombardment at Canton.

"Poor girl," Sophie murmured. "What will become of her, I wonder."

Anne shook her head. "Or her baby."

"Her life's ruined."

"It's so unfair." Lizzy pulled on a lock of her mother's reddish hair, spoiling Anne's coiffure—and lightening the solemn mood that had fallen between the two women. "Do you have to go right away, Sophie? Stay and have a cup of tea with me, can't you?"

"It's late. I'd love to, but I'd better go home."

"Next time."

"Yes, of course."

"Good night, then." They touched hands, and Sophie went down the flagged path toward the green.

A half-moon silvered the grass and diffused the yellow wink of fireflies rising and sinking in the oak trees. The whispery splash of the Wyck inside its steep banks was a comforting, familiar sound; Sophie barely heard it. She had unhitched Valentine from the cart earlier and left him tethered at the far edge of the grass, within reach of the river so he could have a drink. She heard the tinkle of his harness and smiled, picturing him shaking his head, catching her scent and already impatient for home. A moving glimmer of white caught her eye. She slowed her steps and peered into the gloom.

Valentine wasn't where she'd left him; he was hitched to the cart, and Jack Pendarvis was holding his head and rubbing his nose. And feeding him an apple.

It was the white of his shirt she'd seen in the dimness. As she drew closer, he and Val lifted their heads, hearing her at the same time. The pony whickered a friendly welcome. Mr. Pendarvis watched her come and didn't say anything.

She stopped three feet shy of him, resting her hand casually on the pony's rump. "You've put Valentine in his traces." Her voice came out sounding too low and intimate. "Thank you," she tacked on, louder.

"Don't mention it."

Only a second or two passed while they stared at each other, but to Sophie it seemed much longer. "Well. I'll be going home now." When he didn't move, she said, "Was there something you wanted?"

"Will you lend me that book?"

"This?" She looked down at the tan leather cover of *Emma*, then back up at Mr. Pendarvis. "You don't want to read this."

"What makes you think I don't?"

There wasn't a doubt in her mind that he was mocking her.

But she was determined not to let him lure her into an argument. "I don't believe it's quite your cup of tea."

He folded his arms, leaning lightly against Val's shoulder, as if he didn't have a thing in the world to do except talk about books late at night on the village green. "And what would you say, Miss Deene, is my cup of tea?"

She pretended to consider. "There are some adventure books in our subscription library. Pictures, mostly, but a few with simplified text. The children find them quite stimulating."

Breathless from her own daring, she watched his face, the quick changes in it from surprise to anger, and finally grudging amusement. His slow, knowing smile unsettled her, did something ticklish underneath her breastbone.

"When I was a boy, Miss Deene, the Methodist minister in our village used to tutor me in reading and mathematics. When I did well on my examinations, he'd reward me with presents, a poem he'd written in Latin, or little cardboard pictures of the saints, or Brighton Beach, or the Houses of Parliament." His low voice was deep and pleasant, his accent a lighter Cornish burr than she was used to. "Once he gave me a book. I don't know where he got it—he was a very old man and nearly as poor as we were. The book was called *The Life and Times of Bartholomew Bailey, a Virtuous Boy,* so it's possible the reverend didn't know what he had."

"What was it?"

"A book about a magic boy. Bartholomew was the same age as me—eight—and he could make himself appear and disappear in unlikely times and places—Egypt among the pharaohs or the North Pole. The American frontier. The Bastille in 1789."

"Ah," Sophie breathed, intrigued in spite of herself. "How lucky you must have felt."

"Lucky." His voice gave the word a strange gravity. He stepped closer until their hands, both absently stroking the pony's smooth flank, were nearly touching. "Bartholomew could talk to animals, too. His dog was his best friend. He understood what deer and rabbits said, and horses, and birds." He looked away; a self-mocking smile quirked his lips on one side. "You understand that this book was a miracle to me. Magic. My salvation."

She nodded, although she wasn't really sure she understood at all.

"I kept it with me all the time. I even slept with it. No one in my family knew about it; it was a secret. Magic," he said again 'in a whisper, and Sophie felt a little shiver, not unpleasant, on the skin of her arms. "I had four brothers. One day they caught me."

"Reading your book," she guessed.

"Worse. Talking to a tree. Something else Bartholomew could do."

"Oh, dear. Were they younger or older, these brothers?"

"Older, all of them. They . . . made fun of me."

"Yes."

"In self-defense, I made a mistake: I told them about my book. Everything, in detail." He ran a hand over his jaw, and they were standing so close, she could hear the prickly rasp of his whiskers. "The more I talked, the worse it got. I *believed* Bartholomew could fly through time and space, and have long conversations with Jupiter—that was his dog. When my brothers laughed at me, it was worse than humiliating. It was . . ." He trailed off, and his hand lifted and fell in a gesture of futility.

"A betrayal," Sophie murmured.

"Yes. Because I knew finally that they were right and I was wrong. Dogs can't talk and boys can't fly. And I was a fool."

She clasped her hands behind her back, peering into his face. Even though he was tall, thick-muscled, and broad-shouldered, disconcertingly male, it was easy to see the eight-year-old boy in his strong, hard-boned face, the shadow of disillusionment in his clear gray eyes. And even though she suspected the story he'd just told her had an unflattering moral, she felt a deep sympathy for the child whose brothers' mockery had spoiled his sweetest dream.

"I wasn't making fun of you tonight," he said quietly. "But that book of yours is as big a lie as *The Life and Times of Bartholomew Bailey.* Dogs can't talk, Miss Deene, and ladies who look down on other people because of their 'stations' aren't heroic. They're stupid and arrogant."

"You don't understand."

"I think I do."

"No, no, and—I could never *make* you understand."

"Because I'm a poor, uneducated copper miner?"

She ignored that. "You're making a comparison that isn't fair, a false analogy. An analogy is a—"

"I know what an analogy is," he snapped.

She flushed—but she wanted to ask *how* he knew, and if he knew, then how could he be a poor, uneducated copper miner? She shook her head quickly, frustratedly; this was hopeless. She was in an argument she couldn't win, even though she was still sure she was right, and it was beginning to seem as if every encounter she had with Mr. Pendarvis put her in this disagreeable position. "It's very late," she said shortly. "I must go home."

He put out his hand. "I'll drive you."

She blinked at him. "What? Oh, no. Certainly not."

"You shouldn't be out this late by yourself. I'll drive you."

"I always drive myself."

"After dark?"

"Yes. Anyway, you'd have no way to get home afterward; my house is almost two miles from here."

"I'll walk."

"No, it's out of the question. Thank you very much, but no."

Some kind of smile turned up the corners of his lips; even in the dimness, she didn't think it was a pleasant smile. "Is it my uncouth manner that offends you, Miss Deene? Can you smell the stink of mud and ore on my clothes?" He leaned in closer. "Or is it that you're just scared of me?"

What she could smell was clean soap on his skin, the sharp tang of apple on his breath. Was he going to touch her? She wanted to step back, put a safe distance between them. But she stood still and made herself look straight into his eyes. "I believe we've gotten off on the wrong foot somehow, Mr. Pendarvis. I've never deliberately offended you. But I am completely capable of driving home by myself, and I would refuse an offer of assistance from anyone, regardless of his . . . station," she said deliberately. "And one other thing. Since we met, your society has—has provoked in me any number of things, but please do let me assure you, sir, that fear is *not* among them."

Why did she feel relieved when he chuckled at that? She couldn't imagine, but he had a warm, low laugh, and the mellow sound of it went a long way toward dispelling the tension in the air between them. In truth, she was glad the things she'd said, and the stiffness with which she'd said them, hadn't insulted him. Jack Pendarvis was proud, she'd begun to realize, and as prickly about his dignity as she was about hers. So. They had something in common.

He put his hand out again—to help her into the pony cart, she thought, so she took it. But instead he kept her hand in a light, firm clasp while he said softly, suggestively, "You'll have to tell me someday what other things my society has *provoked* in you, Miss Deene." Impudent! Before she could think of a response, he added, "Are you going to lend me that book, after all?"

She pulled her hand forcibly out of his. "No, I am not."

"Why not?"

"I fear the subtleties would be lost on you."

"Ah, now, Miss Deene." He shook his head sadly. "That's a hard thing to say to a man you just finished apologizing to."

"*Apologizing.* Why, I did no such thing. How you could possibly—" The white flash of his teeth silenced her; with a start, she realized he was teasing. Thoroughly confounded now, she set her foot on the high step and reached for the reins. Mr. Pendarvis put his hands on her waist, but she sprang up into the seat with such alacrity, she barely felt them. "Good night to you, sir."

"G'night, Miss Deene. Be careful going home. Have you a

lantern? There's a moon tonight, but it's still dark as a blathering sack."

The Cornish idiom arrested her, and brought home something, one of the many things, that puzzled her about this man. Sometimes, because of his manner or a certain irony or self-consciousness in his speech, it was almost as if he were *playing* at being a "poor, uneducated copper miner."

She sighted down her nose at him. "I've had my clerk write to the mine agent at Carn Barra, and I expect a reply any day now. It will be interesting to find out what sort of worker you were in your last place."

No reaction; all he did was stick his hands in his pockets and raise his eyebrows at her. She thought he looked amused.

She was tired of looking at him. Without another word, she slapped the reins down and Val took off—so quickly, Sophie's neck snapped back uncomfortably. She hadn't gone far before she began to think of all the things she should've said to him. To put him in his place.

# V

The hole Connor fell through was big enough to swallow a horse.

Or so Tranter Fox estimated while he was hauling him out of it. "Didn't ee spy that great plank, Jack? 'Tis yer own fault fer slitherin' down in thur when any man can see there'm a board wide as two counties acrost un. Did ee slip? Christ, ee're heavy. Quit heavin' and give over yer arm. Now take yer feet t' squinch out o't. That's it, that's it. There you be. Phaw! Ee're one bleedin' mess, Jack, sink me if you ain't."

The murky glow from the candle in Tranter's hat—Connor's had gone out—shed just enough light to reveal the literalness of his words: Connor was a bleeding mess. His left side felt fiery-hot, and warm blood was running down the inside of his left arm and dripping off his fingers.

"Best go up," Tranter advised. "Ee don't look hale, not a'tall, and wounds're like to fester quick down here in the hot and wet. Go up, get Annie Whited t' tend you, there'm a brave lad."

"Who's Annie Whited?"

"One o' the bal girls, but she knows sommat o' nursing and the like. We go to 'er fer snicks and breaks, whereas surgeon's the one fer awful things, bleedin' t' death and whatnot."

But Connor stayed down, resuming work on the pit they had been costeaning since yesterday. The stinging pain in his side was bearable, and he could still swing his pickax. Besides, he and Tranter were a team, their fortunes linked not only by the mining contract they'd signed, but by the comradeship they'd forged while they sweated and labored together under the ground. They got paid by the fathom; if Connor deserted him, his partner's wage would suffer.

By lunchtime, though, his shoulder had stiffened so much, he couldn't hold onto his drill. "Go up, man," Tranter berated him. "Are ee daft? Quit moolin' and get up to grass. I ha'n't no use fer a corpse on my spell, and I ain't carrying un up if ee swoons on me."

There were only four hours left on their core. Connor decided to go up.

By the sixth ladder, he was dripping with sweat and his left hand slipped and slid, leaving bloody prints on every other rung. At the mine entrance, the sudden cool air made him light-headed; blinking in the blinding sunlight, he had to lean against the open trapdoor for a minute to get his bearings. On the far side of the rubble-strewn yard, past the engine house and a couple of outbuildings, the bal girls or "maidens" dressed the mined ore with bucking irons, bruising and hammering the metal into pieces no bigger than fingertips. Annie Whited would be among them, and the only question in Connor's mind was whether he should go there as he was or wash up first in the changing shed. A mule pulling a wagon load of chains and bell cranks rumbled out of the way, and he spied the grass captain twenty yards away, having a chat with his employer.

She saw him at the same time. She wore a pale lavender dress with a square collar, white, and a violet sash around her waist. He watched her shade her eyes with her hand, frowning at him, then suddenly reach out and clutch Andrewson on the wrist, cutting off whatever he was saying. Andrewson turned, saw Connor. The expressions on their faces confused him until he looked down and saw the blood. There was a lot of it, soaking through the coarse linen of his smock, staining the left side the color of rust. It surprised him—he didn't hurt enough to have bled that much. But when he looked up again, too quickly, he almost lost his balance from dizziness.

Sophie was bearing down on him, with the grass captain hurrying along in her wake. "What happened?" she demanded from ten feet away. "Are you hurt badly?"

"No," he denied, then added, "I doubt it."

She stopped in front of him, wide-eyed, taking him in at a glance. "How did it happen?"

"I fell through an old adit." He felt a mixture of belligerence and embarrassment, the former because she permitted such a hazard to exist, the latter because an experienced miner would have avoided it. "Fox pulled me out. I scraped my side, that's all, and cut my arm on the plank over the hole. It's nothing." She'd gone pale; she had the long tube of a rolled-up map in one hand, and she was unknowingly crushing it between her fingers. "Tranter said Annie Whited could fix me up. I'll just go and wash up, then find her."

"I sent Annie home an hour ago," Andrewson said. "She was drunk," he explained, shrugging, when Sophie turned to him.

"Dr. Hesselius had to go to Tavistock this morning," she said, dismay in her voice. "I heard him say so at my uncle's house last night. He'll be gone by now." She and Andrewson stared at Connor helplessly.

"I'll go and wash," he said again, and started around them for the changing shed.

"Go with him," he heard her tell Andrewson. "Then bring him back to my office."

"Yes, ma'am."

The sight of him, slow and stiff-legged and bloody, attracted a number of grass workers on the short walk across the yard to the changing shed. The men went in with him and wanted to know, while Andrewson helped him out of his hardening smock, all about his mishap. Gritting his teeth against the stinging shock of cold water sleucing off his open cuts, he explained what he'd done—fallen into a drainage hole through his own clumsiness. No one made fun of him; everyone had advice on how best to take care of his wounds. Slightly cheered, he accepted the clean shirt Andrewson threw over his shoulders, and together they made their way back across the yard to the countinghouse.

After the bright noonday sun, the small inner office was shady and relatively cool. "I don't know where she's got to," Andrewson muttered, seeing the room was empty. "Set and wait for her, I guess—I've got something that needs tending to." And he gave a nod and was gone.

Connor wanted to explore; the walls and shelves of Sophie Deene's office were covered with the paraphernalia of her trade, maps and ore samples, crosscut diagrams, books on mining and copper speculating—as well as a smaller but more interesting array of personal items, such as a framed sketch on the wall of the man he was sure now was her father, a thick, mannish fountain pen in an inkstand on her battered desk, an amateurish, pink-glazed clay sculpture of a rose—a Guelder?—that she used for a paper-weight. The subtle odor of roses couldn't be from the vase of purple flowers on the window ledge; this was a vaguer scent, softer and yet more pervasive. Her scent.

She bustled in then, putting an end to his inquisitive survey of her effects. She carried a basin of water and a clean white towel over one arm, and he speculated that, as the lady owner of Guelder, she probably had a private lavatory all to herself somewhere on the mine premises. "Sit down," she commanded, setting basin and towel on the edge of her desk.

A boy came in, sandy-haired, tall and gangly, holding out a paper-wrapped parcel to her. "Annie had this in 'er tuck-away, Miss Deene," he said, his Adam's apple bobbing in his skinny neck.

"Thank you, Matthew."

The boy shifted from foot to foot while she opened the parcel and rummaged around in its contents. "Miss Deene?"

"Yes?"

"I'll be fourteen on Wednesday."

"Happy birthday," she said distractedly, holding a brown bottle up to the light and squinting at it.

Matthew blushed. "No, ma'am, I mean, I'll be able t' go down then. Wi' my dad. If you can use me, that is."

"Oh." She glanced at him briefly. "Tell the grass captain, then.

And come to me again on Wednesday, and we'll discuss your wages and so on."

His face brightened. "Yes, *ma'am*," he exclaimed, and for a second Connor thought he was going to salute her.

"You could hire him at ten," he mentioned after the boy had gone, trying not to wince while he shrugged off his shirt.

"Legally, yes. But I don't send children down in my mine."

"That's noble of you."

She sent him a look. "Matthew's parents wouldn't agree with you. He can earn three times as much in the mine as he does now as a jigger. They'd have happily seen him underground at nine. Will you come over here, please? It'll be easier for me if you're sitting on the desk." She slid a pile of papers back from the corner, and he got up and went to her.

Together they examined his injuries. His scraped side hurt worse, but his arm was probably more serious; he'd torn a gash in it, probably on the rough wooden plank, that ran from just under his armpit to the crease in his elbow.

"The bleeding's almost stopped. But I have to clean it, which will probably make it start again."

"You don't have to do this."

She looked up. "Don't you trust me?"

"Not particularly."

"I've done it before. When Michael Tavist smashed his hand with a hammer, I'm the one who bandaged it for him until Dr. Hesselius came."

He smiled at the pride she couldn't quite keep out of her voice. "Have at it, then, by all means."

"Hold still, then; even if it hurts, hold still."

"Yes, ma'am." He did well, bore it all with manly courage, until she started dabbing something brownish and evil-smelling on the cuts in his side. "Ow. *Ow.* What the hell is that?"

"Please don't swear."

He squeezed his smarting eyes shut for a second. "What . . . is that?"

She glanced down at the glass vial in her hand, then back up to his face. "I have no idea."

For the barest second, they almost smiled at each other. Then a man barged through the open doorway, and the rare friendly moment was gone.

It was Jenks, the mine captain. A stocky, compact bull of a man, he had a fierce black beard that seemed to bristle when he was angry. The mine shafts daily rang with his shouted profanities, which were famous for their variety and vulgarity, and Connor had often wondered how he tempered his obscene utterances for the benefit of his ladylike employer.

"Murdoch's team and Bean's team didn't meet up," he announced without a greeting. With only the briefest glance at Connor—who must have presented a curious sight, half-naked, perched on the edge of Miss Deene's desk, and still bleeding from her amateur ministrations—Jenks stomped past both of them to the opposite wall, where a huge map of the whole of Guelder mine stretched between rough pieces of lathe for frames, and slammed his meaty fist down on a faint series of lines in the lower left corner. "Didn't meet up!" he repeated, incredulous. "They're six feet apart if they're an inch, the toads, hang me if they're not." He hammered his fist down again.

*Toads? Hang me?* Connor wanted to laugh, but Jenks's eyes, glittering with fury, kept his face sober.

Sophie set down the bit of flannel she'd been daubing his ribs with and went to look at the map. From Connor's vantage, there was nothing to see but a lot of vertical and horizontal scratchings made with a piece of charcoal, with a lot of erasures and overwriting. She and Jenks had a hurried conversation, pointing at lines, pressing their faces to the map, as if they could change the bad news by getting closer to it. Ignorant as he was, Connor got a rough idea that two teams of tributers had been simultaneously sinking shafts, one beneath the other, perpendicular to a crosscut above the southwest lode, preparatory to opening the lode so it could be worked for ore. They hadn't "met up," which meant the shafts, being driven from above and below, had failed to connect. Missed each other. By a fathom.

No wonder Jenks was angry.

Sophie and the mine captain were the same height, but Jenks outweighed her by about seven stone. He was an intimidating man when roused, spreading ire like sparks from his whole beefy body; underground, the men gave him a wide berth when he was on a tear, which was often, and not a few were really afraid of him.

"Mr. Jenks," Sophie said quietly, making no effort to stand back, out of the way of the almost visible aura around him of frustration and anger. "How did this happen?"

"I don't know yet. Each man is blaming the other. I suspect it's Bean who's off worse, but it could be it's the both of 'em."

"If it's both of them, a likelier reason for the error is that the specifications were wrong to begin with."

Jenks opened his mouth, shut it, and turned a darker shade of beet red. A vein popped out in his forehead. Connor watched its erratic pulsing and wondered if his head was going to explode.

Sophie turned back to the map. "The vein stone in that portion of the southwest is soft. Relatively. How long do you think it will take to align the two shafts?"

Jenks considered. "A week."

"With both teams working?"

"No, the one. And o' course, it'll change the angle."

"By how much?"

"Three, four degrees. Maybe five."

"Try for three. Put both teams on it, one working at either end, and get it done in four days. If you can."

Jenks squinted hard at the map, then at his boss. "Four days?"

"If you can."

The livid vein pulsed more slowly until at last it disappeared. "Three and a half," the mine captain rumbled.

"Even better."

"I'll make it a race. I'll tell 'em the team that drives first to the meet point gets an extra half crown per foot for each man." He dipped his big, shaggy head. "That is, if you agree."

"Why, that's an excellent idea, Mr. Jenks. I'm glad you thought of it."

Connor wouldn't have believed it if he hadn't seen it: Jenks, who never smiled and always scowled, actually grinned at her, showing a mouthful of large, perfect white teeth.

"What happened to you?" he asked on his way out.

"Slipped on a plank. Fell in an adit at the forty."

"Hmpf." Without even a sympathetic head shake, Jenks stomped out of the room.

Sophie was staring at the map again. She'd been calm and un-ruffled in front of Jenks, but now she was nibbling her bottom lip, one hand on her hip, unconsciously twisting a lock of hair with the other.

"Is it a serious setback?"

She turned, and the worry line between her brows smoothed out. "Oh, no," she denied, moving back to him, retrieving the flannel and rinsing it in the basin. "It's the sort of thing that happens often enough that it would be foolish to get upset about it."

"But it's a nuisance."

"A bit more than that." She pressed her lips together, as if she'd said more than she intended. "Six feet in four days without blasting must seem like fast work to you, Mr. Pendarvis," she mentioned, changing the subject as she leaned over him again and resumed cleaning the scrapes on his side.

"How's that?"

"Because the ground is so much harder in Cornwall than it is here. Generally speaking."

He made a vague sound; it was news to him.

"I visited the Charleston mine in St. Austell a few years ago, when my father was still alive. There, of course, a portion of the mine is open for several fathoms, so the study of a lodestone's characteristics for once doesn't have to be done by candlelight. I found it fascinating. Have you ever been there?"

He decided to tell the truth and say no. "But I imagine that would be interesting, seeing how the copper veins lie and so forth."

"The tin, you mean. Charleston is a tin mine."

"I meant tin." Before she could bring up another topic he didn't know anything about, he asked her about ventilation at Guelder; the subject would figure in his report, after all, plus it might keep his mind off the way her left hand felt, resting on his forearm, or the brush of her hair when a strand of it floated across his chest. The rustle of her clothes when she moved. The scent of her, faint as a whisper, potent as an aphrodisiac.

"Yes," she answered, "I've contracted for a new ventilator that ought to improve the circulation of air, and especially of smoke after a blast. It sounds simple, just a pipe, a valve, and an internal cylinder, but I'm told it can pump out twelve thousand gallons of air in an hour. If it really works, I may buy another one."

"And, of course, that would be a purely humanitarian gesture on your part, toward the health and safety of the men you employ."

She looked at him blankly. "What?"

"It wouldn't have anything to do with the fact that you'll save money with every degree you lower the temperature in the mine with your new ventilator. That would be an afterthought. Just a happy by-product."

Her hands stilled; she straightened. Her fine blue eyes studied him for so long, he wanted to fidget. "Why do you dislike me so much?"

"I don't dislike you." He felt churlish; he felt like a fool. He wanted to know why his liking her or not mattered at all to her.

"I think you do, but I don't understand why. I can't think of anything I've ever done to hurt you."

Now he did fidget. The honest confusion in her face made him ashamed. "You've done nothing. Nothing at all. I'm—I've been worried about my brother." The explanation slipped out so easily, he decided it must be only half a lie.

"Your brother?"

"He's a miner, too. Was a miner—he can work no longer because his lungs are gone. Consumption."

"I am very sorry." It rang true: sympathy softened every feature. "Does he live in Cornwall?" she asked.

"No, he's here in Wyckerley with me."

"You take care of him."

He smiled slightly. "In a way. It's a new role for me. He's older than I am. It . . ."

"Seems strange," she finished softly. "And . . . it makes you sad."

"That's it."

They exchanged a long, thoughtful look, and he imagined his face reflected the same subtle surprise hers did, because they were speaking for once without subterfuge or hostility. Almost like friends.

"This is all there is for a large bandage," she said, recollecting herself. She held up a white square of cloth, like a split pillowcase, which she'd found in Annie Whited's bundle. "I'm not sure it'll go around you."

It did, barely, and he enjoyed her efforts to tie the two ends together across his chest. She glanced up at him once, then back down, quickly, and he noticed her cheeks were a deeper pink than usual. Interesting. All this intimate nursing hadn't fazed her while they were sniping at each other; but now that they were being civil, she blushed.

"The cut here is much deeper," she said briskly, turning her attention to his arm. "I'm afraid it'll have to be sewn."

"Is that your professional opinion, Doctor?"

Her eyes twinkled. "It is. If I were you, Mr. Pendarvis, I would go straight—"

"Well, well, what 'ave we 'ere? Pick me liver! If I'd've knowed what were in store fer the disabled, by Jakes, I'd've hurtled myself down the main shaft ages ago." Tranter Fox, tracking mud onto Miss Deene's clean-swept floor, whipped off his miner's helmet and sent her his biggest gap-toothed grin.

"Good afternoon, Mr. Fox," she greeted him, pressing down a smile. "What brings you up at this time of the day?"

"Consarn fer my dear friend, ma'am," he intoned solemnly, coming closer, pretending to examine Connor's bandaged ribs and the still-oozing cut in his arm. "How're ee faring, Jack? Ee've got a angel o' mercy tending to yer wounds, I see. If you was t' pass on right now, at least yer last eyeful on earth ud be a beauteous one."

Sophie snorted.

"That's a comforting thought," Connor allowed. "I'll try to hold on to it as I'm slipping away."

"Do that." He stuck his hands in his pockets and rocked on his toes, darting secret glances at Sophie when she wasn't looking. "What are ee doing for the invalid, ma'am? If I may be so bold as to ask."

"Nothing much, only cleaning the cuts. And putting some of this on," she added, holding up her brown, vile-smelling bottle, "to make sure he stays awake."

"That's the ticket," Tranter cackled, rubbing his hands together. "Keep 'im on 'is toes."

"Exactly."

They smiled at each other—and for Connor, the raillery between them was a revelation. It confirmed the crush Tranter was reputed to have on his employer, and also revealed a side of Sophie that Connor had thought he might never see again, the girlish, lighthearted side.

"Don't you have three hours or so left on your core, Mr. Fox?"

"Yes, Miss Deene, but I were that et up wi' worry, I could barely hold up a pick. Had t' see how the boy were doing, like, or go mad from the strain."

"Ah. And now that you've set your mind at rest, there's probably nothing to prevent you from returning to your work."

Tranter screwed up his face, thinking hard. "Prob'ly not," he finally begrudged. He edged toward the door. "Now, Jack, ee want to be layin' out fer a day or two or three, lest you open up and bleed all over everything. Don't worry about me being on my own, not fer a second, for there'm plenty o' things I can be—"

"I'll see you tomorrow," Connor interrupted.

"Oh, will ee? Well, ain't that fine. That's—"

"I very much doubt that," Sophie said severely. "In my opinion, Mr. Pendarvis, that would be very foolish."

"Very foolish," Tranter echoed, nodding adamantly. "I very much doubt ee'll do any such thing. You listen to yer nurse, Jack, and obey 'er wise words. Miss Deene, she'm knowed far and wide for 'er wisdom, see, not to mention 'er loveliness, which she'm famous for, too, and a base, low miner like yerself, or *my*self, come t' that, couldn't do better' n take 'er advice in all matters, great and small. Because she'm truly a pillar o'—".

"Thank you, Mr. Fox," Sophie cut in, laughing. "Good afternoon to you now."

Tranter bowed from the waist. "Yer sarvant," he said to the floor, and sidled out of the room. .

Before he could consider his words, Connor said softly, "I like to hear you laugh."

She kept her head down and made no answer.

"You were laughing the first day we met. Do you remember?"

She'd been dabbing gently at the cut on the inner side of his biceps, supporting his arm in the crook of her elbow, so that his wrist rested lightly against the side of her breast. Because of what he'd said, the innocent contact was too personal now: she stepped away to rummage in the paper parcel for another bandage.

"How's Birdie?" he asked smoothly.

"Ah, Birdie. She was very taken with you, you know."

"Was she?"

"She still speaks of you."

"What does she say?"

"She calls you 'the nice man with big hands.' "

Connor chuckled. He waited until she had to touch him again, to wind a strip of gauzy white cotton around his arm, to say, "Will you go for a walk with me next Saturday afternoon, Miss Deene?"

Her face was a study. He saw pleasure light up her eyes before she averted them and said quickly, "Oh, no. I can't."

He studied her profile, the aristocratic nose with its fine white nostrils, like porcelain, and her pretty mouth, the lips meeting at just the right, seductive angle. She wore her hair in a little net at the back of her neck today, a snood, he thought it was called, but a few long, wavy wisps had escaped, softening the severity of the style. Her refusal to see him came as no surprise. He shouldn't have asked her anyway.

But he was tired of doing what he was supposed to do. "We wouldn't go far," he pressed lightly, "just along the river in the village. You'd be perfectly safe."

She lifted one eyebrow at that, and the side of her mouth curved slightly. But she said again, "No, I can't." He stood up, so abruptly she started. "You must forgive my impertinence. I'll not ask you again." Grinding his teeth against the pain, he tucked the loose end of the gauze strip roughly inside the neat bandage she'd made. He looked around for his shirt.

She snatched it from the desk before he could reach for it. "Mr. Pendarvis," she said, and the low urgency in her tone stopped him. "I can't meet you because—I *can't*. Next Saturday is Midsummer Day, and I'm the precentor of the children's choir—we've a program planned outside on the green. If it doesn't rain, there's a festival as well. It's—an important day in Wyckerley." She subsided, and he could swear she was blushing again. Because she thought she'd sounded too eager to explain herself to him?

He made a great business of having trouble with his shirt, so she would help him put it on. It worked; and then he pretended his left arm was too stiff to bend, so she'd button the shirt for him. While she was doing it, he watched her face, which had gone very still, so close to his, so very lovely. She was anything but indifferent to him, he knew that now. Because he wanted to, he lifted his hand to one of the strands of her golden hair and drew it gently behind her ear. An audacious liberty. What would she do?

Her hands at his chest froze. She looked up, into his eyes, and he saw all her innocence and interest, the trepidation and the excitement, in her level blue stare. He bent his head to her; in one second, he knew they would kiss, and in the next, he knew they would not. Her doing—yes, but his, too, because such a thing was forbidden, and it was unthinkable. Still holding her gaze, unable to break it, he took a step back, then another.

The distance steadied them. She ran her left hand nervously up and down her right arm, clearing her throat. "Go and see Dr. Hesselius tonight. He'll be home by six, I should think. His house is directly across from the inn. The First and Last Inn," she specified—unnecessarily, since there was only one inn in Wyckerley. "You'll go and see him, won't you?"

"Yes."

She nodded, relieved. "And don't come to work tomorrow. He'll probably sew up your arm, and you'll need a few days to rest it."

"No, I'll be in tomorrow."

"But that's *foolish*."

He walked to the door. "Will you pay me for the time I spend recovering?"

"Pay you? No. Pay you when you're not working?" She was nonplussed—honestly bewildered.

"It's a novel concept," he conceded mildly. "Coal miners in Durham are striking for it."

"*Striking*." Her eyes widened in horror; she said the word like a curse.

He couldn't help smiling. Or saying the word again. "Striking." He tipped an imaginary hat. "See you on Saturday, Miss Deene," he said, and left her alone.

# VI

Midsummer Day, June twenty-fourth, wasn't what it used to be. Twenty or thirty years ago, people from all the neighboring villages in St. Giles' parish flocked to Wyckerley for the annual festival, which in those days had also served as a midyear hiring fair. But that function had gradually fallen into disuse, superseded by bigger, showier fairs in Tavistock and Plymouth, and now Midsummer Day in Wyckerley was chiefly an opportunity for the locals to have a half holiday, gather on the green on a typically glorious day, and amuse themselves with games and entertainments, contests and music, refreshments, a rummage sale, and anything else the All Saints Ladies' Vestry Committee could think of—because the proceeds of the day went toward financing church programs for the rest of the year.

The rummage sale this year, thanks to a vigorous solicitation campaign for donations led by Anne Morrell and Emmaline Nineways, was, by eleven o'clock in the morning, a rousing success. Villagers eager for bargains scoured the tables set up in the grassy back garden of the vicarage, choosing from a wide array of secondhand treasures. Two items were deemed to be so especially desirable—Captain Carnock's collection of military memorabilia and a dozen of the blacksmith John Swan's finest handmade fishing lures—that written bids were being taken on them for an auction to be held at the end of the day.

"I want that camera," Anne confided out of the side of her mouth as she poured two cups of tea from a heavy urn and handed one to Sophie. "Your cousin bought it in Exeter a year ago and she's never used it, and now she's asking *four guineas* for it."

"Highway robbery," Sophie agreed, glancing at the item in question, a Knight and Ottewill double-folding camera with a collapsible bellows covered in black waterproof cloth. "How much did she pay for it?"

"Well, that's not the point, is it? It's not *new*, and whether she used it or not, the price should reflect that. I think it should be a third lower. To take into account depreciation."

Sophie smiled at the illogic in her friend's reasoning. Anne could afford a brand-new camera—she was an heiress—but it was like her to hold out for a bargain on a used one. Especially if she could get the better of Honoria in the process. "What did you contribute to the sale?" Sophie asked her, taking a coin from her pocket and a biscuit from a covered tray. Tea was free at the rummage sale, but biscuits and scones were three pennies apiece.

"You mean besides my backyard? Books, mostly, plus a lot of bric-a-brac and curios that looked as if they'd been gathering dust in the vicarage for a few hundred years. Junk, really," she admitted, "but I don't feel guilty about donating it anymore. People are *buying* it, Sophie, and not even haggling over the price." She broke off to smile and say good morning to Miss Pine and Mrs. Thoroughgood, who were carrying their purchases over to the table where Mrs. Nineways sat, taking money and making change from a biscuit tin. Sophie noticed with satisfaction that Mrs. Thoroughgood was buying the plaster fruit compote she had just this morning convinced Mrs. Bolton she couldn't bear to see on the dining room sideboard one more day. "What did you contribute?" Anne asked her a moment later.

Sophie made a face. "Clothes, what else? Scarves and hats, the prettiest silk shawl. Kid gloves, four pairs. Two chemisettes I've never worn."

Anne laughed. "You've *got* to stop buying these things."

"I know, I know." But clothes, Sophie liked to think, were her one and only vice; no dress shop was safe from her, no fashion catalog. The problem was that she rarely went any place fancy enough for her new finery, and as often as not she ended up giving it away.

"Mrs. Morrell, Miss Deene, how lovely to see you!"

It was Jessie Carnock, the captain's new wife. Whenever she saw her, Sophie marveled anew, for the former Miss Weedie looked less and less each time like the shy, nervous, middle-aged spinster she'd been only four short months ago. Marriage had transformed her. She was *pretty* now, her gray-flecked yellow hair positively girlish in its charming disarray, her rather long, pink-cheeked face full of animation and enthusiasm. "The sale is going so well," she exclaimed with a little bow—her arms were too full of booty to shake hands. "Someone's bought my thimble collection, Emmaline couldn't remember who, and Margaret Mareton just purchased my jade plant—imagine that! It was the captain," she said confidingly, leaning toward them, "who suggested we might like to donate it."

"He didn't care for it?"

"He said it was eating up the hallway!" She laughed merrily, turning her face up to the sky, and the sight was so unusual, so unexpected, Sophie and Anne could only stare at her in amazement. Sobering, she told Anne, "Reverend Morrell's prayer on the green this morning was very fine, just the right beginning to the day, we all thought."

"Was it? I didn't hear it; I was madly setting up tables with Emmaline and the others. I hope he didn't go on too long."

"Oh, *no*," Mrs. Carnock denied, a little shocked. "Not at all, oh, not in the least."

Eyes twinkling, Anne lowered her voice. "You'll never guess what Reverend Wilke said to Christy about Midsummer Day." The ladies bent closer. Reverend Wilke, the fiery Evangelical preacher from Horrabridge, was known for his colorful rhetoric. "He said it was a pagan ritual celebrated by the ungodly, and that from sunup to sundown today Wyckerley will be 'an abode of moral darkness.' "

Sophie laughed; Jessie gasped, then laughed with her. "Well, there is dancing later," Sophie acknowledged. "Around a *bonfire*, no less."

"Pure wickedness," Anne agreed, and they laughed again.

"Sophia!" The sharp falsetto voice put an end to their gaiety; the ladies' smiles turned formal as they turned to greet Sophie's cousin Honoria. "Sophia, it's nearly noon—you must come round to the green, it's time for Father's speech."

"Oh, but I've said I'll help out here at the sale until the singing," Sophie equivocated. Her uncle's speeches always made her tired.

"Nonsense, you have to come. It's expected. Anyway, haven't you had enough of *commerce* for one morning?" she asked with an artificial laugh, while her dark eyes glided with delicate distaste over the tables of used merchandise and the villagers who were rummaging among them. She disapproved of Midsummer Day as thoroughly as Reverend Wilke, although not on moral grounds: Honoria deplored the opportunity it afforded for this unseemly blurring of social class boundaries that ought, in her very definite opinion, to remain discrete.

Sophie regarded her with tolerant exasperation. In some ways Honoria was a handsome woman, taller than Sophie and with a stately way of carrying herself, shoulders flung back, chin high. She was vain about her thick brown hair, naturally curly, which she arranged in finicky circles across her forehead to mitigate an abnormally high brow. Her color was high, too high, and Sophie wondered sometimes if she toned it down with rice powder. She was nearsighted but wouldn't wear spectacles; as a consequence, she squinted and blinked at the world when she wasn't staring at it down the generous length of her sharp-pointed nose.

Sophie protested again, and Honoria pinched her lips together like a darned buttonhole, the stubborn expression she'd been bullying her cousin with since their childhood. "Father will not understand," she pronounced heavily.

There was a pause.

"I'll be happy to help out here so you can go and hear the mayor's speech," Mrs. Carnock offered sweetly, innocently.

Caught. Avoiding Anne's humorous eye, Sophie said, "Oh, very well, then." She thanked Mrs. Carnock with as much grace as she could, and followed her cousin up the flagged path around the vicarage to the green.

Uncle Eustace's speeches were always the same: intelligent, suitable to the occasion, and slightly condescending. Sophie no longer blushed for him, though. After six years as their mayor and chief magistrate, the villagers were used to him; indeed, he'd grown so adept at projecting his own superiority, most of his constituents had come around to accepting him for exactly what he thought he was: better than them.

"And so, in that very spirit of benevolence and cooperation, we come together today," he was droning, standing on a platform in front of the stone cross, "gathering as neighbors and as friends, striving as one in this labor of affection and duty to endow for another year the plans and programs of our most beloved church . . ."

Her attention wandered. Under the oak tree across the way, a knot of men, miners from Guelder and Salem, shifted impatiently, anxious to get back to their quoits match. She recognized Tranter Fox and Charles Oldene. Lawrence Brill, her uncle's mine captain. Big, beefy Roy Donne with his shirt off—trying to impress Cora Swan, no doubt. Her gaze focused suddenly, and she controlled a start. Jack Pendarvis was there—he was one of them.

She'd wondered if he would come. "See you on Saturday," he'd told her in her office four days ago. All morning, off and on, she'd been looking for him.

Shielding her eyes with her hand, she watched him. He stood out from the others, although she couldn't have said precisely why. It wasn't his clothes, which were plain and unremarkable. He was with the men, and yet he was aloof from them, but not because of anything standoffish in his manner. It was something subtler that she couldn't quite put her finger on, but she knew she wasn't imagining it. She'd noticed it before, in the way the miners treated him—affectionately, but more formally, a little more respectfully. The way men treat a leader.

Then again, perhaps she was imagining it. Deceiving herself, pretending he was different from the others because she wanted him to be, *needed* him to be different in order to justify her interest in him. In reality, he was probably treated differently only because he was a newcomer and the men didn't know him yet. Yes.

No.

She didn't know.

He was smiling, saying something to Tranter, hands in his pockets, making scuff marks in the hard-packed earth with the toe of his boot. All of a sudden he lifted his head and looked straight at her. She felt her face heat, realizing it was the intensity of her stare that had drawn his attention. Snared, she couldn't look away, and her heart pounded in her chest. Was he daring her? No; his eyes were searching and alert, not mocking. The moment stretched to the other side of bearable—and then her uncle saved her by finishing his speech, and Sophie was able to turn away naturally, to clap her hands with the others in polite applause.

But when Honoria started speaking to her, she used her cousin's straw hat for a screen, behind which she could look at him. He wore a collarless blue shirt with tan trousers and braces. She thought of the day she'd patched him up in her office, that mixture of alarm and excitement she'd felt while she'd done it. It wasn't the first time she'd played nurse for a miner with cuts and bruises, but it was the first time there had been physical tension between herself and the injured man. Tension so thick she'd felt suffocated by it.

She'd learned from Jenks that Dr. Hesselius had put six stitches in Mr. Pendarvis's arm, but they hadn't prevented him from returning to work the next day, just as he'd told her he would. The wound, she saw, hadn't affected his quoit-throwing ability; fascinated, she watched him stride to the line and take aim at the opposite pin. He had a side-arm delivery she hadn't seen before—curlers in Wyckerley preferred the underarm throw. The nine-pound quoit sailed high and fast, landing in the clay circle; metal clanged against metal, but Sophie was too far away to see if he'd hit the pin or someone else's quoit. A cheer went up from the Guelder men gathered around, and Tranter Fox yelled "Two!" A ringer, then.

Honoria's voice, like a stern schoolteacher's, finally distracted her. "Sophia, are you looking at those men? Stop it this minute. One of them has his *shirt* off."

Coloring, Sophie said, "Don't be so silly," more sharply than she should have, and turned her back on the curlers. Suddenly her cousin grabbed her forearm and dug in her nails. "Honoria, what—"

*"They came,"* she breathed in an ecstatic undertone, staring past Sophie's right shoulder. "Oh, how gracious, how delightfully condescending. But"—her face changed from awe to worry—"*should* they have come?"

"Who?" Turning, she saw Lord and Lady Moreton, arm in arm, standing near the riverbank while they exchanged words with the mayor.

"No. No," Honoria decided, "they ought not to have come."

"Why ever not?" wondered Sophie, who was glad to see them.

Honoria made her "Are you mad?" face. "For heaven's sake, isn't it obvious? This is a most *common* occasion, completely beneath Lord Moreton's notice. The rough element"—she looked around, feigning a slight shudder—"is capable of anything at any moment. No, no, it's most unseemly of his lordship to attend."

Sophie sighed with irritation. It wasn't worth an argument, but she could have pointed out that half of the "rough element" Honoria disparaged were the men and women who worked for her father's mine, the ones whose honest labor put food on her table and clothes on her back. "Don't be silly," Sophie said again, although she knew that was a futile suggestion, and started away to greet the Verlaines. Honoria hurried after her.

In fact, she beat Sophie to them, and had already dropped into a low curtsy when she arrived. "My lord, my lady," she effused, clutching her hands to her bosom as if overcome with the honor their presence bestowed. "Welcome to—to Midsummer Day," she said inanely. "Isn't it a beautiful day? It's as if the heavens knew you were coming and commanded the weather to be fair."

It was either smother a laugh or drop through a hole in the ground from embarrassment. Sophie chose the former, and was rewarded by Sebastian Verlaine's answering grin as he stuck out a forthright hand to shake.

His wife's smile was subtler and confined to the eyes, but Sophie imagined she was no less tickled by Honoria's absurdity. "This is a treat for me," she confided in her low, rather reserved tone of voice. "It reminds me of the Midsummer fair in Ottery St. Mary, the village where I grew up. Once my brother won the smock race, I remember, and the prize was a baby chick. We kept it for a whole year."

Everyone smiled at the innocent pleasantry, even Honoria. Lord Moreton asked his wife which fair was bigger, Wyckerley's or Ottery's, and which was better. While she answered, Sophie studied them with veiled interest. They'd been husband and wife only half a year or so, and the marriage had shocked Wyckerley to its toes—but then, Wyckerley was easily shocked. Still, Rachel Verlaine's scandalous past, not to mention the fact that she and Sebastian had been living more or less openly with each other before the marriage—the fiction that she was just his "house-keeper" had fooled no one—guaranteed that they had been the storm center of unrelenting gossip for months. But he was an earl, and now she was a countess, and titles had a wonderful way of smoothing the harsh edges of unkind memories. If they had been common people, in all likelihood they would never have lived down their pasts, at least not here. But they were aristo-crats; hence, no less a pillar of Wyckerlian respectability than Honoria Vanstone was now smiling obsequiously at both of them, shamelessly bent on winning their favor.

Lord Moreton spoke of the Lady Day fair in the Rye neighborhood of his childhood, and of how he and one of the grooms in his father's stables had sneaked off to it for three years running. He was a sinfully handsome man, effortlessly charming, easy to talk to; marriage had lessened his haughtiness, but there was still a rakish tilt to his smiles and a devilish edge to the languid lift of his brow. He seemed always to be touching his wife, her hand or her elbow, the small of her back, and Sophie found being with them exciting and unsettling because of the physical energy that crackled between them.

For her part, Lady Moreton was always quiet and reserved—outwardly; Anne Morrell maintained that once she knew and trusted you, she was warmth itself, the kindest of friends. Sophie could believe it: the horrific nature of Rachel's past excused caution in the present. She was not quite beautiful, but with her dark, silver-streaked hair and her odd, almost colorless eyes, she was certainly striking. But it was her manner that fascinated, the gravity behind her smiles, the barest hint of melancholy that still lingered in her eyes even when she laughed. Sophie wanted to know her better.

But there wasn't time now. "I must go," she said with real regret. The clock chiming in the church tower reminded her—"The children's program is supposed to begin in twenty minutes, and it will probably take me that long to find them." They parted; the Verlaines said they would see her again, and Honoria waved good-bye with a satisfied simper, happy to have their lordships all to herself.

Hurrying across the green toward the vicarage, she was accosted by Tranter Fox. "Miss Deene," he cried, "Miss Deene! I'm sended t' tell you!"

"What is it?" She stopped in her tracks, old habit causing her to worry if something had happened at the mine.

"Ma'am, yer very own team have won! The champeenship," he explained when she looked blank.

"Oh, *good* for you, Tranter," she said warmly, smiling at his excitement. In truth, his news pleased her: the competitor in her was delighted that "her" team had beaten her uncle's.

Tranter blushed, and she wanted to touch him, pat him on top of the head or pinch his cheek, because he was so appealing. He barely came up to her chin, and she was sure she weighed more than he did. But he flirted relentlessly, swaggering and posturing like a London dandy, and embellishing his attentions with outlandish compliments that always made her laugh. "We beated 'em flat out, three out o' five, and we was playing to twenty every time. Now the boys're waitin', ma'am, to present you wi' the game quoit."

"The game—oh, lovely." He looked so earnest, she didn't dare smile. Together they walked toward the oak trees, where six miners, the "Guelder Hurlers," had just "drobbed," as Tranter said, the Salem team—she'd forgotten their name, and they'd drifted away in defeat anyway. A knot of spectators, male and female, was gathered around the victors, admiring and congratulating them. Roy Donne separated himself from the rest and came toward her, buttoning his shirt, clearing his throat, and Sophie remembered he was the team captain.

"Miss Deene," he began, and the men behind him fell silent. "The Guelder Hurlers are happy to present to you—"

" 'Delighted,' " Tranter broke in in an undertone. "Say 'delighted.' "

"The Guelder Hurlers are *delighted* to present to you the game-winning—"

"To you, our *leader*."

"To you, our leader, this—"

" 'An' most respected employer, who we'd be nothing without.' "

Donne made a deep growling noise and waited. When Tranter kept quiet, he resumed. "We're delighted to present you with the game-winning quoit—"

"Match-winning."

Donne rounded on him. "Who's giving this speech, Tranter, you or me?"

"Well, if ee can't do any better'n that, me," and he nimbly plucked the iron ring out of Donne's hand. Spinning around, he made Sophie a low bow while the captain muttered ineffectually and the others snickered. "Miss Deene, us're honored and proud t' give to you, our leader and most favorite lady, who we admire a turrible great deal fer not only yer fair beauty but also yer wisdom and . . . and smartness, not to mention yer generosity, like, for letting us toil in yer wonderful mine for the greater glory of, um . . ." Tangled up, he paused to think, and Roy Donne took the opportunity to snatch the match-winning quoit back.

"Here," he said bluntly, and held it out to her.

She took it—and almost dropped it, unprepared for how heavy the flat metal ring was. A speech seemed to be called for. "Thank you—thank you. I'm very proud of you all. This annual match between Guelder and Salem began years ago, as you know, when my father was living. He enjoyed it very much, and he was always very gratified when his men won—as I am. I'm sure you're also aware that my father established a tradition, one that I have every intention of continuing." She heard hopeful murmuring and saw speculative looks. "Tonight at the George and Dragon, I'm pleased to stand for three rounds, one for each winning game, of cider, ale, and brandy for you and your friends."

A boisterous cheer went up—so widespread that it was obvious that everyone within the sound of Sophie's voice considered himself a friend of the Guelder Hurlers.

She happened to glance at Jack Pendarvis then, whose eye she had been avoiding. He was smiling—but whether he was amused with her or by her, she couldn't tell. She stood still, and he began to walk toward her, not hurrying, pulling on his jacket as he came. When he reached her, neither spoke for a curious moment that was, surprisingly, more friendly than nerve-wracking. She half expected him to say something cutting about her speech to the quoits team—in his ears, she suddenly realized she might have sounded patronizing—and so she was completely unprepared for what he did say.

"You look beautiful."

She looked off to the side, empty-headed as a girl, trying to marshal her thoughts. Phrases drifted through her mind—*Please don't speak to me this way*—*How dare you?*—*Why, thank you*—but in the end she took the coward's way out and pretended he hadn't spoken at all. "How are you feeling, Mr. Pendarvis? Have you recovered from your injuries?"

"Yes, I've recovered. The doctor was impressed by your handiwork. He said he doubted Florence Nightingale could've patched me up any better."

She smiled, pleased and amused. Florence Nightingale was a national heroine these days; hardly a week passed when a story about her admirable exploits in the Crimea didn't appear in the Plymouth *Gazette*. "I'm so glad." Another pause. "Well. I'd better go."

"Why?"

"Because . . ." She forgot.

"Walk with me."

She remembered. "The children—they're singing. At noon. I have to go and gather them up." And while she was at it, she'd better gather up her wits.

"Afterward, then." He smoothed his black hair back with his palm, jutted his chin at her a little. "Will you walk with me, Miss Deene?"

It was half dare, half request, and the combination demolished her last feeble scruple. "Thank you. I would enjoy that, Mr. Pendarvis."

There were six songs in the children's musical program for Midsummer Day, four with harmony, two with one-verse solos, and one, the grand finale, with instruments. It was this last song, "Tell Me How the Roses Bloom," that presented the children with their biggest challenge, but also the one that would carry them to glory if they performed it successfully. Sophie could see their excitement mounting as the simpler songs were dispensed with and the moment of truth drew closer and closer. At last it was time. With no more bustle and commotion than absolutely necessary, the instruments were passed out: two small drums, four cymbals, a triangle, a cowbell, and three whistles. As usual, a few of the children felt compelled to try out their instruments before the song began, to see that they were still working; Sophie had expressly forbidden this nervous practice more times than she could count, but she waited for silence patiently, resigned by now to the inevitable. Bringing up her little baton, she engaged the attentive gaze of every child, smiled brightly, whispered one last encouragement, and dropped her hands—the signal for the Burch twins to smack their cymbals together so the song could begin.

They did it—they even did it simultaneously, a feat they'd only managed in practice a few times—and after that everything went perfectly. Describing how roses bloom was only one of the song's challenges; it also demanded musical interpretations of how raindrops fall (fingertips on drums), skylarks sing (whistles in alternating glissandi), and bullfrogs jump (cowbell and drum, the subtlest depiction, and the one requiring the most open-mindedness on the part of the listeners). Every musical hurdle was met and overcome, with an ease Sophie could only call deceptive, considering how rehearsals had been going as recently as yesterday. She had a bad moment at the end when Birdie, a whistle blower, decided to improvise how snowflakes fall along with the triangle player. But even that worked; the audience assumed she was the wind and the snowflakes were caught in a blizzard.

After three years as choir precentor, Sophie was an expert at classifying applause—polite, relieved, pitying, surprised, occasionally pained. The only word to describe the applause that burst out after "Tell Me How the Roses Bloom" was *delighted*, and the sentiment was mirrored in the grinning faces of the children, who bowed and curtsied—Birdie blew kisses—as if they'd just brought down the curtain at Covent Garden. Laughing with pleasure and relief, Sophie bowed with them, and then, to her genuine surprise, Tommy Wooten came around from the second row and presented her with an enormous bouquet of dahlias. More applause.

Mothers surrounded her, claiming their children, congratulating her. Miss Mareton's play followed the singing program almost immediately, and Sophie found herself standing next to Mr. Pendarvis while she watched it. How had that happened? Had she drifted over to him or had he drifted over to her? A combination, perhaps. She found it difficult to follow the plot, such as it was, with his tall, hard body standing so close. Miss Mareton was the Sunday school teacher, and thus the play had a religious theme. It seemed to be about Saint Peter at the Gate, although the story line was a little muddy owing to the fact that the children recited their lines pretty much inaudibly. The song Sophie had taught them, a simple tune of Miss Mareton's composition, went off fairly well, though, and that had been her main concern.

Birdie portrayed an angel in the production. When it was over, she ran toward Sophie with her arms outstretched. But instead of flinging herself against Sophie's knees, as was her habit, she skidded to a comical halt in front of Mr. Pendarvis, gilded paperboard wings aflutter, and stared up at him in fascination.

"It's the man," she breathed to Sophie, but never taking her eyes off Jack. "He unstuck your hair, Miss Sophie, remember?" To the "man" she whispered, "I thought I dreamed you!"

He put his hands on his knees so they could be at eye level. "I thought I dreamed *you*," he said seriously. "Know why?" Birdie shook her head. "Because you're the prettiest little girl I've seen in a long, long time." He dropped his voice to a matching whisper and confided, "I thought you were an *angel*."

Birdie's mouth dropped open. Only a moment passed, though, before a surprisingly adult coyness replaced her amazement. She actually simpered as she stuck her hands in her apron pockets and twisted her stocky body slowly from side to side— the perfect six-year-old coquette. But then it was all too much for

her. She gave a sudden high shriek of laughter, clapped her hands
to her pink cheeks, and bolted.

Mr. Pendarvis's low, tickled laugh provoked Sophie to laugh
with him. They looked at each other and smiled naturally, with
no tensions or hidden animosities. But then he said, "Shall we?"
and she was afraid he would touch her, take her arm or her hand.
That she was socializing in public with one of her own miners
was going to look bad enough to the people of Wyckerley who
cared about such things—which was most of them; if he was also
seen to be taking liberties with her, however innocent, those pre-
disposed to shock would be shocked all the more. Reminding
herself of Birdie, Sophie put her hands in her pockets, and she
and Mr. Pendarvis set off at a slow amble across the green, not
touching.

# VII

Self-conscious at first, intensely aware of him, matching her steps to his, Sophie feigned nonchalance and spoke of the weather. Walter Tall, she informed him, was the oldest living soul in Wyckerley—eighty-four—and he claimed to have kept a count of the times it had been fair on Midsummer Day during his lifetime. "He says today makes the sixty-seventh sunny day and the seventy-third dry one," she said, aware that she was prattling. "Old Mrs. Cleary, though, who's eighty, disputes that and says Walter's gone senile." She threw him a glance, and was relieved to see that her chatter was making him smile. "Did you celebrate Midsummer in your village in Cornwall?"

Mark Stark, whose father was the baker, accosted them just then, carrying a tray of funnel cookies. "Tuppence apiece, four for sixpence," he chanted, and Mr. Pendarvis asked Sophie if she was hungry. She admitted she was, and he bought eight cookies. Mark gave him a paper to carry them in, and they ambled toward the river bridge, munching as they went.

"I grew up in Trewythiel," he drawled, leaning against the ledge and staring down at the ripple shadows the sun made on the water. "I don't expect you've heard of it."

"No."

"It's mid-county, a little bit east of Redruth." He paused, as if debating with himself whether to tell her something. "Trewythiel is in a poor district. We had no fairs, and few holidays that I can recollect. And we had no cricket team, that's for certain." She followed his gaze to where two teams were playing the game on the flattest part of the green. Christy Morrell was the batsman on the near side; while they watched, he bowled the last over and ran to change places with Robbie Woodworth, his opposite across the wickets.

She'd never given it much thought, but cricket, even the casual, loose-structured way it was played in Wyckerley, was, relatively speaking, a gentleman's game. These twelve men and boys playing it on the village green weren't the ones who had hurled quoits an hour ago for a prize of three rounds of ale at the George. These were the husbands and sons of the village's "right sort," as Honoria would put it, the men who wore waistcoats and cravats to work, men whose hands stayed clean all day because they labored with their minds, not their muscles. What would it be like to live in a place where there were no such men, and no women who belonged to them?

"Do you come from a large family?" She knew next to nothing about Mr. Pendarvis, it suddenly occurred to her.

A moment passed. He kept his eyes lowered, and his face was very still. She began to wonder what in her innocent question had disturbed him when he looked up and answered in a monotone, "I had four brothers and a sister."

"I always wanted a sister," she said lightly. "Or a brother; I'd have settled for either." She found herself telling him, "My mother died soon after I was born, so it was just my father and I. I wasn't lonely, though. Not really. Not much. Because we were so close."

She rarely ran on like this, and certainly never to a person she hardly knew—but before she could chide herself for it, he said, "You miss your father," with such simple compassion that her embarrassment fled.

"I do. Every day. He was my best friend."

"I'm sorry."

She could see that it was true, and she murmured, "Thank you."

"My best friend is my brother."

She smiled. "Which one?"

He said, "Connor," after a curious pause. "I told you about him."

"I remember."

"We don't have much in common." He frowned, and stared down at his hands, which were methodically clenching and unclenching the stone ledge of the bridge. "Nothing, in fact. But we would do anything for each other."

"You said he was ill. Why doesn't he go home to Cornwall?" None of her business, of course, but she wanted to know. "Couldn't your family take better care of him there?"

"No, he . . . My family . . ." He raked his fingers through his glossy black hair. "He'd rather stay with me."

"Ah." Now she was even more curious, but something in his manner told her more questions on this subject would not be welcome.

She watched him crumble a cookie and drop crumbs from the bridge to a huddle of black ducks below, and after a minute she joined him. Two speckled babies kept fighting over the unexpected feast, feinting and circling in the gentle river current, clucking at each other. Their antics tickled Sophie; she started to giggle. She picked out one of the chicks and tried to lure him with manna away from his rival, but the maneuver failed when the whole family went with him. With a helpless laugh, she looked up at Jack—and his expression made her heart skip a beat. She looked down at the ducks, to hide her face.

"I can't get enough of that," he said in a low, intimate voice that did nothing to slow down her pulse rate. "The sound of you laughing, I mean. I like it better than music."

Sophie owned a mine; she supported herself. She employed a hundred men. People in the community respected her for qualities like competence and perseverence. She was twenty-three years old. Why was it that, on the extremely rare occasions when Jack Pendarvis said something sweet to her, she turned into a speechless, blushing ninny?

"We used to have swans in the Wyck," she said seriously, "but they ate up all the watercress—which grows in the river year-round, you know, because our winters are so mild—and so the town decided to raid the nests and steal their eggs until the population went down. It worked too well, some of us think, because now there aren't *any* swans, and that's really a—"

"Sophie, there you are! I've been looking for you."

In a way, it was good to see Robert Croddy striding up the hump of the bridge toward them: it meant she could finally stop talking. In another way, though, she resented the interruption.

"Where have you been?" he asked with his tight, square-toothed grin, stopping in front of her. "I looked for you after the singing, but you disappeared."

"Not at all. I'm right here." A pause. No help for it. With a strange reluctance, she said, "Robert, this is Mr. Pendarvis. Mr. Croddy."

"How do you do."

"How do you do."

They didn't shake hands.

"Well." Robert threw the tails of his coat back and stuck his thumbs in the shallow pockets of his expensive waistcoat. She was used to the gesture; he did it to show off the gold of his watch fob. When she wore high-heeled shoes, she and Robert were the same height, a fact he disliked, she'd always suspected. He had a strong, fleshy face, and his hair, his eyes, and his lips were all the same color: pale ginger. Ladies of her acquaintance thought him quite a handsome man, and she supposed his powerful body and a certain earthy, grounded quality about him were attractive. In a way. But she'd always found it disconcerting that he simply had no neck, none at all. He reminded her of a bull.

Ignoring Mr. Pendarvis, he said, "I thought we might have a bite to eat. The food won't be much, but it's for charity, so we'll try not to notice." Again the tight grin, smug this time. It annoyed her, and she felt offended on behalf of all the ladies who had been making puddings and meat pies and batches of lemonade for days, out of nothing but the kindness of their hearts.

"No, thank you. I've already had something." A cookie was something.

"Well, come and sit with us anyway, while we eat. I'm with His Honor under the trees," he said, pointing across the green. "Honoria's brought umbrellas and chairs, so you'll be perfectly comfortable."

Robert enjoyed called her uncle "His Honor." That annoyed her, too, although not as much as when he called him "Eustace." The two men were friends of a sort, yes, and Robert owned a part interest in Salem mine. But since he was at least twenty years younger than Uncle Eustace, Sophie could never think of the first-name familiarity as anything but a rather tasteless presumption. "No, thanks," she said again. "But I'm sure I'll see you later."

His ginger eyes flickered to Mr. Pendarvis, then back, alert now, asking a silent question. She kept her smile pleasant, bland, despite the tension she could feel thickening slowly around them. Robert wasn't her beau—she had no time for beaus anymore—but it occurred to her that he might *think* he was simply because he had become her escort, by default, to the few social functions she did find time to attend. Now, naturally, he wanted to know who this male stranger was, and why she didn't excuse herself from his presence and walk off to sit under the trees with Robert and her family. She tried to imagine saying to him, "Mr. Pendarvis is one of my tutmen at Guelder, and we're spending the afternoon together." Just the thought made her cheeks burn. Not that Jack's identity could stay a secret for long, whether she blurted it out now or not; she doubted that it would take Robert more than five minutes to discover the unsavory truth after he left them. But she had a craven wish not to be there when it happened.

"Well," he said again, as if giving her a last chance. She just kept smiling. "I'll see you later, then."

"Yes, later."

His face darkened. Without even a glance at Mr. Pendarvis, he spun around and left them on the bridge.

Sophie, who had been avoiding looking at Jack as determinedly as Robert had, looked at him now. She knew him now, a little, enough to recognize that what lay behind the stiffness of his jaw and the hard gleam in his eyes wasn't coldness or rancor, but bruised pride. The novel idea that he and Robert seemed to be, at least for a moment, rivals for her favor gave her a quick, illicit lift. But a second's reflection corrected her error. It was hardly likely that Robert Croddy *as a man* had put Mr. Pendarvis's nose out of joint. No. Knowing him, she thought it infinitely more plausible that it was Robert's class (middle; "hopelessly" middle, Honoria would say, but with unquenchable ambitions to rise to the upper middle, or even someday—Sophie was positive this was the secret Robert held in his deepest heart—to the *gentry*), that had turned him, within seconds of their meeting, into Mr. Pendarvis's enemy.

"Mr. Croddy is a business associate of my uncle's," she said evenly, breaking a taut little silence.

"I know who he is."

"Oh, do you?"

"Not much about you doesn't get talked about underground, Miss Deene. You might say you're the favorite topic of conversation among us poor, humble miners."

She didn't understand his mood. His tone was cool, but there was a twist of self-mockery in his lips that skewed her reaction to him and put her off balance. "That's hard to imagine," she said lightly. "I can't think of anyone who leads a less interesting life than I do."

"Don't you like your work?"

"Oh, I love it. What I meant to say is, no one leads a less *gossip-worthy* life than I." She smiled back at him, elated to see that she'd somehow restored his good humor. Buoyed by that, she felt reckless. "I was fibbing to Mr. Croddy, of course, when I said I'd already eaten. The truth is, I'm starving."

95

He had a fleeting, slightly crooked grin, just off-center, completely charming. It came and went quickly, but a twinkle in his eyes remained when he said gravely, "The food won't be much. But since it's for charity, we'll try not to notice."

She laughed—she couldn't help it. Robert deserved it, she rationalized. And besides, Mr. Pendarvis liked to hear her laugh.

Dining alfresco was easier if one balanced one's plate while seated on something, a blanket, a bench, a lawn chair. Mr. Pendarvis suggested they go and sit on the long flat rock by the riverbank, but Sophie resisted, for complicated reasons. A moving target was harder to hit—that was one reason, and the experience with Robert had taught her that she and Mr. Pendarvis did much better together when they were alone. Then, too, she had some idea that staying in motion could dilute, or at least postpone, the public perception that they were a couple, with all the attendant complications that would inevitably follow. So they strolled from booth to booth while they nibbled on spiced prawns and green pea tarts, sampling the mutton pie here, the fancy buttered eggs and anchovies there. They stood among a group of children to watch a puppet show, Sophie confiding behind her hand that the string pullers above the makeshift curtain were none other than Cora and Chloe Swan, the blacksmith's pretty daughters. That meant nothing to him until she reminded him that he'd met them, two weeks ago at the penny reading. What a difference a fortnight made. They exchanged a look, and Sophie imagined Jack was thinking the same thing she was: the fascinating contrast between the prickly antagonists they had been and the wary friends they seemed to be becoming.

They wandered back to the bridge, sipping from paper containers of sweet lemonade. "Who is that girl?" he asked casually, leaning against the ledge, gesturing with his cup.

She turned slightly. "What girl?"

"There, in the blue dress. Small, with black hair."

"Oh, that's Sidony Timms." Pretty Sidony worked as a maid in the dairy at Lynton Hall Farm. Lately she'd been keeping company with William Holyoake, Lord Moreton's bailiff—but the man with her now, a tall, gaunt individual who was saying something to make her giggle and blush, wasn't William. Sophie narrowed her eyes, studying him; she was quite sure she'd never seen him before—so why did he look vaguely familiar? "I wonder who that man is," she murmured, more to herself than to Mr. Pendarvis.

"He's my brother."

She turned back in surprise. "Your brother? Really? Well, no wonder."

"No wonder what?"

"I thought he reminded me of someone." Fascinated, she scrutinized Connor Pendarvis. He had Jack's height, his black hair, and fine, strong features, but illness had sallowed his skin and melted the flesh from his bones. He was still handsome—and charming, evidently, judging from Sidony's smitten demeanor—but he was so ill, and he looked so much like his brother. Watching him gave Sophie a queer feeling.

"I think they're flirting," she remarked, for something to say.

He grunted. "Miss Timms had better have a care. My brother fancies himself irresistible."

"She's the dairymaid at the Hall Farm," Sophie told him, smiling. "And she's not the least bit silly, but I must admit she looks it right now." Sidony was staring into the middle distance with one finger on her cheek, apparently mesmerized by whatever Mr. Connor Pendarvis, bent over her like a great black stork, was murmuring in her ear.

"Dairymaid, is she? My brother knows his place, then. It seems I'm the only Pendarvis who has trouble recognizing his betters."

Sophie stared at him, thinking, *So we're back to that again.* But she didn't say it, because she was weary of the argument it would start. Their conversation seemed to go around in loops, always circling back to the subject of social status.

Her heart sank a little lower. Thirty feet away, Honoria was sailing toward them, skirts in her hands, chest out, dark eyes trained on them like an eagle's before a midair strike. She thought of warning Jack—but of what? Imminent insult? Besides, Honoria was her cousin, her kinswoman; one didn't say, "Uh-oh," to bare acquaintances at the approach of a relative.

"Sophia."

Honoria was incapable of calling Sophie "Sophie," and had been all their lives. As a child Sophie had once committed the grave error of calling her "Honor" for short, a lapse never to be repeated after the humorless lecture she'd been treated to on unseemliness, frivolity, and ill breeding. "Hullo, Honoria. Did you enjoy your picnic?"

Wasted words; Honoria waved her hand in the air, as if erasing them, and said, "Sophia," again, with even more displeasure, surging to a halt in front of them. Her color was high and her eyes were flashing: always a sign that she was ready to do her duty.

Sophie tried another diversion. "May I introduce Mr. Pendarvis? Mr. Pendarvis, this is my cousin, Miss Vanstone."

She realized from his tone—formal, wary—that he didn't need a warning. "A pleasure to meet you, Miss Vanstone."

Honoria ignored him. "Sophia, will you come with me, please?"

"Mr. Pendarvis is one of my—"

"I know who this person is. Come, Sophia, my father is waiting for us."

Cheeks flaming, Sophie spaced her words carefully. "I'm afraid that won't be possible. As you can see, I'm engaged." Honoria's features went stiff with alarm. "But perhaps I misunderstood," Sophie added. "Perhaps you were inviting both of us to join your party."

"You did not misunderstand."

"I see. In that case, I decline."

Standoff. She couldn't imagine Honoria making an actual scene; surely this was as beastly as things were going to get. She stood still, returning her cousin's furious glare impassively, waiting for her to turn around and stomp away.

She'd underestimated her outrage. "You cannot mean to stand here any longer with this person," she enunciated in a low, shocked, venomous tone. "Surely you cannot. I insist that you come with me now, Sophia, this instant."

Her acute embarrassment fell away, like a heavy coat she was suddenly too hot to wear, and wholesome anger took its place. "Honoria, please leave us. Mr. Pendarvis is my escort."

"Sophia—"

"I will not join you or my uncle this afternoon." Sometimes anger made her reckless. "And I won't join you this evening. Mr. Pendarvis has invited me to watch the bonfire dance, and—I've accepted."

The horror in her cousin's face would have been amusing if the situation hadn't been so ghastly. Her mouth opened and closed twice, but no words came out. She backed away, as if from the scene of an accident, whirled, and ran off to tell her father.

Sophie's relief that she was gone mingled with a strange elation. Curbing an impulse to laugh out loud, she leaned back against the cold stone of the bridge and smiled up at Jack in shaky triumph. "She's gone. Thank God." He didn't smile back. In fact, his lips were pale with anger. "Oh, I'm so sorry," she said hurriedly. "My cousin was unconscionably rude to you. She's insufferable sometimes. I do apologize—"

"Did you think I'd be glad that you told her we were together?"

"What? I—"

"The worst thing you could think of? The thing guaranteed to shock her and send her on her way?"

"No, you don't—"

"That wasn't a kindness to me, Miss Deene. That was condescension. Sorry, but I'm not flattered, and I'm not able to thank you for it. Excuse me." He made her a stiff bow and walked away.

Sophie blinked in shock and gathering dismay. "Mr. Pendarvis!" She'd whispered it—he didn't hear. She ran after him, then slowed her steps self-consciously. *"Mr. Pendarvis."*

He stopped, halfway across the green, heading who knew where, and slowly turned. Acutely aware that they were probably being observed by a dozen people, she approached him casually; but she couldn't keep the distress from her face, or from her voice when she said softly, "I must speak with you. *Please.*"

He streaked his fingers through his hair again, as upset as she was. "Speak, then."

"No, not here." She looked around, flustered. "The church-yard—follow me there. In a moment. Will you?" He nodded once, and she left him.

She felt blind, deaf; people waved and spoke to her as she hurried across the grass toward the church, but she barely acknowledged them. She had been accused of a sin she truly didn't think she'd committed, and she was wild with the need to justify herself. But that was only part of it, and not even the biggest part. Worse was that she'd hurt Jack, truly hurt him. And he'd let her see it. For once he hadn't hidden behind coolness or cynicism. What was between them wasn't fencing or posturing anymore, it was real.

The lych-gate grated on rusty hinges as she slipped inside the graveyard, hidden from the green and the vicarage by high, centuries-old yew hedges and then the crumbling churchyard wall itself. Voices and shouts became a murmur, muffled by the heavy blanket of shrubbery and stone. She went along the cinder path past the monuments and headstones, some of them new, some nearly as old as Wyckerley itself. Her father was buried here; she saw his granite marker, and the wilting clutch of daisies she'd laid on it early this morning—but she hurried by, moving toward an angle in the path that would hide her from view if anyone but Jack came in through the gate behind her.

A distant peal of feminine laughter came to her from the vicarage garden. The rummage sale would be winding down by now, and she remembered her promise to Anne that she would help clean up afterward. What on earth was she doing? She felt breathless with the impropriety of this, the riskiness, the calamitous nature of the consequences if she were found out.

She heard the scrape of the gate, the soft thud of footsteps. Her yellow dress would give her away in an instant—but surely it was he. She stepped into the path.

He saw her and stopped, and the nervousness that swept over her then brought home the full significance of what she was doing. But discretion had come too late. He started toward her again, and she drew back, behind a screen of dense green holly. A thrush that had been singing in the copper beech abruptly fell silent. Mr. Pendarvis appeared in the angle of the path and came to her.

She spoke before the intimate stillness could unnerve her even more. "I'm sorry. I think you were right. What I did—it was an insult to you, but you must believe that I didn't intend it to be. I didn't think. *Truly* I didn't mean to condescend. You—you have me thinking things that are *new* to me, and I . . . well. I apologize to you. That's all. I'm sorry."

He shook his head, and for an awful second she thought he was going to scorn her. "None of this was your fault. I was wrong to be so angry. My brother calls me stiff-necked, and I always deny it. But this is one of those times when I know exactly what he's talking about."

When he smiled, the cloud of anxiety around her lifted, and she felt light and airy, quite weightless, dizzy with relief. "You mustn't forgive me so easily," she laughed shakily. "What you said on the green—"

"You're easy to forgive. And . . . you have me thinking new things, too."

"Do I?" It was a double entendre, she was almost certain. His handsome face was serious, but his eyes held a meaning she couldn't possibly misconstrue. She was resting her hand on the trunk of a locust tree, running her fingers along the rough fissures in the bark. She could claim agitation but not surprise when Jack took her hand and held it in both of his, gently, anything but possessively. He studied it, the white back and then the pink palm, and when he traced his thumb lightly across the crease of her life line, she lost her breath. She didn't move, had no desire to snatch her hand back. This was different, nothing like the other times when the tension between them had been half-sexual, half-antagonistic. For her he had let down a wall, and behind it she saw a man she couldn't resist.

Their eyes met, and she knew they were going to kiss. Slowly, giving her a chance to break away if she wanted to, he bent toward her. She closed her eyes when their lips touched, the better to contain the excitement welling up at the simple, feather-light brushing. He wasn't holding her hand anymore, he was lifting the hair from the back of her neck and caressing her there with his fingers, while his mouth grazed and nuzzled her mouth, taking the most delicious kisses.

They pulled away, just a little, to look at each other. If she had seen anything in his eyes like triumph, anything like complacency, she'd have bolted, heartsick. But all she saw was the same gladness she was feeling, and it gave her the courage to tell him, "I didn't come here for this—"

"I know."

"But I'm not sorry. How could I be?"

"Sophie," he whispered, lowering his gaze, touching her cheek with his fingertips. She loved the strong, masculine slash of his eyebrows, the shiny lushness of his long black lashes. The sound of her name on his lips. She brought her hands to his shoulders, let her fingers drift to his throat. She could see his pulse beating; she wanted to put her mouth there, just there, under his jaw. But he dipped his head and caught her in another sweet, drugging kiss, and the thought drifted away. They pressed closer, held each other tighter. She felt his urgency, the same as hers, the same craving to know more. *Who are you?* they were both asking in these deep, wordless kisses. *Tell me. Show me.*

"We must stop," Sophie managed at last, breathing fast, feeling his warm breath on her face.

He kept her in the circle of his arms, holding her fast. "I want to see you," he said boldly. "Not tonight. I won't dance with you round a fire while everyone you know looks on, gossiping about you."

An inkling of the difficulties involved in being with this man began to intrude on the thoughtless joy. "I don't know. I've never . . . I don't know *how* . . ."

"Tomorrow." He smiled at the worry in her eyes. "Say yes, Sophie."

"Yes. But where?"

He shook his head, leaving it to her. "Anywhere you like."

She pulled his hand away from her cheek, so she could think. "After church. Do you know where Abbeycombe is? It's an old Roman ruin, south of here, maybe a mile, set back from the Plymouth toll road."

"I'll find it."

They kissed again. "I can only stay for a little while," she whispered against his lips.

"But you'll come?"

"Yes, I'll come. I promise."

# VIII

But she broke her promise.

Sunday was perfect, a replica of the day before, with cotton-puff clouds scudding across an azure sky, and sunshine like a warm blessing from some affable, even-handed god. Connor arrived at their rendezvous early, and had plenty of time to wander among the tottering stone arches and roofless corridors of the ancient abbey, beguiled by the stillness and the deep melancholy of the place. Yellow and purple wildflowers poked through the rubble, making a gay carpet. He found himself picking a bouquet for Sophie, like an eager swain waiting for his sweetheart.

But he was hardly that. He was a liar and an impostor, and everything he did or said to her was under false pretenses. He knew only one honorable way out of the complicated web of lies he'd not only spun but gotten hopelessly tangled up in, and that was to tell her they couldn't see each other again.

He'd been telling himself that since this morning, and he wondered now at how long it had taken him to reach such an obvious conclusion. But he hadn't been in his right mind. Those minutes in the churchyard with Sophie had temporarily deranged him, and he'd spent the time since then in a kind of cloud of sensual, romantic arousal. Until this morning, when his wits had finally come back, along with the first clearheaded realization of what he'd done.

He had no good explanation for his behavior, and no excuse. Jack was the ladies' man in the family, not him. Chasing women had never figured in his image of himself, or distracted him from the vision he had of his own future. He was a serious man; he had responsibilities, a mission, life goals more important than self-gratification. He couldn't *marry* Sophie Deene, and so he had no business keeping company with her in any way except professionally. Of course even that relationship was based on a fraud, but he'd squared it with his conscience long ago by declaring that the noble end justified the messy means. But consorting with her as a would-be lover went beyond the pale and could not be justified.

So. Today he would end it. He sat down on a flat granite stone and tried to think of a good way to tell her. It wouldn't really be that difficult, and he wasn't so vain as to think she would need consoling. And yet . . .

He smiled unconsciously, twisting a daisy stem, remembering how she had looked in the churchyard in that moment when she'd seen him on the path. Her face flushed, her eyes bright with trepidation and . . . excitement. She'd known exactly what she was risking by meeting him, there in the eye of the storm, the dangerous center of her village, her universe, where the walls could so easily be breached by any casual intruder. She'd courted disaster, and she'd done it for him. So she could apologize to him. That was the moment when he'd lost his bearings.

Afterward, touching her, kissing her—that had been a gift, magic, an indescribable pleasure. But her sweetness, the graciousness in her halting words when she'd said she hadn't meant to offend him—that's what had changed everything. Seduction had been the last thing in his mind, but when she'd leveled the last barrier of hostility and distrust between them, nothing had seemed more natural to him than holding her.

He had no watch, but the angle of the sun between two rust-colored columns told him the afternoon was slipping away. She was late. "After church," she'd said. The Sunday service at All Saints was over by twelve-fifteen, twelve-thirty at the latest. Even if she walked instead of rode, even if friends delayed her to talk, she ought to have been here by now. He got up, restless, and began to pace.

What if she didn't come? No, she'd come; she'd given her promise. Even if it was only to tell him they couldn't do this, she would come. He kicked at rocks, then flung them at the crumbling stone walls of the abbey. When he tired of that, he watched squirrels chase each other in the thicket of vines and ivy crawling over the rubble. The cranking of crows in the oak tree branches was angry and impatient, and his mood began to match the sound. It couldn't be true; she couldn't be doing this. If she regretted her promise, she would tell him that to his face, wouldn't she? Something must have delayed her, an emergency at the mine or—no, unlikely; Guelder shut down on the Sabbath. Well, something else, then, a last-minute complication she needed to attend to. She must know that he would wait. "I'll come," she'd said. "I promise."

When the sun wavered and sank behind the trees on the western hillside, he knew she wasn't coming. Still, he stayed where he was, marking the progress of the shadows as they inched, darkened, lengthened across the rough stones, dousing the light in the faces of the wildflowers he'd thought were so pretty before. He watched the bouquet he'd picked for Sophie wilt, droop, die. He wanted the lesson driven home, clear and unambiguous, so he let another full hour drag by while he contemplated his own folly. He was wearing his best coat and trousers, which he'd carefully brushed last night, wishing they were newer, sprucer, in better fashion. Jack had lent him his only good necktie, and he'd felt self-conscious putting it on this morning, thinking of all the times Jack had worn it in hopes of seducing some comely young thing he'd set his horny sights on. He had shaved with extra care, even trimmed his hair with a pair of scissors borrowed from one of the miners in the cottage. He'd cleaned his shoes, cleaned his teeth. Scrubbed his hands and fingernails until the last of the black mine stain was gone. God help him, he'd put some of Jack's rosewater cologne on his clean, smooth cheeks.

It was good to think of these things, good to let the hot humiliation wash over him like fire. He would never forget it, and the memory would stand him in good stead if the temptation ever came again to believe in a mirage.

But he wasn't angry. He told himself that all the way home. Anger wasn't called for, wouldn't have been appropriate. Had nothing to do with his decision to finish his report on Guelder mine, the one that had been stuck inside a book in his room for the last three days.

He didn't make anything up, but he didn't leave anything out. In dry, factual language, he set down every safety and health hazard and economic inequity he'd observed in the weeks he'd been employed at the mine. The worst was the system of ladders, so he began with that. Now a hundred and sixty fathoms deep, Guelder still relied on the old fifty-foot ladders it had been using for twenty years, virtually perpendicular, fathom after fathom, with no resting place except the narrow sollar platform and a manhole leading to the ladder under it. Calculating, he reckoned that at a hundred and sixty pounds, a man climbing from bottom to top exerted a constant force equivalent to raising the weight of one ton in the space of a minute. The consequence was exhaustion, which led to carelessness, which resulted in accidents. He cited the example of Tranter Fox's partner, who had recently fallen off a ladder at the thirty level and broken both legs.

Wages were low. Tutmen and tributers earned an average of fifty shillings a month, but ended up paying about forty percent of it back to the company for supplies—candles, powder, fuses, drawing and dressing costs, use of the grinder, sampling and weighing costs. Was it a coincidence that the mine owner's uncle held a de facto monopoly by virtue of operating the only store where a miner could buy supplies unless he went to Tavistock? Where, incidentally, the prices for his candles and fuses and so on were cheaper; Connor knew that because he'd checked.

The heat was intolerable at the deepest levels, where men routinely lost three or four pounds of body weight at a single eight-hour core. Although the owner had recently installed a ventilator, it was inadequate; at the lower fathoms the temperature never went below eighty degrees. Studies were still under way, but no one could dispute anymore that bad air contributed to the condition known as miner's consumption. Dr. Barham's report found that in four varied mining districts, out of one hundred and forty-six miner deaths, seventy-seven had been the result of consumption. And Mr. Lanyon's report claimed miners died an average of sixteen years earlier than agricultural laborers.

There was no training at Guelder, no system of apprenticeship. No hot food available in winter, and no warm room for grass workers except the smith's shop or the drying room where the miners hung their clothes. When accidents happened, there was no doctor; injured miners had to rely on the dubious nursing skills of a female grass worker, who might or might not be sober when her services were called upon. Otherwise, the mine owner herself had been known to dispense rudimentary first aid in her office, a contingency that, while no doubt kindly inotivated, couldn't inspire much confidence in the injured worker.

Worst was an attitude of tolerance toward accidents and catastrophes, which were generally viewed as inevitable or unavoidable. Indeed, the mine captain himself had spoken of the loss of life of one or two men a year as "natural wastage." Until that sort of complaisance was recognized and eliminated, the author of the report could see little hope for real change.

Jack came in while Connor was folding the pages and stuffing them in an envelope. He hadn't realized how late it was; he'd lit a candle earlier, but now it was pitch-dark outside, time to light the lantern.

Jack was smiling, but he looked tired. "So," he opened, heading straight for the bed and flopping down. "How were yer afternoon wi' the lady mine owner? Eh? Hurry and tell, I've a story o' my own."

"Tell yours, then, because mine's short. She didn't come."

"What? The devil!"

Connor shrugged, affecting a nonchalance Jack probably saw through. "I thought she might not. It wasn't definite."

"Oh, it weren't? The devil!" he cried again, angry for him. Jack's loyalty was a constant in Connor's life he usually took for granted, but he appreciated it now.

"Anyway, it's over and done. No need for us to talk about it."

"No? Well, whatever ee say, Con." He was sneaking glances at him, making sure he was all right.

Connor laid the envelope aside and hitched his chair around so they were facing each other. "What have you been doing? You look like you're guilty of something."

"No, I ain't, but not for lack o' trying. Remember that gel I were talking to at the fair? Sidony is 'er name. Sidony Timms. Never knowed a gel called Sidony afore, did you? Pretty, ain't it?"

"She's the dairymaid at Lynton Hall Farm."

Jack's blue eyes went wide. "How do ee know?"

"I heard. Miss Deene mentioned it."

"Aha. Well, she'm that, all right, and today being Sunday, she had a holiday. So who walked her all over creation after church, do you guess?"

Connor folded his hands behind his neck. "Did you, now. And what did you get for your pains?"

"Nothing like what ee're thinking wi' yer foul, wicked mind, my lad. Miss Timms, she'm above yer low suspicions."

"I expect she's above yours, too, then. So it's *Miss Timms*, is it?"

He grinned. "In the morning. By afternoon twur Sidony. Sidony," he said again, breathily, and fell over backward on the bed. "Do ee know why she limps?"

"Does she limp? I didn't know it."

"Didn't ee see? Yes, she'm lame, but it ain't turrible, not near as bad as she thinks. Twur 'er father that crippled her, years back, beatin' on 'er. The vicar took 'er away from him and put her at the great house wi' the lord. Moreton, as he is now, although he were D'Aubrey then. So now she'm doing brave, and happy as a pirate."

"You like her."

"Oh, I do, Con. She'm clever as can be, and sweet-natured, and I like the way she looks up at me through her black eyelashes, smilin' like she were walkin' wi' some grand gentleman. She have a way about 'er, that's pat."

"Has she no other sweethearts, then?"

"Hm. Ha." He scowled. "She have. Fellow called Holyoake. He'm the bailiff at Lynton." He sat up and began to rub his bony knees. "But he'm old, forty, like, and she'm not twenty. I don't take 'im into account."

"Does she take him into account?"

Jack shot him a candid glance. "She've a grea' deal o' loyalty to 'im, see, on account o' him being kind to 'er. I'm thinking 'tis more a friendship for her. For him . . ."

"He's in love with her."

He shrugged. "As to that, I couldn't say. Never met the man and don't care to, neither. I don't," he repeated, "take 'im into account." He got to his feet slowly, giving the humorous, exaggerated groan that Connor knew masked real discomfort. "What are ee scratching at? Another letter to the Rhads?"

"I finished the report."

"You never! This early?" He looked at him quizzically, and Connor turned back to his desk. "So, 'tis truly done, then? Ee didn't hurry it along, did ee, Con?"

"Hurry it along?"

"Because she turned you down." Connor looked up sharply, and Jack raised his hands. "Not but what ee wouldn't be entitled, and not that I'd care one whit—her and her mine can rot for all o' me. I'm only sayin'—"

"I know what you're saying. The answer's no, I didn't tinker with the report."

"No. No, o' course ee did no such thing. 'Tis something *I* might do, Con, but never you. I'm sorry."

Connor scrubbed his face with both hands, muttering a tired curse. "Ah, Jack. Forget it."

But later, after Jack had gone to bed, he read over what he'd written and added a postscript. The mine owner spoke of installing more ventilators in the near future, he wrote, and if that happened, his findings with regard to heat and the cleanness of the air would alter significantly. In addition, morale was high. Wages were low—but not in comparison to other mines in the immediate vicinity. There had been no forced layoffs in recent memory. And although the law allowed boys to work underground at the age of ten, no child at Guelder went down until he was fourteen, and then only as a helper, working the windlasses or wheeling barrows.

He sat for a long time, listening to the hiss of the oil lamp, the muffled cadence of Jack's snores through the wall. The church clock struck eleven, each tinny thud ringing loud and clear in the late night hush. When the last note died away, he made a decision.

"This report is preliminary," he scrawled at the bottom, underlining the words. "In the interests of accuracy, completeness, and absolute fairness, the preparer needs more time. For purposes of the mining bill Mr. Shavers plans to bring in at month's end, it is hoped that the two previous papers furnished on Wheal Looe and Tregurtha in Cornwall will prove sufficient. In any case, this investigation of Guelder mine should not be taken as final until a supplementary report is furnished in"—he tapped the pen against his lips thoughtfully—"approximately a fortnight."

The next morning, he looked for Sophie before he went down to work, but didn't see her. Sometimes she could be found outside, early, exchanging a few words with the bal girls, examining the dressed ores from the day before. Not today.

At dinnertime he climbed up, under the pretense of changing the shirt he'd torn on a piece of scaffolding. Why he wanted to see her, he couldn't say; maybe to show her he was just the same, completely unaffected by her . . . "betrayal" was too strong, even though that's what it had felt like. Her change of heart. But he couldn't find her, and when he asked one of the men in the smithy if she'd come in today, he said he didn't know.

No one below knew anything either. When the cores changed, Connor loitered in the yard, passing the time of day with the new men while he kept an eye on the mine office door. Just when he'd run out of reasons to hang around any longer, the door opened. The grass captain came out, and Connor accosted him as he was walking toward the engine house.

"Mr. Andrewson! I haven't seen Miss Deene today. Tranter Fox and I had a question about our wage," he fabricated, "and when we asked Jenks he told us she'd be the one—"

"She's not here. She's home sick."

"*Sick.*"

"Well, not sick, more stove up. She got in an accident yesterday. Doctor doesn't know when she'll come back." He started walking again. "You have problems about money, talk to Dickon Penney, he'll be—"

Connor moved between Andrewson and the engine house, cutting him off. "She's hurt? What happened to her?"

The captain eyed him curiously. "Driving accident. Fell out of her gig, going for a ride after church. I heard she can't walk. You see Mr. Penney, he'll answer your question about wages." He stuck his pipe back in his mouth, nodded, and left Connor standing in the yard.

Stone House lay about a mile from the mine, north of Wyckerley on the toll road. Connor had passed the weedy entrance once before, on his way to Tavistock, but he'd never ventured through the crumbling granite gateposts—the gate was long gone. He hurried up the carriageway, wondering a little at the raggedness of the borders and the pitted wheel ruts in the worn, dusty gravel. The lane was straight and level until the last second, when it curved up and sharply right, hiding the house behind a stand of low-branching willows for another thirty yards. Its eastern side came into view first, high and many-chimneyed, covered with ivy, rather grand-looking. Then the drive turned again, and the humbler front revealed the building's farmhouse origins. It wasn't at all what he'd expected.

The gabled roof was worn blue slate, so old the individual tiles looked as if giant teeth had been gnawing on the ends. A small porch that served for an entrance was the reverse of stately, but undeniably welcoming. Roses were climbing up the two and a half stories of Dartmoor stone, which had weathered and mellowed to a soft shade of honey yellow. The windows, mullioned and studious-looking, made an odd contrast to the rest of the house with its heavy eaves and blocky, earthbound aspect. He'd thought she would live in a newer place, maybe something like her uncle's Tudor-style mansion in the village High Street. This old house . . . the only word for it was cozy, and that didn't quite fit with his image of fashionable, no-nonsense Sophie Deene, mine owner.

The front door was wide open. He knocked on it, and knocked again, louder, when no one came. Across the narrow foyer, he could see worn wooden stairs from the second floor widen out in a graceful arc at the bottom. He took a few steps into the hall. To his right was a formal parlor, and to his left an informal one, the friendlier, seedier one it was obvious everyone used; he made out blackened fireplace stones, comfortably worn furniture, a thinning carpet. A dim corridor to the left of the staircase led to the back of the house, and he could see the lighted doorways of more rooms. "Hullo," he called. "Is anyone at home?" No answer. But he could smell food cooking, the odor mingling with the scent of roses on a side table in the foyer.

He went back outside. Broken flagstones made a path through dark, overgrown shrubbery, leading to the back of the house. He followed it around, coming out on a crescent-shaped stone terrace in front of a glass-walled sunporch. Self-conscious, he shielded his eyes with his hand and peered inside. Empty.

The odor of roses was stronger now. He turned around toward the garden—and there was Sophie. Thirty feet away, past a high hawthorn hedge bordering what looked like an old apple orchard, she lay on a low wicker divan, sleeping.

His heavy boots sounded loud on the two shallow steps to the garden, and louder still on the white pebble path to her clearing in the screened, latticed, and trellised maze of roses that seemed to be taking over everything. He stopped eight feet shy of her, acutely conscious of the house and all its windows at his back. She'd hurt her foot—it rested on a plaid pillow at the bottom of the divan, bare except for a strip of gauze around the ankle. She wore no shoe on her other foot, only a sheer white stocking, and for the life of him he couldn't stop staring—at her long, pretty feet and trim ankles, and that startling four inches of naked white calf below the frilly hem of her petticoat. But she couldn't be hurt badly; she was fully dressed, and the ground around her was littered with the debris of her recent occupations—newspapers, a sewing basket, crumbs and a half-eaten piece of cheese on a plate. She had a closed parasol at her side, a book lying open on her chest. A straw bonnet hung by its ribbons from her slack fingers. He went closer.

The white of her eyelids looked delicate, vulnerable; they quivered once, as if she was dreaming. Her lips were not quite touching; he watched the flare of her nostrils, the rise and fall of her bosom with every slow, quiet breath. She looked paler than usual, more fragile. She'd piled all her hair on top of her head in a hasty-looking knot, and half of it had slipped out and fallen around her shoulders, loose golden curls shining like coins in the waning sunlight. Seeing her like this was an illicit thrill he wasn't ready to give up. He took another step toward her, and gravel rasped under the sole of his foot. She opened her eyes.

And smiled. His level, predictable world tilted sideways. But Sophie's lucid blue gaze, calm, dreamy-eyed, unbearably lovely, steadied him even while it drew him closer, captured him, and bound him to her.

"I was watching you sleep." He barely spoke above a whisper; she didn't move, but she was so intent, she seemed to strain toward him with her body. "I didn't want you to wake up, because then I'd have to stop. You are . . . beautiful," he finished, smiling a little because the word was so inadequate. "I wish I could touch you. If I thought we were alone, I'd have to kiss you. Would you let me?"

She didn't move; the invisible thread that held their gazes had hypnotized her, too. Finally she whispered, "I'm afraid of you."

It floored him. It evened the score, because he was afraid of her, too. But she was braver: she could admit it, and he couldn't.

He came to her, knelt beside her on the grass. "You've hurt yourself," he said softly. "I'm so sorry."

She shook her head, touching the side of her face with her fingertips. He saw two things then: a bruise on her cheekbone, just in front of the ear, and a long white bandage on her forearm, uncovered when the sleeve of her dress fell back. "It's nothing, really." Her voice was husky from sleep. "A silly thing—an inconvenience. Really nothing, I promise." She must have felt his alarm, or noticed the chill that was creeping over his skin.

"My God, Sophie," he breathed. "Andrewson said a driving accident."

She pushed herself up straighter, clutching at the book that still lay on her breast. He took it from her, his hand brushing the open pages, warm from her body. "It's nothing," she said again. "I was daydreaming, and I drove too far after the path turned rough—should've stopped the cart and walked the rest of the way. There was a rock, an *enormous* rock, big as Gibraltar—I have no idea how I missed it. One of the wheels hit it, and I flew up in the air like a jack-in-the-box." She was smiling, rueful—but he felt the chill again. "Luckily I let go of the reins, or there's no telling what I'd have done to Valentine. He has a very tender mouth."

He sat back on his heels, and somehow he managed to keep his hands to himself. But they wanted to touch her, comfort her. Comfort him.

"I landed in the ditch, and at first I thought my ankle was broken. Sweet Val—he came back, but I couldn't manage the step on the cart, so I had to unhitch him hopping on one foot; can't you picture it?—and finally got up on him by standing on the same rock that upended me in the first place."

"Where did it happen?"

"At that place where the road gives out and it turns into a rock quarry," she said humorously.

"On the way to Abbeycombe?"

"Yes." She sounded surprised by the question. "You were waiting for me, weren't you?"

He nodded, looking down at his hands, half-afraid that if she saw his face, she would know all the bitter, unjust things he'd thought about her while he waited.

"Well," she said with a light laugh, "at least it wasn't raining. So—anyway—the rest isn't very interesting. I rode Val to Dr. Hesselius's house, and after he patched me up, he took me home in his carriage."

"What did he say about your ankle?"

"That it's probably not broken, just sprained."

"Probably?"

She waved her hand in the air. "Maybe a tiny fracture, a 'hairline,' he called it, but he's not sure. But, of course, he's very conservative; if you so much as sneeze he wants to put you to bed."

Connor looked at her skeptically; he was familiar with this minimizing, deprecatory talk. Jack was a master at it.

"He says I shouldn't walk at all for a week, maybe even two. Which is absurd. I've told my uncle to find me some crutches, and I'll probably be back at work in a couple of days."

He said nothing; it wasn't his place to argue with her. Or tell her she was being ridiculous, which was what he wanted to do. "And this?" he said, lightly touching the bandage on her wrist. "And this," his fingers barely grazing the bluish swelling on her cheek.

She closed her eyes for a second. "A nuisance," she murmured. "Nothing hurts anymore except my ankle, and that's only when I move it. Dr. Hesselius gave me medicine that makes me do nothing but sleep. I've stopped taking it."

"So you're a bad patient."

"Not at all. I just know how I feel better than anyone else does."

He couldn't help smiling at that, she sounded so much like Jack. She smiled, too, and for a little while he was lost again, not a coherent thought in his head.

She sobered, and the humor faded from her eyes. "Mr. Jenks is coming. I've just remembered. I asked him to come at five o'clock."

The spell broke. Without a word, Connor got to his feet. Jenks mustn't find him here, of course. Nor anyone else. He became aware for the first time of his uncouth miner's garb, his dirty hands, dirty hair, the mud caked on his ungainly boots. "I'll say good-bye, then," he told her, trying not to sound stiff. "I'm sorry you were hurt. Glad you're on the mend. If there's anything I can do . . ." He forced a laugh. "Well, that's not too likely, is it?"

"Yes, there's something." She sat up straight, wincing, holding one hand out toward him. "Come and see me tomorrow. If it's fair. I'll be right here." Her sweet, hopeful smile could have eclipsed the sun. "Will you come?"

He promised.

# IX

He came every day after that, always in the hour before dusk, always to her mother's rose garden. She began to watch the skies anxiously from about noon on, because if it rained he wouldn't come. That was their rule, although they never spoke of it. She told Maris and Mrs. Bolton that he came on "mine business," and they believed it, because anything else would have been unthinkable. She made sure no one else paid her a visit at the same time by inviting her cousin or her uncle or solicitous friends earlier in the day, and by asking Jenks or Dickon Penney to come (on *real* mine business) at night.

So they were alone, or as alone as it was possible to be outside in the garden, in full view of the house or any passing servant, including Thomas who lived over the carriage house. After the first day, he came to her in his best clothes, his hair still damp sometimes from bathing. She offered him some biscuits once; he devoured them, and she realized he was starving. After that, she made sure Maris brought out a plate of sandwiches and a pitcher of orange tea or lemonade before he came.

They never touched. They talked. They sat in chairs beside the rose-covered garden house, she with her left foot propped up on a pillowed stool, and told each other everything they'd been doing—which in Sophie's case was not much—since the day before. In the beginning, naturally, their chief topic was copper mining, the thing they most had in common. But after he left, it would strike her that she'd done most of the talking, and she would wonder at the notion that, for a miner, he didn't seem very interested in the actual process of mining. He cared more about mine *conditions*, ancillary issues like heat and air, whereas she spent her life puzzling over the mysteries of vein stones and fissures, champion lodes and elvan courses, thinking of ways to eke more ore out of a finite underground cache.

Gradually, though, their talks began to range over wider ground, touching on subjects she would never have guessed he cared about. How clever he was for a self-educated man. He'd always read a lot, he explained when she marveled at it, and changed the subject. He rarely spoke of his family, and she wondered if there was some secret there that embarrassed him. But despite her intense curiosity, she respected his reticence and didn't pry. Instead, she found herself telling him about her own childhood, the closeness she'd shared with her father, her devastation when he died.

"He must have had a lot of faith in you to leave you the mine," Jack said one afternoon, sitting beside her under the acacia tree, surreptitiously feeding Dash tiny pieces of ham.

"He did. He told me I was destined for great things, and he said it so often I almost came to believe him." There was no "almost" about it; she *had* come to believe it. But she thought saying that out loud might sound conceited. "I suppose he spoiled me—Honoria says he did, anyway. He treated me more like a son than a daughter, telling me I had a 'masculine' mind, making sure my education wasn't frivolous. But do you know, I had no idea he was thinking of giving me the mine until the night he died."

"How did it happen?"

"He collapsed at his desk in the countinghouse. They brought him home, and he died a few hours later. It was his heart—it just—gave out." She blinked the tears out of her eyes, unashamed. "He was conscious until the last moment. I think even *he* was surprised when he asked me if I wanted Guelder— we'd both assumed Uncle Eustace would take it over if anything happened to him. When I said yes, he changed his will right then and there, with Christy Morrell for a witness."

She found her handkerchief and blew her nose, shaking her head at herself, smiling through the tears. "Afterward, that's all that made losing him bearable for me. He always believed in me, and never stopped being proud of me. Carrying on and trying to make the mine profitable gave me a reason to do something besides grieve. And I've never regretted my choice. In fact, I can't even imagine living any other way."

Another slight disingenuity; like any woman, she often thought about marriage and children, a quieter life, domestic contentment. But she always pictured them in the vague future, seductive contingencies she didn't have time for right now. Someday, but not yet.

The shadows lengthened slowly, inexorably; Jack would have to leave soon. She watched him lift Dash onto his lap and pet him, scratching him under the chin until the cat flopped over on his side and purred in ecstasy. "Does this animal do anything except sleep?"

"No."

He smiled, leaning back in his chair. He was quiet today, content to listen to her and say little himself. There was a secret about him, something hidden and unspoken. But she never feared or distrusted him, and she felt strongly that whatever he was keeping to himself couldn't hurt her. She was sure of it, and she always trusted her instincts.

"Feel like going for a stroll, Sophie?"

Lately they'd been taking a slow, *very* slow turn around the garden, she using a cane while leaning heavily on his arm. Dr. Hesselius had been right and she'd been wrong: the injury to her ankle was severe, and her cocky plan to be back at work in a day or two seemed, in retrospect, foolish in the extreme.

Jack helped her to stand and gave her her cane, which she preferred to her crutches when he or Maris were around to lend assistance. Anne Morrell had found a wheeled chair for her somewhere in the parish, and when she was tired she rolled herself around in it in the house and the upper part of the garden. She was a nuisance to herself and everyone around her; she felt like a senile old lady, and she suffered her invalidism with little patience and not much grace. And yet . . .

And yet she didn't really want to hurry her recovery. Sometimes she lied and told herself she wanted this holiday from the mine because it was the first she'd had in almost three years. But that wasn't really it. The truth was that she didn't want these hours with Jack to end. She couldn't name—chose not to name—what was happening to them, but she knew it would change once she went back to her old life. Her real life. This was an idyll, a time out of time, not completely real and yet completely irresistible. She wanted to hang on to it as long as she could.

She was teaching him the names of the roses. "Sweetbriar," he guessed, pointing to the white and pink eglantine sprawling over a trellis along the path side.

"Correct. And that?"

"Mmm . . . moss rose?"

"White damask."

"Damask. I knew that. This is maiden's blush."

"Yes."

"And that's Glory to thee John."

"Gloire de Dijon."

"And General Jack-me-not."

"General Jacqueminot," she laughed, letting her temple rest on his shoulder just for a moment. How could she give up these sweet, slow walks? She loved the sturdy feel of his arm as they ambled along, the smooth texture of his coat under her fingers. She loved it that he smelled like fresh soap and water, and she loved the way he looked down at her, his gray eyes warm and smiling, seeing nothing but her. If anyone saw them, Maris or Thomas, Mrs. Bolton, they would have to know that "mine business" was the last thing on their minds. She might be the below-stairs talk of the town by now. She almost didn't care. Anyway, she doubted that the news had spread any higher—to Uncle Eustace, for example. What if it did? She knew how he would react, but how would she? Would she defy him for Jack's sake? She didn't know. She was living dangerously, and she almost liked it.

They had walked farther this time, past the hawthorn hedges and into the old orchard. "You'll have to carry me back," she joked—and gave a low, delighted shriek when he bent and picked her up right off her feet.

"I don't want to carry you back. I want to carry you over there and kiss you."

They were almost kissing already, their mouths only a breath apart, their faces smiling and tense with the same flushed anticipation. "Over where?"

"Behind those trees."

"No, *those* trees," she said breathily, pointing vaguely. "There's a bench—we can sit—"

It was what they had both been wanting for days, and the only wonder was that they'd waited so long for it. She looped her arms around his neck and pressed her forehead to his cheekbone, shutting her eyes tight, trembling already. The novel sensation of being borne along, will-less, appealed to her on some level of herself she hadn't indulged in for so long, she'd forgotten it existed. He found the bench, white-painted wrought iron, rarely used anymore, and sat down. But he kept her on his lap, an intimacy she hadn't anticipated. His laughing eyes reassured her, and when he pressed his face to the side of her neck and inhaled, sighing, "Ahh," on the exhale, as if he'd never smelled anything sweeter, she laughed with him from sheer happiness.

She'd been wanting to touch his hair because it was dark and shiny, like rich black satin. She played with the ends that curled a little above his collar, and pushed her hands through the hair at his temples, relishing the cool, sensuous tickle between her fingers. He was sliding one of his hands slowly up and down her backbone; his other arm lay heavy across her lap, his hand curved possessively around her hip. She knew the precise moment when he realized she wasn't wearing any corset or stays—she was an invalid, she'd rationalized for the last several days; she was allowed to recover in personal comfort in the privacy of her own home. His hand on her spine stopped in midcaress, and his face took on a rapt, intent look. They'd gone beyond flirting, but she couldn't resist a mischievous, knowing smile when his startled eyes found hers. "Ah, Sophie," he murmured, as if she'd given him some generous gift. Then he kissed her.

Memories of the last time they'd done this washed over her in a wave of sweetness. His lips were familiar now, not so stunningly new that she could barely let herself revel in the thrilling feel of them against hers. She could savor the subtleties of kissing him, all the blood-stirring nuances like long and short kisses, soft and hard, little nibbling kisses and deep, lingering, burning ones. She sighed his name, and he seemed to stiffen. "Hush," he said, and before she could think about that, he nudged her lips open with his tongue.

This was new. She went still and let him caress her inside her mouth, startled at first by the strangeness of it, the unimagined intimacy. Her body knew before her mind did that this was pure pleasure, pure seduction. "I'm melting," she whispered, opening her mouth to him, letting him take whatever he wanted. Thoughts spun away, and there was nothing but sensation. She stirred, restless, wanting him to touch her with his hands, and she sighed when his fingers drifted from her cheek to her throat, and then her chest, bare above the square white collar of her gown. "Jack, Jack," she breathed—and he broke the kiss and pressed her head to his shoulder.

Gradually she caught her breath. She could feel the thud of her pulse slowing in time to his, and she put her hand on his chest, inside his jacket, soothing herself with the strong, steady beat of his heart under her palm. Above their heads a bird was trilling, cheerful and oblivious to their intense drama. The scent of apples mingled with the sweeter smell of Jack's skin, and his hair, and his soft breath on her forehead.

"I was angry that day you didn't come to Abbeycombe," he said suddenly. She lifted her head to look at him. "I don't know why I want to tell you this. I wasn't going to."

"You were angry with me?"

"I thought you'd decided not to see me again. Come to your senses."

"Oh, no."

"It hurt," he said simply—a dear confession. "I blamed you."

She smiled, forgiving him. "I think I've been out of my senses since we met."

He looked up from playing with her fingers. "Yes," he said seriously. "Yes, it's like that."

"Yes, it is." Because she wanted to, and because she didn't like the worry in his eyes, she brought her mouth to his and kissed him passionately, pressing against him, holding him tight. Her body heated up in an instant, wanting more, and she made herself stop kissing him to whisper against his lips, "What will happen to us, Jack?"

"Don't talk, Sophie. Don't talk about that."

Each time he came after that, they eventually wandered, casually, seemingly by chance, into the fragrant apple orchard. But there was nothing casual about the way they touched each other as soon as they were alone and invisible. They were on fire. Sophie couldn't think straight when he was away, couldn't think at all when he was there. They began to talk less, touch more as the warm summer days drifted by. It wasn't only the world of differences between them that made the future seem so complicated and hopeless. The mystery Jack carried inside him also kept them apart, in every way but physically. They were both constrained, equally unable to speak of what they were feeling. For Sophie it was at once the most exciting and the most distressing time of her life.

It came to an end on a hot July afternoon, with no warning except a soft *tap, tap, tap* from the direction of the house. She paid it no heed, didn't associate it with the sound of her uncle's cane until it was too late. She was too intent on securing the last flower in Jack's clover wreath and then putting it on his head, which lay pillowed in her lap. "You look like Julius Caesar," she told him, artfully arranging his hair in curls around the whitish blossoms. She put a kiss on his forehead, another on his nose. "No," she said, reevaluating, "not Julius Caesar. Brutus."

He sent her the tender, amused smile she couldn't resist. "Lend me this," he growled, gently pulling on her ear. She gasped when he gave the lobe a playful nip with his teeth, then hummed with excitement when he soothed it with his tongue. "Sophie," he whispered, making her shiver. "*Et tu*, Sophie."

She blinked down at him curiously, rubbing her knuckles across the whiskers of his chin. "How is it you know . . ."

She never finished the question. She broke off to listen, and before she could associate the faint swish of grass in the distance with footsteps, her uncle's voice sounded out loud, clear, and frighteningly close by.

"Sophie? Where are you? Sophie!"

She scrambled up in a flurry of skirts and petticoats, heart hammering, barely suppressing a cry. She gave her hair a frantic swipe—it was loose and full, disheveled from Jack's fingers—and darted to the opening in the hedges. "Here, Uncle, I'm just coming!" He was across the way by the garden house, looking for her inside the dark doorway. He turned when he heard her, tall and severe in black, his citified top hat fitting squarely on his sleek head. He started toward her.

She threw a glance back at Jack. He'd gotten to his feet. He was watching her, waiting for her to walk away, toward her uncle, so he wouldn't know he was here. The look on his face pained her—the face she'd just caressed, the hard, straight mouth she'd softened with kisses moments ago in a slow, teasing line. She saw resignation in his eyes, and cynicism. But the worst thing she saw was good-bye.

"I'm here," she called again to her uncle, needlessly. "I'm here—with Mr. Pendarvis !"

It wasn't like the last time, when she'd flaunted her association with him to her obnoxious cousin like a dare or a slap in the face. There was still bravado in what Sophie had done, a trace of the rebellious girl challenging propriety, convention, and authority all wrapped into one imposing figure: Eustace Vanstone, mine owner, magistrate, and mayor. But Connor couldn't be angry with her this time. Because there was no condescension in this act, only courage.

But what had it accomplished? He picked up a stone and flung it as far as he could into the yellow hayfield bordering the lane he was tramping, thinking of Vanstone's face when he'd seen him walking out of the orchard behind Sophie. Puzzlement, suspicion, dismay, and finally horrified certainty—they'd all flitted across his cold, dignified features, as easy to read as an alehouse signboard. Sophie had stuck to her story—"Mr. Pendarvis has been keeping me up to date on some business at the mine"—but evidence to the contrary was everywhere, and Vanstone was no fool. She even had grass stains on her dress. And she'd limped out without her cane; Connor had to hand it to her, aware that his tie was loose and his waistcoat wasn't buttoned. They looked guilty.

But nothing was going to be said about it in front of him. He'd tarried as long as he could, trying to gauge Sophie's state of mind, trying to understand whether staying was helping or hurting her. In the end he'd decided on the latter, but his leave-taking didn't feel right either.

But, of course, there was nothing else to be done. The wonder was that it hadn't happened sooner—their discovery. They'd been playing with fire and, like children, they'd grown more careless the longer they'd put off disaster. He took most of the blame for himself. He could have stopped coming at any time and saved her. She'd been the passive one, bored and restless with nothing to do; she probably welcomed his visits in part just for the diversion. But he'd stuck his head in the sand and ignored his conscience, not to mention his common sense. How had this happened? How could he have forgotten, even temporarily, the serious goals that had always sustained him for the sake of some wildly improbable dream? He was awake now, thanks to Eustace Vanstone, and he was ashamed of himself.

He'd done everything wrong. Lied to Sophie about who he was. Lied to the Rhadamanthus Society about needing more time—he could have finished his report on Guelder mine last week, *two* weeks ago. And there was no solution, no way out. If he told Sophie his name wasn't even Jack and everything about him was a fraud, what good would it do? The truth would hurt her more than the lies already had. The only honorable thing to do was go away. It wouldn't take much to revive her old bad opinion of him; she'd feel as if she'd been blind for a while and now she had her sight back. And she'd forget him fast, look back and wonder what could have possessed her that summer. But for as long as he lived, he knew he would never forget her.

Jack was waiting for him, lying on Connor's bed. He wasn't asleep, though; he was staring up at the ceiling. "You had another letter from Rhads," he roused himself to say, reaching over to the night table and tossing an envelope to Connor at the bottom of the bed. He looked worse than usual, gray-faced and exhausted, and lately he'd started to lose weight again.

"How are you feeling, Jack?"

He gave his usual shrug. "About the same"—his usual answer. "Aren't ee going to open it?"

"I already know what it says." The society wanted his final report on Guelder, and they wanted it now. A few days ago he'd sent an addendum to his so-called preliminary report, advising them that the mine owner was "actively considering the installation of manmachines" to replace the dangerous, antiquated system of ladders that had been in place for a quarter of a century. "Actively considering" was an exaggeration of gross proportions, but not, he told himself, an outright lie. "Just think about it," he'd said to her, days ago when they were still talking to each other about substantive things like mining, and he was still pretending to himself that one of the reasons he visited her was to educate her, subtly and artfully, on revolutionary mine safety techniques. But when she'd heard how much the new mechanism would cost, she'd set the subject aside. "Just give it some thought," he kept insisting, and finally she'd thrown up her hands and agreed, laughing. Hence, the "active consideration" he'd felt justified, just barely, in adding to his report.

"What have you been doing all day?" he asked his brother, shaking him by the boot.

"Lyin' here mostly. Thinkin' o' last night."

"What happened last night?"

Jack stacked his hands behind his head on the pillow. "I were wi' Sidony. We . . . well, we done it. In a hayfield near to Lynton, all in the moonlight. She stopped wi' me till morning almost. Con, she were a virgin."

"Was she?" He looked at him curiously. Jack wasn't a man to boast about his female conquests, but he wasn't particularly demure about them either. At the moment he didn't look proud or modest; he looked . . . moved. And confused. "Don't tell me you've gone and fallen in love with her," he said softly.

"Love," he snorted, but his eyes were uneasy. "Ha. That's a rich one. Very rich. Me in love. Oh, yes."

"Well, then. How was she?"

He sat up jerkily, and the blood suffusing his ashy face made him look healthy for a few seconds. "Don't talk like that. She isn't like that, Con, so just leave it, see?"

"All right."

"She'm different, understand?"

"Yes."

He looked away, sheepish. He made a point of lying back down on the bed very casually, separating himself from that agitated fellow who cared a damn about Sidony Timms. "So. Tell me about yer afternoon wi' the lovely Miss Deene."

Rather than answer, Connor pretended he gave a damn about his mail and ripped open the envelope from the Rhadamanthus Society.

"Well, what? What's it say?"

Connor looked up, stunned. "They want me."

"What do they—"

"They want me to come to London and work for them."

"The devil."

"Shavers' bill won't be brought in this session after all, so the report's gone all to hell. Now they want me to come and write speeches for them."

"In London, you say?"

"Speeches for Shavers to workingmen's clubs, and articles, and broadsides—I'd be paid to lobby for them."

"Oh, Con. 'Tis perfect for you."

"Yes."

It was the solution he'd felt too hopeless even to look for. His "professional" life, such as it was, had ended here in Wyckerley after the society decided not to finance his report on the copper mine in Buckfastleigh, and he had never been able to see the future for himself, or Jack, beyond the last day he would spend at Guelder. He'd felt as if his life had come to a halt since the death of the Falmouth attorney to whom he'd been articled as a clerk two years ago. Now the thread was picking up, the natural progression becoming visible again, *possible*. He should feel relieved, elated—but there was a weight on his spirits he hadn't anticipated. The price for getting his life back was going to be very high.

"I'll have to go."

"Yes, o' course ee'll have t' go. When?"

"Right away. They say immediately. You'll come with me, won't you?"

Jack pressed a fold in the knee of his old corduroy trousers with his thumb and index finger, staring at the crease with great interest. "I dunno, Con, I can't say. Gi' me leave t' think on it."

# X

On Friday, it looked like rain. Through the glass doors of the sun-porch, Sophie watched moody gray clouds blowing up from the south, and despaired. Channel winds usually portended a storm. If it rained, Jack wouldn't come.

Rose petals littered the terrace, pink and ivory, coral and blood red, skimming across the stones, spinning in mad little whirlpools propelled by the breeze. The treetops swayed, and the birds called out the nervous warning song they sang before a storm. Sophie stared at the pale, hollow-eyed reflection of herself in the glass and thought, *Who are you?* She hardly recognized her face; she looked like a stranger.

He had to come. They couldn't leave things the way they were, and this was their last chance. After today, her life would have to go back to . . . what it had been before. Normal, she'd almost thought, but *normal* had come to mean seeing Jack every day. Today that would end, though—if he came—and tomorrow people would come to her tea party, Sunday she would go to church, and on Monday she would return to Guelder. Then what?

No answer. She only knew he had to come, he had to. Uncle Eustace hadn't insulted him yesterday, not in words, but he hadn't needed to. Everything in his manner had declared his disapproval of Jack's presence in her home, and his disgust with Sophie for countenancing it. She ached when she thought of how that must have made Jack feel. She knew him now, understood his pride as well as she understood her own. She longed to see him and tell him none of it mattered, her uncle wasn't like her, nothing had changed, they could still . . . they could still . . .

"Oh, God," she mumbled, pressing her cheek to the cool glass. She opened the door and let the wind blow in her face. It even smelled like rain. "Oh, God," she whispered with her eyes closed, and the breeze snatched the words and blew them away.

By noon, the wind had dropped and the racing clouds had slowed to a stately march. At two, the sun came out. At five, Jack still hadn't come.

"He's not coming." She said it into her hands as she paced in the garden, not wanting Maris or Mrs. Bolton, if they happened to be looking, to see her talking to herself. But her mind felt too full of worry to keep the words in, and saying them out loud gave her some relief. Not much, but some. "Maybe this is how people go crazy," she muttered into her palms. What was happening to her? She was frantic to see him, and she wasn't even sure why. On the face of it, nothing had changed. They'd been caught, and yet their afternoons together had been about to end anyway. She had a secret, unexamined fear that she was losing him, but that wasn't what was causing this strange urgency. The truth she wasn't ready to face was how much losing him was going to cost.

She heard a step on the stone terrace. Afraid to hope, she turned toward the house slowly, schooling her flushed features into calm.

Ah, Jack. He stood on the top step, watching her, and she felt her heart lift in her chest like a bird taking flight. Too late now for caution or second thoughts. Everything about him was beautiful to her. And everything was falling apart, but she couldn't stop the glad, thankful smile that went out to him like an open hand, or a candle in a window whose soft glow said *welcome*.

His smile was slower, sadder. She disregarded it and moved toward him, meeting him halfway. She loved his long-legged walk and the hard, tough set of his shoulders, his graceful hands. The way his hair grew. She stopped in front of him, longing to touch him. "I thought you weren't coming," she said with her hands clasped under her chin. "I'm so glad you came."

"I shouldn't have."

"I know," she agreed without thinking. "Oh, but what does it matter? I don't care, Jack, I truly don't—I had to see you!"

"Sophie," he whispered, and lifted his hand toward her—then dropped it back to his side. "Can we sit down? I have to tell you something."

She'd thought he would want to go into the orchard, where they could be private. This was better, and of course he was right—but she had a sinking feeling of disappointment.

They sat in their usual place beside the garden house. She didn't need the pillowed stool for her foot anymore; she hardly even needed her cane. Odd, no doubt, to feel regret because an injury had healed, but she did.

"What happened after I left you?" he asked, leaning toward her, his eyes dark with concern.

"Nothing. You mean did he scold me? No, nothing like that. He's not my guardian," she said with an unsuccessful laugh. "And I'm not—"

"What did he say to you? Tell me."

"It doesn't matter. I don't care what he thinks."

"Tell me."

"Jack, can't we leave it? I don't want to say what he said. It was nothing terrible, and nothing you can't imagine, I'm sure. But—don't make me say it. Why spoil this last day for us?"

"It is our last day, Sophie," he said quietly. "But how did you know?"

"I didn't mean that. It doesn't have to be. But this—" She lifted her hand, gesturing at the garden, the house. "It's probably . . . I don't know if we . . ." She flushed with embarrassment and distress. She was falling in love with a man she couldn't even invite into her house.

"No. No, it is our last day." She started to speak, but he leaned toward her and said, "Listen. There's an organization called the Rhadamanthus Society. Perhaps you've heard of it."

She nodded. "They're socialists, aren't they?"

"They're reformers."

"My uncle says they're socialists."

He smiled grimly. "Your uncle thinks the queen's husband is a socialist. But we won't argue about that now."

"No. What do they have to do with you, Jack?"

"They've offered me employment."

She sat back in her chair. "They've *what*?"

"They think I could be helpful to them," he said, and his voice was stilted. "In their efforts to improve health and safety conditions in mines. Because of my experience. As a miner."

"But—how do they even know about you?"

He looked away, rubbing the back of his neck with his hand. "Oh, I . . . wrote them a letter once, a long time ago. They printed it in their broadsheet, and that started a correspondence."

"You never told me."

"I didn't think of it."

The thought that he was leaving something out floated through her mind for a second, then sank beneath a wave of anxiety. "Are they in London?"

"Yes."

"Would you go there?"

"Yes."

She put her hand on her throat. "Are you going to do it?"

"I think I must."

"When?"

"Right away."

"I see. And so you've come to tell me good-bye."

"Sophie."

She stood up and started to walk away from him, holding her hot cheeks. She heard him behind her and quickened her steps. At the entrance to the orchard, she threw back over her shoulder, "Don't come after me, Jack, please don't—"

He didn't obey. She craved solitude, but when he stopped her blind flight by putting his arms around her and pulling her back against him, she wanted that even more. "I'm all right," she kept saying, pressing his hands to her middle, "I'm all right. Oh, Jack." She turned her head to kiss him, his hair, his cheekbone. "I don't blame you for going. It's an opportunity to better yourself, and you must take it. I know that." She turned in his arms, facing him. "But—what if I asked you to work for me? Not as a miner—something else. You could be Jenks's assistant, or Dickon Penney's." He started to shake his head. "Or anything—you could be anything, Jack, you're so clever—"

"No, Sophie, no. I can't work for you."

"But why?"

"I can't. It's not possible. Don't ask me."

More than the words, the look in his eyes and the strong grip of his hands on her shoulders convinced her there was no use in arguing. Rather than cry, she went into his arms and held tight. He'd known all along, then, that this was the end. But to lose him like this, *really* lose him, never to see him again—how could that be right?

"Don't go," she begged, her mouth muffled against the collar of his coat. "Jack, can't we find a way?"

His arms around her tightened painfully. "Sophie, it would never work for us. You and I . . . how can I stay?"

"Stay . . ."

"Darling." He put his cheek next to hers. "I can't."

She let her breath out in a long, hopeless sigh and pulled away to look at him. The same misery she felt was in his face, the same sorrow. She took his hand. "Stay with me tonight, then."

His handsome brows came together. He said very softly, "What?"

She laughed. It was as if she'd just dived from a great height, and the hard part was over. All she felt now was breathless. "Come to me tonight, Jack. You want me, don't you?"

"I—" He couldn't say anything else.

"You won't leave me like this."

"Sophie, no."

"Yes. Stay with me." She had both of his hands, and she was squeezing hard. "My housekeeper goes away on Fridays, and I'm alone. Except for Thomas, but he wouldn't know—he never comes to the house after dinner. You could come tonight."

He started to say no again, but she put her fingers over his mouth. "Please. It's what I want. I'm not asking for anything else. Come to me, Jack, come when the moon rises."

She couldn't sit still. Twice she tried to wait for him on the sofa in the day parlor, and both times she jumped up after two minutes and began to pace. She straightened the books on the bookcase, blew dust off the candlesticks on the flap table, took her handkerchief to the crystal of the eight-day clock on the mantelshelf. Should she change her clothes? Would that be silly? But why was she so nervous? She wanted to be serene, confident—but she was jumping out of her skin. Maybe she ought to take a glass of sherry. Or brandy; there was still a bottle in her father's liquor cabinet. She'd started for the door before she caught herself. How absurd. Courage in a glass was the last thing she needed right now.

She began to pace again. *Oh, what have I done?* Everything had seemed so clear a few hours ago, and now it seemed completely mad. She was going to give her innocence away to a miner. She might be in love with him, and he might be the cleverest miner she'd ever encountered, but that was still what he was and what he had been all his life. Did it matter?

Of course it mattered. She couldn't lie to herself, any more than she could help being who she was. At school in Exeter, she'd belonged to a club called the Daughters of Victoria—"Doves"— and one of the club's many precepts on ladylike deportment had been that true gentlewomen had congress with the lower classes only for the purposes of trade or charity. The notion that a gentlewoman might own a copper mine had, of course, never entered a single Dove's mind.

A soft knock sounded at the front door. Her heart leapt into her throat; she patted at her hair in the mirror over the mantel, dismayed by the two bright pink spots on her cheeks and the glitter in her eyes—pure nerves. She didn't want him to see her this way, full of fears and second thoughts. The knock came again. She smoothed her skirts, squared her shoulders, and went to answer it.

It was Robert Croddy.

Staring at him, dapper in plaid trousers and a coat with a yellow flower in the buttonhole, Sophie felt all the excited color in her cheeks drain away. "Robert! What are you doing here?" she blurted out ungraciously.

He had his arm curled around his hat, holding it to his chest in a stiff, formal posture. He looked ridiculous; she couldn't help imagining him giving the hat a good strong flick with his wrist and sending it flying like a discus. He sent her his tight-lipped smile. "May I come in?"

"No!" Getting a grip on herself, she tried to smile back. "I'm sorry—I'm alone tonight. I'd invite you in, but it wouldn't be proper. I'd better not." Looking past his shoulder, surreptitiously frantic, she could see nothing but his shiny black chaise in her drive, hear nothing but the impatient stamp of his horse. The platinum face of the full moon stared at her from above the dark treetops.

"No, no, of course not. Certainly not. Forgive me, Sophie, I had no idea you were alone." He frowned. "Why are you alone? Where are your servants?"

"My housekeeper is often absent on Friday evenings," she said coolly, hoping to convey that none of this was any of his business. "Was there something you wanted?"

"Only to tender my regrets. I see I should have sent a note."

"Your regrets?"

"I won't be able to come tomorrow."

"Tomorrow?"

"You invited me," he said stiffly, "to tea."

"Oh! Yes, of course, forgive me—I was dozing over a book when you knocked, and I'm not quite awake yet."

He bowed. "I won't detain you."

"I'm sorry you can't come tomorrow," she remembered to say as he was turning away.

"Thank you. Some last-minute business makes it impossible."

She wondered what his business might be, but didn't ask; that would only make him stay longer. Anyway, Robert never liked to speak of the details of his father's brewery business, or even his investments in her uncle's mine, for that matter. He was old-fashioned in that way. He was *in trade,* as the pejorative saying went; but unlike Sophie, he was ashamed of it.

She lingered a moment by the open door after he went away, hoping the cool, quiet night would calm her. Behind her, a lamp glowed on the table in the foyer. She'd left it there on purpose, because she wanted Jack to come to the house tonight, not the garden. The crunch of Robert's carriage wheels on the gravel drive faded away. Out of the stillness and the dark, a form materialized, just beyond the hedges in the circle of the drive. Sophie froze—until the moonlight made bluish shadows in Jack's black hair, spilled silver on his shoulders and his long, handsome legs. She smiled. All her doubts drifted away like dead leaves in a spring river current.

He took the steps in one long stride, and she moved back, away from him, inviting him in with her body. That he should be here, alone with her in her house, her hallway—it took her breath away. It was almost a minute before she realized he wasn't smiling back at her.

"Maybe I should have come later." His hard voice shattered her mood, like a rock thrown through a mirror. "I didn't know you'd have a man here ahead of me."

"Oh, Jack." She reached for his stiff hand, and kept it even when it wouldn't soften. This was all wrong, ridiculous, not at all the way it was supposed to be! "Come in," she told him, drawing him into the parlor. He stood in the center of the room, looking around at her things, her furniture, his face tight with an emotion she didn't fully understand. "That was Robert," she began, "Robert Croddy. You met him before at—"

"I know who he is."

"He just—he's never come here before like this, at night, I mean. He wanted to tell me he can't come to my tea party. He—he—" She was through explaining. "Jack, are you *jealous* of him?"

Her incredulity finally brought him to his senses. He smiled at the floor, then lifted his sheepish gaze to her. "Hell, yes. I'd like to stuff him in a beer barrel and throw him in the river."

She laughed. He still had her hand. They came together in a warm, perfectly natural embrace, sweet and welcoming. She hugged him, feeling the relief wash over her in waves. "I sent him away," she whispered, pressing her palms to his chest. "The perfect suitor. Rich, handsome—"

"Ugly."

"Strong."

"Fat." He kissed her on the mouth. "Stupid."

"Yes, but rich."

"Not so rich. Which one of us is holding you in his arms?"

She rested her cheek on his shoulder. Robert *was* the perfect suitor, and she'd sent him away so that she could entertain the attentions of a poor Cornish copper miner. She was giving him *herself,* and he'd been jealous. If she were found out, she would be ruined. Ruined. All the risk was hers, none of it Jack's.

Suddenly she felt so frightened, she wanted it over with quickly. She held his face and kissed him again and again, her eyes shut tight, desperate to lose her mind, give herself up to sensation. She felt his surprise before he pulled her closer and his mouth turned greedy. This was what she wanted—surrender, possession; to be overcome. She tried to say his name, but his ravenous kisses prevented it. She slipped her hands inside his coat and rubbed them up and down his spine, molding the curves of his muscles under the satin back of his waistcoat. He wore a belt, and she put her thumbs inside it first, then all her fingertips; she couldn't really feel anything except his shirt, but the bold intimacy fired her imagination. And his—he brought his hands down to her bottom and caressed her, kneaded her through her gown. Her knees went weak; she was trembling, she could barely stand. His open mouth glided across her face to her ear, and she shivered from the delicious sensation. She could have slid down to the floor then and lain with him on her mother's old flowered carpet. But he kissed her again and murmured in her ear, "Sophie, love, is there some place we can go?"

They caught their breath while they held each other, swaying a little. She wanted to stop making decisions, but new ones kept being required of her. She'd asked him to come, and he was here—wasn't that enough? Her mind, that coward, had shut down every time she'd begun to imagine what making love with Jack would be like, and so she had never envisioned a place where they would do it. Here? In her room? Her father's room, where the bed was bigger?

In the end she chose the most natural place. "Would you like to come to my room?" she asked, with her forehead resting on his, their hands clasped between them.

"I would." He kissed her fingers, one at a time. "If you're sure about this."

She didn't say anything. She just led him out of the parlor and then up the dim staircase, and let that be her answer.

She lit a candle from the one she'd brought with her and set them both on the table beside her bed. She tried to see the room through Jack's eyes, and for the first time it seemed childish to her: the virginal white coverlet on the tester bed she'd slept in for twenty years, the shelf of school books and pictures of girlfriends, framed certificates and prizes she'd won at various levels in her women's academy. She'd been the May queen in Wyckerley for two years, at ages sixteen and seventeen, and she still had the silly, ribbon-strewn straw hats she'd worn in the processions tacked to her wall. She was still using the dressing table her father had given her when she was ten, even though the stool was too small and the mirror was so low she couldn't see herself unless she bent over in half.

Jack was standing by her bureau, looking at the pictures and photographs on top. She went to his side, and pointed to a framed miniature in watercolors. "This is my mother. Wasn't she beautiful?"

"Yes. You look like her."

"Thank you. Other people say that, too. I can't see it myself. These are my parents." She touched another picture, this one an oil painting. "They'd only been married a month. I love this picture, because they look so happy."

"Is this Guelder?" He pointed to a sepia-colored daugerreotype, frayed and fading under the glass.

She nodded. "Fifteen years ago, not long after my father leased it." She was fond of that picture as well, because in it the mine looked like nothing but a tumbled-down engine house and a ladder sticking out of a hole in a great muddy yard. Over the years, Tolliver Deene had turned it into a fine, profitable business, and she was following proudly in his footsteps.

She leaned against Jack's arm lightly, wishing he would touch her. She was back to being nervous again. She wanted to be swept away, she wanted to stop *talking*. But he wasn't going to seduce her, she could see that; he was going to let it be her choice every step of the way.

Right, then. She left him and crossed to the bed, bent over and blew out both candles on the table. She'd forgotten the moon was full; the room wasn't nearly dark enough. With a deep breath for courage, she began to undress.

At first she was afraid he wouldn't come to her, that he would stand still and watch—and she couldn't have borne that. But his big, shadowy body moved toward her slowly in the dark, and his hands when he touched her, to help her with the buttons at the back of her gown, were warm and sure. He opened her dress and eased it over her shoulders, and she could feel his breath on her skin, ticklish and exciting. "I'm sorry, Sophie," she thought he whispered. "I can't resist you."

She turned to face him. "I don't want you to be sorry. I don't want you to resist me." She kissed him, fighting against the last of the reluctance she could feel in his body, hear in his voice. If they were really going to do this, she wanted it to be a celebration. *But how can it be? He's going away!* She shut her ears to that, shut her mind. Thank God she trusted him. If they never met again, she wouldn't regret this. She had saved herself for him, Jack Pendarvis, and the fact that he couldn't stay and marry her, be her lover forever, might be tragic but it was also irrelevant. "This is right," she told him, "it's right, Jack," and she believed it with her whole soul.

Her certainty was his undoing. Even when she called him by his brother's name, Connor couldn't stop. Too late now; he had no choice but to believe she was right. And love her, and give her the best of himself.

"Ah, Sophie," he breathed, filling his hands with her hair. She had on a soft cashmere chemisette under the bodice of her gown, and he tugged it down over her breasts, revealing the dainty white corset cover she wore—with no corset under it. "Such pretty clothes you always wear. I don't know anyone else who dresses like you." She liked that, he could tell by her smile. A row of tiny pearl buttons ran down the front of the last garment. He leaned in close while he unfastened them one by one, and she put her hands on his neck, stroking him softly, kissing his hair. Moonlight silvered her bare skin, and made her breasts look cold and untouchable, like some impossibly lovely marble statue. The reality was different. While she held her breath he caressed her, and she was warm and silky-soft, her fine-textured nipples coming to life in his palms. He couldn't believe he was seeing her like this, Miss Sophie Deene, the object of near-constant fascination among the miners, and plenty of coarse but heartfelt wishful thinking.

"The men speak of Guelder as if it's a woman," he told her, nudging dress, blouse, and slip over her hips. "Like a ship. 'She's killer hot today,' they'll say, or 'She fought us for every inch last night.'"

"Do they?" She tugged at one end of his necktie, smiling.

"Sometimes I'll catch myself thinking they're talking about you." He frowned at the waist of a pair of white cambric drawers, wondering where the fastener was. " 'How is she today?' a new man will ask me on the ladder, and I'll have to stop myself from saying, 'You wouldn't believe it, she's even prettier than yesterday.' "

Sophie laughed, and sighed, and put her head on his shoulder. He found the little lace ribbon and pulled on it, untying an inside bow, and the drawers slid to her knees, then her ankles. Nothing left but her stockings—she'd already stepped out of her shoes. He set her away from him a little, to look at her, and she shivered once but kept her hands at her sides, not trying to cover herself. "Are you cold?" She shook her head. "Sophie, you're beautiful," he told her, wishing he knew more words. She was perfect, exactly as lovely as he'd known she would be. "Beautiful. But you know that."

"No, I don't, Jack."

Her hushed voice gave her away—she was scared. And he was an idiot for not realizing it sooner. He put his arms around her and held her gently, cupping her shoulder blades, tracing the fragile bumps of her backbone with his fingertips. "It's all right. Everything's going to be fine." Her body softened enticingly. She gave him a kiss, and he deepened it, keeping her still with a hand on her waist while he shrugged out of his coat and started on the buttons of his shirt. Then she turned away from him to pull down the covers of her bed. She sat on the edge, her gaze skittish but interested when he stripped off his trousers. He'd wanted to take her stockings off for her; but watching her do it, her hands slow and her eyes dreamy, almost absentminded, was even better.

She scooted back, making room for him, and they lay down. There was only one pillow. Her narrow mattress sagged slightly in the middle, so they rolled together naturally, their hands eager and welcoming. "I've thought about this," she confided, barely brushing the healed white scar on his side with her fingers. "I've wanted it. Jack, I think about you *all the time*."

"I think about you constantly," he whispered back. "Since the first time I saw you. Do you remember that day as well as I do? I thought I'd never seen anything so lovely. Not just your body, which is beautiful, and not just your beautiful face and your beautiful hair—Sophie, you have the most *beautiful* hair. It's like sunlight, it's like yellow flowers—"

"Oh, Jack." She huffed out her breath, delighted and embarrassed.

He laughed with her, pressing a kiss to her forehead. Her right breast fit his left palm just right. He fondled her while he said, "But that wasn't it. I was with my brother that day, and we both felt it."

"What?"

"It's hard to explain. The way you were with the children. Your gentleness. Grace. Sophie, you are . . . sweet."

"Not always." Her face was a study. She was smiling with her eyes closed, intent on what he was doing—stroking his middle finger across the pink tip of her nipple.

"Do you like it?" he asked needlessly, and she answered by biting her bottom lip and moaning. He put his mouth on her, murmuring, "And this?" before he sucked gently at her little peak, soothing it with his tongue. The soft sounds she made fired him, and he thought again that this was a miracle, being with her in her girlish bed, touching her and making her sigh.

"How long," she breathed, then trailed off, distracted.

"How long . . . ?"

She cupped his cheek with her hand. "How long do we do this before we really . . . before the real thing?"

"As long as you want," he answered recklessly.

"Oh. I thought . . . I didn't even know people did this. Does everyone?"

"Mmm, don't know." He was caressing her silky flat stomach in circles around her navel. "What did you think they did?"

"Just the one thing. I didn't know there was all this . . . beginning part. Isn't it nice?"

"Very nice." He trailed his fingers down to the soft mesh of her pubic hair, playing with the little curls, listening to her breathing change. She turned her head to kiss his mouth—or maybe to hide her face when he fluttered his fingers so gently against her. She parted her thighs for him when he asked her to, and he stroked her slowly, intimately, making her gasp.

"Jack?"

"Mm?"

"You said as long as I want."

"Mm."

"Now . . . let's do it now . . ."

He kissed her as he came over her, whispering, "Open your legs, Sophie." She hadn't touched him yet; he used his own hand to guide himself to her. She was unique in his experience; he'd never known what to expect from her. At the last second, he said, "Tell me if I'm going to hurt you." The confusion in her face was his answer, and he knew he'd been a stupid fool for asking. "Ah, Sophie, I'm sorry."

"Why, Jack?"

Was it better to warn her? "Because I have to do this." Steeling himself, he pushed into her all at once, and she gave a gasp and a startled cry. "It's over," he assured her, after a second of such intense pleasure he couldn't speak.

"It's over?" she quavered.

He couldn't keep from smiling. "The pain," he explained. He framed her face with his hands and kissed her softly, again and again. "Now, nothing but pleasure. I promise."

## XI

Brandy at midnight—what a decadent delight. And the smoky, prickly taste was only part of the pleasure; the best part was sipping it in your night robe with your lover, while you gave him a tour of your house.

"This was my nursery," Sophie told Jack, leaning against his shoulder, just to touch him, and holding the candle high in the doorway so he could see into the spacious, blue-and-yellow-papered room. "Needs dusting," she observed. Needed airing out, too; the mattress on her old crib was probably responsible for that mildew smell. The crowded shelves brought back a flood of memories. "That was my favorite doll." She pointed to a yellow-haired china doll in a blue brocade gown, enthroned in a miniature upholstered chair, the place of honor in the doll collection. "Her name was Norah. I pretended we were sisters."

"She looks like you."

"It would have thrilled me to hear that when I was seven years old."

He slipped his arm around her waist. "You had a rocking horse."

"His name was Midnight. We went on a lot of rides together."

"Did you take Norah with you?"

"Sometimes. Sometimes the cook would pack lunch for me in a little box, and I'd eat it on Midnight, pretending I was an American cowgirl riding the range." Jack smiled at her. "I was spoiled, I suppose. Compared to most children." Compared to him, she was thinking. She'd had a hundred toys; most of them were gathering dust on shelves in this room—books and puzzles, blocks, games, chalks and paints, paper dolls, stereoscopes. She thought of the book Jack's tutor had given him, the one about the boy who could make himself invisible. His brothers had spoiled that book for him—but at least he'd had brothers. Maybe she hadn't been so very much better off than him after all. At least not in that one way.

"This was Mrs. Turner's room," she pointed out, continuing the tour. "She was my nurse. And this—this was my father's bedroom." Unconsciously she dropped her voice, as she always did when she came into this room. She'd given most of his clothes away to the parish, but otherwise the spare, stately bedchamber looked just as it had on the night he died. The heavy mahogany four-poster's curtains were closed, and sometimes—not so much anymore—she imagined that her father was sleeping behind them; that she was bringing him tea or the newspaper, and he would yawn and stretch and say, "Morning, Sunshine," the way he used to.

Jack put a soft kiss on her temple. "You still miss him."

"I do. Would you like to see his study? Or—is this dull for you, Jack? It's all right, we don't—"

"No, I'd like to see it."

"Truly?"

"Of course."

She took his hand and they went downstairs, carrying the candle and their brandy glasses. She was barefooted; Jack had on his trousers and waistcoat, no shirt. She felt wicked and free and sophisticated. "I love this creaky old house," she confided. "I've been wanting to show it to you for so long."

"It is a wonderful house," he agreed, to her delight. "It suits you. But don't you ever get lonely here all by yourself?"

"Oh, no. Well—yes, sometimes. But I'm not really by myself, I have Mrs. Bolton. And Maris, and of course Thomas."

In her father's study, she handed Jack the candlestick while she went to close the curtains—the room was at the back of the house, and she was afraid Thomas might see the light from his bedroom over the carriage house and wonder about it. She turned back, and tried to picture the study through Jack's eyes. "Everything's a bit dingy," she realized. "Honoria's always scolding me for not doing something about the house—refurbishing it, you know."

"But you don't want to?"

"I wouldn't mind. But I've been turning all the profits from Guelder back into the mine. There really isn't any money right now to do anything with the house." She ran her hand over the cracks in the leather of the chair behind her father's big desk. The floorboards creaked under the tassled rug, which had a worn-down path from door to desk. But Sophie loved everything about this room, especially the two walls of shelves crammed with books, facing each other on opposite sides of the door.

"Have you read all of these?" Jack held the light high to read the titles.

"Not all. Most of them, though. They're mostly about mining." He grunted and shook his head, and she imagined he was thinking she was a very odd sort of girl.

"You love the mine," he said, smiling at her, coming toward her and sitting down on a corner of the desk.

She sat beside him. "Of course. It's my life."

"Why do you like it so much?"

"Mmm . . . my father loved it." That sounded like a strange answer, but it was the truth. "And . . . I like doing something well. Something that matters. I like the feeling of being proud of myself."

"Yes," he said, nodding. He understood that.

"My father used to tell me I could be anything I wanted to be, because I was as smart as a man." She smiled self-consciously, trying to look modest, as though she didn't believe it herself. But she did. "We were partners. It felt like—like a conspiracy. Us against the world. When I lost him, the mine is what saved me." She fiddled with the belt of her silk dressing gown, thinking how natural it felt to be telling Jack these things about herself. Of course they were lovers now, but she hadn't anticipated that he would become quite so much a *friend* afterward. "Do you like being a miner?" It seemed curious that she'd never asked him that question directly before.

"No, I hate it."

His vehemence startled her. But after a second, she felt glad. "Then why do you do it?" That question she *had* asked him before, and he'd always cut her off to avoid the subject. But things were different now—surely; being lovers must change everything. "Why, Jack? I've never understood it, not from the beginning. You could be so much more, you could be—"

"Why does it matter to you so much?"

"*Why?* Don't you know why? Oh, Jack—"

"Let it go." He put his hand on her thigh and spoke softly. "We'll talk about it later. I want to talk about it, but not tonight."

"All right." She put her fingers through the spaces between his. "But tell me why you hate it. At least tell me that."

The look he sent her was faintly incredulous. "Sophie, have you ever been down in a mine? Gone down in it on the ladders with the other miners?"

"Yes, of course." But only once, she had to admit. She'd been nineteen, and for five years before that she'd begged her father to let her go down in Guelder. On her birthday, he'd finally said yes.

"Did you like it?"

"I don't know. Yes," she decided. "Yes, I enjoyed it." But enjoying it hadn't seemed relevant at the time; she'd simply wanted to know what a copper mine was like. Jenks had taken her down to the twenty level, and she'd watched a tribute crew costean to the twenty-five. Everything about it had fascinated her.

Jack was staring at her. "You *liked* it? What if you had to go down every day? Think about it, remember what it was like. Every day, Sophie, every—oh, hell. I said we'll talk about it later. But not now, not tonight."

"Fine."

They went down to the kitchen, and the slight strain between them lasted until they began to fix a midnight snack. Then it floated away, forgotten under the weight of more interesting dilemmas, like whether butter or mustard was the right accompaniment to slices of pork on thick pieces of Mrs. Bolton's barley bread. They sat side by side on a bench at the scarred and scrubbed oak table, sipping tea and brandy and munching on their sandwiches. They talked about food they liked, food they hated, the best meals they'd ever eaten, why they thought the reputation of English cuisine for being the worst in the world wasn't fair. Laughing with him, bumping shoulders, saying silly things, Sophie reveled in the easiness of the conversation. Except for the interesting fact that they were intimate now and had just made sweet, spectacular love with each other, being with Jack was like being with a dear and trusted friend. She felt there was nothing she couldn't tell him about herself, and more than ever she wanted to know everything about him. The brandy was making her a trifle light-headed, and she asked him if he'd ever been drunk.

"Really drunk? Only once. I'd just turned sixteen, and my brothers took me to Redruth to celebrate my manhood."

"Wait, now. Do I need to hear the rest of this story?"

"You asked for it."

"But I have delicate ears."

"I know." He pulled her hair back and kissed her on the ear, a loud, smacking kiss that made her squeal. She retaliated with a hard squeeze on his thigh, where she knew he was ticklish. "Anyway. As I was saying. They took me to a tavern called the Black Bull. That I remember. The rest starts out hazy and ends in the pitch-black."

"Heavens. What were you drinking?"

"Blue ruin. Gin." He gave a mock shudder. "Never been able to stomach it since. Can't even bear the smell."

"What does it feel like, being inebriated?"

"It feels like bloody hell."

"Yes, but that's afterward. What about when you're just start-ing out?"

"Then it's fun. Haven't you ever been drunk?"

"Certainly not."

"Never?"

"Of course not. Even if I wanted to, which I don't, it couldn't happen, because my cousin is always with me on drinking occa-sions."

"So?"

"So? You've met her, Jack. Could you let go of yourself and have a jolly good time with Honoria watching you?"

"That's a good point."

She put her hand on his bare arm. "How different we are," she mused. "Do you think about that, too? How unlike we are?"

"Yes."

They fell quiet, thinking their separate thoughts. When they finished eating, Sophie washed the plates and put them away so that Maris wouldn't find them in the morning. Hand in hand, they went upstairs and wandered out to the sunroom, to watch the moon go down.

"Look how bright out it is. Almost like day."

"We could go into the garden," Jack suggested. "Would you like to?"

"Yes, but we'd better not. If Thomas woke up, he might see us."

"Or hear us."

She shook her head. "He's deaf."

Below the terrace, white foxgloves and Canterbury bells gleamed in the moonlight, and tall white Madonna lilies. The ever-present scent of roses perfumed the still air; somewhere nearby an owl hooted; bats wheeled and whirred over the apple trees in the orchard. Jack's arm around her shoulders felt solid and real, and yet Sophie couldn't stop thinking about the strange-ness of him, his essential separateness from her. A man and a woman, joining together physically for the first time—beyond the nearly unbearable excitement, how could they know what was real about the other and what was only fantasy, wishful thinking? Early love was like a fever: it destroyed the critical faculties and made you giddy. Jack was so thrillingly alien, so *other,* and she felt absolutely driven to learn all his secrets. Impossible to say if they were as opposite to each other as they seemed to her right now. She hoped not, but only time would tell. Did they have time?

"I'm afraid, Jack."

"Why?"

"Because I don't want to lose you." She came into his arms and held him close, shivering a little, and he murmured to her and stroked her back. "I know you have to go, and it's all right." Then her arms tightened reflexively, and she told the truth. "No, it's not. I thought I could do this and say good-bye to you afterward. Oh, God, Jack—"

He kissed her mouth, slowly and tenderly, stopping the words, and she understood that he was as sad as she was. But he didn't want to talk about it, and perhaps his way was right. Why think about what a mad idea this had been *now?* Why ask herself why she'd deliberately opened herself up to hurt and heartache when she still had him, when his kisses and his hands and his whispered words were irresistible? To have him tonight, to be lovers, to lie together—all the pain in store for her was worth it, because she loved him.

"Lie down, Sophie. Here."

He urged her toward the long, rush-covered chaise by the window. Her heart began to beat faster. Memories of what they'd done before made her feel breathless, as if there weren't quite enough air in the room. She lay down, and was surprised when he knelt on the floor beside her. "There's room for you," she whispered, smiling tensely.

"Not yet." His dark silhouette loomed over her, formidable against the bright night behind him. She felt him tug at the sash around her waist, and then the warm slide of his hand on her skin. He didn't kiss her. His eyes were all she could see of his face, lucid and intent, while he stroked his fingers across her stomach. He pulled away the lapel of her robe to bare one breast, and her toes curled while she waited for him to touch her. Just his fingertips, making the tiniest circles, then the gentlest little pinches. She put her arm over her eyes to keep him from seeing her—to bear it—to make it more intense. Now his lips, plucking lightly, driving her higher, and now his tongue, caressing her, his teeth, making her gasp from the excruciating pleasure. He was squeezing her other breast with his hand, and she wanted more of everything, had to have his weight on her. He took her arm away so he could kiss her, deep, drowning kisses, long and ravenous, burning into her, breaking her down. He had his hand in her hair, and he put the other one between her legs and began to knead the skin inside her thigh almost roughly, using his nails, squeezing her there, and she couldn't recognize the sound of her own voice when she cried out to him, called out his name. He stopped her mouth with another hot, luscious kiss, and in the middle of it he opened her with his fingers and stroked her, all sleek and wet, throbbing for him. Her eyes were shut tight, she was shuddering, and the edge was coming closer, closer. Jack crooked his fingers inside her and at once she flew up and over it, soaring and soaring, out of herself, shot through with absolute pleasure. How could she live through this? It was exquisite, it was too much—slowly it released her and she began to float back to earth, and then she wanted it all over again.

He was taking little nibbling bites of her ribs, the undersides of her breasts. His mouth tickled. "Good thing Thomas is deaf," he mumbled against her wet skin, and when she realized what he meant, she put her hand over her mouth and blushed crimson.

Some time or other, he'd taken off his waistcoat. Now he stood up and took off his pants. She watched him, mesmerized, thinking that if she hadn't known him, known how gentle he could be, his big, powerful, utterly male body would have frightened her. It unnerved her more than a little as it was, but her trepidation was wedded so perfectly with sexual anticipation, she liked it. Thrilled to it.

She sat up to shrug out of her night robe. Jack's scorching gaze made her skin burn everywhere. She held out her hand and he took it, and put his knee on the side of the chaise. She started to move over, make room for him beside her, but he smiled, and lowered himself, and lay on top of her. "Ohh," she breathed, so glad they weren't going to wait. She curled her legs around his, rubbing the hair on his calves with her ankles. "I love this," she told him, touching him with her hands, starved for the feel of him. Kissing him was like a compulsion now, a thirst she couldn't quench. Everything they did was just right, everything was natural.

Her head fell back when he came into her; the shock of it, the unbearable intimacy made her gasp. She felt his mouth at her breast, and the deep, premonitory shudders started over. As good as it had been with him the first time, this was better, because she wasn't new at it anymore. She was experienced. She knew how it would end.

She felt the end coming when he slid his hand under her body and pulled her up tight against him. Braced on one forearm, he drove into her deep, deep, and she was possessed, lost. She cried out, "God!" and "Jack!" and words that didn't make sense, grinding against him, her body arcing back like a bow pulled taut. The climax came slowly, teasingly—*is this it? is this it?*—and then took her all at once. Blind and breathless, she let it have her. She heard the echo of someone's hoarse voice, huffing ecstatic groans she could scarcely imagine coming from herself. She felt drenched with pleasure, utterly sated with it, there wasn't an inch of her body that wasn't pulsing with it.

Jack made a low growling sound in his throat. All his muscles contracted. She clutched at him—he pulled away from her. She felt him slipping out of her body, and she moaned at the loss, "Oh, no, Jack," such a sad abandonment. But he wrapped her up in his arms and surged against her, and she knew what he was about when she felt his stunning, powerful release, the lunge of his hips, the hot liquid rush against her belly. She could hear him grinding his teeth, and it thrilled her to think that she knew exactly, *exactly* what he was feeling in this endless instant of time, "Darling," she called him, holding his spent, panting body close, layering exhausted kisses across his damp forehead. "Oh, Jack, I love you. God help me, I do."

His head came up. "I love you, Sophie. I swear it."

He said the words as if he didn't think she would believe them, as if she needed convincing. But how could she doubt it? It wasn't in her to disbelieve. Not this, not Jack. She had no idea what was going to happen next. She only knew that she would never, ever regret this night.

It came to him while he was watching the ceiling in Sophie's bedroom lighten from black to blue, then gray. The answer.

The shrill chirp of morning birds grew louder in proportion to the brightening light, and it pleased him to think that the solution to his dilemma was becoming clearer in proportion to both of them. Of course. How simple. Why had it taken so long to see it?

She stirred, pressing her cheek against his shoulder, clicking her teeth once. He smiled at her, at his arousal, at everything—and turned his head on the pillow to kiss her, just a soft brush of his lips across her brow. She sighed in her sleep. He whispered, "Love you," and he could swear she smiled.

He would tell her who he was and ask her to wait for him, until he made something of himself. Then they could marry.

She'd do it. She would. She loved him—*loved* him. She'd said it at last, the first one to say it, much braver than he. But he'd had some idea that he was saving her, protecting her by not saying it. Stupid of him; love was too precious to hide, regardless of how noble one might have decided the motive for hiding it was. Now everything was clear to him. He would confess to her his deception, which she would eventually understand and forgive—his mind skated over the details of that—and then he would go to London and make his way. His fortune. The Rhadamanthus

Society could stake him in the beginning, and he would enjoy writing for them, helping them formulate progressive labor policy. But eventually he'd save enough money to resume his studies, and then he'd return to the law, his first love, the dream of his youth. His family's goal for him. How many years would it take—three, four? It would be hard to wait, but Sophie would do it, and her faith in him would make it easier.

He felt euphoric in the wake of the decision. He thought of kissing her until she woke up, and then telling her. Now the secret was almost intolerable, worse the closer he got to being rid of it. To be himself with her, to hear her call him "Connor"—simple pleasures, never to be taken for granted again.

But she was sleeping so sweetly. And the secret was so complicated. Better to tell her in the morning, when they were fresh and had all their faculties.

Or was it?

Yes. *He* needed to be fresh, that was certain. He might want *her* drowsy and uncritical. But what he had to tell her would be hard, no way around it, and he was going to need all his wits to do it right.

He slid down lower in the bed, bending his knees when his feet hit the footboard. He wasn't comfortable this way, but he wanted Sophie's head next to his. Wanted to feel her soft breath on his cheek. He couldn't get enough of her, and he couldn't bear the thought of losing her. Tomorrow—today, rather—if he did everything right, he wouldn't have to.

But they overslept.

A sound woke them both at the same moment, and at first there wasn't a thought in his head except how pretty the sun looked on her hair, splashed across their shared pillow. They smiled into each other's eyes. Then the sound came again, like wood banging on wood—and Sophie shot straight up in bed like a spring.

"Maris!"

They scrambled out from under the covers, both of them nude, and stood, frozen, on opposite sides of the bed, gaping at each other in silent panic. He didn't know who started it, which one of them laughed first, but it wasn't long before they were pressing their hands to their mouths to stifle helpless, uncontrollable mirth. "Shh! Shh!" they kept commanding each other, to no avail. Sophie darted around the bed, pink-faced, snorting. "Get dressed!" she hissed at him. "I'll tell her to go down and get me some coffee—she's on the steps, sweeping, she does it every morning—Hurry, get dressed!" She snatched his shirt off the floor and threw it at him, found her dressing gown, shoved her arms through the sleeves, and yanked the belt tight, then ran out of the room.

He was tying his shoes when she came back. The hysteria was over; she'd recovered her composure. So had he. "She's gone down to the kitchen. Go straight out the front door, Jack, and she'll never know, but you have to go *now*."

"We have to talk."

"Yes, but not now!"

He stood up, went to her. "When?" She looked blank. "This afternoon. In the garden."

"Yes, yes, all right."

"Two o'clock?"

She nodded—then shook her head violently. "No, I forgot, I'm having a tea party this afternoon!"

He cursed. "Tonight, then."

"Yes, tonight. Oh, Jack, *please* go now."

He hated this. There wasn't even time to kiss her. She went with him as far as the staircase, and hung on the post at the top. Excitement, nerves, tenderness, they were all in her beautiful face. He pulled her into his arms for a fast, hard hug, thinking of all the things he wanted to say to her, things about the future as well as the past, how much he loved her, what last night had meant to him. No time. "Tonight," he whispered, and she said it back.

The sixth stair creaked so loud, it sounded like he'd stepped on a cat's tail. He glanced over his shoulder at Sophie. She was all eyes, both hands covering her mouth, face turning red again. So much for his dignified exit.

In the open front door, he couldn't resist a last look back. She was sitting on the top step, bent over to see him, her arms crossed over her knees. She mouthed something and blew him a kiss. Outside, sprinting down her worn gravel drive, it came to him what she'd said: "I love you, Jack!"

# XII

"I said, we were right, it's startin' to rain."

"What?" Sophie looked up from the teaspoon she'd been polishing for the last few minutes. "What, Maris?"

The housemaid heaved a sigh. "For the third time—good thing you moved yer party inside, because 'tis blackenin' up and startin' to rain."

"Oh." She glanced out the parlor window. Maris was right; the sky, which had been blue all morning, was filling with great, rolling storm clouds, and the first drops of water were already hitting the glass with loud, smacking thuds. "Yes. Good thing." She went back to her spoon, missing the white roll of Maris's eyes.

"What's wrong with you?" the maid asked curiously. "Yer a million miles away from here. Didn't you sleep good?"

Sophie kept her head down and said she'd slept fine.

"Well, I'm going down to start them biscuits you like so much. Mrs. B.'ll be here any minute, so there's plenty o' time yet for her to do the quince pie and whatnot. Yer doing the flowers, right?"

"Hm? Mm hm."

"Miss Sophie."

"Yes?"

She put her hands on her hips. "For the Lord's sake, go upstairs and lay down fer half an hour. Believe me, you could use it."

Sophie put the spoon down and reached for a fork. "Nonsense, I'm not tired at all. Go ahead, I heard you—you're making biscuits and I'm doing the flowers. There's no rush; we've got an hour and a half before they come."

"Don't forget, you have to put clothes on."

She looked down at her night robe, back up at Maris. "I won't forget."

After Maris went away, Sophie wandered over to the window to look at the rain. It still might clear up; it was one of those changeable days, cloudy one minute, sunny the next. She wished she'd extended invitations to this tea on any other day but today. How could she keep her mind on her guests? She couldn't even polish silver. She was a wreck.

What if she made Jack a partner in Guelder? Or—what if she simply gave him the mine? She could accomplish that easily enough just by marrying him: a woman forfeited all her assets as soon as she said, "I do." It sounded mad, giving him the mine, but he would surely stay then. Not for the money—he wouldn't care a straw about that—but for the responsibility. He wanted to better himself, make something of himself. This business with the Rhadamanthus Society or whatever it was called was just one opportunity. She could offer him another, much better one. He wouldn't have to go *down* in the mine if he hated it so much. Just run it, with her. He could even make some of the improvements he was always harping on, ladders and ventilators and such things.

The rain stopped. She turned away from the streaky window and walked out into the hall. For a long time she stood still, staring back into the parlor without seeing it. What was it she was supposed to be doing? Oh, flowers. But she hadn't finished the silver, and she'd left the dirty polishing cloth on the tea table, the tea service only half-done.

Suddenly she put her hands on her cheeks and squeezed her eyes shut, the better to stand the shock of anxiety that jolted through her like an electric current. *Marry Jack?* Had she gone mad? She couldn't, couldn't; the idea was insane.

Maybe the reason didn't do her credit, but she was honest enough to admit to herself what it was. If she married Jack Pendarvis, her place in society—which she had taken for granted all her life, her right by birth and by talent, by grace and intellect—would be forfeited. Wyckerley was tiny, but she had grown up here; this provincial village was her whole world. In truth, she was used to being one of the three or four gentlewomen at the top of the social pyramid. Cousin Honoria would disagree, but Sophie recognized no one above herself except Anne Morrell and Rachel Verlaine. If she allied herself with Jack Pendarvis, she would lose her place. She would be nobody, less than nobody, because of the height from which she'd have fallen. It was unthinkable.

What, then? An affair? She sagged against the archway, hopeless. She wasn't a secretive person. If she and Jack continued as they were—assuming he would even agree to it, which was doubtful—the strain of constant concealment would wear her down, and either kill the passion between them or cause her to make a mistake and reveal herself.

Catastrophe. She'd be a fallen woman—she'd have to go away. She would disgrace her father's memory.

There was only one solution. She would have to give him up.

Empty-headed, she walked through the house to the sunroom, out to the terrace, down the wet path to the garden house. She found her apron and put it on, found her cutting shears and basket and carried them to the annual border at the back of the garden. China asters would look pretty on the tea table. Nasturtiums for the sideboard, stocks for the tall vase in the foyer. The smell of the cut stalks was sharp and reedy; the juice made her fingers sticky.

Maybe she would make bouquets for the ladies, flower gifts for them to take home. Wandering over to the perennial beds, she cut more blossoms, sweet Williams and love-lies-bleeding, larkspur and pinks, wallflowers, gillyflowers, and Canterbury bells. The rain had made the heads heavy, the stalks plump and full. Sweetness perfumed the humid air. Should she cut dahlias for the glass bowl on the bannister? Her basket was full; she'd have to . . . she'd have to . . .

She was on her knees in the soft dirt, squeezing wet loam between her fingers, weeping. She couldn't stop. It frightened her; she never lost control like this. Tears clogged her throat, blinded her, ran down her cheeks in rivers. The sound of her own choking sobs shocked her so thoroughly, she finally subdued them. In the breathless, shaky aftermath, a strong certainty entered her heart.

She couldn't give him up. The consequences didn't matter, nothing mattered. She was lost to him, and she would bear whatever it cost to have him. She loved him. She wouldn't give him up.

An exhausted calm drifted over her. She wiped her hands on her apron, climbed to her feet. She'd been wasting time; now she'd have to hurry—she had guests coming in less than an hour. Good: the sooner they came, the sooner they would go away, and then Jack could come to her. It was all she could think of. Hurrying up the path, she started sifting through lies she could tell Mrs. Bolton, to get her out of the house again tonight.

Connor didn't go to the mine that day; that part of his life was over. But he didn't know what else to do with himself. He was exhausted, but he couldn't sleep. Jack was in bed, having one of his bad days, so there was no one to talk to. The time between now and six o'clock stretched before him like a dry, featureless track winding into the desert for a million miles. Nothing made him more restless than wasting time, but when he tried to use these empty hours by planning ahead or simply looking into his own future, his mind filled with chaos. Nothing was clear and distinct except memories of Sophie, last night.

Too late to debate with himself whether he'd done right or wrong by taking her to bed. What mattered were the consequences. Making Sophie his lover was going to change the course of his life, in ways he couldn't foresee. His plan to tell her the truth about himself, which had seemed so brilliant in that unreal hour before dawn, looked fraught with peril in the clear daylight. But there was no help for it, and no alternatives. Before anything else could happen, that exceedingly unpleasant duty would have to be gotten out of the way. He still couldn't contemplate the possibility of failure. Sophie was gentle and kind and sweet; he would rely on those qualities, as well as her tolerance and fair-mindedness, and in the end she would forgive him. He just wished it was over with. As much as he dreaded it, he could hardly wait to tell her everything, so they could begin again on level ground, without secrets.

But mostly he just wanted to see her again. Five more hours— eternity. Love was an extraordinary feeling, and in his case it seemed to be comprised of equal parts euphoria and anxiety.

He heard a tap at his door. Not Jack—he never knocked first. Barefoot, buttoning his shirt, Connor came off the bed and crossed to the door.

The girl in the dim passageway looked familiar, but he didn't recognize her until she took off her wide straw bonnet. Small and pixyish, her rather wild black hair almost hid her piquant features. "Mr. Pendarvis?" she said in a soft voice. "I'm Sidony Timms. I brought you yer mail—'twas out in the box."

Surprised, Connor took the envelope she handed him, noting absently that it had no sender's address. Something from the Rhads, then. "Thank you."

She blushed, and looked down at the hat brim she was mangling with her thin fingers. A moment passed.

"Would you like to come in?"

She had a dazzling smile. She flashed it gratefully and moved a few feet into the room. There was only one chair. He gestured to it, but she shook her head and mumbled, "No, thank you." More hat mangling. Finally she looked him in the eye. "I'm sorry for bothering you, but I was wondering if I could ask you something. It's about Connor."

He passed a hand over his face. Wheels within wheels; for the first time it dawned on him that unmasking himself would mean unmasking his brother as well. "What is it?"

"Oh, sir, I'm that worried about 'im," she said in a rush. "I know he's sick, but he won't ever talk about it; and the times I ask him straight out, he turns snappy and gets mad at me. But I have to know. I care for him, Mr. Pendarvis," she said simply. "Will you please tell me if he's very, very sick?"

Her small, clenched hands and worried eyes moved him, and brought him to another unwelcome realization: his lie to Sophie wasn't the only potentially hurtful fraud perpetrated by the Pendarvis boys on innocent Wyckerley women. As gently as he could, he told the girl the truth. "You know that he was a miner until a year ago." She nodded. "He contracted a consumption of the lungs, and since then he's been unable to work. He's seen two doctors, and they both said they don't know what his prognosis is. Whether he'll recover or not," he explained when she looked blank.

"But is it serious?" She swallowed hard, but she had to whisper to say, "Might he die?"

"It is serious. I pray he won't die."

She bowed her head. He almost took her hand, for comfort, and to tell her that they were feeling the same pain. But she looked up then and asked haltingly, "Does he ever speak to you about me?"

He cleared his throat, uncomfortable. "He . . . well, he . . ."

"I'm sorry," she blurted, red-faced, turning quickly and heading for the door.

"Wait. Miss Timms—"

"Thank you for speaking to me!"

"*Wait.*"

But she wouldn't wait, and she was quick as a rabbit; rather than run after her and embarrass her even more, he let her go.

Alone again, his thoughts were black and unpleasant, and exactly twice as guilt-ridden as they had been before. He tore open the heavy brown envelope from the Rhadamanthus Society for a diversion, and carried the contents to his bed. The director's short letter on top confused him; he had to read it twice before the message sank in. "Time ran out for our bill, as you know, but we decided to circulate the report now in order to begin shoring up support for the next session. Again, we are grateful to you for your conscientious labor and dedication, and look forward to working more closely with you in the near future."

Under the letter was a thick pamphlet, cheaply bound in cloth-covered paperboard, the *RS* logotype centered in gilt letters, and below it, "Journal of the Rhadamanthus Society, Quartus II, A.D. MDCCCLVII." Dread congealing in his stomach, Connor opened the pamphlet. There was his report.

It was the centerpiece of this quarter's journal. He had titled it, "An Investigation of Mining Hazards in Cornwall and Devonshire," but the society had renamed it, "Englishmen in Danger: A Factual Account of Deplorable Conditions in Copper Mines by an Eyewitness." They'd ranked the three mines he'd worked in and written about, and Sophie's came out the second worst, between Wheal Looe and Tregurtha. It was all there, a cold-blooded indictment of the heat and the ladders, the bad air, the medical inadequacies. There was even an implication of financial collusion between Sophie and her uncle, because his store was the only source of mining supplies within ten miles of Guelder. Connor hadn't written that—and some of the words in the rest of the piece weren't his either. They'd taken the basic facts and embellished and dramatized them, adding a tone of high moral outrage. They even criticized a "High Church vicar," without naming him, for allowing "these deplorable circumstances to take place" in his village without taking steps against them. Connor had mentioned the social makeup of St. Giles' parish, its population and so forth, including the fact that it had two churches, Anglican and Methodist. The journal's rewriters, all radical Wesleyans, had seized on that, but hadn't bothered to include the fact that the Methodist preacher had never "taken steps" against abuses either. Nor did they mention that two years ago, Christy Morrell had gone down in the mine alone and saved Tranter Fox's life.

As horrified as he was, Connor had to admit that the piece

was effective. Devastatingly so. It would do exactly what the society intended—arouse the average workingman's ire, at the same time it moved recalcitrant Commons members to act on the reform bill Shavers would offer in the next term.

By rights, Connor should feel glad, victorious. He'd struck a blow against the forces of greed and negligence, those faceless owners and adventurers who might finally, because of his work, be held accountable for a thousand men's deaths, including his own father and two of his brothers. What he felt was cold fear.

"Everything's all right, isn't it, Sophie?"

"Yes, everything's fine. Why do you ask?"

Anne Morrell accepted the small glass of Madeira Sophie handed her, shook her head at the plate of biscuits she offered next. "I don't know. Nothing, no reason."

But Sophie wasn't fooled. Her shrewd friend had spoken softly, and she'd waited until they were out of earshot of the others before asking her gentle question. She'd noticed, of course, that Sophie's eyes were puffy and her manner, although she was trying hard to concentrate on the things her guests said to her, was distracted. But as close as they were and as much as she trusted Anne, she was incapable of confiding in her now, and not only because the circumstances prohibited it. She was in the center of the most difficult dilemma of her life, and until she found a solution, it would remain literally unspeakable.

"I wonder what's keeping Honoria." Lily Hesselius spoke up from behind Sophie's shoulder, startling her. "Not the rain, that's certain. We could have had our tea outdoors after all, Miss Deene." She had a girlish giggle that wasn't always appropriate. A relative newcomer to Wyckerley, Lily was the doctor's much younger wife, and some wagging tongues disapproved of her flighty manners, and especially her habit of flirting with her husband's male acquaintances.

"It still might rain," Anne countered. "When the clouds blow up from the south, anything can happen."

Sophie smiled to herself at the thought that Anne was defending her, and at her tone of expert Devon weather forecaster—Anne was even newer to the village than Lily.

"Oh, no, you don't." All three ladies turned to see Reverend Morrell bearing down on them from the far side of the room. "This isn't going to turn into one of those parties where the ladies steal off to whisper secrets and leave the men staring at each other. I've been sent to tell you that you must come back and save us."

The women tittered, aware that he was joking, but were flattered in spite of themselves. That was Christy for you, thought Sophie. He didn't even have to try to make people feel good; he accomplished it just by his presence. Her glance stole to Anne's face, and she wasn't disappointed: that look of wry tenderness softened her lovely green eyes, the way it always did when her husband came anywhere near her. Sophie wasn't given to envy, an unsatisfying failing if ever there was one; but if anyone could make her feel its fruitless pangs, it was the Morrells. Their happiness together was prodigious and unqualified; they were the talk of the town.

They all drifted back to the others—Captain and Mrs. Carnock, Dr. Hesselius, Margaret Mareton and her parents. Lily wondered again what was keeping Honoria and her father, and the captain said there was no bench business today that he knew of—he and Uncle Eustace were local magistrates, along with Sebastian Verlaine. Mrs. Carnock—Jessica—was looking positively fashionable in a teal green carriage dress, with a silk mantel thrown back dashingly over her shoulders. They'd recently returned from a holiday in Southampton, Sophie recalled; shopping for clothes for Jessie must have been on the agenda. As usual, she hung on her husband's every word, even though at the moment the captain was treating Dr. Hesselius to an account of his military experiences in the Aliwal campaign of '46. The doctor, a mild-mannered, bald-headed man whose gentle brown eyes behind thick spectacles camouflaged a sharp and lively intelligence, sent his wife a smile along with a subtle message—softly stroking the seat beside him on the sofa—that he wanted her to join him, or possibly to save him. Lily didn't see it, or she chose not to; in any case, she ignored him, and began telling Anne about the wonderful new console table she'd just ordered from a cabinetmaker in Bath.

Sophie nodded and smiled, spoke when spoken to, refilled teacups, and helped Maris pass plates. The hands of the clock on the mantelshelf seemed to have stopped; twice she surreptitiously checked its time against that of the watch pinned to the bosom of her dress. She caught herself staring blindly at her guests, the friends and neighbors she'd known most of her life, lost in imagining their separate reactions if they knew the truth about her and Jack—what they'd done, what they might do next. All of them would be shocked, many would be scandalized; some would feel obliged to distance themselves from her. Could she bear it? Yes, if she had to. But she prayed it wouldn't come to that.

She heard the sound of carriage wheels, and saw Thomas through the west window, walking slowly around to the front of the house. Uncle Eustace and Honoria had finally arrived. She put on a pleased smile, but her thoughts were much less gracious: because of their tardiness, her tea party was bound to go on for at least an hour longer.

The thud of footsteps in the entrance hall was loud, fast. Before Sophie could rise from her perch on the arm of Anne's chair, her uncle appeared in the arched parlor doorway. Conversation halted, and everyone stared. Anger radiated from him in waves; his sharp, handsome face was mottled with it. He had his cane in one hand, a rolled-up paper in the other, swatting his thigh with it with loud, violent smacks. *He knows,* Sophie thought reflexively. *He knows about Jack.*

He was staring at everyone as if he didn't know who they were, as if he'd forgotten about her party. "Uncle?" she ventured, taking a few steps toward him.

He fixed his furious gaze on her, and she stopped in her tracks. "I hope you're satisfied."

Behind him, Honoria bustled into the room. "Did you tell her?" Her dark eyes glittered with excitement. Eustace ignored her.

"What on earth is the matter?" Sophie tried. "Is something wrong at the mine?"

"You could say that."

Her panic shifted. "Is someone hurt? Has there been—"

"Read this!" he thundered, thrusting the scrolled paper at her.

She looked down at a small bound pamphlet with gilt lettering on the cover. Her uncle's grip had broken the cheap spine and torn the first page. She read the word *Rhadamanthus* on the cover, and immediately her original foreboding returned. With stiff fingers she opened to the contents and read the title of the first article, "Englishmen in Danger: A Factual—"

"Pendarvis wrote it!" he roared. "Read it!"

"Jack?" she said, numb. "Jack wrote this?"

"*Jack?*" He advanced on her. "You call him *Jack?*"

Christy Morrell stepped to her side, looking big and alert. She felt grateful; she'd never known her uncle to be physically violent, but he looked capable of it now. "You're in it, too, Reverend. He doesn't name you, he only slanders you! Read it, damn you, Sophie. The good part begins on page ten—that's when he gets to your mine."

She made an effort to control her voice. "What makes you think Mr. Pendarvis wrote this?"

"Because he all but says so. Who did you hire on the twelfth of June? *Read it.*"

But she had already started to. *I began work as a tut laborer at Guelder mine in Wyckerley, St. Giles' parish, the county of Devonshire, on 12 June 1857. The mine owner, Miss S. Deene, offered a wage of £5 per fathom, and a £2 subsist, which I repaid on 30 June from my second week's earnings.* She kept turning the pages, hardly able to see the words. Her eyes swam in and out of focus, picking out dreadful phrases—*heat so enervating, a man faints nearly every day—miner's consumption a direct consequence of the thick, unbreathable air—complete disregard for even the minimal comfort of grass workers, such as a hot drink at dinnertime in the winter.* Her uncle's strident voice became a blur. She found herself in a chair with no recollection of sitting down, and Anne Morrell bending over her with a worried expression. "It's a mistake," she heard herself say, "he couldn't have done this. It must be someone else. How did you get this paper?"

"Clive Knowlton gave it to me," Eustace snapped. Knowlton was the district MP. "Every member of the Commons got one, so they'll know how to vote when this *Rhadamanthus Society*"—his lips curled with revulsion—"puts its socialist mouthpiece up to bringing in a bill on mine reform next term. They've sent it to the newspapers, too. By Monday everyone in the county can read it!"

She felt sick. Words swam in her vision—"unsafe," "intolerable," "inhumane." She put her head in her hand.

"What do you know of him?" Eustace demanded, standing over her. She couldn't think. "You hired him. Who is he? Didn't you know he was an impostor?"

"He's not. He's who he says he is."

"Did you try to find out? Did you ask for any proof that he was—"

"Yes! I wrote to Carn Barra, and they knew him. He'd been ill, hadn't worked in half a year. Everything he told me was true." She stood up. "It's a mistake, it must be someone else. I *know* him," she said boldly. "He would not do this to me. To us." Behind her, Honoria made a shocked sound. Sophie ignored her and said with shaky confidence, "If there's been a—a spy at Guelder, it was not Jack Pendarvis."

"No, it wasn't Jack Pendarvis."

There was a collective gasp as everyone in the room turned toward the man standing stiff and straight in the threshold, the dim hallway at his back. Sophie almost ran to him. She put her hand on her heart, going weak-kneed with relief. She didn't speak, but she sent Jack a message with her eyes: *I knew it.*

"But I wrote that report," he said in a rough voice, looking only at her. "I am Connor Pendarvis. I used my brother's name to gain employment at Guelder mine."

Time stopped for Sophie. She couldn't make sense of his words at first, kept trying to make them mean something else. She whispered, "No, Jack," shaking her head over and over. "Don't say that. Oh, no, Jack."

Connor couldn't see anything but her. He watched her face go from white to bright pink as the truth sank in. Her eyes had been frightened before; now they were glassy and blank. She had a weird, stiff smile, and she was shaking her head in spasmodic jerks, staring hard at him, not blinking, not crying. He couldn't go to her, but he couldn't stand still and watch her disintegrate before his eyes. "Sophie, I'm sorry."

He didn't see the cane, only heard it, slashing through the air an instant before it sliced across his cheek. White, blinding pain; a woman's scream. Another blow across his right forearm staggered him. He looked up to see Christy Morrell wresting the stick out of Vanstone's fist with a deft, muscular movement.

Connor drew back his own murderous fist and someone else, a man he didn't know, stepped between him and Vanstone, spoiling his aim. He cursed, feeling the hot blood slide down his face, his neck, inside his collar. Morrell pressed him back with his hands on his chest, pushing harder when he resisted. "Get out," Vanstone was shouting, while the unknown man hung onto his arm. "Get out."

Sophie hadn't moved. Her face looked frozen, her eyes wide and shocked. Slowly, so slowly, she turned her back on him. She was shaking. Connor saw her rigid shoulders, the brittle-looking nape of her neck, and he knew he was finished.

"She's not at home."

Sophie's maid blocked the doorway, tall as a tree, mad as a

bull terrier. Maris, her name was. Connor used to like her, liked exchanging quick pleasantries with her in the garden when she brought him a glass of tea or a plate of sandwiches. She had a long, plain face and kind eyes, a lanky, lean body, and oddly graceful hands at the end of long, sharp-jointed arms. Loyalty was an admirable quality, in the abstract; in Maris, to Connor, it had become insufferable.

"She's home," he contradicted her. "I can see the light in her window." And in his mind, he could see every detail of her room.

The maid was unmoved. "She's not at home."

"Did you give her my letter?"

"I did."

"Did she read it?" He flushed, angry and embarrassed because of what he'd been reduced to—questioning the housemaid to gain intelligence about her employer.

"As to that, I'm sure I couldn't say." She had both hands on the edge of the door, preparing to shut it in his face—again. This was the third time he'd come. He gritted his teeth, controlling his temper, aware of how often it had got him into trouble.

"Tell her I'm not leaving." He stuck his foot in the door—to hell with his temper. "Tell her I'm not going anywhere until she comes down and speaks to me. Have you got that?" He leaned in, baring his teeth. "Tell her I'm here, and I'll bloody well stay here till hell freezes over."

Maris blanched but didn't budge. He could see her indecision: she couldn't close the door because his shoe was blocking it, but if she left her post and went away to deliver his message, he might force his way into the house. Bloody well right, that was exactly what he would do. "Listen here," she blustered. "You can't come in, I'm telling you, because she don't care to see you." He didn't move. "I'm fetching Thomas," she tried next. "He might not look it, but he's terrible strong, so you'd best have a care and get along."

"It's all right, Maris."

The maid whirled at the sound of her mistress's voice, and

Connor took advantage of the opportunity to push the door all the way open. Sophie stood on the last step of the staircase, holding on to the newel post with one hand. His anger collapsed when he took in her paleness. She was fully dressed, and her hair was perfect, but her red-rimmed eyes gave her away. His heart twisted in his chest.

Maris was gnawing her lip, indecisive. "You sure, Miss Sophie? I can run for Thomas. Between us we—"

"No, it's all right. I'll speak to Mr. Pendarvis in the drawing room."

A telling word choice; two nights ago it had been the "parlor." Connor feared he was going to fare much worse with Sophie in the "drawing room."

He watched her glide across the hall without looking at him, and when he followed her into the room, she backed away from him in the archway to make sure they didn't touch. She closed the sliding doors and turned around, keeping her hands behind her back. She looked bruised and untouchable.

He'd been thinking of what to say to her for the last twenty-four hours. Now he couldn't remember anything, not a single one of his excuses. No loss there; they'd all sounded stupid and self-serving. The awful suspicion that what he had done was truly indefensible had kept him in a state of dread, unable to think straight.

"Sophie, I'm sorry."

That got him nowhere. She continued to stare, glittery-eyed, waiting for his next keen-witted utterance. Nerves had him prowling the room, picking up objects and setting them down. She never moved, and her complete stillness was a silent, lacerating reproach. He made himself stand still in front of her, empty-handed, and say, "I lied to you. I did it in cold blood, and nothing excuses it. Some of the things in the journal I wrote, some I didn't. The society printed a preliminary report. They had no right to do that, and I've disassociated myself from them."

He streaked his hands through his hair, goaded by her unresponsiveness. "I was going to tell you all of this last night. I've hurt you, and I swear I never intended to. I thought I could make it right between us, but—I ran out of time."

He took a step toward her. She literally shrank from him: her eyes widened and she squeezed back against the doors, rattling them. He halted in shock. "For God's sake, Sophie. Are you going to say anything?"

"Have you finished?"

He stared at her. "Yes."

"Then you can go."

Her icy calm was a facade, but it was working, freezing him to death. "Stop it." His voice came out harsh. "Stop doing this."

"I want you to leave."

"Not until you talk to me. Say something to me, Sophie, tell me what you're thinking."

"Get out of my house." She moved then; he thought she was leaving. He reached for her arm, and she whipped away from him in a violent white blur of hands and elbows. "Don't touch me," she warned in a dead, lethal whisper. "It makes me feel sick."

Her face wasn't her face—he couldn't bear to look at it. He stared at the gold locket around her throat, the links of the chain disappearing into the blond hair at her neck. "Don't say that. Everything—Sophie, nothing else was a lie, only—"

"All of it."

"No."

"You were my lover. I took you to my bed, and you let me call you 'Jack.'"

There it was. "I—"

"*In bed*. You let me say it to you. You're a coward and a liar. I'll hate you for that as long as I live."

She meant it, and everything she said was true. He hadn't told her the truth about himself because he'd been afraid he would lose her. He had been a coward. His shame was so bitter and complete, it made him belligerent. "What difference does a name make? I meant everything I said to you. You said things to me, too. If they were true, you wouldn't recoil from me like this. It's your pride that's been broken, not your heart."

"You're right," she flared, "but you're still a liar. All you cared about was seducing me."

He lifted his arm toward her, then let it fall. "You can't believe that."

She didn't hear. "Your summer conquest. Who else did you entice? Too bad the mine owners at Tregurtha and Looe aren't women, you could have had them, too."

"You're deluding yourself," he snapped. "Think back, Sophie. Who asked me to come here in the dead of night? 'Come when the moon rises,' you said. I never seduced you and you know it."

"*Bastard.* I'm ashamed of myself for having anything to do with you. Do you know—I hate myself even more than I hate you, because you taught me how low I could sink. I'll spend the rest of my life repenting what I did with you—like a sinner with a hair shirt. You're my penance. I committed a sin with you, a low, grievous error, and I'm too mortified to confess it."

There was a haze in front of his eyes; he could barely see her through it. "I was right about you the first time. You're shallow, and vain, and self-involved, and bourgeoise. The report in the journal was too kind—you're the worst kind of capitalist because you soothe your social conscience with nonsense—leading the church choir, teaching your condescending 'literature' to a handful of sleepy, Sophie-worshiping burghers one night a week, believing you're Lady Bountiful, while down in the mine you didn't do one damn thing to acquire, men are losing their youth and their vigor a drop every day, becoming weak, demoralized, and diseased. And you could stop it if you tried, if you cared more about human beings than being the belle of this backward, provincial, small-minded town you're so goddamned proud of—"

She slapped him. He flinched, because the blow caught the livid scar her uncle's cane had left on his cheek. He didn't think she could go any whiter, but she did. "Get out," she whispered, drawing away in revulsion, from him, from what she'd just done to him.

He couldn't wait to get out. And he couldn't speak, although he knew they would never meet again. Her face was too hurtful to look at any longer. He pulled the doors open and left her.

# XIII

An accident at the mine brought Sophie back to life, or a semblance of it. Afterward she wondered how much longer she'd have stayed at home under the pretense that she had reinjured her ankle, seeing no one, too lethargic to put on her clothes, keeping to the house because the garden brought back unendurable memories. But Moony Donne came close to losing his head in an explosion, and even though he would recover, and even though the resulting cave-in hadn't caused any lasting damage, the incident brought home to Sophie the truth that she couldn't continue in seclusion forever.

Besides, the shock that had numbed and cushioned her emotions at first was beginning to wear off. Every day it grew harder to avoid considering the possibility that everything she had ever believed about herself, every quality she'd ever convinced herself was admirable, was in fact a sham. Rather than look that monster in the eye, she would gladly stop being a recluse and return to Guelder.

But nothing was the same. Once before when happiness had been wrenched away and her life was in turmoil, the mine had saved her. This time it did not. Days passed before she could bring herself to acknowledge why, and the reason made her more despondent. Since childhood, she had seen Guelder through her father's eyes, but now she was seeing it through the eyes of Connor Pendarvis.

It changed everything. And she was as loath and unwilling as a martyr forced on the rack to repudiate her faith, but she wasn't blind and she couldn't deny what her opened eyes saw. Or what her ears heard: she questioned her men—not the managers, the miners themselves—about their working conditions, and when they gave her cheerful, evasive answers, she delved deeper, would not settle for politeness or uneasy justifications. Naturally no one wished to impress her as a complainer; she could understand that. At times, though, she had the unnerving sense that some of the men were trying to protect her, like gallant but misguided swains, because they were concerned that the truth would upset her. Increasingly it embarrassed her that she hadn't gone down in her own mine in six years, and then only as the merest tourist.

So she went. Jenks, hardly able to keep his disapproval to himself, acted as her guide. He took her to the twenty level, walked her around two galleries, and started back up. When she explained that she wanted to go down to the one-sixty and see everything, he couldn't contain himself. "You'll get dirty," he protested, holding his candle aloft, making a gesture at her clothes. She replied that she had a fair idea that mines were dirty places, and that she'd left her ball gown at home this morning. "You'll tire out," he tried next; "you'll never have the wind to climb up again. It'll take hours to see everything—whatever would you want to do it for anyway?" His attitude made her angry, not because it was impertinent, but because it came too close to her own way of thinking not very long ago. It struck her as willfully ignorant now, and arrogant as well. But she only said, "I'd like to go down, Mr. Jenks," and the burly mine captain snorted, shrugged, and took her.

It wasn't a revelation, exactly. She saw nothing she didn't already know about, came upon no shocking surprise. But there was a difference between looking at a map of the slope of a mineral lode or a diagram of a scaffolding system, or listening to a miner describe the clay-slate he'd dug out over a six-day marathon to unearth a seam of pure copper—there was a difference between that and experiencing the black, dripping, smoking, booming guts of the mine with her own five senses. In that way, it *was* a revelation, and she had a long time to ponder it as she struggled back up the straight, muddy, killing ladders, pausing at every sollar to rest while Jenks gazed off into space a respectable ten steps below and tried not to let *I told you so* show in his dark, glaring features.

Two long days and three sleepless nights later, she made up her mind. Jenks read about it in a memorandum she drafted to him, Andrewson, and Dickon Penney. Using the capital currently earning interest for funding exploratory excavations, management—Sophie—intended to contract for the construction of man-machines to replace the longest ladders, as well as an improved ventilation system at the deepest levels. Effective November and lasting until March, hot soup at midday would be available aboveground for anyone who cared to come up for it, at a cost of three pennies a bowl. A heated shed would be built for the use of grass workers in wintertime, and washing facilities for the miners would be expanded and improved. In addition, she was authorizing a committee of six men, three of them ordinary miners, to study safety concerns, including contingencies for emergencies, and draft a report in three weeks with recommendations for changes.

The news traveled fast. Before the cores changed in the afternoon, she saw, through her dusty office window, Uncle Eustace ride into the mine yard on his big bay mare. Sophie had a fair idea that he wouldn't approve of the changes she was proposing, but she was unprepared for the violence of his opposition.

"You've lost your mind," he declared flatly, striding around her tiny office like a tiger, so wrought up he forgot to take off his hat. "If you were trying to ruin yourself, you couldn't have chosen a faster way. Capital cannot be used like this—capital must be turned back, reinvested in the enterprise that created it in the first place, at least until the business is on an unshakable footing. I never thought I would have to tell you this. Guelder—"

"You don't have to tell—"

"Guelder has only begun producing well in the last two years. Anything could happen. If your working veins dried up tomorrow, what would you use for money to dig elsewhere? What good would your 'man-machines' be if they led nowhere? You're operating legally right now, there's no law in the world requiring these so-called improvements."

She stayed in the chair behind her desk, out of harm's way, and answered him as calmly as she could. "I'm sorry, but I don't agree with you. I think it's the perfect time for improvements, while copper prices are stable and the mine is producing well. If it slows down in the future, at least its substructure of—of safety and convenience will be in place, and I'll be able to concentrate solely on new sources of ore."

"Do you have any idea how much these machines will cost?"

"It's substantial."

"It's hundreds of pounds—a thousand pounds!"

"It's been done at the Fowey Consols, and the investment was returned in miner productivity within a year. *With* a profit."

"The Fowey Consols is ten times the size of Guelder!"

"I'm aware of that. I can't do it all at once; the machines will have to be phased in gradually. Even so, there will still be money for venturing—not as much, I admit, but barring catastrophes or a sudden fall in the price of—"

"You cannot bar catastrophes," he thundered, banging the tip of his cane on the floor like a war club. "Use your head, Sophie. What does Penney have to say about all this?"

"He's—considering it. He's taking it under advisement." So far Dickon Penney, her mine agent, had been too stunned to react.

"Hah! He's delighted, I'm sure, to learn that you've turned your mine over to the miners."

"That's a bit of an—"

"What's next? A union? Sharing of the profits with your bal girls?"

"You know that's—"

"This isn't only your own throat you're cutting. I could stand by and watch you bleed to death if it were—but what you're proposing affects every mine owner in the district."

"Good," she said grimly. "It's long past time for most of these measures. They're not only common sense, they're common decency."

"You're deluded."

"How long has it been since you went down in your own mine?" she dared to ask.

He smacked his palm on top of the desk and leaned in toward her, his hard, handsome face red with emotion. "I heard about that. Everyone in the county has heard about your little tour by now. You speak to me of *decency.*"

"What are you saying, Uncle? What did I do that—"

"I'm saying I'm ashamed of you."

She gripped her hands together in her lap, desperate to hold on to her composure. "I'm sorry. I think you're angry because I didn't consult with you before I made these decisions. I'll tell you the truth—I didn't ask for your advice because I knew what it would be. I'm sorry if that offends you, but Guelder is mine, and I'm doing what I believe is right for it. And for me, and the people who work for me."

His cold, careful anger was infinitely worse than his hot rage. "I know who's responsible for this," he said quietly, venomously. "Don't mistake me for a stupid man, Sophie."

She stood up. "I don't want to have this conversation any longer."

"You were seduced by that Judas." Her heart stopped until he added, "He's polluted your mind with his socialist rubbish. I can understand how it happened—you're a woman, your sensibilities are soft, not focused; you can't see reality in the way a man can."

"That is the most—"

"I was against Tolliver leaving the mine to you, as I'm sure you know, and nothing has happened to change my mind since then. In fact, quite the reverse."

"Are we to be enemies, then?"

"Enemies?" He frowned, disconcerted. "No, of course not. I think you've embarked on a path of monumental folly, Sophie, one that may have disastrous repercussions throughout the entire district. But you are still my niece," he finished, as if that said everything.

She could think of nothing else to say. They parted with equal stiffness, and she sat in her chair for a long time afterward, reliving the unpleasant exchange. But gradually her mind began to clear. The worst, she could almost hope, was over. The decision was made; she'd taken the first irrevocable steps toward doing a thing she knew in her heart was right. It didn't matter quite as much anymore that it was Jack—Connor, rather—who had put the idea in her head. She felt better than she had in many days. Perhaps she could bear to think about him now. If so, that would be the first step in the process of forgetting him.

That night, Maris came into the study, where Sophie was poring over figures in her new draft budget, trying to change the totals by glaring at them. "Somebody here to see you. I put 'er in the day parlor."

"Who, Maris?"

"It's that Timms girl."

"Who?"

"Sidony Timms, the dairymaid over to the Hall."

Feeling a queer sort of dread, Sophie went to greet her visitor.

The interview didn't last long. Sidony, pretty and sweet, shy as a turtle, had come to ask a question. "I was wondering, ma'am, if by any chance you might know where Mr. Jack Pendarvis is living now."

Sophie could barely speak civilly to her. "No, I don't."

"Oh." She hung her head. "I was hoping you might, being as his brother worked for you."

"No."

"Con—Jack, I mean," she corrected with a blush, "said as he'd write to tell me where he was going once he got there. But he hasn't yet, and I . . . I . . ." Her dark eyes filled with tears.

Sophie knew sympathy and mortification in equal measures. Awkwardly patting Sidony's shoulder, she faced the fact that she and this girl, this dairymaid, were in exactly the same situation. If Connor Pendarvis had wanted to humiliate her, he had succeeded with a vengeance.

"I don't know where they've gone, Sidony," she said gently. "If—if I should hear from Mr. Pendarvis," she added with a twisted smile at the unlikelihood of that, "I'll be sure to let you know."

"Thank you, ma'am. I wouldn't've come here and bothered you and all, except I thought you might know. Con"—she made a face—"*Jack* made a promise that he'd write to me. And since he's so sick, I was thinking he might've got worse, might even . . ." She covered her face with her hands and wept.

Sophie didn't know what to do. "I'm so sorry," she said helplessly. "I thought—forgive me, but I had assumed that you and William Holyoake had an under—that you . . ." She subsided, embarrassed.

Sidony lifted her face, wet from fresh tears. "I know. I know, and that's what makes it all worse. William's my best friend, and until I met Jack I thought we'd get married. Oh, I'm so mixed up," she whispered, wiping her cheeks, miserable. "I've hurt William so much, and now Jack's gone and won't even say where. Before he left he told me he wasn't good enough for me and I should forget him. But I can't, even though I wish I could, because that would solve everything." She fumbled a handkerchief out of her pocket and blew her nose. She was petite and lovely, with long black hair that gleamed blue in the lamplight. Sophie remembered her at the Midsummer Day fair, the way she'd blushed and laughed at the things Connor's gaunt-faced brother had whispered in her ear. Had she given Jack everything? Something told Sophie that she had. The Pendarvis men went about getting what they wanted from women in different ways, but both ways were devastatingly effective.

Sidony went away after Sophie told her, as disingenuously as the first time, that she would pass along any information she might receive about Jack's whereabouts. The rest of the night, she had plenty of time to reflect that the older Pendarvis, whatever his other shortcomings, at least had had the decency to tell the woman he was exploiting that she was too good for him. Such a refinement had never occurred to his lying, false-hearted brother.

"I've decided to stand for Clive Knowlton's seat at the by-election," Robert Croddy told Sophie one evening a week later. They were standing in her foyer, saying goodnight to one another; he'd brought her home in his carriage after a glum and uncomfortable dinner at Wyck House, her uncle's home in Wyckerley.

The news amazed her. "Clive Knowlton is resigning? But why? Anyway, he's a liberal," she said naively. "Aren't you a conservative, Robert?"

He smiled at her indulgently. "I'm a Whig, and that's what counts. Knowlton's leaving to take Holy Orders, and he has the power to name his successor. If I can gain his patronage, there won't be any need for an election."

"I see," she said thoughtfully. "And do you think he will favor you?" Knowlton, one of two Members for the Tavistock borough, was a wealthy, influential, deeply respected gentleman, who had been returned to the House of Commons in every election since before Sophie was born. That he would choose Robert Croddy to succeed him seemed . . . unlikely. Not that there was anything wrong with Robert. But still.

He moved closer, lowered his voice. "What I've told you is in confidence, Sophie. Only a few people know that Knowlton means to resign. As of now, the field is empty, and I intend to take advantage of that."

"Ah. Well, I wish you luck, of course."

"Your uncle is backing me."

"Is he?" That made sense. Uncle Eustace voted the Whig party because in this district it was politically expedient to do so, but he was a Tory in his heart of hearts, or so Sophie had always assumed. "Then I expect you'll have a very good chance, indeed."

"Yes, I think so."

"Well," she said when he didn't speak for a moment but made no move to leave. "Thank you for bringing me home. Will I be seeing you . . ." She trailed off. He'd put his hand on her shoulder. He'd never touched her before. With a start, she realized he was about to kiss her. "Robert—" His lips found hers after a fumbling second; she stood still, not pulling away. It was a dry, firm, businesslike kiss, not altogether unpleasant. When it was over, she didn't feel anything. Nothing at all.

Robert felt something. "Marry me, Sophie."

"*Oh,*" she said, shocked into near speechlessness. "*Oh.*"

"You won't regret it. My father's business will come to me in the course of things, and then I mean to become a man of *real* substance. Knowlton's seat only insures it. I'll sell the brewery and make respectable investments, a gentleman's investments. I'm on the rise, Sophie. Marry me and I'll make you proud of me."

She knew he was in earnest because he'd slipped and called his father's business "the brewery"; always before it was "the firm," or sometimes "the family concern."

"Robert," she stuttered, "I—I don't know what to say."

"Say yes."

"No—no. This is—" So sudden, she almost said. But there was no point in giving him false hope or pretending time might change her mind. She pulled herself together. "I'm extremely flattered by your proposal, and touched that you would think of me in that way. But . . ."

"Don't say 'but,' Sophie. Marry me. I do love you."

Could it possibly be true? In her distress she studied him, his powerful body and tense posture, his bland, familiar face creased with an emotion that *seemed* to be no stronger than concern. No, no, it couldn't be true. What a relief; refusing him wouldn't break his heart, then.

"You do me a great honor," she said gently, laying her hand on the sleeve of his coat. "Please understand, it's not you—I'm so fond of you, Robert. I have the highest regard for you, of course, and our friendship means a great deal to me." She was overstating the case, but it seemed a time for exaggeration. "I don't think I will ever marry, though. I'm already set in my ways, and I should make a most unsatisfactory wife. Especially for you."

"Why? Why especially for me?"

Because he would expect too much of her—he would want her life to be subordinate to his. Alternatives would never occur to him. How she knew this she wasn't sure, but she knew it. "Because you deserve better. I feel it strongly, that you would regret it if we married. I haven't a doubt that you would try your best to make me happy, Robert, but I'm just as sure that I would make you miserable. Please let me say no without spoiling our friendship."

His ginger eyes narrowed on her, and she thought he was angry. But he was only pondering. "All right," he said almost cheerfully, certainly without any evidence of heartache. "We'll leave it for now, if that's what you want."

"No, what I—"

"But I'll ask you again, and then again if that's what it takes. You're what I want, Sophie. And you're wrong about us. I'm exactly what you need. But if you can't see it now, that's all right. I can wait."

She smiled and shook her head, but said no more, on the grounds that it would be unkind to contradict him. They bade each other good night with more affection than she would have thought possible, considering the circumstances, and she went up to her room to think it all over.

She could have said yes. Would it have been so terrible? Perhaps he was right, perhaps they were made for each other. What difference did it make that they didn't love each other? Love only got in the way. A messy, irrelevant bother. A crimp.

She had never been cynical about love before. It was another part of Connor's legacy, something else to despise him for. The fact that she could think about him now, think of him at all, must mean she was healing. Numbness had helped see her through the last weeks, that and the long, hard hours at Guelder. Robert's proposal—somehow it had opened the locked door between her and memories of Connor. Tonight she believed she could bear them.

The trick was to look back on her time with him as just another life experience and try to learn something from it. Turn it from a painful, degrading episode into something positive. She had lived through it. She had kept her reputation intact—miraculously; when she remembered the risks she'd taken, she thought she must have been mad. She regarded it now as a fever, a time of insanity that had blinded her to the dangers of exposure—and all for a man who wasn't worthy of her anyway.

She, of course, had plenty of flaws, and under Connor's tutelage she had become intimately familiar with a number of new ones. But he was worse. He'd lied to her from the first day they'd met. In fairness, she couldn't claim that he'd seduced her, but he had certainly betrayed her. Even allowing for his impersonation, even granting him the *possibility* that that masquerade was morally defensible—a questionable grant, she would go to her grave thinking—he had still committed an egregious sin when he'd deliberately begun a personal relationship with her. She may have committed one, too, when she'd allowed it, but at least her transgression had come out of true affection and healthy desire. She had sacrificed everything, including her virtue and her respectability, because she'd thought she loved him. He had no such excuse. There was nothing in his heart except lust and deceit, and she could never forgive him. She would try not to think of him again, except as an object lesson: don't trust men, and don't give yourself to them in any setting other than marriage. If she'd had a mother or a father, perhaps she would have known that already. She was twenty-three years old; she *ought* to have known it. She knew it now.

She lay in bed for a long time, dry-eyed but full of sorrow, watching shadows move across the ceiling. Maybe Robert's proposal could be a turning point for her. It was time to try to be happy again. But how? She was no longer lighthearted, no longer a girl. Connor Pendarvis had stolen her youth and made her a wary and suspicious woman. A sad woman, although she constantly beat back the sadness as well as she could. She felt old and tired, dried up inside, and she had to be on guard against flashes of memory that blotted out the here and now and flung her into the past. She would see him in the rose garden with Dash on his lap, remember how his hands had looked stroking the cat's inky fur. Or how his sideways smile lit up his face when she said something funny. Once he'd told her a silly joke about a Cornishman, a Welshman, and a Scotsman, and they had both laughed until the tears came. Those were the treacherous memories; they broke her heart and made her cry.

How could she get out from under this weight of sorrow and regret? When would the pain fade and give her her life back? Hating him helped; she clung to her conviction that he was a monster like a lifeline, hostile to the smallest impulse to see anything mitigating in what he'd done. That was the way. Absolute truth didn't matter; survival mattered. For now, she was surviving by making Connor her bitterest enemy. Demonizing him. It didn't work, not really, but it was the only weapon he'd left her.

The next day was Sunday. She was late to church, so she sat in the back, not in her customary pew in front by the window. The late August day was stifling hot; Christy's sermon was fine, but long. Afterward, she understood that there had been clues before, signs she ought to have recognized. But she had ignored them, been too listless or distracted to notice.

Fainting in church could not be ignored.

She was pregnant.

Nightmare. Fear as like a cold drug in her veins, freezing her, making it impossible to think or plan, even move. After the service, after she recovered from her most public swoon, she found herself in the churchyard, kneeling on the moss beside her father's tombstone. She put her hands on the cool grass over his grave, instinctively seeking his comfort, desperate for him to save her. If only he could! She didn't know she was weeping until she felt Anne Morrell's arm around her shoulders. "Forgive me, Sophie—you don't have to tell me—but is it that man, that Mr. Pendarvis, who's making you so unhappy?" She denied it violently, again and again, and Anne stopped asking. "I'll go and get Christy," she said, rising, but Sophie pulled her back down. "Please don't. Just stay with me." She couldn't speak to either of them. They were her best friends, and she couldn't speak to them. Her shame was grievous and absolute.

She went to the mine the next day, and she was soothed a little by the familiar routine, as well as her own pretense that nothing was amiss. But with everyone to whom she spoke—Jenks, Dickon Penney, her blacksmith, everyone—she found herself wondering, *What will he think when he finds out? Will this one revile me? Will this one stand by me?* On the following day she nearly fainted again; luckily she was alone, and recovered quickly by putting her head down on her desk. But it dawned on her that she wasn't eating, nothing at all, and in fact the thought of food revolted her. Was that normal? She couldn't ask anyone, not even Dr. Hesselius. Not yet. She was too frightened. Panic ruled her; she couldn't see into the future past the hellish minute she was in. The next day she couldn't go to the mine at all.

The idea of a baby, unthinkable at first, began to tap at the corners of her mind, a shy, tentative visitor unsure of its welcome. She had always loved children, always wanted them— someday. But oh, God, not like this! There should be joy, ecstatic anticipation, the humbling certainty that one had been blessed—but all Sophie could feel was stark terror. Because she was ruined.

Connor's cruel jibe, that she cared for nothing except being the belle of her "backward, small-minded village," haunted her. It wasn't fair, but there was truth in it, and she was too demoralized to deny it or try to justify herself. "Lady Bountiful," he'd called her. Yes, she'd felt like that sometimes. And she'd liked being liked; sometimes she'd even enjoyed being envied. But had she sinned so terribly that the devastation of her whole life had to be the price for her pride and folly? She knew the rules, had understood since childhood, as every girl did, what penalty a woman paid when she "fell." Of course it wasn't fair; she knew that, too—as every girl did—but what did it matter? Social morality was like a great, impersonal machine, grinding up all transgressors whether penitent or defiant, naive or cunning, punishing them all with exactly the same efficiency and indifference. So how did she feel about her "backward village" now? The perspective from the bottom was nothing like the one from the top. Whom could she trust not to trample her? How could she stay here? What would become of her?

She was exhausted, ill. She lay on her bed until Maris came in to cluck and fret over her, then she went outside to escape her.

Summer was ending. The climbing tea roses still bloomed, and the bourbons, too, and would until the frost, but most of the others were gone. Thomas had been dutifully cutting off the dead blossoms, but not raking them up and taking them away; the wilted heads lay in brown heaps along the path sides, dreary and dismal-looking, portending autumn. Sophie sat in a chair and contemplated her house, her derelict orchard, her mother's lovely old garden. She thought of the night she'd taken Connor on a tour, showing him her father's study, her old nursery, confessing to him how much she loved her "creaky old house." "It suits you," he'd said. Yes. It did. If only she could turn back time, be that carefree girl again. How innocent she had been, and how complacent. She hadn't known what she had until she lost it.

Crying again. Self-pity could easily become a habit. She wiped her cheeks with her handkerchief—and turned her face away from the house when she heard footsteps on the terrace. If Maris saw her in tears again, she'd—

"Sophie!"

Not Maris. Robert Croddy.

She jumped up, shaking out her skirts, imagining what she must look like. She sent him a gay wave, and he walked down the steps toward her. He didn't much resemble her idea of a Member of Parliament, at least not an elegant one; too stocky and short. He looked more like a sheriff, one you wouldn't want to cross.

Her bright, pasted-on smile was a failure: the first words from his mouth were, "What's wrong?"

"Nothing! I'm taking the day off, that's all. This morning I felt a little tired, so I decided to indulge myself."

"They told me at the mine you were sick."

"You went to Guelder? Why?"

"To invite you out to lunch in my new curricle. Come and see it, it's in your drive." Her face must have fallen. "I'm sorry; never mind, you can see it another time. Come and sit down."

"Really, I'm fine."

"Sit." He had taken her arm, and he was pressing her back into her chair firmly, solicitously. He drew another chair close and sat beside her. "It's that fall you took from your gig; you've never fully recovered from it. You didn't give yourself time to heal, and now it's caught up with you."

An interesting diagnosis. Untrue, but sweet. She was surprised when he reached for her hand, but it was the genuine sympathy in his face that was almost her undoing. She swallowed the tightness in her throat and said in a low voice, "Robert, truly I'm all right. And I'm glad you came—I needed the company." It was almost true; she needed another person's voice, the business of another person's life temporarily eclipsing hers. "Tell me about your new curricle. Did you buy it in Devonport?"

"No, in Plymouth. It's bright blue. I bought it to match your eyes."

She laughed weakly, sitting back.

"Do you think I'm flattering you? It's the truth. I bought it imagining both of us riding in it, Sophie. As man and wife."

"Oh, Robert."

"It's all right, you don't have to say anything. That wasn't a new proposal, merely an extension of the old one." His tight-lipped smile came and went, intending to set her at ease. She was touched by his gentleness, his unwonted delicacy. He began to tell her about his new chaise, the status of his candidacy for Parliament, what her uncle had said about his chances. She couldn't follow any of it; her mind was traveling a different path, racing down it like a thing being chased. Her skin felt prickly, and her hands were damp with sudden perspiration. She stood up all at once, in the middle of his sentence, something about a constituency party association, and writs being cried. "Sophie?" He got to his feet, too. "What's the matter?"

"Nothing. Nothing." She forced a smile. Her heart was pounding in her ears—was she going to faint again? She walked away from him, went to the garden house and leaned her back against the warm, chalky bricks. He came toward her slowly, and his body seemed to get bigger and bigger, filling her vision, blocking out everything else. The concern in his face steadied her and brought her back to herself. "Robert," she said, so quietly he came even closer. "Do you . . ." No, she couldn't ask him if he loved her. She didn't believe it, and she didn't want to hear him say it again; it would have embarrassed her. "Do you really want to marry me?" she asked instead.

His fleshy features stiffened in surprise. "Sophie," was all he could say.

"Do you?"

"My dear girl." He'd have taken her hand again, but she had both of them clasped behind her back. "You know I do."

She wet her dry lips with her tongue. How could she tell him? What were the words? She almost balked then. She saw herself breaking away from him and streaking across the lawn into the house, the orchard, anywhere. She braced her knees, which were trembling—and then she saw her resemblance to a soldier, back to the wall, face to the firing squad. A laugh came out of her mouth, a giddy, scary sound that had Robert frowning at her in concern. "I'll marry you if you still want me after I tell you something," she said in a staccato rush.

"You'll—what? You'll marry me?"

"I have to tell you something first."

"What?"

She stared at him, poised on the brink, teetering; this awful risk terrified her, but if she succeeded the nightmare would go away. She didn't look any further than that.

"What?"

She opened her mouth—but the flat truth wouldn't come out. Not head-on; she needed to approach it sideways.

"If you knew I had done something wrong. Something you couldn't approve of. Something you despised. Do you think you could forgive me?"

He couldn't answer—of course he couldn't. He just stood there, blinking at her.

"Robert, I've made a terrible mistake. I've shamed myself, and I've shamed my family. But I promise I would be a good wife to you if you would forgive me, if you could take me anyway. And— no one would ever know but you. And me."

He looked frightened. "What is it you've done?"

Too late to stop, but a premonition of disaster made her blood run cold. "I'm pregnant. It's Connor Pendarvis's child. We were together only once. I thought I loved him."

There. Even if he spurned her now, the part of her that hated lies and deception was eased by the confession. She'd suffered from the need to lie almost as much as from the thing she'd needed to hide.

She could see the blood drain from his face. Then she could see it return, more of it than before, turning his thick-skinned cheeks a ruddy bronze. The possibility of violence occurred to her for the first time; she looked past his broad, strong shoulder at the empty garden, the house so far away. There was a faint white line around his upper lip. Hardly moving his mouth, he said, "Connor

Pendarvis? Are you talking about that miner? That *miner?* Are you talking about that man who worked in your mine?"

She bowed her head. She could taste defeat on the back of her tongue; it tasted like salt. "He wasn't a miner. He was . . ." A thief. "He wasn't a miner."

*"You were intimate with him?"*

He didn't shout the words, but they struck her like stones all the same, forcing her back against the brick wall. "I've told you. Only once. And now I'm with child. Robert." She held her hand out to him, not to beg him, but to offer a truce. "Will you have me anyway? I'd make you happy—try to. Will you?"

He whispered. "My God," and turned his back on her.

She let her hand fall to her side. It was finished.

"God," she thought he muttered again. Suddenly he whipped around again. *"Whore,"* he said wonderingly. "He was a miner, and you let him fuck you." She recoiled, hunching her shoulders. "You're a *whore,* aren't you? You're nothing but a *whore."*

"Don't. Robert. Go. I shouldn't—" Her throat closed up.

"To think I wanted you to be the one. You to be my wife. I thought—" He looked up at the sky and laughed. "Perfect, I thought. She's perfect."

"Go away. This is—so hurtful. Go away now, I'm begging you."

The meanness in his ginger-colored eyes was unfamiliar to her, and yet somehow it didn't really surprise her. "So that's what you've wanted. All along. Now I get it. How stupid I've been." He took a step toward her.

Pure, uncluttered instinct had her yelling, "Thomas! Come out here, please!"

Robert stopped, and after a second his clenched hands softened. He looked stunned, as if he'd shocked himself. "You don't need help," he said hoarsely. "Don't worry, I wouldn't touch you now if you asked for it."

He looked stiff and jerky and oddly dignified as he stalked off toward the terrace and the path that led around the house to the drive. *I should have married him,* she thought, watching his broad back recede, the expensive tweed of his coat, the resolute swing of his sturdy arms. *Should have chased him years ago and caught him. Then I'd be safe.*

The awful present came back in a wave. "Robert!"

He halted, and turned around with glacial slowness—laughable slowness, she'd have thought at any time but now. His cocked sandy eyebrow asked what she wanted now.

She stumbled toward him a few steps, wringing her hands—partly an act to win him over, part true, sheer terror. "Despite—Even though you—May I—" His dignity might be intact, but hers was in tatters. She swallowed hard and steeled herself. "I have always believed you to be a gentleman. You're angry, with every right. May I have your assurance that when you are calm again, the things that have passed between us today, the—confidences I have given to you in good faith, will remain a secret between us alone?" A stiff speech, practically medieval; it made her blush. But she was in an old-fashioned situation, and formal words came most naturally.

He sneered at her. To think she'd ever liked him—ever even been civil to him! "Don't distress yourself. Your sordid 'confidences' are so distasteful to me, Miss Deene, I assure you I won't be repeating them to anyone. They make me ashamed of the hopes I once entertained. They make me feel like a fool." He bowed to her slowly and ironically. She couldn't deny that his exit was effective.

"Good riddance," she muttered shakily, collapsing in her chair. She'd rather be chained up in the stocks and pelted with stones for adultery than bound for life to such a man.

Oh, but everything was worse now, a state of affairs she wouldn't have thought possible. Was he a gentleman? *Could* she rely on him to be discreet? The bottom was dropping out of her life. Through the thickening fog of fear and desperation she could see one last rope dangling, barely within her reach. If she grabbed for it and missed, all would be lost. But if she caught it and it held, the price of her salvation might be more than she could pay.

# XIV

"Huh-huh here's the ruh rest o' the fuh-fuh forty-fourth. Ye'll hah-hah have it cah-cah copied oot by muh-muh-muh-muh—"

"Morning."

The white beetling brows of Angus McDougal, Q.C., drew together over his thin blade of a nose. People who finished his stammering, incomprehensible, infuriating sentences earned his ire, not his gratitude. Connor knew that, from a dozen personal experiences over the last few weeks, but he simply could not help himself. His employer was driving him wild.

"Aye, muh-muh-muh mornin'," the Scotsman confirmed deliberately. To pay Connor back, he decided to say more. "I wuh-wuh wasn't puh pleased wi' yer last truh-truh trans scruh-scruh scription, Mr. Puh-Puh Pendarvis. Chuh chapter fuh-fuh forty-three had ink bluh-bluh blots in the margins, and some of it wuh was illeg-leg-legible."

"I'm sorry, sir. I'll try to do better with forty-four."

"Aye, suh-suh see that ye do." He put a white envelope on the corner of Connor's desk. "I fuh-fuh-fuh forgot t' gie ye this luh-luh letter. Came in yeh-yeh yesterday's puh-puh-puh—"

"Post." He bowed his head in contrition, at the same time he bit down hard on the knuckle of his right index finger. He felt like screaming.

"Post," McDougal said coldly. From the pocket of his seedy, pipe ash-littered waistcoat he took out a key. "Ye'll lah-lah-lah-lah lock up at six, will ye?"

"Yes, sir." He did it every night, and every morning McDougal asked for the key back.

"No' a minute sooner," he warned, sticking a bony finger in Connor's face. He wasn't by nature a mean man, but he seemed compelled to act out his own Dickensian fantasy of the irascible, eccentric lawyer, full of maggoty habits and exasperating mannerisms. His stuttering brogue was intensely annoying, but it was only one of his quirks; he had a hundred others.

Like forgetting what day was payday. His Scottish frugality was the real article, no affectation. Through the opaque glass of the half window, Connor watched his thin, black-coated form slip through the street door and recede into the rainy evening, but he didn't call out a reminder. The day had been long and unusually tedious. He would rather be broke, he decided, than endure another minute of his employer's conversation.

The letter in the envelope was nothing more than a scrawl on a half sheet of cheap vellum. "A quick note, probably illegible because I am on a train, to say again that Mr. Thacker and I enjoyed our dinner with you on Thursday evening. Please be assured that I'll be in touch with you in the quite near future. Yrs., etc., Ian Braithwaite."

Cryptic, to say the least. So had his visit been, sudden and out of the blue, last week. Braithwaite was a party agent for one of the liberal arms of the Whigs. He and Thacker, his associate, had read Connor's piece in the Rhadamanthus Society's quarterly and been impressed by it, they claimed. They'd come up from Plymouth, apparently for the sole purpose of taking him out for a meal. They'd had a long, wide-ranging conversation about politics and reform, and when it over Connor had no idea why they'd gone to the trouble. "Have you ever thought of standing for public office yourself, Mr. Pendarvis?" Braithwaite had wondered once over the cigars and port. But the subject lapsed after Connor denied ever considering any such thing. If there had been a point to Braithwaite's visit, he'd never come to it, and Connor had put the incident out of his mind.

At least he'd gotten a free dinner—no trifling matter these

days. And at least one good thing had come out of the debacle in Wyckerley. What an unpleasant irony: at a time when his personal life was in fragments, his professional reputation, such as it was, at least in the small reformist circles in which he was known at all, had never been worth more.

"I'm clerking for a solicitor here in Exeter," he'd told Braithwaite. "It's temporary, just until I make up my mind about a number of options I'm weighing." Vague; not an absolute lie, although close to it. And it sounded so much better than, "I'm transcribing the mad, illegible notes of a has-been attorney on the *Reformatio legum ecclesiasticarum* for room, board, and eleven shillings a week while I try to put my life back together."

He rubbed his tired eyes, flexed his aching shoulders. The light in the small office was fading; it would be six soon. Even if he'd wanted to work late, which of course he didn't, McDougal didn't permit it: he was too stingy to pay for lamp oil to light the room after dark.

A knock at the door made him jump. McDougal had no appointments today, none at all, and walk-in clients were all but unheard of. Who could it be? A woman; he could see that from her outline in the murky glass. He grabbed his jacket from the back of his chair and went to answer the door.

He recognized her at once. They'd met two days ago, when she'd engaged McDougal to probate her late husband's will. "Good evening, Mrs.—" His mind went blank.

She had a slow, foxy smile, small teeth, suggestive eyes. "Irene Wayburn. Good evening, Mr. Pendarvis." She enunciated his name carefully, a gentle reproach because he hadn't remembered hers. Slipping off her glove, she gave him her bare hand. "May I come in?"

He blinked. "Yes, of course. Mr. McDougal's not in, though. You've just missed him."

"Oh, what a pity."

Connor widened the door, and she brushed his arm as she passed through.

She smelled of rain and perfume. The meanness of his cramped, cluttered office oppressed him as he tried to see it through her eyes. There was only one chair besides the one behind his battered desk. He pulled it away from the wall and asked if she cared to sit down.

"Oh . . ." She put her finger on her cheek and tapped it thoughtfully. "I think not. I doubt that I'll be staying long."

"How can I help you, Mrs. Wayburn?"

The foxy smile came again, and this time he had to smile back, because her frankness was irresistible. "I've brought some papers Mr. McDougal asked me to hunt up in my husband's files. Here they are." She took a thin, light envelope out of her purse and handed it to him.

"I'll see that he gets them in the morning."

"Thank you." She watched him for a moment, appraising him without a trace of embarrassment, her arms folded across her waist. Her features were heavy and a little coarse, but she had beautiful skin, pale and creamy, almost ethereal-looking, like a nun's skin. Medium height, full-breasted, full-hipped, she wore her sexuality like a pretty new coat she wanted to show off. Had she always been this way, he wondered, or had it taken the demise of Mr. Wayburn to set her free? "A few things have occurred to me since Mr. McDougal and I had our initial consultation," she said. She had a nice voice, pitched to a low, intimate note. "Things about my husband's state of mind when he made his last will. I'm not sure if they're relevant or not, but I feel I ought to confide them to . . . you."

"To me?"

"Well, to someone. To you, as McDougal's assistant. I thought perhaps over dinner. They may be important. Time may even be of the essence." She cocked an arch eyebrow.

Connor rubbed his chin, then his mouth to cover a grin, while he returned her bold, open stare. She was tempting. Very tempting. Why not go with her? There would be no entanglements afterward, and neither of them would indulge in sentimental regrets when it ended. What she was offering would be simple, quick, and basic. Why not?

"I can't."

"Oh." She pouted her lips. "Sure?"

"Yes. I'm very sorry," he said truthfully. "I have no doubt that it would be . . . most enjoyable. But it's not possible."

"Ah, well. *Quel dommage,* as they say." She was over him already; she heaved a wistful sigh for form's sake. "Maybe another time." She closed her reticule with a businesslike snap and moved around him toward the door. "Don't forget to give Mr. Mc-Dougal the papers, will you, Mr. . . . ."

"Pendarvis. No, I won't."

They smiled at each other one last time, and then she was gone.

Within minutes, he regretted his decision. Why hadn't he grabbed for the free gift the Widow Wayburn wanted to give him? Who the hell was he saving himself for? It wasn't as if women were flinging themselves at him every day, it wasn't as if he had scores to choose from. *Jack* was the ladies' man in the family. That was the way it had always been, and Connor couldn't imagine it being any other way. Didn't even want it any other way.

But Jack was gone, down to Exminster to find work with a gang for the late harvest, so that he wouldn't be a "burden." All the talking, cajoling, and finally shouting that Connor had done hadn't accomplished anything. He wasn't sick, Jack maintained; he would *get* sick if he kept on as he was, useless and in the way. He needed to work, needed to make some money of his own. It was a matter of pride. Connor understood that, but he'd have kept him here anyway if he could. But with Jack there was never any use arguing. Bullheaded, the family always called him. The last two Pendarvis boys had a lot in common.

Exeter Cathedral's tower clock struck six. McDougal's dingy law offices were in a courtyard off the Magdalene New Road, within sight of the beautiful cathedral—but much closer in spirit to the Female Penitentiary and the Unitarian and Jewish Burial

Grounds a few blocks to the north. Connor lived in one room over the office, entered from rickety wooden stairs outside at the back. He hated his room. His job. His life. He thought of taking a walk through the city or along the Exe before going upstairs for the night, but the chilly rain and darkening sky dissuaded him, along with a deepening depression that made the least exertion seem onerous and exhausting. Locking the door with McDougal's key, he went up to his room.

He lit it with tallow candles because that was all he could afford. He hated the smell, and the strain they made on his eyes when he read by them, but at least candlelight softened the room's ugliness a little. His bed was a lumpy divan wedged under the eaves. A deal table with uneven legs served for his desk, reading area, and eating place. There were no bureaus or chests of drawers; he kept his clothes in a box at the foot of the bed or hung them on a nail behind the door. The one dirty window wouldn't open, and its view of the other buildings facing the shabby courtyard wasn't edifying. At least the neighborhood was quiet tonight, no neighbors brawling, no dogs fighting. He rinsed the ink from his hands in the basin on the washstand, took off his coat and tie, and unbuttoned his vest.

For a long time, he stared at his face in the mottled mirror, thinking sullen thoughts. What kind of man was he? He used to know, or think he knew. A serious man, he'd have said, one with principles, strong convictions, goals that meant something to him. He'd been told so often that he was the hope of his family and the pride of his village that he'd eventually come to believe it. A barrister or a journalist: those were the two great professions he had decided would take him closest to his ultimate goal, and his ultimate goal was nothing less than the furtherance of the cause of reform and social justice for all working people. In the mirror, he watched his mouth twist into a thin, ugly smile. What a pathetic joke. If the end justified the means, he could say that he'd succeeded, on a small scale. But it didn't. Instead of striking a gratifying blow for the cause, he'd committed the worst ethical blunder of his life. He felt *drenched* with guilt, and he was no closer now to justifying what he had done to Sophie than he had been six weeks ago. *It's over,* he told himself constantly; if he couldn't forgive himself, at least he could forget the whole sordid incident, just let it go. But it wasn't possible.

The strange thing was that he was still angry with her. All the blame was his, and yet every time he thought of the things she'd said at their last harrowing meeting, his skin felt hot. Fury and mortification came boiling up in him, as if the encounter had happened yesterday or an hour ago. *You taught me how low I could sink. I'll spend the rest of my life repenting what I did with you.* Maybe he deserved that—yes, all right, he deserved it—but her absolute disgust still infuriated him. Sophie was a snob, and he believed in his heart that not a single moment had passed during their summer-long acquaintance, not even the night they had made love in her narrow bed, when she didn't consider him her social inferior. He himself had much to answer for, but he couldn't forgive her for that.

Dinner was a piece of mutton pie, purchased two nights ago from a cookshop in the next alley. He ate it cold because there was no stove in his room, and if there had been he couldn't have afforded the coal to heat it. Afterward, he stared at the pages he'd been trying to write for the last six nights; it was a paper on the child labor law, and he was writing it for publication in the journal of the Liverpool Workingmen's Association. But almost immediately the words blurred in front of his eyes. He was tired, his eyes hurt, his head ached—but that wasn't it. He'd lost his edge, that angry energy that had gotten him through university and then law studies, and the dreary, grinding poverty of them both. The Rhadamanthus report ought to have buoyed him. He'd heard from several sources that it had hit its target; if Shavers' bill passed next term, he could truthfully say that he had helped get it through. Helped to save lives. Yet that gave him only a chilly, abstract kind of pleasure. He saw himself as pitiful in his bare cell of a room, a hypocritical monk with no life, pretending he was biding his time until something meaningful came along, saving his pennies for an elusive dream of one day returning to studying the law. He disgusted himself. He should have gone with the gay widow, Irene whatever her name was. Better to drink and womanize, go on a tear, pretend he still had an existence—*anything* was better than this pathetic, mean, embarrassing excuse for a life.

He took up his pen, pulled his one candle closer to the sheets of paper on his desk. Old habits die hard.

He must have dozed off. He awoke from a dream in which Irene was knocking at his door again, and this time he kissed her in the threshold and picked her up. In the dream she weighed a ton; the staggering load of her helped jolt him into wakefulness. Disoriented, it took him a few seconds to realize that that intermittent tapping sound really was a knock at his door. Well, well, he thought. It could be no one but the widow. And this time he would agree to anything she wanted, anything at all. His chair scraped on the bare floor in his haste; he rushed to open the door before she could get away, grabbed the knob, flung it open.

Was it another dream?

No. It was Sophie.

At first he was too stunned to speak and could only gape at her in the dark doorway. He felt a slow warmth begin to creep into all the cold places, like a man with a chill drawing closer to a blazing fire. He could hardly see her face; she wore a long black cape with a hood, and her eyes were in deep shadow. Her soft, unsmiling mouth unlocked a storehouse of forbidden, carefully unexamined memories. He whispered her name. To have her here—to see her again like this—at once nothing else mattered, nothing but this moment. "Sophie—"

"May I come in?"

Her voice, ice-cold and hostile, dashed all his stupid, fledgling hopes in an instant. His own face froze. He made a facetious gesture of welcome and opened the door wide.

He couldn't stand her seeing where he lived. He watched her straight back and stiff shoulders, the slow, disdainful turn of her head as she took in the cramped, dark, miserable little room, and he wanted to disappear, or bolt out the door, or kick every piece of furniture to splinters. When she finally turned around to look at him, his hackles were up and he was ready to fight. Nobody put him in this bloody-minded, humiliating place better than Sophie Deene, and in that moment he hated her for it.

"I can see this isn't a social call. What did you come for? Do I owe you money?"

Even in the dim candlelight he could see her turn pale, and he felt a painful pinch in his chest. She never used to be so thin-skinned; for a second he wondered if she was unwell.

If so, she recovered quickly. She glanced around with deliberate distaste, and her lips curled when she answered, "Luckily I didn't come for the view. You don't seem to have landed on your feet, *Connor*. It almost looks as if you've gotten what you deserve."

He folded his arms, smiling nastily. "I don't have time for this, *Miss Deene*. What is it you want?"

She faltered. Her hand fluttered to her throat and hovered there, as if she might unfasten the top button of her cape. Her eyes skittered away. When she turned her head, he couldn't see her face anymore, because of the hood. "May I have a glass of water?"

"Sorry, I'm fresh out." He frowned at her motionless profile. "Can you stomach flat ale? I've got that in abundance." He owned two mugs; miraculously, one of them was clean. He poured warm, stale ale into it from a covered stone pitcher he'd gotten filled yesterday at the local public house. To make Sophie look at him, he stood at her elbow, mug in hand, and waited for her to turn.

"Thank you." She took a minuscule sip without shuddering, then set the mug down on the table. "Writing more tracts?" she asked, eyeing his messy spread of ink-blotched papers. "Or are you really an attorney when you're not pretending to be a tut-man?"

He sat down on the edge of his bed because he knew it was rude. "I'm not a lawyer." For no reason he could think of, he added, "I was articled to one once, in my careless youth. But he died. And then other circumstances got between me and the rest of my legal education." She said nothing to that, just stared at him. "How did you find me?"

"Your brother mentioned your address in a letter he wrote to someone . . . someone I know."

"Who?"

The corners of her mouth flattened. "Sidony Timms."

He pulled one foot up on the edge of the bed and wrapped his arms around his knee. So she'd been reduced to questioning Jack's dairymaid lover to learn his whereabouts. He should have felt some sort of satisfaction at that, but he didn't. His curiosity intensified. Was she really here with him in his room, unchaperoned, in the dead of night? "Why did you come, Sophie?"

There was a picture on the wall over the washstand, a cheap print, poorly framed, some sort of landscape—he could hardly remember it. But Sophie was examining it as though it was a masterpiece hanging in the Louvre. She couldn't bring herself to say whatever it was she'd come here to say, and a foolish, battered hope flickered in him again, like a beaten boxer who won't stay down even though his legs can't support him. Connor knew the hope was stupid and pitiful, but it wouldn't die.

"I've got an appointment," he lied after a full minute crawled by in silence. "I have to go out in a little while, so if you could come to the point . . ."

She turned, bracing her palms on the rickety stand behind her. The look on her face shut him up. "I would have done anything not to come here," she said in a low voice that broke at the end. "All that's gotten me through the last weeks is thinking I would never see you again. Believe me—"

"Yes, I get the point," he flared. "Then why did you come?"

Her throat worked. She swallowed, her glance darting from place to place, anywhere but on him. She was in misery, and the cause suddenly struck him like a hammer blow to the back of the head. "I—find that I—" She had to close her eyes to say it. "I'm going to have a child."

He couldn't get up. His foot hit the floor with a thud, like an exclamation point to her low, shaky sentence, but otherwise he couldn't move.

"Well." She turned her back on him. "I had hoped for something more from you, but I don't know why. I should know by now that you're incapable of simple decency, the—"

Finally he got to his feet. His mind was in turmoil. "Are you telling me this," he said loudly, to cut her off, "because you believe I'm the father?" She hunched her shoulders, and immediately he was ashamed. Why were they hurting each other like this? "I'm sorry, I didn't mean that."

"Go to hell."

He raked his fingers through his hair, afraid to go to her but wanting to touch her, or at least see her face. "What are you going to do?"

She turned back, and it was a mixed relief to see that she had herself under control again. "Besides coming here and telling you, do you mean? Beyond that, I don't think that's any of your business."

"Oh, come now. What you want from me is a declaration of devotion and a quick marriage proposal. Am I right?"

"On the second count. But I beg you not to attempt the first under any circumstances. These days I'm nauseated enough, and I don't think I could bear it."

His eyes glittered, but Sophie had no idea what he was thinking. He looked strange to her in his gentleman's clothes, the tools of his profession—pens, papers, books—scattered around his small, untidy room. He wore glasses; she saw them on the table next to his inkstand. His hair had grown long and shaggy in the weeks since she'd seen him last. He looked like an impoverished don holed up in his college, surviving on books and biscuits. Connor, his name was. It suited him.

"Let's be clear," he said, moving toward her. "You're having my child, and you want me to marry you."

She considered insulting him by saying something scathing about the inaccuracy of the word "want." But then she reminded herself that nastiness was a luxury she couldn't afford. If he had wanted to see her humbled, he'd certainly gotten his wish: Lady Bountiful was groveling at his feet. "If I had any other choice, I would take it. I'm under no illusions as to how you feel about me; you made that clear at our last meeting. If it were only myself, I would endure anything before coming to you with this request. But now there's the child, and it must come first."

He didn't speak. If he refused her—she shrank from imagining what would happen next. Perhaps he was already re-encumbered, she thought, remembering the attractive woman who had come out of his downstairs office not long ago. She'd seen her while she'd huddled in a dark doorway across the street, waiting for the courage to knock on his door.

"You needn't live with me," she said harshly. "Stay here and continue your important reform efforts—" She stopped, curbing again the impulse to insult him, this time with sarcasm. "I'm asking you for your name, for the sake of this baby. Marry me, then never see me again if it suits you."

"Does it suit you?"

She let too much time go by before answering, and her tone of voice wasn't adamant enough. "Yes."

Again he said nothing, and the silence became unbearable. She had to turn away. "There's money in it for you," she said, feeling weary to the bone. "A yearly stipend if you like, monthly if you—"

His ungentle hand jerked her around by the arm to face him. "How much do you hate me? That much, that you think I would take money for this?"

"It wasn't my intention to offend you. I don't know anything about you. I've learned to take nothing for granted." His grip loosened; he let her go, and she saw remorse in his eyes. "Will you do it?" she asked while he was in this softer mood.

He watched her for a moment. "I'll let you know. It's a big step; I'll have to think it over," he said, then smiled at the indignation she couldn't hide. "Where are you staying?"

She wanted to curse him, spit in his eye. She named the small, discreet hotel in Friars Walk where she'd taken a suite of rooms.

"Friars Walk," he repeated, pretending he was impressed by the address. "Then you'll be comfortable while you wait for my answer, won't you?"

She moved around him toward the door, pulling her cloak tighter around her shoulders. If she stayed here another minute, she was afraid she would strike him.

Her exit took him by surprise. She was already outside on the stair landing when he called to her, "Sophie, wait. I'll come with you."

"No, don't," she threw over her shoulder, hanging onto the railing as she clattered down the wooden steps in her half boots.

"Wait!"

She was running now. "You know where I am. Send a note, because I don't want to see you!"

The foggy darkness was her friend; it swallowed her up quickly. She walked back to her hotel with no fear, just gladness because she was alone, and because the encounter she'd been dreading was over. Nothing could get worse now. Surely it couldn't.

The next, day a messenger delivered his letter.

*Dear Sophie,*
*I accept.*
*I assume discretion is the watchword, but will otherwise leave all of the arrangements to you. Do you desire an*

*elopement here in Exeter, with the sheepish couple return-
ing to Wyckerley after the foul deed is a fait accompli? I'm at
your service; only apprise me of your wishes, and I will do
my utmost to comply with them.*

Yr. obed. svt.,
Connor Pendarvis.

# XV

Christy was reading a book by the light of a candle he'd brought over from the altar and set on the back of his pew. Sophie envied his absorption, and especially his calm. She couldn't even sit down. Every time she tried, she popped back up after half a minute and started prowling again, trying to walk off her nerves. If the monotonous clack of her footsteps on the worn stone floor of the nave annoyed Reverend Morrell, he never showed it.

She thought he must be the kindest man she'd ever known. Certainly he was the easiest to confide in. She thought of his compassion when she'd confessed to him the trouble she was in, and his gentle counsel, his refusal to moralize or condemn. He'd petitioned the archdeacon to waive the banns so the wedding could take place immediately. He wouldn't lie and put down in the church registry a false date for the nuptials, but he'd done everything else he could to accommodate her. Such as holding the ceremony at ten o'clock at night. And sending his deacon and his churchwarden away on trumped-up business at opposite ends of the parish, to eliminate the unlikely possibility of inter-ruptions. Just then he looked up from his book and smiled at her, and she smiled back, comforted in spite of herself. They had talked and talked until there was nothing left to say, and now they were waiting. For the bridegroom to show up for his wedding.

She assumed he was coming. He'd never said, never re-sponded to the letter she'd sent to him from Wyckerley telling him the date and time of the "foul deed." If he didn't keep his word, if this had all been a lie, if he literally abandoned her at the altar . . . She pivoted and started on another round of pacing.

She didn't even know what would happen after the wedding. Would he go away immediately? Might this be the last time they ever saw each other—that is, if he came at all? Or would he stay for a little while and then go away, under some pretext they concocted in advance? And how would she explain her baby's arrival a mere seven and a half months after the wedding? Christy told her not to worry about things she couldn't control, but that was easier said than done. Anne said anyone who ostracized or gossiped about her could go to hell for all she cared. But that kind of defiance was easier in the abstract, too. Sophie wasn't like Anne. What people thought of her mattered, and it always had. She'd even been afraid at first to tell Anne the truth, for fear of losing her friendship.

But that had proved a baseless worry. "I could tell you things about myself that would shock you," Anne had shot back, to console her. "I won't, because it's not only my secret. But you can't alienate me, Sophie, and you can't make me stop loving you, or wanting you for my friend."

Was ever a poor, miserable girl in trouble blessed with kinder friends?

She was staring at the dim portrait of one of the Stations of the Cross, so murky in the half light that she couldn't even tell what it was, when she heard the sound of carriage wheels outside in the street. She whipped around, heart pounding, and saw Christy lift his head from his book. She hadn't imagined it, then—he'd heard it, too. *Thank God,* she thought reflexively— then wanted to take it back. Christy said the Lord had forgiven her, but she lacked his sanguine faith. She hadn't been able to pray since she'd found out about the baby.

Footsteps on the stone porch. Christy came to stand beside her in the aisle; she squeezed his hand gratefully, then turned her gaze toward the door.

She could hardly see him at first, just the flash of a pale face and white shirt in the dark vestibule, and for an awful moment she feared he'd sent someone else, a proxy. But it was Connor, walking neither fast nor slow down the aisle toward her, his set face giving away no clue to what he was feeling. When he stopped in front of them, he said, "Sophie," without touching her, and offered his hand to Christy. The two men shook solemnly, and then Connor said, "Reverend Morrell, may I have a word with you alone before we begin?"

"I was going to suggest it myself," Christy said mildly. They excused themselves and walked toward the sacristy, leaving Sophie alone.

Her nerves stretched tighter. She couldn't imagine what they were saying to each other. But she was so relieved that he'd come, she had to sit down. She was shaking, she realized, and thinking the most inane thoughts, such as if her hair looked all right, and if he had noticed her dress.

The men returned. She rose to her feet, thinking Connor looked even more subdued than before. Christy said, "Let me go and get Anne. I'll only be a moment," and strode off again toward the sacristy.

To keep a nerve-racking silence at bay, Sophie said quickly, "Anne's going to be the witness—Christy says we only need one. She's with Elizabeth now, her little girl. She has a cold, Elizabeth, I mean, so Anne's staying with her. Otherwise—" She took a deep breath. "Otherwise she'd have been here before. Anne, I mean. Waiting with me." *No*, she realized, *silence is better*, and resolutely closed her lips.

"You look beautiful."

She felt an inward jolt, and then a foolish blush stealing into her cheeks. "Thank you." She smoothed the skirt of her simple green gown with self-conscious hands, not looking at him. "How was your trip?"

"I took the train to Plymouth and then hired a carriage. I drove myself."

"I see."

"Have you been all right, Sophie? I never asked you, that night in Exeter."

She assumed he meant her physical health, the state of her pregnancy. "Yes, yes, I've been in perfect health."

"That's good. I'm glad."

She stole a glance at him. He had his hands in his pockets, although he looked anything but relaxed. His dark suit looked cheap but brand-new. He'd had his hair cut. For some reason that moved her. She heard herself blurt out, "Thank you for coming."

"Did you think I wouldn't?"

"I thought you would—but—"

"But you worried anyway."

"It seems to be what I do best lately."

They almost smiled at each other.

"I'd have come sooner if I'd thought you needed me. To face anything, I mean. Has it been—difficult for you, has anyone—"

"No, no," she assured him, "there's been nothing to face. No one knows, so . . ." She trailed off, then added, "But thank you."

"You're welcome."

Silence.

"What did you say to Christy?" she asked, to break it. "Unless it's private. Excuse me, you needn't——"

"No, it's not private. I apologized to him for what the piece in the Rhadamanthus report said about him. I didn't write it." He combed his fingers through his hair, a gesture of uncertainty she'd grown much too fond of. "No, I did write it, but someone else added the implication that he wasn't a caring minister. I told him I'd never intended that. He accepted my apology."

Of course. He would.

"Do you know what he had to say to me?"

She returned his gaze levelly. "I can guess."

"You probably can. It was a manly conversation about honor and duty, and my intentions toward my betrothed. He let me off quite easily, all things considered."

She couldn't tell which one of them he was mocking, himself or her, or Christy. Before she could think of a reply, the Morrells trooped into the church, all of them, Elizabeth sprawled asleep on her mother's shoulder. Anne walked purposefully, without hesitation, to where Sophie and Connor were standing, and planted herself in front of the groom.

"We've never formally met," she announced in soft but carrying tones. "I'm Anne Morrell. Christy's my husband. And Sophie is my friend."

As gauntlet-throwing went, it wasn't particularly subtle. Connor disarmed her by putting out his hand, and Anne had no choice but to take it. "No, we've never met. But I made your daughter's acquaintance the first day I came to Wyckerley. I didn't know who was prettier, Elizabeth or Sophie. I still haven't made up my mind."

"Hmpf," said Anne, but he'd taken a lot of the fight out of her. "You're worse than Sophie warned me you would be."

"Much worse," he agreed.

She shook her head at him, and sent Sophie a complicated look, humorous and anxious, full of feminine resignation over the shortcomings of men.

Christy had finished lighting more candles on the altar; now he cleared his throat softly, signaling it was time to begin. As they drifted toward him, Sophie reflected on the difference between this ceremony and the one in her girlish daydream, the one in which All Saints Church was filled with friends and flowers, and sunshine, and she was clinging to her father's arm and smiling, the envy of everyone, as she walked slowly toward her faceless Galahad. This silent, furtive service in the dead of night certainly put proud Miss Sophie Deene in her place. The only thing she was thankful for was that her father wasn't here to see it.

Connor stood at her right, Anne at her left, gently bouncing Lizzy, who had begun to whimper. Christy's low, stirring voice sent a little thrill of excitement or apprehension through Sophie's breast, and her heart gave a violent leap. "We have come together in the presence of God," he began, "to witness and bless the join-ing together of this man and this woman in Holy Matrimony." She hazarded a glance at Connor. He looked stonefaced and calm—but when he touched her, took her hand to pledge to her his troth, she realized he was trembling, too. It put a different light on things. For the first time she tried to put herself in his place. With Christy's soft promptings, he made his vows to her. "In the name of God, I, Connor, take you, Sophie, to be my wife, to have and to hold from this day forward, for better for worse, for richer for poorer, in sickness and in health, to love and to cherish, until death do us part. This is my solemn vow."

There was no ring. Before she knew it, Christy was pro-nouncing them husband and wife, thoughtfully omitting the "You may kiss the bride" directive, and the wedding was over. They signed the registry right there in the chancel, and afterward Anne asked if they would like to come to the rectory for wine and cake. Sophie hesitated. When Connor said nothing, she declined, with the vague excuse that it was late, they were all tired—but the truth was, she had no idea what would happen next. Would Con-nor go back to Exeter tonight? Tomorrow? Would he come home with her and be her husband? It was mortifying not to know; she would go to any lengths to avoid saying out loud to Anne—Christy already knew—that she had no idea what her husband's plans were with regard to herself.

So they said good night with hugs and handshakes, and in Anne's case, surreptitious tears. Connor took Sophie's arm, and they went outside to the front of the church, where there was no crowd gathered to wish them well, or throw rice, or catch So-phie's bouquet. The night was misty and damp and absolutely still. A moment passed, and then she noticed the small, one-horse cabriolet Connor had hired, tied to a post at the edge of the green. Next to her own pony gig. Ha, she thought, without humor. Would they ride off in separate directions now, never to meet again?

Connor was frowning at the two conveyances. "Wait here a

moment." He let go of her arm, trotted down the steps, and jogged around the corner of the church out of sight.

She waited.

Two minutes later he returned, slightly out of breath, and waited for her to come to him at the bottom of the steps. "Christy's offered to stall your pony overnight," he explained as he handed her up into his carriage and lifted the hooded top. "I said I'd come and get him for you in the morning."

Well, she thought. At least he was seeing her home.

The ride to Stone House was accomplished in silence after their first few attempts at casual conversation fell embarrassingly flat. She imagined his stilted observations about the weather and the condition of the road sounded as ludicrous to him as hers did to her, and before long they both lapsed into muteness.

At home, he stabled the hackney while she went inside and tried to think of what she ought to do now. It was after eleven o'clock; she'd told Mrs. Bolton not to wait up for her. The housekeeper had learned not to ask questions; if Sophie's absences from home alarmed or puzzled her, she didn't show it.

Now what, she wondered. Should she offer her husband a drink? Or food; maybe he was hungry. She rarely kept spirits, but there was some wine in the pantry. She brought it into the formal parlor and was pouring out a glass when she heard his footsteps on the porch. She wondered if he would knock at the door. No, he was coming in, walking through the hall as if he lived here. She composed herself; by the time he saw her through the archway and came toward her, she had her face in order.

"Aren't you having any?" he asked when she handed him the wineglass.

She shook her head. "The baby—I thought it might not be good for him. Her. Whatever." So much for her composure. She walked to the mantel and lit candles, fidgeted with the clock. In the mirror, she could see him watching her. At last she turned around and asked straight out, "What do you intend to do?"

"What do you mean?"

"Are you staying the night?"

He looked blank. "Staying the night?"

"I don't know what you mean to do," she admitted, clutching her hands together, trying not to wring their. "About—anything. Is this a marriage? Are you staying? Going away?" She drew a breath. "Please don't let's quarrel tonight, Connor." It was the first time she'd called him, without sarcasm, by his name; she said it self-consciously. "My housekeeper sleeps downstairs. I'd like to keep our difficulties between us, if that's possible."

He set his glass down carefully on the low table. "I wouldn't care for a fight tonight myself. You want to know my intentions. I'm surprised you didn't see my case in the back of the carriage. I thought I'd send for the rest later. Not that there's that much to send for."

"Later? Then, you're staying? With me?"

"If it suits you. I think that's the conventional way most marriages begin."

She had to look away. Her emotions were in complete chaos these days—because of the baby, she supposed. All of a sudden she was weeping, and she didn't even know why. She heard him behind her, felt his hands lightly touch her shoulders.

"Why are you crying?"

"I don't know."

"Do you want me to go?"

"No. I don't know what will happen. I don't want you to go." His hands slid down to her arms in a clasp she remembered very well. There was a heightened, suspended moment in which she felt that anything could happen. And then he let her go, and she heard him step back, away from her.

"It's late."

She turned back to face him. "Yes. You've had a long trip, you must be tired." New waves of anxiety washed over her. This time she wouldn't ask, she would tell. "My father's room has been made up. You can sleep there."

"I know where it is. You go up, I think I'll stay down here a little longer."

She stared at him. This was what she wanted, so why did she feel so frustrated and awkward? "Good night, then."

"Good night."

In the doorway, she paused. "Connor."

"Yes?"

She made a helpless gesture with one hand. "Thank you."

"For doing the decent thing?"

She didn't answer. He toasted her with his wineglass, and once again she didn't know whom he was mocking, her or himself. All in all, she thought as she crossed the hall to the staircase, everything had gone well. Perfectly, in fact. She walked up the steps as if lead lined her shoes, as miserable as she'd ever been in her life.

Wyck House, Eustace Vanstone's pretentious Tudor mansion on the village square, had an iron fence around it to separate its neat, sterile garden from the cobbled road, not to mention passersby in the High Street. Excluding Lynton Great Hall, it was the grandest house in the district, and Connor had never expected to be strolling up its neat stone path at all, much less with Sophie Deene—Sophie Pendarvis, make that—on his arm. She'd mentioned over breakfast that morning—while her maid and her housekeeper thought of excuses to return again and again to the dining room so they could stare at him—that she thought it best to announce their marriage to her family at once, before someone else announced it first, and asked him tentatively if he would care to accompany her to her uncle's house in an hour or so. "Not at all," he'd lied, and his reward had been her visible relief and, better hidden but just as unmistakable, her surprised gratitude. He didn't care for the implication: that anything he did that was decent or even civilized came as a wonder to her.

She knocked once at the painted black door and stood back, shoulders squared, chin up—a heretic confronting the Inquisition judges bravely. She'd made an effort to look solemn and contrite in a plain gown of blue-gray silk, with wide white cuffs that made him think of the Puritans. But she hadn't been able to resist a gay paisley shawl with a dashing fringe, and her hat was downright rakish. For himself, he had on his wedding clothes again—dark blue Prince Albert coat and trousers, paid for with the last of his puny savings. He'd had to borrow his necktie from Jack, as well as money for the train and the hired carriage. What would his new bride think if she knew that the sum total of his fortune was down to about twenty-four shillings?

She knocked again, louder, when no one answered the door, and sent him a grim smile. She was beautiful, always beautiful, but she looked tired, as if she'd gotten as much sleep as he had last night. He'd lain awake for hours, thinking of her across the hall in her room, her bed. Thinking of what would become of them. Thinking of their baby. The future was like a dense gray fog his imagination couldn't penetrate at all.

Rustling behind the door; it opened. "Good morning, Fay," Sophie said brightly to the uniformed maid who curtsied to her. "Is my uncle at home?"

"Yes, ma'am, he's in his study. Shall I go and tell him—"

"No, no, I think we'll surprise him. We'll just go in, it's all right." Her hand was damp when she slipped it into Connor's to pull him around the ornate staircase and down the long hallway toward the rear of the house. They stopped at a door that was slightly ajar, and she tapped on it, peering in through the crack. "Uncle Eustace?"

"Sophie" came a voice from inside. "Come in. This is a surprise."

Connor heard her draw a deep breath. She squeezed his hand once, hard, and let it go, and they walked into the room together.

Vanstone was in the act of getting up when he saw Connor. He halted in midair, buttocks poised comically over his chair, staring in disbelief. "What's this?" he demanded, straightening. "What is this?" Even working at home alone on a Saturday morning he was fully dressed, as if for a business meeting, in frock coat, striped pants, satin vest. He had keen, ruthless eyes, and he'd struck Connor from the first as a man he wouldn't want for an enemy. But Connor had a scar on his cheek that said it was too late to make him a friend.

Sophie was smiling a terrible, painted-on smile. "Uncle Eustace, we've come to tell you something. I think you will be quite surprised. I hope you'll be pleased." She was stalling; she fluttered her hand over her throat, determinedly smiling that ghastly smile. "Mr. Pendarvis—Connor—and I, we've—married each other."

"You've what?"

"Yes, it was very sudden, we did it last night, in fact, in the church. Christy did it. An elopement, I suppose you would call it, only we—didn't go anywhere, to Scotland, I mean, or anyplace like that." She forced out a laugh. "And now we've come to ask for your blessing."

He couldn't speak. He stared at them in horror, second after second, trying to believe what she'd told him. Connor knew she was trembling even though he wasn't touching her. He hadn't realized how much her uncle's good opinion mattered to her, and he wondered if she'd known it herself until this moment.

"Why?" Vanstone finally managed to get out.

Sophie said, "Why?" back, as if she didn't understand the question.

"Why in the name of God did you marry him!"

"Why? Because," she faltered, "we . . . I . . ."

Connor said, "For the usual reason. Because we love each other. We've been corresponding since I left Wyckerley. I kept asking her to be my wife, and finally she said yes."

Vanstone uttered a truly vile curse, and Sophie went even whiter. "Please, Uncle, I know there's been unpleasantness in the past—"

"Unpleasantness? This man's a Judas. You can't have married him."

"I have, and I'm asking you—"

"Have you forgotten what he did? Have you taken leave of your senses?"

Connor gritted his teeth, but kept his mouth shut. He was taking his cues from Sophie, and anger apparently wasn't allowed. They'd come here to make obeisance.

"I'm asking you to try to forget what happened in the past," she said tensely. "It was—a misunderstanding, and I've put it behind me. We want to start our new life together with the blessing of the people we love. Please, can't you wish us well?"

"No, I can't," Vanstone said, and Connor had to give him credit for bluntness. "I can give you a piece of advice, but I doubt that you'll take it: Find yourself a lawyer today and have this marriage annulled." Sophie just looked at him in misery, and finally he relented enough to come out from behind his desk, even sat on the edge of it with his hands clasped in his lap. "What are your plans?" he snapped at Connor. "Will you work, or live on my niece's money?"

Sophie started to answer, but Connor cut her off. "I haven't decided what I'll do." Vanstone snorted. "I have a university education. I read the law for three years with a solicitor; in two more, I'd have been eligible for the examinations. My wife's money is mine now," he said belligerently, "and if I choose to use some of it to finish my studies, I will. I'm telling you this for Sophie's sake, not because I believe it's any of your business."

Vanstone scowled and said nothing, stroking the silvery ends of his mustache.

"I don't care if you approve of me or not," Connor was goaded into saying. "But—"

"I don't."

"But Sophie's asked for your blessing. She wants it. It's important to her. May she have it?"

After a long pause, Vanstone said, "No," and Sophie bowed her head. "But she can have my hopes for her. I hope you're happy, Sophie. I'm sorry to say I don't think you will be. I think a time will come when you'll need my help. I'll give it to you if I can, and I make a promise to you now, that I'll try very hard not to say I told you so."

She smiled feebly. "Thank you for that, then." She twisted her fingers, glanced helplessly around the room, as if searching for something that could keep her there a little longer. She didn't want to go, but Vanstone wasn't making it easy to stay. "Well," she said, and went toward him uncertainly. He stood up and let her kiss him on the cheek. Connor he just glared at, not offering to shake hands.

On the way out, Connor had time to reflect that they'd been lucky on two scores: no one had hit anyone, and they'd never had to speak to the awful Honoria. A success, then.

But it wasn't over. As the maid closed the front door behind them, Sophie suddenly muttered, "Oh, my God," and turned her back to the street.

"What is it?" he asked, alarmed. At the end of the walk, coming toward them through the wrought-iron gate, he saw Robert Croddy.

"He knows."

"Knows what?"

"About the baby."

"How could he?"

"I told him."

"You—" There was no time to say more. She told this—*jackass* about the baby? He couldn't believe it.

"So you've come back," Croddy sneered, planting himself in the path, blocking the way. He had on a morning coat with tails, a silk tie, a top hat—doing his best to live down his heritage. "I didn't think you'd have the gall to show your face around here again, Pendarvis. Is he bothering you, Sophie?"

Her short laugh was just shy of hysterical. "No, he's—"

Connor stepped in front of her, cutting her off. He'd had enough. "You're bothering me," he said goadingly, forcing Croddy back a step, then another, by butting chests with him. "Keep away from me, you sodding beermonger, and keep away from my wife."

"Your *wife*?" He looked around Connor's shoulder in astonishment. Then he made a mistake: he laughed.

His big square chin made a wide-open target, and Connor's fist smashing into it made a most satisfying *crunch*. Pain, sharp and bracing, radiated all the way up to his elbow. He watched Croddy stagger back a few steps, drop, and hit the hard ground on his rump.

"Stop it!" yelled Sophie, trying to grab Connor's arm. Beyond the gate, a man and woman were gaping at them, and others in the street had stopped to stare. Croddy wasn't going to fight back; he just sat there on the stone path, holding his jaw, glassy-eyed. Sophie started to go to him, but Connor snatched her hand and pulled her around him, through the gate and out into the street.

Ignoring the shocked spectators, he half shoved her into the seat of the pony cart, then sprang up beside her. She twisted around to gaze back at Croddy; when he snapped the reins, the horse jerked forward, and she had to grab at the seat to stay aboard.

He whipped the pony into a canter, much too fast for the sleepy center of Wyckerley. Pedestrians and ducks scattered. When they got to the Tavistock road, he didn't slow down. "Why," he demanded over the clatter of hooves and wheels, "did you tell that horse's ass about the baby?"

She'd taken her hat off so it wouldn't blow away. Looking straight ahead, she answered through her teeth, "It seemed the decent thing to do for the man to whom I was proposing marriage."

He saw red. He couldn't speak—he didn't know any curses vile enough for his fury. When he glanced at Sophie, she looked wary, almost frightened of him, and he was just foul-minded enough to be glad.

"What are you in such a goddamn hurry for?" she wanted to know, voice quaking with the jerking of the gig.

She never swore; she must be furious. So was he. "Why, Sophie," he snarled back, "I'm in a hurry to get away on our honeymoon."

"Our *what*? Where are we going?"

He snapped the reins, giving poor Val a good smack on the rump. "To Cornwall," he said with relish. "I've met your family, sweetheart. Now it's time you met mine."

# XVI

Connor's family was dead.

Sophie didn't find that out for three days, though, the length of time it took them to travel half the long leg of Cornwall to the village of Trewythiel. They took a southern route and skirted the dreary moorlands, for which she was glad; her mood was already bleak enough. The pace they set was leisurely in the extreme—the first night they got no farther than Liskeard—and she wondered if he was being careful because of her condition. If so, his concern came a little late. But she didn't ask, didn't so much as inquire about their destination, and he didn't tell her. They were furious with each other, and it seemed they had both chosen silence over shouting this time to express it.

At Liskeard there was no train, and no coaches until Monday. That left nothing to do on Sunday but sightsee. After they looked at the stained glass in St. Neod's and the tower of St. Martin's, and after they wandered through the public gardens on the site of an old castle, there wasn't much to do. But they had taken separate rooms, thank God. Playing the tourist with a person to whom one wasn't speaking was more exhausting than Sophie could ever have imagined possible. By early afternoon, she pleaded fatigue with perfect truth and escaped to her room, and didn't come out of it until Monday morning.

They traveled the short distance to Lostwithiel by coach, then caught the train for Truro. Two things immediately dampened her spirits even further. The pretty hotel they found near the train station had only one room to let for the night, and Connor took it, without hesitation or consultation. At least until now the worry that this was going to be a honeymoon in any real sense had been mercifully absent. Now it was mercilessly present, and she suffered from it (in silence, unwilling to give him the satisfaction of knowing she was a nervous wreck) for what remained of the day. The second bit of unpleasantness had to do with money. Their departure from Wyckerley had been hasty and unexpected; she'd had time to pack only a few clothes—at least by her lights; her new husband had expressed amazement at the number of bags she'd managed to fill in an hour—and she hadn't even brought along her maid. She'd taken all the money there was in the house, which wasn't much, and handed it over to Connor without a second thought. In Truro, in their one small hotel room, he informed her with unprovoked harshness that they were out of cash, and that if she expected him to pay for meals, lodging, and transportation for the remainder of the journey, he would either have to get a job or she would have to wire her bank in Tavistock for more funds. The source of his hot, unexpected anger eluded her until she thought, for the second time, to put herself in his place. Then she understood. It was a matter of pride.

They sent a message by telegraph, and received a reply that a check transfer could be accomplished by morning of the next day. Marveling privately at the wonders of modern technology, they spent the rest of the day exploring the town.

Sophie wanted to see the coinage hall and compare it to the one in Tavistock. If they had been an hour earlier, they could have witnessed a ticketing—an auction of tin and copper ore by local mine owners to the great metal companies in the district. As it was, she only saw the building, and discovered that it was bigger and newer than the ancient one she went to twice monthly with Dickon Penney.

The afternoon was chilly, and the sun was setting across the harbor, dry in low tide, with large vessels having to anchor three miles out. In a glum mood, they walked back to their hotel, lost in their thoughts, barely speaking. Sophie could not imagine their lives past this minute, not together. She was plagued by flashes of remembrance, poignant, mind scenes of the good times they'd shared, and once in a while she remembered much too well why she had loved him. But they were so very different. Under any other circumstances they would never have chosen each other, certainly never married. They might have been attracted, but common sense or an instinct for emotional survival would have gotten in the way and saved them from making a lifetime commitment.

And yet here they were, striving to stay true to themselves while they struggled not to kill each other with coldness. Was he as horrified as she? And did he harbor the same secret hope that somehow, against logic and all the odds against them, they could find a way to make this marriage work? Since they couldn't talk to each other, there was no way to find out.

They ate dinner in the hotel's private dining room. She was hungry and the meal was good, but as the minutes passed, what little conversation there was became sparser, tighter. She caught him staring at her, and she didn't like the speculation in his eyes. He was waiting for something, and it didn't take her long to realize what it was. Her nerves were in shreds by the end of the meal, but she didn't get up from the table; instead she took minute sips from a glass of watered wine, wondering how she could make it last for infinity. Something in his expression assured her he was aware of, probably amused by, her discomfort. "I have a say in this," she burst out suddenly, apropos of nothing.

"Not much of one," he shot back, understanding her perfectly.

"Because you're my lord and master?"

"Now you're getting the idea."

"In a pig's eye."

They both got up at once, chairs scraping, looking like duelists ready to fire.

"If you would care to discuss this, I suggest we do it out of sight and hearing of everyone in the room," she hissed.

"You took the words out of my mouth."

Later, lying rigid on her side of the invisible but inviolable dividing line down the center of the bed, she feigned sleep by breathing deeply, and entertained depressing philosophical thoughts about Pyrrhic victories. Would it have been so wrong to make love with him? They were married; the damage—although she didn't like to think of their baby as "damage"—was done. What matter that they didn't love each other? Millions of loveless couples engaged in marital relations, and no one thought it was wrong. Was she trying to punish him? Well, yes; she had to admit she was, partly. The other part was some gesture toward delicacy, a reluctance to engage in intimacies with a man who had used and betrayed her. But what good did such sensibilities do in the long run, really? Wouldn't it be better to go through the pretense of a normal marriage and hope that somehow, in time, through habit if nothing else, the pretense would become reality?

Besides, "used and betrayed" didn't ring as true to her as it once had. It had become a cliché from overuse. Seeing Connor, being with him day after day, and now night after night, had started to chip away at the neatness of his image in her mind as a conscienceless seducer. Gradually, unfortunately, she was beginning to see him as a man.

In the morning, she'd have sworn she hadn't slept a wink all night and believed it, except for Connor's insistant voice, "Wake up, Sophie," and the gentle shaking of his hand on her shoulder. She rolled over to look at him. "What time is it?" she mumbled, blinking sleepily.

"Early."

"You're already dressed."

"We're leaving now. Get up and dress while I go out and hire us a carriage."

"Where are we going?"

"We're going home."

"Home?"

His smile was a little grim. "My home. Trewythiel."

\*      \*      \*

Six Pendarvis graves lay in a corner of the sunken, neglected churchyard of St. Dunston's, under the writhing arms of a dead locust tree. Mary and Egdon must be the parents: they were the oldest. There were Jude and Diggory as well, beloved sons, who had died within a year of each other, and a tiny marker for little Ned, "asleep at birth." The newest grave, only a year old, was Catherine's. She was eleven.

Connor had moved away from Sophie, to stand at the opposite side of the mournful heaps and thin granite headstones; otherwise she'd have taken his hand. "How did they die?" she asked softly.

"My father had the miner's consumption," he answered without looking at her. "Jude fell off a rotten ladder at seventy fathoms. Diggory died in an underground flood. My mother . . . she just died. Of grief, we said. But it was a blessing, because she missed having to watch Cathy fade away to nothing. Cathy had a frail heart."

Sophie covered her mouth with her folded hands, stricken. She could feel his pain, and she didn't want to. She didn't want to forgive or understand him, but pity and compassion were undermining her resolve while she stood there. "So," she said. "It's only you and Jack now?"

"Just Jack and me."

And Jack was ill with the disease that had killed his father. She'd have gone to Connor then, put her arms around him and held him whether he wanted it or not—she wanted it—but he dropped to his knees and began to brush dead leaves off the grave nearest him. She hesitated, then knelt on her side and copied him.

They worked in silence, and when they finished cleaning the graves he still didn't speak, only stood for a moment with his head bowed. Then he turned and walked away.

She caught up to him at the edge of what passed for the main street in Trewythiel, a mean little avenue, rutted and full of horse and dog offal, edged with a handful of narrow, leaning cottages. He was staring off to his left, shading his eyes, and she followed his gaze to the last cottage before the lane turned out of sight. "I grew up in that house," he said, pointing to a small, ugly, thatch-roofed building of gray stone. It had no garden, at least in front; the low doorway opened directly onto the street. He looked at her, as if waiting for her to speak. She didn't like the knowing twist of his lips when he saw that she had nothing to say.

An old woman was shuffling toward them in the street, clothed in black and muffled in a shawl, tapping the ground with a stick in front of her tiny steps. Sophie thought she might be blind. She kept her head down and would have passed them by without looking up if Connor hadn't said suddenly, "Mrs. Gregg?"

She halted. "What's that?" She peered up at him, scowling in confusion, not suspicion. "Who is it?"

"It's Connor Pendarvis. Do you remember me?"

"Connor?" She wasn't blind. Her leathery face creased in a sweet, sudden smile. "Little Con. The smart one. Yes, o' course I remember you. You took all my Malcolm had in his head and then went off and left us. Tell me, did it do you any good?"

His quick laugh sounded abashed. "No, not much."

"Hah. Malcolm's gone, you know. Eight years now."

"I know. I was sorry to hear it, Mrs. Gregg."

She nodded. "No one replaced him. They send a curate down from Truro every two Sundays to preach. The rectory's no fit place to live anymore; I've had to move in with my niece."

He murmured something sympathetic. Sophie made a connection and realized who she must be—the widow of the Wesleyan minister Connor had once told her about, the man who had taught him to read and write. The one who had given him a book about a magic boy.

"Did you hear they closed up the mine?"

Connor nodded. "Jack told me."

"Might as well've closed up the village while they were about it. Nothing's left now, not that there was much before. We're all just waiting for each other to die. Who's this?" she asked without a pause, pivoting to face Sophie.

"I beg your pardon—this is my wife."

Sophie took the old woman's dry hand in hers, murmuring that she was happy to meet her.

"Pleased to meet you, too." She sent Connor a stern look. "And you said all that learning didn't do you any good."

"I misspoke," he acknowledged, smiling.

"So what have ee come down here for?" she asked. "To see the graves?" He nodded. "Well, there's naught much else for you, I don't expect. Nobody lives in your house, nobody a'tall. You were right to get out, young Con. You look like a gentleman, and you've married this fine young lady. Now ee'd do well to get out o' Trewythiel and never look back, because it's finished."

She left them after a sudden, brusque leave-taking—so that she wouldn't cry, Sophie suspected—and they watched her small, dark figure hobble down the lane and out of sight. Their mood was somber as they walked back to the carriage they'd left in front of the ancient, crumbling church. Connor handed her in, and they drove slowly out of the village, heading north.

"Let's not go back to Truro," Sophie said out of the blue.

"What?"

"Let's go south, Con. I want to see the coast."

They'd come to the crossroad at the bottom of the village. She couldn't remember the last time she'd seen him smile. "Then that's what we'll do," he said, and turned the horse toward the sea.

They went to Lizard Point, the southernmost tip of the county. Of the country, too, he pointed out with Cornish pride, and she pretended she didn't know that already. The village of Lizard had a tiny inn called Crawler's—named after the proprietor, they were assured, not the migratory mode of the town's namesake. After depositing their luggage in their small room, whose chief asset was a balcony overlooking the Channel, they set out, by mutual consent, for a walk along the cliffs. The clean, fresh wind blowing in from the west felt like a tonic, and Sophie stood on a headland above Kynance Cove and let it whip at her skirts, her hair. She shut her eyes when they teared, and imagined the wind was blowing away all the sorrow and regret inside her, all her unhappiness. If only they could start over. That wish was almost a chant now, she'd had it so often. But trouble didn't go away because you wanted it to, and she was cursed with a long memory.

Still, when Connor took her hand to help her over a fall of rocks in their path, she let him keep it afterward, even though the way was smooth. Anyone passing by would probably mistake them for lovers, she mused. Honeymooners. Not that there were many people about to see them; the tourists who came to look at the colored veins of the serpentine rock or explore the cliff caves were gone now, because summer was over. It was their loss, because out of the wind, on the lee side of a boulder or a crevice in a sunny angle of the cliff, it was as warm as July.

The tide was ebbing. They found a cove sheltered from the wind by a line of black rocks slanting into the sea like crooked teeth, and sat down in the soft, warm sand to look at the waves. Bags of cloud sailed high in a sky the same pigeon's egg blue as the water. Connor lay on his side with his head propped on his hand. His stillness and the faraway look in his eyes dimmed the beauty of the scene for her, because she could feel his melancholy as sharply as if it were hers. She wanted to save him, protect him from it, but she couldn't. Madness to want it anyway. "Tell me about your family," she said, half expecting him to rebuff her.

Instead he smiled. "What do you want to know?"

"What was it like when you were a boy? Were you happy?"

"Sometimes."

"Were your brothers kind to you?"

"Sometimes."

"And your parents?"

"Always."

She felt relieved. "Why were you unhappy? Sometimes."

He sent her a look through his long lashes, assessing her interest. Then he sat up and began to sift sand through his fingers. "Things were expected of me."

"What kinds of things?"

He kept his head down, but she saw his lips quirk. "Great things."

More silence. She sighed. She wasn't going to pull the story out of him word by word; if he wanted to tell her, he could tell her. She wound her arms around her knees and stared out at the white-lipped waves.

"We were poor," he finally resumed. "You've seen Trewythiel—you can imagine what it was like." But he glanced at her briefly, and she knew he was thinking the same thing she was: no, she really couldn't. "Practically everyone in the village worked in the tin mine at Feock, including the women and children. My family was no exception. When the price of ore was high, we lived all right, and when it dropped, we starved."

"Did you work in the mine?"

"No, not me. I told you, I was special. I was the youngest son, the golden one. I went to school, not the mine. And when there wasn't any money for school, Reverend Gregg tutored me for nothing. You met his wife today. His widow."

She nodded. "Did you hate it?" she asked in spite of herself, too interested to keep quiet. "The schooling, not being allowed to do what everyone else did?"

"No. And yes. I loved the reading and studying, but I was also ashamed of it. I tried not to enjoy it, tried to make it a burden. That way I didn't feel as guilty for not doing anything useful to help my family survive."

"What did they want you to be?"

"A gentleman and a scholar." He gave a short laugh. "No, I'm joking, of course. They were deluded, but they weren't insane. What they wanted for me—it was never named, never put in words. But everyone knew I was the hope for the future. I was supposed to find a profession—the law, politics, journalism—that would give me enough power to make things change."

Sophie's eyes went wide. "You were a *communist*," she realized all at once.

This time his laughter was truly amused. "Do you even know what a communist is, Sophie?"

She opened her mouth, then closed it, blushing. She had no idea. "Something very, very bad."

"And how do you know that?"

"You know how." She smiled sheepishly. "My uncle."

His eyes twinkled—he liked her best when she was being honest. She liked herself best that way, too. "Someday we'll have a long talk about communism," he promised. "But for now, just believe me when I tell you it's not my philosophy. I want reform, not revolution."

"All right, I believe you." She watched him lie down, clasping his hands under his head, and close his eyes. "So," she prodded, afraid he was going to sleep. "Go on, finish telling the story. You told my uncle you went to a university. How could you afford it?"

"I was given a scholarship. Not much of one, but then, it wasn't much of a university."

"Where was it? Is it?"

"Was it—it's closed. Manchester. Afterward, there was no money to study at one of the Inns of Court, so that left articling myself to a lawyer for five years, at the end of which I'd be a solicitor, not a barrister. It was disappointing, but I told myself it was the next best thing."

"You wanted to be a barrister?"

"Desperately."

"What happened?"

"After three years, the man I was apprenticed to died." He rubbed his eyes with his hand, momentarily hiding his face. "Right after that, my mother died. She was the last—there was no one left but Cathy."

"And Jack."

"And Jack. But Cathy was sick, and Jack couldn't take care of her and make a living at the same time. So I moved to Truro—"

"Where had you been living?"

"Falmouth. I moved to Truro, because we had an aunt there and she'd said Cathy could stay with her. I began clerking in a law office. The pay was miserable, but it was better than nothing— which was what I'd earned before."

"Nothing!"

"Room and board; that's what apprentice lawyers make. And then . . . then she died. She was eleven years old." He put his forearm over his eyes, and all she could see was his mouth, the lips tight with pain. "That was the worst. Worse than any of the others. Much worse. Because she was so young. Jack and I . . ." He stopped talking, and she didn't urge him to continue this time. She brushed his sleeve, then took her hand away, not certain if he'd felt the touch or not.

She watched the gulls wheel in the blue sky, their cries shrill against the steady sighing of the surf, and she thought of her father, and how his death had devastated her. What must it have been like for Connor to lose loved one after loved one, each as dear to him as her father had been to her? Inconceivable. She could not imagine it.

He sat up.

"If you don't want to talk anymore—"

"No, I want to finish it," he said with his face turned toward the sea. "I owe you my life story. Such as it is."

"Tell me, then."

"I'll make it quick. I was at loose ends, as they say. My clerk's job meant nothing; in fact, it was intolerable. I was wasting my life. Jack had begun to get sick, but he was still working at Carn Barra. He introduced me to some men—reformists, agitators. Communists, for all I know," he said with a skewed smile. "I liked what they stood for—change—but not the way they wanted to accomplish it."

"Violently," she guessed.

"Some of them, yes. Then a man from the Rhadamanthus Society contacted me—"

"Excuse me, but what does that word mean? Why did they call it that?"

"Why, Sophie," he chided, "I thought an educated lady like you would understand the reference." She only cocked a patient eyebrow. "Rhadamanthus was one of the three judges of the dead in the underworld," he explained. "Don't you remember him from your *Aeneid*?"

"No. But how perfect—they named themselves after a mythological figure who sent souls to heaven or to hell, depending on his mood. You don't find that just a trifle arrogant? A trifle overbearing? Just a wee bit—"

"Yes, I do," he snapped. "I did before and I do now, but unlike you, I was broad-minded enough not to hold their name against them before I found out what they stood for."

She dipped her head in mock contrition. "And what do they stand for?"

"Change, the same as the others. Only they were reasonable, pacific, bent on working from the inside, through the government. Shavers is their man. You and your uncle have no use for him, but at least he doesn't advocate burning down the manor house. Or *strikes*," he said deliberately, using the word to traumatize her, she knew.

"Do you still work for them?"

"No. I told you, I disassociated myself from them. The report they published on Guelder was preliminary, and they knew it and printed it anyway."

"But you wrote it," she said coolly. "Preliminary or not, they were your words."

"Not completely."

"No?"

"I gave them facts, and they turned them into an accusation. They changed the tone."

"Ah. A distinction, forgive me for saying so, without a difference."

"Do you think so?"

"I don't know." She looked away. "I don't want to fight with you, Connor. No, I suppose not," she finally conceded. "But it's not the point anyway, is it? It's not . . ."

"It's not what you can't forgive me for."

She stared at him for a loaded moment, wondering if they would talk about it now, the thing he had done. But in the end, she scrambled to her feet, brushing sand from her skirts. "I think I'll go for a walk," she announced, and left him where he was.

She didn't go far; the cove was small, and girded by impassable piles of fallen rock. He watched her bend to take her shoes off, then lift her skirts to dabble stockinged feet in the white-lace edge of the tide. The wind caught at her straw hat and whipped it off her head; she had to let go of her skirts to grab it back. Just then a wave batted at the hem of her frock, drenching it, and he thought he heard the light peal of her laughter as she dashed back, out of reach of the surf.

Her leggy, wild pony beauty startled him sometimes, took him unawares, because she liked to present to the world an altogether different picture of herself—poised, self-possessed, utterly competent. He loved the mix, all her fascinating contradictions, and he found it intensely exciting to think that she was his. His. The pretty girl darting after a tern along the wet shoreline, graceful as a wand—she belonged to him. No matter what happened. For better or worse.

He thought of the things he'd told her about himself, relieved because the whole truth was out at last. His fear that it would distance her from him even further had proven groundless; she'd heard him out calmly and with no visible horror. She knew it all now, there would be no more unpleasant surprises, at least not from his past. As for the future . . . it jolted him to realize he was looking forward to it. Maybe today, because they had finally let go a little of their pride, could mark the real beginning of their marriage. It was as if they'd taken the first step on a long road, not back to where they had been, before everything went to hell, but toward something new and unexplored, and even better. He hoped.

He couldn't keep away from her. He got up and went toward her, plowing through the sand to the water's edge. She was examining a piece of driftwood washed up by the tide, running her hand over the smooth sides. She didn't see him until he was beside her. Then she smiled, and the color of her eyes was the color of the sea, and the wind teased and played with the ends of her golden hair. "Look," she said, showing him her find. "Doesn't it look like a bird?" He said it did, and stuffed his hands in the pockets of his coat to keep from touching her. The water glittered like a blue enamel plate, scored by the long, slow lines of breakers parading in toward shore. Out to sea, the sun was dropping behind thin veins of gaudy cloud, orchid and gold, yellow and salmon pink. There was a bite in the wind; the warmth of the day was fading with the sun. Good: he wanted it to be night.

"Are you hungry?"

She nodded vigorously, widening her eyes at him as if he'd said something quite brilliant, something perfect. She brushed sand from the soles of her feet and slipped on her shoes. Her bonnet strings were knotted under her chin; he helped untie the knot, thinking of the day they'd met, wondering if she was remembering it, too. They walked home holding hands.

Sophie wouldn't stop talking.

She was putting her nightgown on inside the narrow, three-sided partition that served as a dressing room, and under her constant chatter he could hear the sounds of cloth rustling and snaps unsnapping, shoes hitting the floor. And something else: a brush gliding through her hair? The topic of her monologue had finally shifted from the weather to food, and now she was telling him all about the meal they'd just eaten in the restaurant next door, as if he hadn't been there with her. It was the sea air that made one ravenous, she opined; normally she herself was a rather dainty eater, delicate even. But she always made a point of eating fish when she was at the seashore, any kind of seafood, although shellfish were her favorite, particularly prawns and mussels. One ought to eat a lot of fish when visiting seaside places, because of course then it was freshest, but also because it intensified the experience, didn't it, made one feel more—unified with the ocean, the . . . She tapered off into silence, and he could imagine the blush on her face. He had the smile wiped off his own face by the time she appeared, buttoned to the throat in her dressing gown, her pretty hair down and gleaming around her shoulders. She looked relieved to see him already in bed, his mostly naked body decently covered up. "Shall I close the shutters?" she asked, moving uncertainly toward the balcony.

"If you like."

"Are you chilly?"

"No. Are you?"

"No. The wind blows from the west, so we must be facing south. Or perhaps it's the other way around. Anyway, it's not cold. Do you smell flowers? Marvelous how the fuchias bloom the year-round here. Camellias, too. I can't see the moon—I think it might rain."

She ran down again, and finally there was nothing for her to do but come to bed. She sat on the edge with her back to him to take off the robe she'd just put on. He'd pulled the sheet and blanket back for her; she slid in and covered herself up in one smooth, fast movement.

"Don't blow out the lamp."

She turned back from the night table, looking at him inquiringly. "Aren't you sleepy?"

"Not particularly. It's early."

"I'm sleepy all the time."

"And hungry. And not just because of the sea air."

She smiled slightly, and put her hand on her stomach. "No."

He laid his hand over hers. "We never talk about it. The baby. Are you perfectly well, Sophie?"

"Perfectly."

"Good. What is it like? How does it feel?"

"It felt ruddy awful at first," she said feelingly.

"Were you sick?"

"Yes, very."

"I'm sorry." He gave her hand a squeeze.

"But now—I think I've never been healthier in my life. I feel very strong—when I'm not sleeping. Very . . . alive."

"Are you glad?"

"Oh . . .." She sighed. "I can't say. Yes, sometimes. Euphoric, really. Other times . . ."

"Not so glad."

"It's frightening."

"Yes." He moved her hand aside, so he could touch her stomach. "I don't feel anything at all."

"That's because I'm lying down. I can feel a bulge sometimes. I'm starting to get fat."

He laughed. "Let's see." He drew the bedclothes down, and cupped her belly through nothing but her cotton nightgown. "Oh, very fat," he murmured, stroking her with his palm. The quality of the stillness between them changed, became breathless, and he realized he'd been waiting all day for this. "The night we made love," he said quietly. She exhaled slowly, motionless, expectant. "After the first time, I tried not to make a baby with you."

"I know. But . . . I've heard that once is all it takes."

"Sophie." He softened the pressure of his hand, made slow circles over her belly button. "Can I kiss you?"

She looked at him directly, her clear eyes direct and troubled. Last night she'd refused him, but tonight it would be different. "But that isn't all you want from me, Connor. A kiss. Is it?"

"No," he said, because they were through with lies.

"But nothing's changed, not really."

He fingered a bit of lace edging the buttons along the front of her gown, his eyes downcast. "I thought it had. It seemed to me that something had changed today." She didn't answer, and he could feel her indecision and her fear. He walked his fingers up to her throat and undid the top button of her nightgown, soothing his hand over her warming skin. "I don't know what will happen, Sophie, but I think we have to begin sometime." With his fingertips light on her cheek, he passed his thumb over her closed lips, watching them quiver. "We have to come toward each other."

She murmured something he didn't catch, and put the back of her wrist over her eyes. "This would be more than *coming toward* each other."

He smiled in acknowledgment, because she couldn't see him. Words weren't his best friend right now, so he leaned over her, brought his mouth down until their lips were almost touching. She felt his breath, and took her hand away. Her eyes were still cloudy with doubt. She couldn't say yes to him, and yet she didn't want to say no. He touched her with his mouth, the barest brush of lips, stroking softly, back and forth. Her hand lay palm-up on the pillow by her head; she closed her eyes, and closed her fingers into a fist. He could feel her lips softening by slow, sweet degrees.

At the moment he skimmed the closed crease of her lips with his tongue, she broke the kiss and turned her face away. "Connor, I'm sorry. I can't."

He watched her a second, then sank down onto his own pillow.

"Good night," she said softly.

"Night, Sophie."

He heard the sputter of the lamp wick, the rustle of covers. Sophie thumped her pillow and settled on her side. She may have fallen asleep, but he didn't. She'd been right about the rain. He listened to the sea grumble and hiss under a steady downpour for hours.

It stopped after midnight, but the moon stayed invisible behind a heavy, rolling mist. Somewhere out to sea a bell rang, ding-

ding, ding-ding, faint but incessant, warning ships away from the craggy, fog-bound coast. There was nothing to see in the blackness around the wet balcony, nothing at all. Sophie hugged her arms around her waist, shivering, straining to make out a star or a light somewhere in the Channel, but it was as if she was blindfolded. She put one hand on the slick railing, needing the cold wood to steady herself, anchor herself. She shivered again, because the loneliness inside was as deep and bottomless as the black, black night.

Barefooted, she padded silently back to bed. Connor lay on his stomach, one arm flung out across the mattress, his hair a darker blur against the pillow. Slipping under the covers, she touched him by accident—and that brief, warm brush unlocked all her yearning. "Con," she whispered, and he woke up. She came into his surprised arms.

"You're cold," he said.

"Warm me."

They kissed, and she made him lie over her, holding him close with her arms around his bare shoulders. "Sophie—"

"Let's not talk." She shut her eyes tight so she couldn't see him at all, not even his dark outline. She wanted it to be like a dream, she wanted her will taken from her—she wanted her lover to be silent and invisible, unreal.

With her hands and her lips, she enticed him. She was desperate for him, had to have him, but she wanted it over with quickly. He wanted to take deep, slow kisses from her mouth, but she turned her head aside, murmuring, "No," and she pulled her gown up over her legs and her belly, uncovering herself for him. She heard his sharp, helpless gasp when she reached for him, her fumbling, inexperienced hands urging him to hurry.

He moved over her, and she embraced him with her legs, and cried out when he came into her. He went still, whispering to her, filling her. He began to caress her with his mouth, pressing kisses to her throat, taking tender little bites along the line of her jaw.

She didn't want tenderness, she didn't want to be seduced. "Don't," she said, and jerked her hips against him, making him move inside her. She put her mouth on the muscled top of his shoulder and bit down, while her nails scored his back, his buttocks. She set the rhythm herself, fast and hard, purposeful. Losing herself to it, she held him tight, wouldn't let him stop. Time stopped, and she cried out, something wild and incoherent, to tell him the—*flower* inside her was bursting, she could feel its passion-red petals opening and spreading wider, farther. And then it shattered, and she was lost in the blast of red, blinding pleasure.

Afterward she lay still and passive, determinedly empty-headed, not returning Connor's soft, slow caresses. He said her name in a question, but she didn't answer. "What's wrong?" he whispered.

"Nothing's wrong. That was what you wanted, wasn't it?" She covered a pretend-yawn with her hand and turned over onto her side, away from him. "G' night," she murmured.

He didn't answer.

Her body cooled quickly. She pulled the covers closer around her shoulder, drew her legs up, wrapped her night-gown around her ankles. But she couldn't get warm.

# XVII

They settled into a daily routine of sorts, satisfying to neither, but easy and bloodless, noncombative. The crux of it was that she went to the mine and he stayed at home, and at dinner they told each other about their days. That was when the flaw in the arrangement was most evident. If Connor had been enjoying himself, if studying his law books and drafting articles for political journals had truly absorbed his energies and engaged all his talents, then at least in one respect their lives would have been perfect. But he was restless, she could tell, although he tried to hide it, and his restlessness was undermining the surface placidity of their relationship.

"How was your day, dear?" he asked her one night at dinner a week after their return from Cornwall, in that ironic tone he took when he was being deliberately husbandly.

Between bites, she told him about progress in the various seams the men were currently working, the latest rumor at the coinage hall about copper prices, what Jenks had to say about extending the northwest gallery at the thirty level. He made polite noises, and poured himself more wine from the decanter Maris had left on the table. "Tranter Fox paid a call on me in the afternoon," she went on, eager to find a subject that would engage him.

He brightened. "Did he? How is Tranter these days?"

"Much the same. He has a new partner, Martin Burr's brother Thad. Apparently their pit rate is down this month, and Tranter came up to tell me that the reason is because his heart is broken and he's lost all interest in his work."

Connor grinned. "Rascal," he muttered fondly.

"He still calls you Jack. He said, 'If I'd of knowed young Jack were after stealing the gel o' my dreams flat out from under my nose, I'd of nudged 'im off the ladder at eighty fathoms the first day.' "

She didn't know if it was Tranter's quip or her approximation of his Cornish burr, but one or the other made Connor throw back his head and roar with laughter. Happiness bloomed inside her; she chuckled along with him, delighted.

"What do you think he really feels about me now?" he asked after a moment, toying with a piece of haddock on his plate. "He and the others. Do they think I betrayed them?"

"No, I've heard nothing like that."

"But you wouldn't, would you?"

"You'd be surprised at what I hear," she assured him.

"Still, I doubt you'd hear from your workers that they consider your husband a traitor."

"Does it matter so much what they think?"

"It matters to me," he said stiffly. "They were my friends."

"Yes, of course. But truly, I don't believe there's any hostility. Tranter was joking, and he asked after you."

"Tranter's only one."

"Yes, but he has a hundred friends. Everyone's fond of him, and in his own way he's influential. You were his partner. If he's not angry with you, I doubt that anyone else is." Besides, she thought, it wasn't the miners Conner had betrayed: it was the mine owner. But she didn't say that, because she didn't want to fight.

"What about you, Sophie? What's it like for you with Jenks and Andrewson and the others?"

She turned her spoon over and over on the tablecloth. "Really, it hasn't been difficult. They were surprised, of course—"

"Surprised?"

She returned his skeptical smile. "All right, shocked. Astounded. I think," she said slowly, staring at the spoon, "that

Robert Croddy has been true to his word." Croddy was a sore subject they studiously avoided; neither had spoken of him since the day Connor had knocked him down in her uncle's front garden. "If he had—been indiscreet about me to anyone, the truth would have gotten around by now to every man, woman, and child in the district. And so—all Jenks and the others think is that I'm a very fascinating person, full of interesting surprises. They thought they understood me, but now they're reconsidering everything they used to think they knew."

Her light tone didn't work. Connor stared moodily into his wineglass for a full minute, at the end of which he said, "Why did you tell Croddy about the baby, Sophie? What the *hell* were you thinking?"

She had wanted very much to avoid this quarrel, but the question galled her. "What the *hell* else was I supposed to do?" she shot back in a near whisper—there was no telling when Maris might come back in the room. "I didn't even know where you were. *I had no choice.* If you're angry because you think I had feelings for Robert, you couldn't be more deluded. He's *nothing* to me. Marrying him would have been the end of me, Connor. I knew it, but I asked him anyway because I was desperate, and because he'd proposed to me himself a few weeks before."

He swore under his breath. "And the son of a bitch turned you down?"

"Emphatically."

"I should've knocked his head off," he said wonderingly. "I should've *killed* him."

She closed her eyes, tired of it. "No more, Con. Please, can we let it go now?"

"All right." A pause. "I'm sorry. About all of it."

"Let's drop it." She wasn't hungry anymore. They sat in silence until Maris came in with the coffee. "So," she said, to lessen the obvious strain while the maid filled their cups. "How was *your* day—dear?"

He chuckled in spite of himself. "Well, I think I'm making

progress. Mrs. B. still can't stand me, but Maris is softening, I can tell."

"Hmpf," said Maris, trying not to smile.

"Oh, yes, I'm sure of it. This afternoon she brought me biscuits and tea without being asked. And this morning she didn't grumble under her breath about what a mess I'd made of the bathroom. That was a first."

Maris gave in and laughed out loud. "What I'd like to know," she said with her hands on her hips, "is how one extra person in a house can make ten times as much work for the poor help. That's what I'd like to know." Smirking, she set the coffeepot on the table and loped out.

While he was still smiling, Sophie said, "The Michaelmas fair is on Saturday. In Tavistock."

"Do you want to go?"

"Do you?"

"Only if you do."

"Well, I don't care. Not especially."

"Let's not, then."

"All right."

The truth was, they weren't quite ready to expose themselves to the world yet. She would never have said they were in *hiding;* they just needed a little more time to get used to the idea of being a couple themselves before they had to go out and prove it to others.

The mention of Martin Burr reminded her of something she had wanted to say to Connor for weeks. Now seemed as good a time as any. "Do you remember what you said in your report for the Rhadamanthus Society about the ladders at Guelder?"

He looked up, wary. "Yes."

"You said a man fell off the ladder at thirty fathoms and broke both of his legs."

"That's right. Tranter told me. It was his partner."

"Yes. Did he tell you the man was flaming drunk at the time?"

"What?"

The look on his face told her he hadn't known, and she was relieved. "Martin Burr—he was stumbling drunk. After he recovered from his injuries, I fired him."

He sat back in his chair. "No, I didn't know that. I swear it."

"I believe you."

"But . . ."

She knew what he was going to say. "But what?" she prodded. Now *he* was the one who didn't want to start a fight.

"It doesn't really change anything," he said reluctantly. "The system is still antiquated and dangerous."

She heaved a sigh. "I suppose you're right." He looked at her in sharp surprise. "Why don't you come and see me at the mine one of these days?" she wondered in an idle tone.

"Come and see you at the mine? Why?"

"Oh . . . you might find it interesting. And it would get you out of the house."

He came the next day.

She was sitting at her desk, pretending to work, brooding about him, mulling over the life they were leading. Sometimes, in spite of its furtive, unreal character, she found it oddly enjoyable. They were learning one another's peculiar quirks and habits, likes and dislikes. Connor, for example, preferred to shave at night instead of in the morning. That seemed to her extremely strange, although she only had her father to compare him to. He was an early riser, and he liked to take long walks by himself. He talked out loud to Dash when he thought no one was paying attention. He didn't snore, thank goodness. He jerked, though, in his sleep, and once he kicked her in the shin and woke them both up. He was quick in the bathroom, which was a good thing because she was slow. Or so he said. And he couldn't understand what one woman could possibly do with so many clothes, or hats, or shoes. He liked to watch her brush her hair. They both preferred to sleep with the window open, exactly two inches. He preferred riding on horseback to driving the pony cart. He didn't drink too much, or smoke, or dip snuff; in fact, he had no bad habits at all that she could discern. And he loved her house—she knew because he'd said so, straight out. Their house, rather. But it didn't seem like his house to her, not yet. Would it ever?

"You look comfortable."

She started, then smiled. He stood in the doorway, grinning at her, looking very handsome. She took her feet off the open bottom drawer of her desk and stood up. "You came," she said gladly.

"Missed you. Are you busy?"

"No." She came around the desk. "Are you? Can you stay for a little while?"

"As long as you like."

"Oh, I see," she said, pretending dismay. "You only came because you're bored with your article."

"It's true that I'm bored with my article," he conceded. "But I still missed you."

Her heart had begun to beat faster, and it wasn't because of his compliments. "Why don't you go down and see Tranter? He's at the forty, costeaning with Thad in the eastern seam."

He made a face. "I didn't really come to see Tranter."

"No, but—think how surprised he'd be to see you. Why don't you go down? Do you care about those shoes? I can find some boots for you if you like, and a hat."

Now he looked confounded. "But I don't want to see Tranter, at least not in the mine. Sophie, it's you I've come to see."

"Drat," she muttered, torn between shaking him and laughing. "Then I'll just have to go down with you." She was aware of his astonished stare while she slipped off her shoes and stuck her feet into a pair of muddy boots she kept behind the door. "Where's my hat, who took my hat? Oh, there." Underneath her shawl, on the coat tree. She put it on her head, made a rueful face at the ruched hem of her rose-colored gown—why hadn't she worn something dark today, something practical?—and turned Connor around by the arm. "Come on, then. It's a perfect time, the cores are changing; you can watch the old men come up and the new men go down."

"Sophie, what—"

"*Come*. You'll like it, I promise." She pulled him out the door and across the yard to the mine entrance.

She was right: he liked it. And she couldn't have waited another day to show him. All week she'd been trying to think of a way to let him know what she'd done without really telling him, or a scheme by which he could find out for *himself,* with her not even being there. False modesty, of course, mixed with some strange, out-of-character bashfulness. But today, here he was, and she couldn't stand it any longer: the suspense was killing her.

She preceded him down the twenty-foot ladders to forty-four fathoms, where the wonderful new machines began, wondering if he could hear the whir of the engines from here. She hoped not; that would give away the surprise too soon. She wanted to tell him to close his eyes until they got to just the right spot, but that wasn't feasible when one was descending a slippery, steep-sloped ladder. So she just stepped off at the last sollar and waited for him to join her, pretending she was calm, not quivering inside with anticipation.

So far, she'd only had time and money to construct man-machines from forty-four down to sixty fathoms, ninety-six vertical feet of eight-inch square iron rods and twelve-inch platforms in constant motion. Eventually, though, there were plans to erect the moving seesaws throughout the whole mine, down to the deepest level and all the way to the top. It would take time, and in the meanwhile she was breaking up the great distances of the old fifty-foot ladders with levels and winzes, and new platforms for fifteen and twenty-five-foot ladders.

She backed off the sollar to stand with her back to the wall of the level—a good place from which to view the marvel—and watched Connor's face when the truth of what she'd done first came to him. Foolish to care about his reaction this much, as if her very life depended on it. She couldn't help it. And he didn't let her down: his eyes went wide and his mouth curved in a soft, tentative, awe-struck smile that said everything he was thinking and went straight to her heart.

The changing of the cores was exactly the right time to watch the man-machines in action. Such simplicity, such cleverness. A man coming up stepped off a stationary platform onto a moving one at the end of a long rod, which took him up twelve feet in a smooth, jerk-free motion to the next stationary platform. He stepped off, and immediately onto another moving platform—or not; if he chose to rest on the fixed platform, he could, and, unlike the ladder system, no bottleneck of ascending miners collected behind him while he loitered. Descending miners did the same thing, only in reverse. It was fascinating to watch the men passing each other in the shaft, the rods zigzagging with wonderful regularity, one miner stepping off at one end while another stepped on at the other. Sophie hadn't gotten tired of it, and she still came down every few days just to look at the amazing process. Truly, they lived in an age of miracles.

Connor was getting over his speechlessness. "Oh, Sophie," she heard him say over the noise of the pumps and the steam engines. He was reaching for her hand when a gruff voice called out, "Hullo, Jack! Is it you?" In the dim light it was hard to recognize the man on the far side of the shaft, rising in midair to the next platform. Connor called "Hullo" back, waving. "Mooney?"

"No, it's Roy!" the man yelled, and took off his helmet to prove it. "What do you think of our new machine?"

"Wonderful!" Connor had time to call out, before Roy Donne raised his hat in a salute and disappeared from sight.

After that, miner after miner greeted Connor with surprise and apparent gladness, and Sophie couldn't help being amused by the names they called him. "Jack, uh, Con—uh, Mr. Pendarvis," was the commonest construction, and she was "Miss Dee—uh, Pendarvis." Men he had come to know well, mostly the ascending ones coming off the first core, began to congregate in the mouth of the short level in which they were standing, doffing their helmets to her and shaking Connor's hand or clapping him roughly on the back. They loved the man-machine and wanted to tell him so, indirectly thanking him for being responsible for its construction. And they just wanted to look at him. Connor had asked her what the miners felt toward him these days, and now it was clear that the answer wasn't resentment or hostility, it was curiosity. Who was this man who had labored beside them for weeks, authored a fiery exposé on mine conditions, disappeared for a month, and turned up again married to their employer? They didn't distrust him; they just wanted to figure him out.

She left them to it. No one even noticed, including Connor, when she slipped away from the all-male cluster and glided up and away on a smooth, reciprocating arm of the new machine. In her office, she looked at ore samples and tried to make calculations on the big map for a while, then gave up and went to stand at her window, waiting for Connor. It wasn't long before she saw him, breaking away from a group of miners and striding toward the countinghouse, waving and calling greetings across the yard as he came. She thought of hurrying to her desk and pretending she was working—but what was the point? When the door to her office opened and he came in, she turned to face him, smiling tensely.

"Where did you go? I turned around, and you were gone."

She shrugged. "No one was talking to me. My feelings were hurt, so I left."

He laughed, kicking the door shut behind him. "Sophie." He came to her, put his hands on her shoulders, and stared at her in the oddest way. "Why didn't you tell me?"

"I don't know. I didn't want to brag, I suppose. And—" this was the heart of it—"I didn't want you to think you'd won. Because I didn't do it for you, Connor."

"I know that."

"I did it because it was right."

"I know."

"And it made sense from a business standpoint," she said aggressively, sticking her chin out. "It was expensive, but once the whole system is in place, it'll *save* money in worker efficiency. In three years it should pay for itself, and in four it will start adding to the profits. So don't think—"

"Don't think you did it out of the kindness of your heart."

"That's right, because I didn't."

"Such a thing would never occur to you."

"It wouldn't. I'm a businesswoman, not a philanthropist. Don't kiss me," she commanded, dodging his lips. "This is not something I need a reward for, I'm telling you, I'd have done it—"

"Hold still. Shhh." He shut her up with a sweet, smiling kiss, until her prickliness dulled and softened away to nothing. Closing her eyes, she folded him in her arms, surprise and happiness flooding through her. It was the first time they had kissed—outside of the bedroom, not as a prelude to sex—since their estrangement. It meant the world to her.

"I heard what else you did. The new ventilator. The safety committee. The—"

"I'm telling you, Connor, that was—"

"Nothing, I know. Sophie, I'm not taking credit for any of it. I understand that you didn't do these things for me, and I don't in the least feel that I've 'won,' or that you've 'lost' or made any sort of concession. I'm just glad. Is that all right? And I just want to kiss you."

"Oh. Well. Yes, that's all right, I've no objection." And she slipped her fingers into his hair and drew his head down, and their smiles merged, and she said, "Mmm," because it was delicious. How lovely, how seductive to touch one another like this, standing up, both of them fully clothed. It meant they liked each other, didn't it? And she'd missed it so much. "Oh, Con," she sighed. She put her head on his chest, to feel his heart beat. "Con . . ."

Very loud throat-clearing had her jumping back like a startled hare, and her husband swearing under his breath. "I knocked," said an aggrieved-looking Tranter Fox in the doorway. "*Twict.*"

Connor spoke through tightly clenched jaws. "Didn't that tell you something?"

"Yes. It told me t' come on in, on account o' nobody could hear me t' holler out, 'Come in!'"

Sophie turned away to laugh, and smooth her hair, and press her palms to her hot cheeks.

"I heard you was here, *Mister* Pendarvis, and I had t' come and look at you."

"How the hell are you, Tranter?" Connor said, grinning now, his composure restored. They shook hands and smacked each other on the back and shoulders, in that strange way men had of showing affection to each other.

"I'm kilt, I'm ruint. Ee've destroyed me, I'm naught but bones and skin, no heart left inside, and all on account o' you. How could ee do it, Jack? Or whatever yer name is. It ain't only me ee've trampled on, neither. 'Tis the soul o' every man who ever set eyes on our own fair and lovely Miss Deene. Ee're a snake in the grass is what you are, and there'm only one way ee could begin to start makin' amends."

"What might that be?"

Tranter's big, gap-toothed grin looked like a trap about to spring. "Why, stand us all fer drinks at the George, what else?"

Connor gave a guffaw, to Tranter's delight. "I see I've got no choice," he told Sophie, holding out his hands with humorous fatalism. "A man's got to begin his rehabilitation somewhere."

"Oh, indeed, a man's got to rehabli—reha—rebuild 'imself somewheres. Come along, Jack, so's ee can get a early start on't. Come on," he urged, hauling on Connor's arm, "time's wastin'. There'm never a time like the present. Time waits fer no man. A stitch in time—"

"I may be late," Connor threw back at Sophie, half in and half out of the doorway. Ignoring Tranter, he added softly, "Will you wait up for me?"

She nodded slowly, with great conviction, and her reward was his devastating smile.

\* \* \*

Sophie's father's study was a precious dowry. Connor, who didn't take the gift lightly, sat in Tolliver Deene's comfortable old leather chair, behind his broad maple desk with the scarred and ink-stained top, turning a smooth, thick, teakwood fountain pen around and around in his fingers. Sophie had given her father the pen, as well as the matching inkstand, pencil, and blotter, on his fiftieth birthday, a year before his death. Sometimes Connor felt unworthy of the legacy, because Sophie had all but canonized Deene, and he was a hard example to follow; but at other times he felt comfortable among the man's books and other effects, even soothed by them. At all times, he wished he could have met him.

But right now, Connor was bored. It was a Wednesday evening, not very late; after dinner, Sophie had gone off to do her chores, household duties, conferences with Mrs. Bolton, so on and so forth, female things he was shut out of in the natural order. Which was fine with him, but it meant he had to work, too, or at least make some show of being usefully employed. But at times like this, when he'd been cooped up in this pleasant room for hours already, it was especially hard to keep from admitting to himself an embarrassing truth: the work he was engaged in these days bored him to death.

How drearily ironic. At a time in his life when he'd never been more ambitious—and that was saying something—his interest in the law seemed to be drying up. He stared at his law books by the hour, trying to feel the old connection, that calm sense of purpose and anticipation that had stood him in good stead over the bad years, when there had been no money and few prospects and not much hope. And now when there *was* hope, because he was determined to make something of himself so that Sophie could be proud of him, his professional future looked like a great black yawning hole. She was unknowingly a more potent influence on him than his family had ever been, and still he couldn't bring himself to care about torts and pleadings, common law versus statute law, demurrers and writs of certiorari. Of course he would study them anyway, and tell himself he was a lucky man to have the luxury to do it. But this new disinterest frightened him. He hid from it, called it a phase, scolded himself for thinking of it at all—when had he gotten so spoiled? But the dissatisfaction wouldn't go away; it lurked like a winter chill in the back of his mind, persistent and cold, and profoundly unwelcome.

Well, life wasn't perfect, and for now, the professional part of his was the imperfect part. The rest . . . he pushed the chair back and stuck his legs over the corner of the desk, folding his hands over his belt, sighing. The rest—was perfect. Or, if not altogether perfect, as close to it as he'd ever thought he would come. It had started the day he'd seen the improvements Sophie had made in the mine. It embarrassed her to talk about it, and he'd had to rein in his surprise and gratitude, but in his heart he had been deeply moved. After that, everything had changed, and finally it was possible to remember why they had fallen in love. The relief was . . . extraordinary.

The difference was the most striking when they were in bed. Sex had become joyful again. They'd added laughter to their lovemaking, and inventiveness, and the most exquisite tenderness. Sometimes Sophie cried afterward, and he never needed to ask why; if weeping weren't an unmanly thing to do, he might have joined her. Neither of them could *speak* of love yet, and there were still reminders of the bitter past littering the path they were treading. But at least they were treading it side by side, and at last they had the same destination.

The baby was bringing them closer, too. They spent hours, usually in bed, thinking up names for it. If it was a boy, Sophie wanted to name him after her father, but Connor didn't care much for the name Tolliver. "We could call him Tolly," she offered, but he pointed out that that wouldn't serve the child very well past the age of ten or so. "Well, it's better than Egdon," she retorted, and of course he had no argument; his father's name was even worse than her father's. If it was a girl, things would be simpler—they could call her Mary after his mother, or Martha after hers—but they weren't really happy with those names, either. They started making lists, and the longer into the night the discussion went, the sillier the suggestions got. Sometimes they worried that Mrs. Bolton, all the way down in the basement, would hear their whoops of laughter and wonder what in the world they were up to now.

"Connor?"

There she was, his beautiful wife, poking her head in the study doorway. The perfect distraction. He took off his glasses, grinning at her with pleasure and relief. "Come in, Sophie, I was just—"

"You have a visitor," she said in her company voice, interrupting him before he could say something personal.

He took his feet off the desk. "I do?"

She widened the door, and he saw who was behind her. "It's Mr. Braithwaite."

"Ian," he exclaimed, jumping up. They shook hands. "This is a surprise," Connor said, adding truthfully, "I'm very glad to see you."

Braithwaite had a shy smile that lit up his thin, studious face. "Sorry to pop in on you at night, and with no notice. I found myself in the neighborhood," he said, coughing behind his hand, "and wondered if we might have a bit of a chat. But I can come again if I've chosen a bad time."

"No, not at all. You've met Sophie, have you?"

"Indeed, I've had that pleasure."

"Ian's a friend of mine," Connor explained, choosing "friend" for lack of a better word, to a politely smiling Sophie. Actually he was more of a business associate, although he wasn't quite that either. In truth, Connor wasn't sure what Ian was. He'd only met him once, the night he and his friend Thacker had stood him to a meal in Exeter.

"Would you care for something to drink, Mr. Braithwaite?" Sophie inquired. "Coffee, or a glass of wine?"

"No, nothing, thanks, I've just had dinner." He waited, and it took Sophie all of half a second to interpret his expectancy.

"Then I'll leave you two to your chat," she said smoothly, backing out of the room. Connor saw the curiosity behind the social facade, but only because he knew her so well. Before the door closed, he tried to convey a message himself—*I haven't the slightest idea*—by raising his eyebrows at her. Those were the kinds of subtleties that tested a couple's true intimacy, he mused to himself before she disappeared. Marriage certainly was a wonderful institution.

He drew up another chair in front of his desk and gestured for Ian to take the one beside it. "How about some cognac? I've got a bottle in my desk."

"That sounds fine," he said readily, confirming Connor's hunch—that Braithwaite had declined Sophie's offer of refreshments so that she would go away sooner. His curiosity mounted. He poured two glasses of brandy and handed one to his visitor, who toasted him and said, "Cheers." Then he got down to business. "I wasn't just in the neighborhood, of course."

"No?"

He adjusted his silver-rimmed spectacles, crossed one long, thin leg over the other. "I came up from Plymouth specifically to speak to you. Thacker would've come with me, but his wife's having a baby. Right about . . . now," he estimated after a glance at his pocket watch. He looked around at the comfortable study, the bookshelves and the warm wood paneling, the photographs on the wall. "We heard about your marriage to Miss Deene," he mentioned casually. "Congratulations—your wife is very charming."

"Thanks. Who's 'we'?"

"I meant the party organization."

Connor frowned at him, at a loss to understand what he was driving at. What did his marriage have to do with Braithwaite's Whig cronies in Plymouth? Jack always said he was too prickly, too quick to take offense when none was intended; but Connor couldn't help thinking that Braithwaite had to be comparing Sophie's house with the mean little room in Exeter where they'd first met, and if so, he must also be speculating that Connor had done pretty well for himself. The implication put his back up. He liked Ian, though, so he hid his temper and kept the suspicion out of his voice when he asked directly, "Was there something in particular you came to tell me?"

"No, something in particular I came to *ask* you." He coughed again, a nervous habit, and fixed his intelligent brown eyes on Connor's face. "I've been authorized to inquire on behalf of the party constituency organization if you have any interest in standing for Clive Knowlton's seat at the by-election."

For ten full seconds, Connor couldn't do anything but blink. All the individual words made sense, but the sentence wouldn't gel; it sounded like gibberish. He tried a laugh, expecting Braithwaite to join in, but he just blinked back, like an owl, behind his spectacles. "Clive Knowlton's seat?" Connor finally got out. "The Tavistock borough? The House of Commons?"

"That's it."

"But—what by-election? Knowlton's leaving?"

"Yes."

"Why? He's been in forever."

"Precisely. He lost his wife last year, and it seems to have taken the fire out of him. He says he wants to study for the Anglican ministry. I'm telling you this in confidence, of course. The party knows, but Knowlton doesn't want to announce his retirement publicly for a few more weeks. Not until Parliament reconvenes in November, you know."

He was speechless again, his mind in turmoil. He kept staring at Braithwaite, trying to see him as a trickster, a practical joker, but it wasn't possible. He was earnest, serious—he parted his hair in the middle.

"As a matter of fact, the conservative branch of the party association is already fronting a man for the seat," he was saying. "You may know him—Robert Croddy."

Stranger and stranger. "I know Croddy."

"Yes. Well, then you can probably understand why we're looking about for someone else."

Connor grunted. "But—why me?"

"The party likes you. From your writing and from our discussions in Exeter, we think you're on our side of the issues. Like you, we favor the manhood suffrage, vote by ballot, annually elected Parliaments, as well as gradual reform—*gradual* reform, that is—of working conditions for the lower class."

Connor had to stand up. "But I'm new here," he protested weakly, going behind his desk for another drink. "I'm not known."

"On the contrary, you're extremely well-known."

"But what I'm known for—is it helpful?"

"We think so. The district's been sleeping. It's long overdue for reform, and men are starting to wake up to that. Knowlton's like an aging father, well liked and respected but not strong anymore, no longer innovative. Even he knows it. Now, you, you have a few handicaps to overcome, but we think you're closer to Knowlton's philosophy than Croddy. Croddy calls himself a Whig, but he isn't—he's an opportunist. He'd call himself a Papist if he thought it would get him elected." His mouth curled under his soft brown mustache, giving away his dislike. If nothing else, thought Connor, they had contempt for Robert Croddy in common. "The fight won't be for the election," he went on, "it'll be for Knowlton's endorsement. It's a safe seat, in other words; the Whigs have owned it for the last half century. In this case, selection means election."

"So whoever Knowlton chooses to succeed him . . ."

"Will probably be the new Member. Croddy's a natural ingratiator, and he's had a head start. He's also got a strong organization behind him."

"And I don't."

"Not yet," Braithwaite said cheerfully. "But these are very early days, and since Knowlton's abdication is still officially a secret, there's not that much Croddy can be doing. So," he said, standing up, too. "The question I'm to put to you is this: Are you interested?"

Maybe he was still in shock, maybe it was the reckless streak in his character, maybe it was the deep-down sense of alignment, of everything fitting together smoothly and perfectly for the first time in his life. Or maybe he was simply out of his mind. In any case, Connor said, "Yes, I'm interested," without thought and without hesitation. But as soon as he said it, his knees felt weak and he had to slug down the rest of his brandy.

Ian laughed. "Good. That's what I was hoping you'd say."

"You mean it's done? That's it?"

"Ah, well. No, not exactly. I'm the party agent, but there are still a few others who'll want to look you over before we make our decision once and for all. Quite a few others, actually. I'll try to make it as painless as possible—dinner meetings, you know, so you don't feel so much like a schoolboy at an examination."

Connor streaked his hand through his hair, nervous already. "I can't get used to this," he said frankly—something in Braithwaite's forthright manner encouraged frankness. "And for the life of me, I can't think why you've chosen me."

"Can't you? Perhaps you underestimate yourself."

He shrugged, but in truth he didn't think that was it. If anything, he'd underestimated Ian's branch of the Whig party, by writing them off as too conservative for him.

"I'm not saying you won't have your work cut out for you, Connor. But the war in the Crimea is over, this business with China is nothing but a skirmish, the Indian mutiny is petering out—it's a peaceful time, relatively speaking. Reform is in the air, and the constituency is in the mood for change. And you," he finished, eyes twinkling, "would certainly be a change."

"Drink to that," he muttered—and he would have, but there was no more brandy. Besides, he didn't want Ian to think he had a drinking problem.

"I hope you don't mind my telling you that your recent marriage made you more attractive to us as a candidate," Braithwaite said, reaching for the hat he'd set on the desk. "It's added a certain, how shall I say, cachet of respectability. And it will serve you well with Knowlton, who's conservatism itself when it comes to matters of personal conduct. By the way, your wife receives above three hundred pounds annually from her property, doesn't she?"

"I beg your pardon?"

"It's the property qualification—something else we're in favor of abolishing, by the way. A man standing for the Commons must, either by himself or through his spouse, earn three hundred a year from his property. You meet that standard, we're assuming."

"I couldn't say," Connor answered stiffly. "I'm newly married; I haven't the least idea how much money my wife has."

"Really? Well, find out, will you? Ways can be got around the qualification, but we'll need to know early on. Well, I must be off." He put out his hand to shake. "I'm glad it's turned out this way. Awfully exciting, isn't it?"

"Yes," Connor agreed, feeling overcome again. "Do you have to go? Stay and speak to Sophie—stay the night. It's late—"

"No, can't, I'm riding back to Plymouth tonight, in fact. There's much to do, as I'm sure you can appreciate. So I'll be off, thanks all the same. And you'll be hearing from me again in the very near future, probably only a day or two. In fact, if all goes well, you'll be spending so much time with me, you'll groan when you see me coming."

Connor showed him out, watched him trot off on the back of a chestnut hackney mare. Then he went to find his wife.

She wasn't upstairs in their room. He clattered back down, calling her. Not in any of the downstairs rooms, including the little sewing nook off the sunporch. Oh—of course. He knew exactly where she was, and mentally smacked his forehead for not going there first. The kitchen.

Correct. He found her sitting at the table, reading a book by the light of two candles. And eating. This time it was potatoes left over from dinner, cold, mashed, and liberally sprinkled with pepper. Last night he'd found her here eating asparagus spears with her fingers, and pieces of a cold beef pudding. Amazing.

She blushed a little. "Huh," she said for a greeting, her mouth full, wiping her fingers on her apron. She swallowed, and daintily touched her lips with the dishrag. "Hungry? There's plenty." She started to get up. "I'll—"

He pressed her back down with his hands on her shoulders, and then he kissed her. She looked so pretty then, her smile so pleased and surprised, he had to kiss her again. "Sophie, the most remarkable thing has happened."

"What?"

He sat down in the chair beside hers. "That man, Braithwaite, he's an agent for the Whig party association in Plymouth."

"Robert's organization?"

"No, they're in Devonport," he said, laughing. "That's the re-actionary branch."

She laughed with him. "I think they prefer the term 'conser-vative.'"

"If the shoe fits." He took a deep breath. "Good thing you're sitting down. In your condition, you might faint when you hear this."

"What?" she cried, mystified.

"Braithwaite and his men are thinking of me for Knowlton's seat at the by-election."

She was floored. "Knowlton's seat? In the Commons?"

"Yes."

"For Tavistock?"

"Yes."

"The seat Robert wants?"

"Yes." So she knew about that. It irked him, but he wasn't going to let Croddy spoil this moment.

"But—that's impossible! I can't believe it!"

He wasn't going to take her incredulity as an insult either. He was only just getting used to the idea himself, after all. "It may not happen. The constituency party association wants to meet me—look me over, see if I spit on the floor, you know, or have three eyes."

"But I don't understand! Why would they choose you?"

"Well, thanks, darling." He felt the edge in his smile and tried to make it more natural. "Your confidence in me is an inspiration."

"I'm not joking, Connor."

"I'm not either."

She bowed her head, contrite. "I mean, how do they think you can win? You're not known in the district."

"Braithwaite says I am."

"But that's . . ."

"Infamy rather than fame? Apparently I'm not held in quite as much ill repute as you think I should be."

"I didn't mean that. I'm surprised, that's all."

"Don't you think I'd make a good MP?"

She narrowed her eyes. He's asked the question in jest, but she was considering it in earnest. "I don't know," she said slowly. "I don't think patience is your best virtue, and so you might find it frustrating. And . . . I'm not sure I can see you making compromises."

He stood up, uncomfortable with her unsolicited candor. "Well," he said brusquely, "it probably won't happen. Braithwaite's probably a raving lunatic—he must be, to have thought of me in the first place. And as you've had the goodness to point out, no one's ever heard of me anyway. Perhaps the whole thing is a joke of your friend Croddy's."

"You're angry."

"Not in the least. I value your realism, darling. Where would I be without you?"

"Connor—"

"How much money do you have, Sophie?"

"How—I beg your pardon?"

"Ha, that's exactly what I said. Ian wants to know. You have to make more than three hundred a year or I can't stand for the seat. Guelder pulls that much down in a year, doesn't it?"

She pushed her chair back, got to her feet slowly, never taking her eyes off him. "You met him before, didn't you? You knew him."

"Ian? Yes, we met in Exeter. He and another chap took me out to a meal. Talked politics."

"Talked politics." He eyes glittered. She turned her back on him. Now *she* was upset, and he couldn't fathom why. "What would have happened," she said tightly, "if you hadn't married me?"

"What?"

"What would have happened to your political ambitions if you hadn't married a woman with three hundred pounds a year?"

He reached for her arm, forcing her to face him. "What the hell are you talking about? I didn't have any political ambitions until half an hour ago!"

"Didn't you? Or was it in the back of your mind all along? Come, tell me the truth—you've got me now, what difference does it make?"

He was too angry to speak.

"I'm not saying that's the only reason you married me," she said wearily, reasonably, as if she were making a great concession. "But come, admit it—wasn't the pill a little easier to swallow when you realized you could make an honest woman out of me and meet the property requirement at the same time?"

"Damn you." If she had spat on him, she couldn't have offended him more, and if she'd stabbed him he would have felt less pain. "Damn you, Sophie," he whispered, and walked out.

# XVIII

They stalked around each other for days. Not speaking made them feel childish, so they said the necessary things and no more—"I'm going out now," "Pass the salt, please," "Good night." In a way, it was worse than the hostility with which they'd begun their marriage, because they'd had an interlude of peace, and this time they knew what they were missing. But neither was capable of breaking through the barrier of hurt pride and new distrust. They were too angry.

Sophie went to the mine early every day and stayed late, even though her constant presence wasn't necessary. She did it to avoid Connor in the house. At night, they didn't go so far as to sleep in separate rooms, but they were careful always to retire at different hours, so that one was either asleep or pretending to be when the other came to bed. That way they didn't have to talk at all, and the possibility of making love, already remote, was eliminated entirely.

Connor had his first meeting with Ian Braithwaite's political associates, and it went well. Extremely well; he was bursting with relief and excitement when the evening was over—but there was no one to share his triumph with. It was a dinner meeting in Plymouth at George Thacker's home, and three other men from the party association. Where was Mrs. Pendarvis, they all wanted to know, and he lied and said she was ill with a cold and not allowed out of the house. Well, they looked forward to meeting her next time, they said, and he felt exultant because there was going to be a next time, and chagrined because Sophie probably wouldn't be there again. Not the way things were going. It wasn't that she'd refused to come. In fact, he hadn't even asked her. Would've cut out his tongue before asking her. If she really believed he'd married her for her frigging three hundred pounds a year, she could rot at home forever for all he cared, and he'd take his political chances without her.

An end to the war, or at least a truce between battles, came from an unexpected source: a letter from Jack. Connor put off speaking to her about it for as long as he could, repelled by the thought of the subject he would have to raise with her—money. But that night he couldn't postpone it any longer; he went up to their room, where she'd retired a little earlier, and confronted her.

"I need ten pounds right away. And tomorrow I'm going to Exeter."

She was sitting at her dressing table, taking off her jewelry, unpinning her hair. She turned around slowly, hairbrush in midair, and stared at him. "Why?"

"Do I have to clear all my expenses with you? Maybe it would be easier if you gave me an allowance. Weekly or monthly, at your convenience."

"I meant," she said coldly, "why are you going to Exeter? All the money's yours now; you hardly need to ask me for it."

He made an effort to be reasonable, rein in his temper. He'd goaded her into this skirmish, even he could see that. He sat down on the end of the bed, smoothing his hand up and down the tall post. Sophie swung back to the mirror huffily and scowled at her reflection. She was still lovely, though. In fact, she never looked more beautiful to him than at times like this, preparing for bed, brushing her hair at her mother's old dressing table. He pressed his temple to the hard wood of the bedpost, swamped with a sudden longing. These moments came and went, he'd discovered; there was nothing to do but wait them out. "I have to go to Exeter to see my brother. The money's for him. He's fallen ill and can't take care of himself."

She turned again to face him. "Bring him here."

"What?"

"You can't take proper care of him in Exeter. Bring him here. He can have my old room. Maris is here in the day, and Mrs. Bolton at night. And you, and me—with four of us tending him, it won't be difficult."

He got up from the bed. He wanted to say something, but all the words he thought of sounded trite and inadequate.

"Is it his lungs again? His consumption?"

He nodded.

"Dr. Hesselius has experience with tubercular diseases. There's a clinic in Somerset, I've forgotten where—Bath, I think. He went there for a few weeks last year for a course of study of some sort, I can't remember the details. At any rate, he knows something about consumptive lung diseases. You wouldn't be bringing your brother into—a medical wilderness, in other words. Well?" she said when he still didn't speak.

"I'll do it. I'll go tomorrow and bring him home." He went toward her. "Sophie."

"Yes?"

"Thank you."

She looked down, started playing with the brush in her lap. "It's nothing."

"No, it's far from nothing." It was like crossing a battle line and walking, unarmed, into the enemy's camp when he put out his hand and brushed his fingers against her cheek. Her eyelashes fluttered. He saw the loneliness and yearning in her still face, and it gave him the courage to tell her the truth. "Sophie, I miss you."

She said, "I hate it when we fight," and he took her hands and pulled her up, into his arms. When they pulled away to look at each other, she blurted out, "I'm sorry for what I said. I don't think you married me for the money, and it was cruel and stupid of me to accuse you."

"Never mind, it's over."

"I don't know why I did it! All of a sudden I was just so *angry*.

And afterward, even when I knew I'd been wrong, I couldn't tell you, couldn't apologize. Because you were so angry with *me*, and that just—fueled the fire. Oh, Con, let's not keep doing this. It's awful, and I can't stand it."

"We'll make a rule," he said, squeezing her hands between his. "When we make each other mad, we're only allowed to sulk like pouty children for twenty-four hours. One day. After that, like it or not, we have to talk. Or shout, or throw plates at each other—anything, but no more silence."

Her radiant smile blinded him. "I love that rule. Especially the plate throwing. I can hardly *wait* for our next quarrel."

Their laughter was as therapeutic as the kisses they lavished on each other, and the soft, reassuring touches. They drifted to the bed and sank down, never letting go. She smelled like the lavender water she bathed in, and he put his face in her hair, filled his hands with it, murmuring to her that he'd missed her, that he wanted her. "But we should talk," she argued halfheartedly, while her hands went inside his shirt and stroked him, making his skin tingle. "About Jack."

"No, later." He kissed her bare shoulder, sliding her dressing gown down her arms, thinking what a miracle it was to be touching his wife again. She sat with a rapt, passive smile, and let him run his hands over her arms and her stomach, her thighs, and when he caressed her breasts she put her head back and sighed.

"We should talk about the seat," she tried next while he kissed her long, soft neck.

"The seat?" he repeated blankly.

"Knowlton's seat. I want you to win."

"Thank you, darling," he said, laughing, making her stand up so he could get her out of her nightgown. "But let's talk politics later, hmm?"

She stood in front of him, naked and eager. "All right," she said, helping him with his shirt buttons, "but I wanted you to know. That I'd vote for you if I could." They came together and fell back on the bed, rolling and turning in a tangle of ardent arms and legs. Sophie landed on top and covered his face with kisses, whispering, "Missed you," between each one. "We'll never fight again, never for the rest of our lives."

"Never," he promised, and he saw the wry, rueful knowledge in her eyes that they were both lying. She kissed his palms, then laid them on her breasts. "So pretty," he murmured, meaning everything about her, but especially her face when he gave her pleasure like this. She was smiling through half-closed eyes, her head tilted to the side, golden hair falling down her shoulder. She made soft humming sounds, and quick little gasps, and when she licked her lips he said, "Come down here," because he had to kiss her.

While they kissed she squirmed on him, kneeing his thighs apart, rubbing her stomach against his. She had his wrists over his head; he pulled one hand free to stroke her long back and her cool, silky bottom. She was playing with his hair, pulling it up and out, arranging it on the pillow to her liking. The result made her laugh out loud, and he laughed with her, not caring at all how silly he looked.

They rolled again, changing places. He lifted her with an arm under her waist, and came into her on a strong, smooth glide. "Con," she breathed, welcoming him, holding his face in her hands. She couldn't say it, but he knew that she loved him—the truth was as plain in her face as smooth pebbles through the clear water of a stream. He took her gently. "We're both inside you, Sophie," he whispered against her lips. "The baby and me, both of us inside you now." That made her cry, and he kissed the tears away with all the tenderness in him.

They rolled to their sides, the better to touch each other. He pulled her knee up and clamped it to his side, pumping into her steadily until she arched her back, moaning. They kissed, and then he broke away so he could watch her come undone. She made that sound he loved, low and desperate, indescribable, and bit her lips into her mouth. With her eyes shut tight, she savored it, keening softly, opening and closing her hands on his chest, and her intense pleasure lit the fuse to his. He drew her closer, tightening his arms around her. "God, Sophie," he gritted out before the storm took him, tossing him like a twig into the wild, swirling place where there was nothing but sensation. He felt her arms around his shoulders, heard her panting gasps, the echo of his. It was too much, he couldn't bear any more—and in that instant the release came, like clashing thunder and blinding light, and the blessed, drenching downpour. In the aftermath he lay still, wrecked on the shore, drowned in her arms. A happy dead man.

They rested. The candles guttered; the moon rose. The room grew cold, and they got under the covers.

"We're too much alike," Sophie sighed, snuggling against him. "That's our problem, Con. We're too much alike."

"A blessing and a curse." He lowered his head and took a lazy swipe of her nipple, just because it was there, with his tongue.

Her surprised squeal turned into an interested hum. "We have the same temper. The same pride. Exactly the same things make us angry." She had her nose in his hair, nuzzling him. "And we're both snobs, but in reverse."

He was listening, but the shapes and puckers her little peak made against his lips had part of his attention, too. "Sometimes you do the stupidest things," she said tenderly, "and they make me furious. But then I think, 'But that's just what I'd have done,' and the anger drifts away. Sometimes."

"Sometimes." He traced a light path from her breast to her navel, and tickled her there until she laughed. The intimacy and the sweetness of this moment made him bold. He said, "I think you love me, Sophie." Before she could agree or disagree, he added, "But I don't think you always approve of me. And I want that. Need that."

"Con . . ."

"Don't say anything, sweetheart. I just wanted to tell you."

"I feel the same," she whispered, shy, stroking his temple over and over. "I know I'm not the sort of woman you'd have married if you'd had a choice. No, I'm not," she insisted when he tried to interrupt. "You'd have chosen someone smarter—"

"Impossible."

"—and more liberal. A socialist, probably."

"Hm, I've never met a lady socialist. It wouldn't have been easy."

"I'm serious, Connor."

"Maybe Karl Marx has a sister."

"Someone with a social conscience. An altruist, a—philanthropist." He had his fingers twined in her private hair, and he was drumming them softly against her most sensitive places. This was a fun conversation, but the drowned man was reviving. "I'm trying to make you respect me," she said in a high voice, locking her thighs around his wrist, "but I can't—change everything about myself, I—"

"I don't want you to change. Nothing."

"You do, though."

"No, I don't." Ever so slowly, he slipped his longest finger inside her. "You're perfect. Look at you. You're the one I'd have chosen, no matter what. Our baby's twice a blessing, because without it we would never have known. We'd have both been too stupid to see."

"Yes," she agreed on a breathy inhale. The drowned man's liveliest part pulsed against her thigh, and she reached for it, blind. "Let's make love again," she suggested, as if the idea had originated with her.

"We could," he ventured, as if he were considering it.

She had more energy: she rolled on top, and they came together again. This time it was different, slower, sweeter. Dreamier. She moved over him like water, fluid and warm, her voice a quiet murmur of love words and soft inducements. He took his hands over her body, searching out the places she liked. Boundaries faded, became insignificant. Her skin, his skin, it was all one, and he didn't care so much now about the ending. He just wanted her close.

But then it changed. She went from water to fire, a radiant flame flickering hot over him, teasing him with the promise of immolation. He caught her fire through his hands, burning on her, and the blaze spread fast, fanned by her quickening breath and the passion in her voice when she sighed his name. They kissed for the last time, and then the fire consumed them, both together, burning up space, time, self, everything. He had a vision: he saw a Roman candle and it was his own body, and Sophie was the dark night all around, and the candle was shooting bright, blinding flashes of fire into the night. He began to laugh before it was over, because it was so grandiose, so marvelous. "Did you see it?" he wanted to know, holding her limp, damp body, blowing strands of her hair out of his face. "Did you see the fire, Sophie?"

He could feel her lips move on his throat in an exhausted smile. "The fire? Mmm."

"No, but did you see it at the end? Fireworks. Pyrotechnics. I was a firecracker and you . . ." It was hard to explain.

"I was the match. No, I was a firecracker, too. I was a Catherine wheel."

He liked that. He laughed again, and she humored him, moving to his side and pulling the covers up, throwing her arm across his middle. He felt like talking, but she was yawning, burrowing against him, her body heavy with fatigue. He held her elbow, stroking his thumb across the soft, soft skin of her inner arm. He put a kiss on top of her head, and she mumbled something sweet and unintelligible. "Sophie," he whispered. No answer. "I love you, Sophie." Her lashes fluttered, but otherwise she didn't move. She'd fallen asleep.

"I'll take it in, Maris," Sophie said, and the maid handed over the covered tray she'd just brought upstairs from the kitchen.

"How is he this morning?" Maris spoke softly out of deference to the invalid, whose door was ajar.

"The same, I think. The doctor's coming in a few minutes."

"I thought he looked better yesterday. Not quite so mooly." It was a Cornish expression Maris had picked up from Jack himself; it meant sickly, as near as Sophie could tell. Peaked.

"Connor says he didn't sleep well, though. And he couldn't eat his supper last night."

The women shook their heads at one another, before Sophie left Maris in the hall and took Jack's tray into his room.

Connor was with him. He'd helped him bathe earlier, and now he was settling him in the bed, plumping the pillows and smoothing the sheets over his scrawny chest. It still seemed strange to Sophie, even after almost a week, to come into her old room and find a man in the bed. She'd removed the most assertively feminine paraphernalia, but it was still a woman's room, *her* room, and Jack would forever look out of place among the chintz-covered chairs and ruffled bed curtains.

He saw her over Connor's shoulder and sent her a welcoming smile—which broke her heart, as all his smiles did, because the awful gauntness of his face made the baring of his white teeth look skeletal. Some people called Jack's disease "decline," and the aptness of the name struck her with cruel force on the day he'd arrived at her house. The coach ride from Exeter had exhausted him; Connor had needed Thomas's help to carry him up the stairs and into his sickroom. He could barely speak—the infection had spread to his larynx—and convulsive coughing had wearied him to the point of collapse. He'd been thin when she'd first seen him last June, but the intervening five months had taken a devastating toll. When he slept, his emaciation and the grayness of his complexion made him look like a corpse.

"Good morning," she said brightly, setting the tray on the bedside table. "And a fine one it is. The sun's trying to come out, and the wind isn't nearly as damp as it was yesterday." She flushed slightly. What a foolish way to characterize this dreary day, whose only real virtue was that it wasn't raining. Dryness and sunshine were the cures for what ailed Jack, but they were in short supply in a Devonshire autumn. She had a cold herself, and hadn't gone to the mine yesterday because of the chilly, daylong drizzle.

"Morning," Jack answered in a hoarse croak, defying doctor's orders by speaking at all; he was supposed to be resting his damaged lungs. "What vile brew 'ave the witch stirred up fer me today?"

"Shhh," Sophie and Connor said automatically, in unison. "I swear I'm going to gag you," Connor threatened, "if you don't hold your damned tongue. I never *knew* a man to blather on like you do, Jack."

"It's porridge," Sophie said quickly, before an argument could start. "And a nice cup of beef juice." Might as well confess it all. "And a raw egg."

Jack made a choking sound, and would have added a lot more to it if Connor hadn't silenced him with a warning glare. Sophie could only sympathize with the invalid, whose sickroom diet ranged from unappetizing to disgusting. He even had to swallow cod liver oil three times a day for his digestion. He called Mrs. Bolton "the witch," although she was only following Dr. Hesselius's instructions.

Connor put the tray on his brother's lap. "Do I have to feed you?"

Jack made a surly face and picked up his spoon. Sophie might have felt sorry for him, except that yesterday she'd caught him feeding his lunch of fresh herring to Dash—who had become, not coincidentally, his constant companion.

Connor slipped his arm around her and gave her a good morning kiss on the cheek. They made idle conversation, trying not to look too much like wardens while they stood over Jack's bed, monitoring his progress with his breakfast. "Is the oatmeal still hot?" Sophie wondered. "Mrs. B. put a little sugar on it, hoping that would taste good to you. Do you like the beef juice warm or cold? Or warm in the morning and cold in the afternoon."

Too soon, Jack lay back on his pillow and closed his eyes. They had learned not to cajole him after a certain point; if he ate more than he could tolerate, he simply vomited it up, and felt worse than ever afterward. At least he'd gotten his raw egg down, Sophie noted, setting the tray aside.

She heard heavy, measured footsteps coming up the stairs. "There's the doctor," she guessed, and Jack gave a comical groan and rolled his eyes.

As usual, Dr. Hesselius looked tired. He had a busy practice and a young, flirty wife, and between them they seemed to be wearing him down. But his manner was calm and unfailingly kind, and he listened more than he talked, a singular trait that made him popular with his patients.

"How are you, Jack?" he asked in a voice that was neither perky nor funereal, only caring.

"He's not sleeping, barely eating, and he talks too much," Connor answered testily. But Sophie wasn't fooled. Her husband had a habit of absentmindedly rubbing his chest when he was with his brother, or away from him but worrying about him, and she'd come to believe it was because his heart hurt.

She touched his arm. "I'll be across the hall," she said quietly, excusing herself so the doctor could examine Jack in private. Connor squeezed her hand and let her go.

She went to wait in her old nursery instead of the bedroom. Her pregnancy was still a secret, so she hadn't been able to do much in preparation for the baby's arrival. The wait was killing her. She had such plans! She wanted new wallpaper, and new paint on the woodwork—bright yellow; Honoria would die—and flowered curtains and a matching cushion for the window seat, fresh white paint on the ceiling, a nice thick rug, and a new mattress for the crib, toys and rattles, a rocking chair that didn't squeak, a bigger bureau for diapers and clothes . . .

She hugged herself, fairly tingling with impatience and excitement. How could she wait six more months for the baby? She was scared to death of it, and at the same time she wanted it now, this instant. Nothing like this had ever happened to her before.

It hardly seemed natural to want a child so passionately. Connor wanted it, too, she'd come to believe, but his desire for it was calm, within bounds—nothing like hers. Would she be a good mother? Oh, how could she not be, when she was longing for the child this much? She wiped her eyes, unsurprised by the rush of tears; they'd become so commonplace lately, she hardly noticed them. Raw emotion was perfectly normal, Dr. Hesselius said, which was reassuring. Connor had been glad to hear it, too; it meant his wife probably wasn't a madwoman.

"There you are." His smile, gentle, tolerantly amused, said he knew everything she was thinking. She'd have gone to him then and kissed him—except Dr. Hesselius was behind him in the doorway.

"How's Jack?" she asked.

"I'm encouraged," the doctor said, coming into the room and speaking quietly. The odor of tobacco smoke hovered around him at all times, and the bowls of at least two pipes could always be seen peeking out over his waistcoat pocket. "His lungs sound better today, for the first time. He says his throat isn't as painful, and that's a good sign."

"But what about his cough? That's no better, and he's still bringing up blood."

Dr. Hesselius reached for her wrist and pulled out his watch, monitoring her pulse while he spoke. "The hemoptysis isn't as alarming in consumption as some of the other symptoms. It's distressing to you to hear it, and uncomfortable for the patient, of course, but fatal hemorrhage from coughing in phthisis is virtually unheard of."

She glanced at Connor, who looked solemn but not fearful, and decided to be cheered by this news.

"And how are you feeling, Sophie? No more faintness, no more light-headedness?"

"No, that's all gone."

"Appetite's all right?"

"Appetite's fine."

Connor snorted. "Appetite knows no bounds."

She made a face at him while the doctor chuckled. They trailed out into the hall. "Your pulse is a little elevated; just a trifle, nothing to worry about. Do you have a cold?"

"Sniffles," she admitted. "It's really nothing."

"Mm hm. I want you to stay home for the next couple of days. You don't have to stay in bed, just take things slowly and quietly."

She put her hands on her hips. "Yes, all right, but this morning I really have to go to Guelder."

"Why?" demanded Connor.

"Because it's payday. I was out yesterday—"

"Nevertheless, I really do think—"

"Can't somebody else pay the men?" Connor interrupted the doctor. "Jenks or Penney? Why does it have to be you?"

"It doesn't have to be me," she said with exasperated affection. "But nobody can get into the safe because I've got the key to my desk drawer—which has the key to the safe in it, which means—"

"Which means *I'll* go to the mine," he announced in the flat, stubborn, don't-argue-with-me-because-you-cannot-win tone of voice he used when he meant business. "Where's the key?"

"In my purse," she said primly. "Which is downstairs on the hall table."

"I'll see you out on my way, Doctor." And without another word, he put his hand on Dr. Hesselius's shoulder and escorted him down the stairs. Leaning in Jack's doorway, Sophie whispered, "He's going to make the most *infuriating* MP."

Word that Connor Pendarvis's brother was staying at Stone House traveled quickly, and a few days later he had a visitor. Sidony Timms arrived in a rainstorm, wet and bedraggled under an ancient umbrella, but with a face blooming with excitement and shy hope. Sophie made her come into the parlor, where a fire was burning, and gave Maris her wet cloak to dry in the kitchen. Sidony wouldn't take a hot drink, but she sat down on the sofa when Sophie insisted, clasping her small hands in her lap. "I can only stay two minutes, ma'am, truly, and I shouldn't ought to've come a'tall, disturbin' you in your house and everything, but—I had to come and ask after Jack. I heard 'e's very bad, and I had to come and find out."

"It's true, Sidony. I'm afraid he's very ill."

"Worse than before even?"

"Yes."

"Oh." She lowered her head, and her glossy black hair, curly because of the damp, hid her face. She looked like a distraught child, small and huddled on the sofa.

"Would you like to see him? It could only be for a minute."

Her head came up, and the light returned to her large, dark eyes. "Oh, ma'am. Do you think it's all right?"

Sophie stood up. "Just for a little while. He's probably awake; he hardly ever sleeps. And you mustn't let him talk—it's bad for his throat, and it tires him out."

They went upstairs, and Sophie put her head in Jack's open door. Just as she'd thought, he wasn't sleeping; he was sitting up against his pillows, staring out the window at the rain. He smiled at her tiredly—but when he saw who was with her, his face took on a look of such gladness and sweet, thankful surprise, Sophie's heart contracted. Swallowing the silly lump in her throat, she said, "Look who's here, Jack."

"Sidony," he rasped, then put his hand on his throat because it hurt.

"Hullo," said the girl, hardly moving from the door. "I came to see you."

Sophie saw that her presence was not only not required, it was unwanted. "Just for a few minutes," she reminded Sidony, and withdrew, closing the door behind her.

Downstairs, she stirred the fire in the grate and stared into the flames, seeing again the way Jack and Sidony had looked at each other. They were in love—anyone with eyes could tell that. Why did it come as a surprise to her? She'd seen Sidony before, the day she'd come here to ask if Sophie knew where Jack had gone. She'd been troubled and heartsick, but Sophie had been too consumed by her own misery and ravaged pride to spare much sympathy for her. Now she felt ashamed: she'd gotten her heart's desire—the man she loved, his baby on the way—while Sidony had only a desperately ill lover and the promise of grief to come.

She heard her on the stairs, and moved toward the doorway to meet her. The girl saw her and tried to smile—but all at once her face crumpled and she burst into quiet sobs.

Without a thought, Sophie put her arms around her. They stood in the dim hallway, both crying, patting one another's shoulders for comfort. "He's so much worse," Sidony mourned. "I couldn't stand to look at 'im, I had to come away."

"The doctor says he's better, though, Sidony. His lungs sound better through the stethoscope."

Sidony brought out a handkerchief and blew her nose. "Mrs. Pendarvis, would it be all right if I came back sometime? I wouldn't stay long, just—"

"Yes, of course. Anytime you like."

"Thank you, ma'am. I think Jack might like it."

"I know he would. You're better for him than his medicine," she declared, and her reward was Sidony's watery smile.

After that she came every two days, always in the late afternoon between tea and dinner, so as not to disturb the household schedule. She never stayed long. Sophie left them alone together, and to hell with propriety: Sidony truly did brighten Jack's spirits, as nothing else had; compared to that, social correctness paled to triviality.

Slowly, slowly, he began to improve. The gargles and lozenges Dr. Hesselius prescribed relieved the infection in his throat, and before long he could speak without too much discomfort—although he was still enjoined to keep quiet as much as possible, to rest his lungs. The fever sweats that kept him awake at night decreased in intensity, and he was able to rest. He looked better as a result, not so gray and wasted, and his new diet was making him gain weight. He began spending his afternoons downstairs, on the couch in the formal parlor because the windows there were west-facing and the fireplace was warmer. Light and fresh air were the elusive antidotes to his disease, and he followed the sun, such as it was in early November, from room to room, hoping its weak, whitish rays would cure him. Maris kept him company when Connor was busy, and Sophie began coming home from Guelder early, at two or so, and played cribbage with him before she went upstairs for a nap. Her pregnancy didn't show yet; it was still a secret. She imagined the men at the mine thought she couldn't bear an all-day separation from her new husband, and in that they weren't too far off.

"I wish my uncle could see me now," she said to Jack one afternoon in the parlor. Connor was away in Tavistock, meeting with his party-committee cronies, and Maris had the day off.

"Why?" Jack looked up from the game of solitaire he was playing on a tray over his lap.

"Because he's always wanted me to take up 'feminine pursuits.' Look at me, Jack. What could be more feminine than knitting baby booties?"

He snickered. "Yes, ee do look motherly like, no doubt o' that. Will ee miss bein' a businesswoman onct the cheeil comes?"

She rested her head on the back of the chair. "Yes, I expect I will. I like it, you know, the . . . purposefulness of it. And I'm good at it," she added. "I like that."

"Mayhap ee'll be good at motherin', too. Which also have a *purposefulness,* so to say."

She nodded. "And Guelder will still be mine. Mr. Andrewson will take over the daily management, but I'll still own it. I'll make the big decisions."

"Well, then. Ee'll 'ave everything, won't ee?"

She smiled at him fondly. He was a rougher, lankier version of his brother, and she'd have loved him automatically for that alone, even without his other lovable qualities. He was so proud of Connor, he couldn't hide it, although he teased him mercilessly and called him "the Honorable Mr. Pendarvis, Member fer the world at large," and other, far less flattering titles. He liked to talk about their childhood, and even though she knew it wasn't good for him, she could hardly bring herself to tell him to be quiet. The tragedy of the Pendarvis family made her deeply sad, but there had been good times, too, and she loved hearing stories of Mary and Egdon and the children, and discovering that the affection in their mean little cottage had triumphed over the poverty.

A heavy knock sounded at the front door, startling them. They looked at one another inquiringly. It wasn't Sidony's day to visit, and the doctor wasn't due until tomorrow. Sophie went into the hall and called down the kitchen steps, "I'll answer it, Mrs. B.!"

It was William Holyoake, dressed in his Sunday clothes, a blue broadcloth suit and black bowtie. For a second Sophie worried that she'd forgotten some church function or other—she and William sang in the adult mixed choir, and William, in addition, had recently become a member of the vestry. He whipped off his hat and smiled rather stiffly, a big, plain, blunt-spoken man, as dependable as dawn. "Afternoon, Mrs. Pendarvis," he greeted her.

"Good afternoon, Mr. Holyoake. Come in," she invited, standing back and widening the door for him.

He hung back. "I've come to ask if I may speak for a minute wi' Mr. Jack Pendarvis."

"Ah." She smiled through her foreboding, realizing at once that he'd come about Sidony. She could feel herself being torn, loyalties divided right down the center. "Come in, please." He obeyed; he was so tall, he had to duck his head in the threshold. If Jack had been upstairs in his room, she could have given him a moment's warning. As it was, William could see him in the parlor simply by turning his head. "Jack," she said brightly, "you have a visitor. It's Mr. Holyoake."

"Don't get up," William said hastily when Jack started to throw off his blanket. "I won't be takin' up much o' yer time." He looked even more uncomfortable than Jack did, and startled as well, as if his rival's physical condition was worse than he'd expected. Sophie thought she saw pity flare in his eyes before he looked down at the hat he was rotating in his big, strong hands.

"Well," she said, smiling determinedly. "If you'll excuse me, I have to go and tell Mrs. Bolton something."

Mrs. Bolton was making a pastry for tonight's herring pie. The whole family was sick of herring, Jack most of all; but Dr. Hesselius insisted it was good for him, and so they all ate it to keep him company. Taking a seat on the bench at the long kitchen table, Sophie made desultory conversation with her housekeeper, taking up a knife and helping to chop dried quinces for the pie, all the while keeping an eye on the clock over the stove. She let ten minutes go by, then five more, before she rose and went back upstairs.

The parlor doors were open, so she went inside. "Jack?" He was staring out the window behind the sofa. He turned to her, and she started forward when she saw the grief in his long, thin face. "Are you all right?" He nodded. She hesitated. "Do you want to play hearts?" she asked—in case he wanted to pretend nothing had happened.

"You know 'im, don't ee?" he asked hoarsely.

"William? Yes, I've known him all my life."

"What's 'e like?"

"Oh . . . he's a good man," she admitted finally.

He bowed his head. "Yes."

"He's . . ." She crossed to the couch and sat down on the edge. Surprised, Jack scooted over a few inches, giving her more room. "He's been in love with Sidony for a long time," she told him frankly.

He nodded. "Ee can guess what 'e wanted wi' me, Sophie. Wanted to know what my intentions was. If they'm *honorable,* 'e says 'e won't stand in my way. That's if Sidony chooses me," he added miserably. " 'E'm rich, ain't 'e?"

"No, of course not, he's . . ." William was the bailiff at Lynton Hall Farm. With a pang, she realized that, compared to Jack, that made him rich indeed. "What are you going to do?"

His ashy complexion pinkened with emotion. "If I could get well," he whispered. "If I could work again. I swear I'd take 'er from 'im and never let 'er go."

She took his hand. Except for the paleness, it looked just like Connor's, big and capable and long-fingered. "Sidony is a lucky woman to have two such fine gentlemen courting her."

Jack sent her a wan smile, and went back to staring out the window.

# XIX

"Good thing we're telling everyone about the baby tonight," Sophie threw over her shoulder as Connor came in from the bathroom, freshly shaved and smelling of bay soap. She pressed her palms over the swell under the basqued bodice of her shaded silk evening dress, regarding herself critically in the wardrobe mirror. Maybe she ought to change into the fawn-colored brocade—its velvet trim obscured the line of the waist better. Then again, why bother? After tonight her secret would be out; she could grow as fat as she liked and not have to worry about hiding it.

Connor stood in front of the dresser, tying his tie. "Oh," she said, turning. "Is that what you're wearing?"

He paused, looking down at the plain, dark blue coat and trousers in which he'd married her. "I thought so. What's wrong with it?"

"Nothing, it's just . . . I thought, tonight, since it's a special occasion, and Knowlton will be there . . ." Why did she have to explain? Tonight was their first formal appearance before the world as a couple. Her uncle had invited them to a reception for Clive Knowlton on the occasion of his retirement. He'd invited Robert Croddy as well, and this would be the beginning of Robert's and Connor's unspoken campaigns to win Knowlton's favor. It was also the night Sophie had decided to announce that she was having a child. Tongues would wag; months would be mentally counted. Any who wondered why the belle of Wyckerley had eloped with a Cornish miner in the dead of night would have his—or more likely her—worst fears confirmed. Sophie would hold her head high and ignore the whispers, but in her ears they would sound like shouted accusations.

To say that it was a significant evening for the Pendarvises was to put it mildly: already her hands were perspiring. She'd snapped at poor Maris for fixing her hair wrong—and now Connor was wearing blue instead of formal evening black, with a necktie so awful she wanted to yank it out of his hands.

"These are my best clothes," he said, trying not to sound belligerent. "This is the first I've heard that they're not suitable. What would you like me to wear?"

She ground her teeth; they would be late if she had to dress herself *and* him. "I've told you, my father's clothes are yours. Why don't you look in his wardrobe for another cravat, maybe something a little more . . . subdued." Something without little yellow checks all over it, she specified in private.

He turned away, but not before she saw his cheeks turn pink. She'd forgotten that there was one person in the world more prickly about his dignity than she was about hers. What a shame it had to be her husband.

"Sorry," she said quickly. "I'm so nervous. I want everything to go well tonight." He made a conciliatory sound, and it encouraged her to add, "It was so kind of my uncle to invite us, since he's invited Robert as well. He didn't have to, he could have let Robert have Clive Knowlton all to himself tonight. I think it's an olive branch, Con. A new beginning for us."

He gave a sarcastic sniff. "Think what you like."

"What does that mean?"

"Dear Uncle Eustace hasn't invited us out of kindness, Sophie. He saw a chance to show Knowlton how much smoother and more polished his protégé is than the Cornishman who married his niece for her money."

"You can never believe anything good about my uncle, can you? He'll always be a villain to you."

"Maybe so. Every time I start to forget it, this reminds me." He stabbed a finger at the scar on his cheek, glaring at her.

"These are the clothes I'm wearing, Sophie. If I embarrass you, that's just too bad."

The evening went downhill after that.

But she was wrong about the whispers and raised eyebrows she'd expected in the wake of her announcement, which she made privately to individuals rather than to the group at large, that she was pregnant. Everyone seemed genuinely, unreservedly happy for her, and if they were hiding secret skepticism, she believed she'd have known it, because on this subject she was as sensitive as a fresh wound. No one, not even Honoria, was crass enough to ask the baby's due date, but if anyone had been, she was ready with her answer: June. And when it came in mid-April, she was prepared to call it premature, and hang the consequences.

Sixteen people comprised Uncle Eustace's "small, intimate supper party." The guest list was man-heavy, as they used to say in her finishing school. But the reason for that was political, not social, and Sophie began to think Connor might have been right about her uncle's motives. Robert Croddy had brought two of his conservative Whig cronies, Mr. Falkner and Mr. Turnbull, who evidently were to him what Ian Braithwaite was to Connor. He was outnumbered by three to one—four to one, counting Uncle Eustace. A conspiracy?

She had met Clive Knowlton only once before, years ago at a civic ball she'd attended with her father. Tonight she doubted if she'd have known him if she'd passed him in the street, he'd changed so radically. His hair had turned completely white, and he'd shrunk in stature by at least two inches. She'd been told that he wasn't ill, only devastated by his wife's passing a year or so ago. Her sentimental heart ached for him. He didn't say much, but he listened carefully to the talk around him, and she thought the sad brown eyes behind his half glasses were shrewd.

At dinner, Honoria seated Sophie between the Carnocks, as far away from Clive Knowlton as it was possible to be, and it amused her to think her cousin found her charms so lethal that she must be kept in quarantine, so to speak. Connor, on the other hand, sat directly across from the MP, a placement that tended to bolster his theory that the secret agenda tonight was to embarrass him. *Ha*, she thought humorlessly. They would find out soon enough that they'd underestimated him. Still . . . she wished to God he hadn't worn that odious necktie.

Dinner was complicated: there were eight courses, including two soups, a turbot with lobster sauce, lamb cutlets, roast saddle of mutton, marrow pâté with asparagus and peas, a green goose, a salad with cucumbers and endives and another of beetroot and anchovies, cream glacé and maraschino jellies, a fruit compote, walnuts, and coffee. Connor handled it fairly well (although once she saw him cut his fish with his knife, a gaffe she hoped no one else noticed), which must have galled Honoria no end—she hoped it did. The only politics discussed were local, and only in the most general and genial of terms. Sebastian Verlaine, Lord Moreton, spoke of the improvements he was considering for his tenant cottages at Lynton, and Christy Morrell talked about the fine harvest the glebe lands had yielded this year, the produce having been distributed among the poor in the district. When talk began to veer naturally toward taxes and poor rates, it was Lady Moreton who steered it gently back to a less controversial topic. Sophie sent her a grateful look. The news of her pregnancy had doubly delighted Rachel, who had confided in secretive tones that she too was expecting. She and Sebastian weren't telling anyone yet, though—but she couldn't resist telling Sophie. She looked beautiful, calm as a Madonna, and as happy as Sophie had ever seen her. Perhaps their babies would be born at the same time. Lovely thought. They could play together, be friends. Connor called her a snob, but who wouldn't be pleased to have a countess's little boy or girl for her child's playmate?

Lost in her thoughts, she was surprised when Honoria rose, signaling it was time for the ladies to withdraw. If Connor was right, the true purpose of the evening was about to begin. She sent him a confident smile, and when she passed behind his chair she gave his shoulder a quick, encouraging squeeze.

Connor watched as the last colorful skirt passed through the dining room door, and listened as the sound of ladies' voices faded and died. Behind him, a manservant poured port into his glass and offered him a choice of cigars from a teakwood humidor.

When every glass was filled, Vanstone held his aloft. "Gentlemen." His guests copied him. "Let us drink to the honorable gentleman who has served us faithfully with integrity, wisdom, and absolute dedication for twenty-seven years. We thank him. We acknowledge humbly that his like shall not be found again. We wish him the happiness and contentment he richly deserves in all his future endeavors."

"Hear, hear" came the heartfelt agreement of every man at the table. They drank, and Clive Knowlton smiled with pleasure and sadness and the innate modesty that had made him beloved in his district.

"Speech!" cried Robert Croddy.

Knowlton glanced at him sharply from under his bristling white brows, but only said in mild tones, "Thank you, gentlemen. I have no speech, only gratitude for my host's too-kind words." He meant it; he closed his mouth and busied himself with cutting off the end of his cigar.

Lord Moreton, whom Connor had seen but never met until tonight, looked too rakish to be an earl. He said something humorous about Knowlton being the only MP he'd ever known to turn down a chance to orate, and appreciative laughter lightened the momentary solemnity.

Vanstone led the talk around to politics, the progress of the crisis in China, army reforms since the Crimean conflict. Gradually the conversation turned from global to regional, and in a smooth transition Falkner, one of Croddy's political advisers, brought up the subject of the property qualification for Parliament. Immediately there was a shift, a change in the atmosphere so subtle, Connor doubted anyone felt it but him—and Croddy and his two henchmen. "What side of the issue do you stand on, Mr. Pendarvis?" Falkner inquired innocently. He was a portly, round-faced, white-whiskered gent, with faded blue eyes that darted swiftly behind folds and bags of baby-pink fat. His political function was the same as Ian's, but in manner and appearance the two men could not have been more unlike.

Falkner already knew how Connor felt on the question of the property qualification, since an article in the Tavistock *Trumpet* two weeks ago had outlined his position on it and half a dozen other current controversies. He said, "I'm opposed to it, sir," turning the smoldering tip of his cigar around and around against the side of a heavy crystal ash bowl.

Croddy cleared his throat. "I favor it. I think tampering with it is tantamount to tampering with the constitution. The framers of the Act knew what they were about in 1710. A man's property showed then, as it still does today, that he owns something that places him above dependence and need. It's the proof of his incorruptibility."

If he hadn't known before, Connor knew it now: Croddy's people had prepped him on the subject of the property qualification, and tonight he was going to debate it. Clive Knowlton had a front-row seat at a preview performance of his successor, trouncing the unskilled, unprepared upstart from Cornwall.

The nine gentlemen around the table were looking at Connor expectantly. Marshaling his thoughts as best he could, he said, "What the framers of the Act wanted to do was exclude Protestants from the throne of England. That and keep the trading class out of the Commons. But the trading class has come up in the world since Queen Anne's day, and the property requirement no longer constrains them. It's obsolete."

"Nonsense," Croddy replied with a huff of amusement. "You might as well argue that integrity is obsolete. I don't say that poverty necessarily makes a man dishonest, but property stands as a pledge for his conduct. It shows he's independent and not open to temptation. Open the Commons up to penniless men, and you open it to bankrupts, spendthrifts, and paupers—a refuge for them, mind you, a *haven*, unless you're also prepared to repeal the laws protecting Members from arrest for debt. Are you, sir?"

"With respect, Mr. Croddy, that's a smoke screen. I don't believe men become more honest and clearheaded as they accumulate more possessions. I believe that as long as intelligent men from the productive and useful classes are excluded from the process of lawmaking, justice for working people will never come."

Falkner sniffed audibly; Turnbull laughed outright. Captain Carnock, the only Tory in the room, or at least the only one honest enough to admit it, said, "Tut," and poured himself another glass of port.

"You speak of smoke screens!" Croddy cried with false joviality. "The point is, the law prevents the entrance into the House of people without the means to devote all their time to parliamentary business. Change that, sir, and you change the very character of the Commons."

"Exactly. It's long overdue for a change."

"I hope you're excluding present company, sir," Knowlton put in, eyes twinkling, and Connor sent him a gallant nod.

"Just as well you're retiring, sir," Croddy laughed. "If men like Pendarvis get into the House, God forbid, it's not a place you'd want to be for much longer anyway."

Connor leaned back in his chair and blew a smoke ring. His adversary wasn't going to provoke him that easily.

"I imagine you ally yourself with the reformers," Croddy went on with undisguised distaste. "Admit it, you wouldn't stop there. If you and men of your ilk—Chartists and radicals disguised as Whigs, if you ask me—if you had your way, next you'd abolish property qualifications for the *voters*."

"I'd certainly try."

Captain Carnock looked shocked, but Dr. Hesselius—a taciturn man; Connor had no idea what his politics were—nodded his bald head in approval. Lord Moreton stroked his chin, regarding Connor with interest. Clive Knowlton kept still, sphinx-like, saying nothing.

"You surprise me, sir. People with your agenda aren't normally so candid in professing it. I call it dangerous," Croddy said loudly, glancing at Knowlton. "Are there any items in the Charter that you do oppose? Any at all? I deplore that kind of radical thinking. The march of democracy must be arrested. I say the manhood suffrage is the last step before anarchy."

"I'll debate democracy with you anytime you like," Connor said quietly, stubbing out his cigar, "but let's finish this discussion first. You'll recall it's about property qualifications." Croddy flared his nostrils at him. "I believe membership in the House is a trust, requiring natural ability, not artificial wealth. Property isn't the safeguard for Members' intelligence and integrity. The real safeguard lies in the hands of the electorate. Why is—"

"Puh!"

"Why is a man who inherits his father's house a better lawmaker than the man who earns a living painting pictures? For myself, I'd rather the Commons were more full of brains than bricks." Croddy snorted. "If we choose an architect—or a general, or a sea captain—by his *merits,* why not elect as lawmakers the men who have the most natural ability to make laws? I maintain such men can be found everywhere, with and without property."

"I'm sure it suits you to do so, sir. I'm sure it suits you very well."

"Now, gentlemen—"

"Are you insinuating something by that?" Connor asked, setting his glass down carefully.

"I'm not insinuating anything at all. I'm saying what everyone here already knows—that you acquired your property qualifications through your wife."

"Robert—"

"And I'm hardly the only one who says you *married* her for them."

When Connor got to his feet, the back of his chair crashed against the wall behind him. Everybody jumped. Croddy stood up, too, hands clenched, jaw thrusting. Sebastian Verlaine rose between them and turned his back on Croddy. "Easy," he said in a murmur, and with his hand he gave Connor's arm a slow, hard squeeze. That and something purposeful in his stern glance settled Connor down, enough so that punching Croddy in the nose didn't seem quite as imperative as it had a second ago.

"I think we might join the ladies now, don't you?" Knowlton suggested to his host. Vanstone rose smoothly and led the way out of the room.

*Bloody sodding hell,* thought Connor, taking a glass of brandy from the silver tray one of Vanstone's ubiquitous servants held out to him. Across the cluttered drawing room, Sophie was trying to catch his eye. He avoided her after a glance at her worried face. She could always tell when something was wrong, and he imagined his own face was looking pretty grim just now. Wait until he told her Robert Croddy had nearly goaded him into a fistfight in the dining room. She'd love that. He downed his brandy in three throat-scorching swallows, and when the servant passed again, he reached for another. Bugger all.

The ladies were talking about opera, although it took him a few minutes to make that out. Talk of *Lucrezia Borgia, Martha,* and *Norma* confused him until someone mentioned *The Marriage of Figaro,* and finally he was able to nail down the topic. Sebastian Verlaine entered into it eagerly; it turned out that he was an aficionado. "Have you seen *Rigoletto*?" he happened to ask Connor, who was leaning with him against the fireplace mantel.

"No, I haven't."

"I saw the premiere in Venice about seven years ago. Magnificent. Do you know Verdi? *Traviata, Il Trovatore*?"

He shook his head. "I don't really know the opera."

Croddy heard. "Really? What do you do with yourself when

you're in London?" He asked it genially, as if five minutes ago they hadn't almost come to blows.

Connor steeled himself. He'd be damned if he'd lie. "As a matter of fact, I've never been to London."

It was a conversation stopper.

"Goodness," said Lily Hesselius, the doctor's flighty wife, after a long, unbearable pause.

"I've only been one time," said Mrs. Carnock softly. Kindly.

"You haven't missed much," Reverend Morrell said—kindly.

Connor felt the heat flare in his face. Across the way, Sophie peered intently into her sherry glass, motionless.

Croddy stirred. He and Falkner exchanged looks. They'd found the opening they were seeking, the chink in the enemy's armor. "But I thought you were a university man," Croddy said with feigned surprise.

"If you mean Oxford or Cambridge, the answer's no."

"Where, then? If you don't mind my asking."

"I attended the Bryce Pennon Workingmen's College. In Manchester." There, that ought to do it. Just the mention of Manchester, the center of working-class radicalism for the last fifty years, set off alarms in tender, middle-class hearts.

"Don't think I know it," Vanstone mused.

"I've heard of it," said Croddy, hardly able to hide his glee. "It's closed, hasn't it?"

Connor nodded slowly. "Yes." He decided to add, "I went there on scholarship."

"Oh. Quite."

"Because my family couldn't afford to send me. My father was a tin miner. So were all my brothers. There, I think that's the worst of it, Mr. Croddy."

The last awkward silence was nothing compared to this one. Except for Croddy, no one could look at him. Even when Anne Morrell deliberately opened a new topic, Sophie kept her gaze resolutely trained on the lacquered fan in her hands, examining the painted scene between the folds with particular, minute care.

Worst was the deep red blush staining her cheeks. Because she was embarrassed for him. Ashamed of him. *Look at me,* he commanded, while around them the chattering voices rose and fell meaninglessly. She never moved.

He could feel a burn in his chest widen, deepen, like a spark searing a hole in dry paper. Until now he'd thought she was with him: Connor and Sophie against the world. What a boneheaded mistake. It hadn't taken much to send her over to the other side, had it? If she'd ever been on his side to begin with.

Or maybe it was the brandy. He saw her smiling at something her uncle was saying in her ear. Connor strolled over to the drinks table and poured himself a tall one.

The group broke down into smaller units, animated pockets of conversation that he moved around and through but never joined. Sophie found him by the long black windows, brooding. "You're drinking too much," she murmured, keeping her back to the room, barely moving her lips.

"Do you think so?" He looked down at the inch of cognac left in his glass. He toasted her before he tossed it back, licking his lips afterward with exaggerated relish. The way her face flinched in nervous shock amused him. "Afraid I'll embarrass you again, sweetheart?"

"Lower your voice," she hissed urgently, moving to block from sight as much of him as she could. "What's the matter with you? Why are you drinking like this?"

"I don't know." He set his empty glass down with a too-loud clatter. "It sure as hell isn't helping. Get your coat, Sophie, we're leaving."

"What? No, we can't—it's too early!"

"I said we're going."

"But we *can't*. It would be rude."

"Stay, then. *I'm* leaving."

He'd had just enough brandy to make the flash of panic in her eyes look comical to him. Moving her aside with his arm, he went past her and started for the door. Knowlton was in his way. "Enjoyed meeting you," he said into his startled face, shaking hands. Honoria was his hostess, so he detoured to where she was sitting on a velvet love seat with the doctor's wife. "Thanks for dinner," he told her, and kept going.

*"Connor."* If you could scream in a whisper, Sophie did it. He heard her behind him. Following him into the hall, she grabbed the back of his coat to make him stop.

"Are you coming?" he asked before she could speak.

Alternatives flickered in her beautiful blue eyes. She decided to dare him. "No."

"Stay here with your friends, then. Since you like 'em so much. Stay all night, why don't you? I'm sure your uncle will be glad to put you up. You and Honoria can sleep together." He spun on his heel and stalked away. A surprised butler saw him from a distance and tried to get to the door to open it for him, but Connor beat him to it.

The wind had come up. A cold, damp blast in his face sobered him slightly. He turned around in the flagstone path. Sophie was coming toward him through the doorway, and the light behind her made her hair glow like a halo. "Come with me," he said. Asking her this time, not ordering.

"Damn it!" She was mortified. "Come back inside, Con, right now! Can't you see this is just what they want?"

"Are you coming with me?"

"No!"

He pivoted. "I'll come and get you in the morning, then," he tossed over his shoulder. "Or you could ask Croddy to take you home. That'd be like old times." He yanked at the reins that were looped over the Vanstones' black iron hitching post. Over Val's welcoming nicker, the door slamming shut sounded like a gunshot.

"Connor's not feeling well," Sophie announced in the drawing room doorway. "He—asked me to apologize for his hasty departure. Good night to you all—thank you, Uncle, Honoria, for a lovely evening. No, don't see me out, he's waiting for me—stay with your guests. Good night—good night!"

They let her go, all of them looking puzzled and uncertain, and Anne more than that—but thank God no one went with her, and after the stone-faced butler helped her with her evening shawl and opened the door for her, she pulled it firmly closed in his face. Because if anyone learned the truth, that Connor had gone home in a huff and left her stranded, she would never live it down.

The moon had all but disappeared. Fast, angry clouds flew across it, blown by the same wind that ripped at her hair and tried to fling her back against the gate. Muttering curses, she put her head down and trudged into the blast, grateful at least that the street was deserted and there was no one to witness her solitary flight.

On the toll road, she could barely make out the verges; more than once she walked straight into a black, prickly hedge. Dead leaves blew in her face, caught on the dangling fringe of her silk shawl. The creak and scrape of tree limbs sounded eerie under the hurtling roar of the wind. She could smell the sea, heavy and wild, calling to something in her that loved a storm. The wind made her stagger, tried to snatch her shawl from her shoulders. "Blast!" she shouted, and the wind blew the word back into her mouth. She had walked this two-mile journey a hundred times, a *thousand* times, but never on a black, blustery night in a thin dress and thin-soled slippers, with no hat and no hood. Anger kept her going. She couldn't wait to get home and yell at her husband.

Then the rain started.

She was drenched in a minute. And she was exactly halfway home—too late to turn back. The violence of the wind astounded her. She tied her shawl over her head and walked backward, gritting her teeth and wiping tears out of her eyes, until the gale shifted and blew in her face again. She tripped over something— a limb, ripped from a tree—and went sprawling in the road, scraping her palms on sharp pebbles and muddying her skirts. She got up slowly, carefully, feeling fear begin to creep inside her, clammy and cold, supplanting the hot anger. *What if I hurt myself?* she thought for the first time. *Oh, God, what if I hurt the baby?*

She staggered on, lurching through the rain until a slashing, sideways torrent forced her to take cover in a coppice of denuded hawthorns. Shuddering from the cold, teeth chattering, she huddled in a wet crouch and alternated between swearing at Connor and begging him to come and save her. But he wasn't going to come, and when there was a second's hush in the mauling, battering rage of the storm, she unwound and set off again, into the teeth of the wind.

# XX

Connor made it between the stable and the house at a flat-out, head-down sprint, but he was still soaked to the skin when he clattered down the area steps and burst through the kitchen door. It took forever to light the lantern because his hands were wet and water kept sluicing off his hat and dousing the match. If Sophie had come with him, she'd be drenched by now; she might have taken cold. So. Behaving like a complete horse's ass had had a compensation.

It was Friday, Mrs. Bolton's night off. He made all the noise he wanted while he built a fire in the stove and put the kettle on to boil. He thought of continuing to drink all night, or until every vivid, burning-hot memory of the Vanstones' dinner party was obliterated from his mind in a drunken fog. They would still be there in the morning, though, only magnified by a sick headache. Besides, alcohol was partly what had brought him to this wretched pass; if he hadn't drunk all that brandy at Vanstone's, he wouldn't have walked out on Sophie like a petulant child. Chastened, he shoveled a spoonful of sugar into a mug of tea and carried it upstairs to the parlor.

There were still some embers glowing in the fireplace. He blew on them with the bellows and threw on kindling, then fresh wood. Stripping off his wet jacket, he unfurled a knitted blanket Sophie kept on the arm of the sofa and threw it over his shoulders. He thought of sitting in the dark, nothing but the fire in the grate for light, no sound but the storm outside blowing and shrieking, while he brooded on his sins. But there was something unattractively self-indulgent about that picture. It was too romantic. He hadn't done anything romantic tonight. He'd behaved like an idiot, and part of his punishment was going to be facing that fact head-on without mitigating frills. So he lit the oil lamp on the table, and a couple of mantelshelf candles for good measure.

Why was he like this? He forgave himself for wanting to beat up Croddy; that was an *honorable* impulse, he decided, maybe not high-minded but perfectly understandable. But why had he flared up at Sophie? To pay her back for being ashamed of him? No—he hadn't really wanted to hurt her. But she'd humiliated him by her embarrassment, pierced him in his weakest spot, his pride. So he'd turned mean and sullen, like a child. Were they doomed to reenact this stupid scenario for the rest of their lives? How could they break out of it? By talking, of course—but how could they talk when they were both so full of anger and resentment they couldn't see straight?

His marriage wasn't the only thing he'd put in jeopardy tonight. How was he going to break it to Ian Braithwaite that his first meeting with Knowlton, the man who held his professional fate in his hands, had been a debacle of enormous proportions? The fact that Croddy hadn't distinguished himself either was no comfort. Personally Connor wouldn't blame Clive Knowlton if he told the party committees to dump both of their candidates and start over.

But it was Sophie who preyed on his mind. It wouldn't have mattered if Knowlton had set a crown on his head tonight and called him Your Highness. When things went wrong between him and Sophie, the world looked gray and paltry and unengaging. He could go through the motions, but he couldn't care.

The mantel clock struck ten forty-five. Rain smashed against the windows like handfuls of tacks, and the wind blew billows of smoke down the chimney and into the room. He got up and went downstairs for more tea, and as he was coming back he heard a noise. It sounded like pounding at the front door, but more likely it was a loose shutter smacking against the house—the wind was strong enough for it. He went to the door anyway to make sure.

At first he didn't even recognize her. With her sodden shawl covering her head and strands of dark, dripping hair plastered to her cheeks, she looked like a beggar woman, or a half-drowned cat. "Sophie!" Her frozen hand was stiff as a claw. He pulled her into the hall, the parlor, pushed her close to the fire. "Sophie, what did you do?" She couldn't speak; her teeth were chattering uncontrollably. He knew the answer anyway. "Idiot," he chided, gruffly tender, hiding his fear.

The dye from her skirts was dripping in blue rivulets and puddling on the floor at her feet. He whipped the shawl from her head and threw it on the stone hearth, turned her around, and started on the buttons at the back of her gown. Her clammy skin was cold and too white; he chafed it with his hands while he got her dress off, then her petticoats, corset, chemise, shoes, stockings, everything soaking wet and heavy as laundry. "Stay here," he ordered, wrapping her in the knitted blanket and pushing her into a chair he drew close to the fire. As an afterthought, he put her bare feet on a pillow. On his way out the door to get her some hot tea, he remembered his own cup. "Drink this," he commanded, handing it to her. But she couldn't hold onto it, her fingers were useless. He held the cup to her bluish lips, held the back of her neck with his other hand, unnerved by the violence of her shuddering. He made her drink all the tea, and then he rebuilt the fire until it was a snapping, spitting blaze. "I'll get more blankets," he told her, and started out again—then halted in the doorway. "No, a bath, a hot bath. I'll put water on to boil. And brandy, I'll get the bottle." Her wind-reddened face was all wide, frightened eyes. She hadn't said a word yet, but she didn't have to; he knew what she was thinking. He was thinking it, too. But he hurried out of the room without saying anything about the baby.

There was a big cast-iron tub in the basement lavatory, but he decided to put her in the smaller copper tub in the kitchen, because that room was warmer. He made her lie back so that nothing but her head and knees broke the surface, and he massaged her stiff arms and legs until she finally stopped shivering and turned a healthy pink color all over. He dried her by the stove, then helped her put on her heaviest flannel nightdress. "I can walk," she protested when he picked her up off her feet. He'd made a turban for her head with a dry towel; she sagged in his arms, looking like a tired, droopy sultana. "I know you can walk. I want to carry you." She sighed, and rested her head on his shoulder, and neither of them said anything about the baby.

He put her to bed, and kept pouring hot tea into her until she held up her hands and said, "No more," in a weak plea. She looked small and frail by the light of a single candle flickering on the bedside table. He pulled the covers up to her chin, and when she closed her eyes he stayed where he was, staring down at her still face. *I love you, Sophie,* he wanted to tell her. *I'm sorry for what I did.* But all he could say was, "How do you feel?"

"Fine." She whispered it tiredly, not opening her eyes.

He bent and put his cheek next to hers. "Go to sleep, sweetheart. Don't worry. Everything's all right." She nodded, then turned away from him, curling up on her side.

He sat beside her for a long time, listening to the whisper of her breathing. Gradually the tension began to let go of him; he relaxed. The wind had died sometime—he hadn't even noticed; the storm was nothing but rain now, falling hard and steady, straight down. He stroked his hand over the thin bulge of Sophie's shoulder under the counterpane. She was sleeping deeply, naturally. She was going to be all right.

The bleeding started just before dawn. She slept all night through tedious, complicated dreams, and awoke in the cold gray hour before daylight with an urgent need to use the night commode. At first the dark stain against the white of the china pot confused her. Her body understood before her brain, and turned ice-cold where she stood. She covered her mouth with her hands, gasping. In an instant she knew it all, everything that would happen, and in the next, she pushed it out of her mind.

She crept back into the bedroom, holding her elbows, hunchbacked, protecting her womb. "Con?" she murmured, too softly for him to hear. She wanted to cry so badly. "Connor." She shook his arm, and he came awake. Before she could say anything else, he threw the covers back and sat up, reaching for her.

"What's the matter?"

He already knew, too; she could tell by his face. "I think something's wrong." If she spoke above a whisper, her voice would crack.

"Why? What is it?"

She hated saying the words. "I'm bleeding."

He blanched, turned sheet-white, but immediately he took her hand, all business, and made her lie down in the bed on his side. The warmth of his body clung to the sheets, comforting her. "It might not be anything," he said, leaning over her.

"I know."

"It's probably not anything."

She nodded. She wanted to grab his hand, but that would prove she was scared. *It might not be anything.*

He was throwing on his clothes, his movements quick and smooth, not panicked. "I'm going for the doctor, Sophie. I'll wake up Jack before I go. I'll be back in less than an hour."

"Can't you send Thomas?"

"It'll be faster if I go."

She didn't want him to leave. When he came to her and cupped her cheeks with his hands, she took his wrists and held him still. "Oh, Con," she burst out, and he said, "Shh," softly, and put his face next to hers. He didn't want her to break down. "I'll be back as soon as I can. Do you need anything?"

"No."

"You're not in pain are you, Sophie?"

She shook her head, whispering, "No, no—it might not be anything," and he said it back. They held onto each other for a long, wordless minute, and then he kissed her on the mouth and went away.

A little later, Jack poked his head in the door. "Sophie?" She sent him a feeble wave and a tightlipped smile. "Do ee want some tea? I'll go and make it. I know how," he added when he saw she was going to protest.

"No, Jack, stay in bed and wait for Connor to come home. Anyway, Maris will be here soon."

He came farther into the room. His dark hair, so like Connor's, was sleep-tousled, and his feet were still bare under his long night robe. "I can make a egg if you want it boiled. Any other way and ee're out o' luck, but boilin' I can do blindfolded." When she couldn't return his determined grin, he sobered. "Con told me. About last night. I'm that sorry, Sophie. Sometimes he'm a rash idiot, and stubborn as stones."

"It's not his fault." She shifted, drawing her knees up. She didn't want to talk, not about this. "Go back to bed, Jack, I mean it. I'm fine—I just want to lie here and be quiet."

"Right, then. Holler if ee needs anything," he said softly, and she nodded. She closed her eyes, and heard the door click shut behind him.

She was staring at the ceiling, praying hard, making God desperate promises, when the cramps began.

Connor was pacing in the narrow hall between Jack's room and the nursery when the door to the bedroom opened and Dr. Hesselius came out. Behind his spectacles, his large brown eyes looked mournful—but Connor told himself that meant nothing. Hesselius always looked like a whipped dog. "Well?" he said aggressively, striding toward him, stopping in front of the staircase.

"I'm sorry. Sophie's losing the baby."

His head jerked in an angry spasm. He couldn't talk. The news felt like a physical blow, even though part of his mind had known it already. He watched the doctor take a pipe out of his pocket and finger the empty bowl, press his thumbnail into the teeth marks on the stem. Connor wanted to slap him in the face. The tobacco smell that hung around Hesselius like a cloud repelled him, and in a quick flare of hope, he saw that he didn't know what he was talking about—he was wrong, incompetent, this was all a mistake.

"The fetus is dead. Complete abortion could take a few hours or a few days. Sophie—"

"How do you know it's dead? Can't you stop it?"

He shook his head sadly. "I'm very sorry. The child is not living, Mr. Pendarvis. I'll stay with Sophie if she wants me to, but at this point there isn't much I can do to help her."

He kept blinking, flailing in his mind for a way to fight this. Because this was going to hurt Sophie to the heart. "Will she be all right? Will she be in pain?"

Hesselius reached for Connor's arm, and looked at the floor while he said, "The fetus is about fourteen weeks old. Sophie's miscarriage will be like a labor, but probably much faster, and there shouldn't be as much pain." He dropped his hand. "I'm very sorry. But she'll recover, and there's no reason she can't have another pregnancy, a normal pregnancy, in the future."

In their room, she was huddled on her side in the big bed. Maris was with her, but when she saw Connor she got up from a chair at the bedside and went out. Her plain, kind face looked tragic; she didn't speak, but she gave him a quick, commiserating shake of the head as she passed him in the doorway.

He sat beside Sophie on the edge of the bed. She hadn't been crying, but as soon as he took her hand her eyes overflowed, wetting the pillow. She used the cuff of her nightgown to dry her face, and turned slightly, to see him better. She was so pale. He didn't know what to say, how to help her. All he felt was misery, and there was nothing he could do. "I'm so sorry." He had to say that, but it only made everything worse.

"The doctor says it's nobody's fault. The baby might've . . ." She squeezed her eyes shut, unable to say the word. "We might've lost her anyway."

"Her?"

Her voice sounded raw, as if her throat hurt. "I thought it was a girl. I don't know why. But I was sure."

He hadn't thought it was anything. It hadn't been real. But now it was, now that they were losing it. He put his forehead down on Sophie's hand, struggling to feel the right thing. He kept thinking, *I don't know what I'm doing, I don't know what I'm doing*.

She made a grating sound and bared her teeth, hunching, drawing her knees up. He huddled over her, frightened. "Sophie?" She clutched his hand painfully. It was like a contraction; after a minute, her muscles went slack and she lay still, panting.

It went on for hours. True to his word, Hesselius stayed with her, but there was nothing for him to do. Connor, the doctor, Maris, even Jack—they kept up a grim, dispirited vigil, taking turns sitting with Sophie. She lay lifeless and silent, not seeming to care who was with her. In the afternoon her contractions became rhythmic and severe, and Hesselius sent everyone out of the room. Jack wanted to stay with Connor, but he couldn't talk anymore. Couldn't keep up the front that he was strong and reconciled and stoic. He had to get away by himself.

He went outside, into the rose garden. Last night's storm had littered branches and debris over the neat paths, ripped the trellises away from the brick wall of the garden house. Everything was wrecked, ruined; the ugly brown corpses of scattered vegetation rustled and scratched in the cold remains of the wind. A thrush, puffed up for warmth, chipped a dry, forlorn song in the leafless orchard. Connor tried to remember how the garden looked last summer, tumbling and fragrant, a rainbow, almost too sweet. Sophie had taught him the names of the old roses: eglantine, damask, maiden's blush, York and Lancaster. She would lean on his arm while they walked so slowly, pretending they were exercising her ankle—but really they'd just wanted to touch. They'd fallen in love in those weeks, here among the roses, and even though he'd been deceiving her, and suffering because of his deception, all his memories of that time were sweet and good, the best of his life.

Ivy vines, lush and fat with shiny dark leaves in summer, clung to the stones of the house like brown, bony fingers, unbearably dreary. The rain had stained the leaves and turned the gray roof slates black. Smoke from the chimneys disappeared in the smoke-colored sky. He gazed at Sophie's bedroom window, but there was nothing to see; like every window but Jack's, it was curtained and shuttered, dark, blind. He shivered from the cold, and the emptiness inside himself.

The sunroom door squeaked; he saw Maris in the opening. "Mr. Pendarvis," she called. From her face and the sound of her voice, he knew it was over. He went toward the house, his feet heavy and slow, shuffling up the terrace steps like an old man.

Sophie wasn't crying anymore. Her face was as pale as a wax candle, and her cold hand when he took it lay in his like a dead stick. He couldn't make her talk, couldn't reach her. She let him hold her, but it was as if she wasn't there. He was as cold inside as she was, but they couldn't warm each other.

But he needed to be with her, so he stayed, even when she turned away from him in her sleep. Sometime in the night the cold woke him. He reached for her, but she was gone.

Alarmed, he got up. He still had his clothes on. Out in the hall, he heard a noise. From the nursery. He found her there, sitting in the rocking chair, pale and insubstantial as a ghost. Unreal. "Sophie?" Her blank gaze went right through him, as if *he* were the ghost. "You'll freeze in here." He made his voice brisk, authoritative. "Come back to bed." She didn't move, didn't even hear, so he bent to pick her up. She strained away, but she was too weak or disinterested to put up any fight; he lifted her easily and carried her back to the bedroom. He put her in bed and pulled the covers up to her chin, and as he was looking down at her, her wide, glassy eyes finally focused on him. She said, "I saw her."

He thought he misheard. "What?"

Closing her eyes, she put her hands over her ears and rolled away from him. His heart was pounding. He was afraid to touch her. He took the blanket from the foot of the bed, wound it around his shoulders, sat down in the chair by the window. The room was absolutely still; he couldn't even hear Sophie breathing. Disconnected from everything, he pounded his fist against his thigh to feel something, pain, anything. Silence, darkness, cold. The fire in the grate had died, but he didn't get up to rebuild it. It wouldn't have done any good.

*Dear Papa,*

*I've been thinking about you so much lately. Tomorrow is Christmas, and maybe that's why. I've been remembering the time you gave me a sled, yellow with red runners, and it was perfect, just exactly what I wanted. It snowed on Boxing Day, and you pulled me up the carriageway hill over and over, watching me slide down, smoking your pipe. I remember how your checked coat smelled, like wet wool and tobacco, and the nubby feel of your rough mitten in my hand.*

*I remember you in summer, too. I picture you in the garden, pretending to drink tea from a tiny cup in the sunshine, surrounded by the dolls you gave me. I'd pretend we were married and the dolls were our children.*

*I miss you so much, Papa. I can't talk to anyone. I wish you were here so I could tell you something.*

*It's a secret. Only Dr. Hesselius knows, but he doesn't count. Oh, Papa—I saw my baby. I saw her. She was small, tiny, no longer than my ring finger, and curled up like a seahorse's tail, the color of sand. Her elbows and knees curved so gracefully, and she had fingers like blades of grass. Your ears. Her eyes were closed, and she looked dreamy, peaceful. And she was real. I touched her with my finger, moved her little arm so gently. The joint of her shoulder moved, and she was perfect, perfect. Oh, Papa, I'm crying*

*inside all the time, and I can't stop. No one knows. I can't
hear what people say to me because it's not important,
nothing at all matters. There's a hole in me where she was,
just a hole. It's as if I've died, too. I'm so lonely. It's like
death, this loneliness, and I can't bear it. I can't bear it.*

Sophie walked out of the Christmas service when the children's choir, under Margaret Mareton's substitute direction,
began to sing the "Cradle Hymn," just before Reverend Morrell's
sermon. Connor stayed where he was, thinking she needed to be
alone for a minute, that the lullaby had been too painful for her
and she would return when it was over. But Christy climbed the
pulpit steps and launched into his sermon, and after five minutes
she still hadn't come back. Jack sat beside him in the old Deene
family pew—it was his first day out. The two brothers exchanged
a look, then Connor got up and went to find her.

She was in the churchyard. He found her by following her foot-
prints in the light snow, the first of the season, that lay on the hard
December ground. She'd left the lych-gate open; she didn't hear
his silent approach. He saw her take something small and white
from her coat pocket—a piece of paper?—and tuck it between the
sere grass and the gray marble of her father's headstone. "Sophie?"

She turned sharply, staring up at him as if she'd never seen
him before. She dusted her hands and stood up, and started to
walk past him.

"What are you doing?"

"Nothing." She'd have kept going, but he stopped her with a
hand on her arm. She stood still, patient, waiting for him to say
whatever he had to say.

"Are you all right?"

"Yes."

"I was worried about you. Why did you leave?"

"I needed some air."

Her cheeks were beginning to pinken from the cold. She'd
lost weight since the miscarriage; her features looked sharp,

pinched, the bones too prominent under the skin. Her eyes were abstracted, and she never smiled a true smile. She shut him out with the look she wore now, and her chilly, remote manner. "Why did you come out here?" he tried again, moving in front of her so she had to look at him.

"Nothing, I told you. Some air. What does it matter?"

"It doesn't matter. I only wanted to know."

Her laugh was only a huff of breath. "Well, I'm out of answers, there's nothing else to tell you." She pulled out of his light clasp. "I'm cold. Can we go in?"

That night, they had Christmas dinner with the Vanstones. Eustace was unwontedly gentle with her, and for the first time since they'd met Connor didn't detest him. Even Honoria behaved well. No one talked about the baby—but then, no one ever did; it was as if it had never existed except in his and Sophie's minds. A kind of brittle gaiety came over her as the evening wore on. It hurt him to hear her false laughter, like glass breaking, and the too-animated sound of her voice.

After she and Honoria rose from the table and went into the drawing room, Eustace leaned back in his chair and said to the wineglass he was squinting at while he turned it around in his fingers, "My niece has had a bad time of it these last weeks. A very bad time. I've wished there was something I could do for her, something I could say. I . . . expect you have, too."

Connor said nothing.

"I've felt . . ." He cleared his throat harshly. "I'm glad you've been there for her, and I didn't think I'd feel that way. To the extent that I might have misjudged you, Pendarvis, I'd like to say right now that I regret it."

Connor lifted his eyebrows, hiding a slight smile at the phrasing. But Vanstone's grudging apology moved him; if this was an olive branch, he would take it gratefully. "To the extent that you and I have anything in common," he answered carefully, "I think it must be a hope for Sophie's happiness. Because we both love her. I suppose that might be . . . the basis for some kind of friendship."

Vanstone kept staring at his glass, his hard face never changing expression. A whole minute passed. "It might be," he conceded at last.

Driving home in the gig, Connor tried to tell Sophie what had happened, that her uncle had made a peace offer to him and he'd accepted it. But the unnatural gaiety had disappeared, and she'd turned back into the silent, aloof Sophie he knew better. He couldn't get a word out of her, huddled in her hooded cloak, staring down at the black ground passing under them.

At home, he said, "We have to talk."

"I'm tired."

"Sophie—"

"I'm tired, Con, I'm so tired. Let me go to bed."

She looked white and exhausted, all the vivacity of an hour ago drained out of her. He took her hands, squeezing them between his to warm them. Her head was bent; her hair hid her face. He brushed it back, put his hand under her chin. Before he could kiss her she craned away, turning from him. "Good night," she said, and went into her dressing room.

"Merry Christmas," he said to the closed door.

The party association leased an office in Tavistock, and Braithwaite gave Connor a key to it. He began to go there during the days, to meet with the committeemen and work on the various articles and papers he was struggling to care a damn about. One afternoon it snowed hard, and he decided not to go home— he could sleep in a chair in the office, or on the floor for all it mattered to him. It wasn't a blizzard, just a snow; he could have made it home if he'd tried. He found Sophie in the parlor the next day, vague and disheveled, still in her nightgown and robe; she greeted him with apathetic confusion, as if the snow and his overnight absence were just registering on her.

He'd hoped for more. In fact, he'd had some idea of shocking her with worry out of the daze of indifference that covered her like a blanket. They never touched, rarely spoke; they occupied the same house, the same bed at night, and yet they never connected, even though the pain they were in must be the same for her as it was for him—he had to believe that. But she wouldn't let him help her, and she couldn't help him. His best friend had deserted him.

In January she went back to the mine. He thought it was a good sign, the beginning of her recovery. She'd let herself go, stopped getting dressed or washing her hair, stopped taking care of herself—so it was a relief to see her looking fit and fashionable again, her old self. But one afternoon she didn't come home at her usual time, and as the hour lengthened his anxiety grew. Something was wrong, he felt sure of it, even when Jack laughed and called him an old maid for worrying. After two hours, he saddled the horse and rode to Guelder at a fast gallop.

He relaxed when he saw Valentine tethered in his usual spot. Sophie wasn't in her office, though, and when he asked, no one could say where she was. "I saw her walking toward the smelting house," Andrewson recalled, scratching his head. "But that was a long time ago, before the cores changed." A bal girl putting in extra time recalled seeing her heading over the crest of the hill, on the path that led to Lynton Hall. "Why's Mrs. P. going up there, I says to Jane. She didn't know neither, and we just went on wi' our work. Never did see 'er come back. She must've, though, for she didn't even have 'er coat on."

He saw her half a mile from the mine, gliding ahead of him along the side of the trail, aimless-looking, lost. When he caught up to her, he saw that she was holding dead leaves in her hand, spread out from the sterns like a bouquet. "I wanted flowers for her," she said when he asked what she was doing. "But everything's dead. This is all I could find." He wrapped her up in his jacket and hugged her close; she was freezing without knowing it. He rocked her, swayed with her slowly in the icy twilight. "Oh, Con," she cried in a high, whispery gasp against his shoulder. "She doesn't even have a grave!" He couldn't speak; his heart was breaking.

If that day had been the crisis point, if she'd wept, if she'd broken down and turned to him for consolation, all the pain and anxiety would have been worth it. But the emotional storm passed, and soon she retreated to her silent, listless stupor, as though nothing had interrupted it Shut out again, he felt worse this time, colder, because for a few brief moments he'd felt her heat.

After that she went to Guelder infrequently, usually on pay-day, because seeing the miners still gave her some kind of satisfaction. Jenks, Andrewson, and Dickon Penney made the day-to-day decisions. For the first time since her father's death, the work of the mine went on without her.

Anne Morrell came often, but her visits didn't cheer Sophie. Connor wondered if she was unconsciously jealous of her friend, because Anne was happy, and her family was healthy and intact. Christy was one of Sophie's oldest and dearest friends, but even he couldn't penetrate her lethargy. She was inconsolable.

In February, Jack moved out of the house. Connor argued with him, tried to reason with him, ended up shouting at him, but nothing could change his mind. He claimed he was well, which was nonsense. He was better, no doubt of that, but Connor knew the true reason he wanted to move out and take a room in Wyckerley was because he believed his absence could somehow make things better between him and Sophie. If he'd thought there was any chance of that, Connor would probably have helped him pack. But he feared nothing could help them now, and he was close to despair. They didn't even sleep together anymore. He'd taken to staying up late in her father's study, then stretching out on the creaky leather sofa with a blanket, and the nights Dash jumped up to keep him company he counted himself a lucky man. If Sophie was sick with grief, Connor was dying of loneliness. They were like two shipwrecked swimmers, unable to touch hands, each doomed to watch the other's slow drowning.

On a raw, sleety, slate-colored morning in early March, as Connor stared out the study window and tried to believe that life or beauty could ever come back to the desolated rose garden, one careless knock sounded at the door and Jack shuffled into the room. Connor had visited him in his rented room in the village, but this was the first time he'd come to the house since he'd moved out of it. Before Connor could get up out of his chair to greet him, he smelled the liquor, stale and sweet, shocking. "You're drunk," he said wonderingly. "I'll be goddamned, Jack, if you aren't bloody corked."

"No, I ain't. Wisht I was, but I ain't. Not for lack o' tryin', neither."

"The hell you're not. Sit down before you fall over. How did you get here?"

"On my legs, how else?" He dropped heavily into an armchair and slid down low on his backbone, bony knees bent and spread wide, arms flung over the sides, his hands empty and slack. "I come t' tell you I'm going away."

Connor's wintry heart went a little colder. "Don't be an ass," he said, too harshly. "You can't leave, you're sick. Why would you want to anyway? What would you use for money?"

"I were hopin' you'd help me out there wi' a little something. Like I did fer you in Exeter, when ee were all fer gettin' married to Sophie. 'Twouldn't be much, and I'd pay it back onct I got work." He gave a hoarse laugh that ended in coughing. "Now, that's a damn lie, ain't it? I wouldn't pay it back, and you know it. On account o' I ain't going to find work."

"What's wrong, Jack? What's happened?" He looked worse than he had in months, thin and gray again, and his cough sounded so pained, Connor couldn't stand to hear it.

He let his head drop against the back of the chair. "I'm done for, Con, that's all."

"What the hell does that mean?"

"I'm glad fer what you and Sophie did, taking me in and what-not. You tell her thanks for me. And tell 'er good-bye, will ee? I ha'n't the heart."

"Jack—"

"Don't fight wi' me, Con. Please."

"Where would you go?"

"Anywheres."

"But—why? Will you just tell me why you're doing this?"

The ragged laugh came again. "Look at me. Have ee got eyes? Who do I look like to you? Heh? Whose face do you see in mine?"

He couldn't answer. Jack's drawn, wasted features were a mirror of their father's in his last days, but Connor wouldn't have seen it if Jack hadn't forced him to, and he would die himself before acknowledging it in words.

"Yes," he said grimly. He stood up with an effort and looked around the room. "What's to drink? 'Aven't ee a drop fer a weary guest?"

"You shouldn't be drinking."

"What the hell difference does it make?"

"I'll tell Maris to bring tea and something to—"

"Sod it, then," he said angrily, weaving toward the door.

"Jack, don't." He touched his arm. "Let me take care of you. Don't go like this."

Jack stood still with his head bent, not looking at him. "I telled Sidony I didn't care for 'er a'tall," he said in a low rush of words. "Telled 'er I never had done, and I'd only wanted her for lovemaking. She cried, Con. It tore out my heart."

"Why did you say it?"

"To let 'er down the right way. Onct I'm gone, she'll go easier to Holyoake now." His voice dropped to a whisper. "Two nights ago she come to my room. We went to bed, but I couldn't do it. Couldn't get it up for 'er. Because I ain't a man anymore."

"Jack—"

"Don't say a word, hear me? Don't say one word."

They stood that way, eyes averted, Connor's hand resting lightly on his brother's arm. He could feel the same violent aloneness coming toward him, that black emptiness that had struck him down after every other loss he'd suffered. "Don't leave me," he muttered under his breath. "Oh, Jack, don't you leave me, too."

Jack's body shook slightly. "If you love me, Con, you won't ask me t' stay."

"I do love you. I'm asking you."

"But I can't."

"Please, Jack."

They were both weeping now, not able to look at one another. Finally Jack heaved a shallow, unsteady sigh and stepped away. "Go and tell Mrs. B. t' make me a great cup of 'er godawful beef tea, then, will ee? That'd sober up a dead man. Which I ain't just yet. After that, I might like t' lie down on that sofa in the parlor, Con. It still feels like mine, see, and I'm in need of a wink or two after all."

The terrible dark edge receded. Relief flooded through Connor, making him feel giddy. They weren't a demonstrative lot, the Pendarvis boys, but he couldn't help giving Jack a quick, rough embrace. The brittleness of his thin body shocked him, though, tempering the gladness. "I'll be right back. Your clothes are wet, you idiot. Sit down by the fire and rest. I'll be back in two minutes." Jack made a face and fluttered his hand in the air. Connor left him in the study, feeling as if he'd just barely avoided a catastrophe.

Mrs. Bolton wasn't in her usual domain, the kitchen, nor in her suite of rooms in the basement; he finally located her in the attic, surveying trunks of summer linens in preparation for the annual spring cleaning. He told her what he wanted, then went to find Maris, to tell her to get Jack's old room ready because, if he had anything to say about it, his brother was moving back into the house. In the end, he was gone much longer than two minutes.

Long enough for Jack to write a note and leave it on his desk.

*Dont com after me Con. Im like a old dog going off to dy by myself. I have to go and I think you know it deep down. But I won't ever leve you in my hart. Your loving brother, Jack.*

# XXI

Sophie was in her room. A need too strong to resist drew him to her, even though his hopes that she had anything to give him had been dashed a hundred times. She lay on top of the bed, not dressed yet, the half-eaten remains of her breakfast going cold on a tray at the bedside. Her occupations, an unread book, an untouched sewing basket, were strewn about on the unmade bed. She barely glanced at him when he came to stand at the foot, wrapping his arm around the tall bedpost.

"Jack was here. He looks bad. Worse than before." She watched him, her face neutral, expressionless. "I couldn't make him stay. He said . . . he said he was going off to die. I don't even know where he's gone." He whispered the last, afraid he might cry in front of her. And yet he wanted her to know how much pain he was in.

She'd been half lying on her side, propped up on an elbow. Now she lay down, head on the pillow, gazing through half-closed eyes at the coverlet. His news had increased her sadness—nothing more.

"He's dying. Do you hear me? He's the last one, the last one, and he's leaving me, Sophie. *Jack's dying.*"

She crossed her arms over her chest, eyes dull. She was locked inside herself, too full of despair even to see him.

Heat felt like a sickness rising in his chest, making his skin crawl. He kicked at the post again and again with his booted foot, yanked at the tumbled bedclothes until they slid out from under the dead weight of her body. The tray flew off the table when he raked it with his arm, and the crash of plates and cutlery made her cringe. He roared his fury in her stricken face, oaths and accusations, confessing his despair, cursing her helplessness. He was afraid to touch her, afraid he would shake her if he took her by her lifeless shoulders while he shouted out his rage at her. And in the end it didn't matter: she never spoke, and he couldn't even make her cry. He'd stunned her, but he hadn't touched her; she was still dead to him. He cursed her for the last time, not even meaning it now, not even caring, and walked out.

Silence. Sophie got up and dragged herself across the room to the window, careful not to step on any of the broken crockery that littered the floor. She pressed her cheek against the icy windowpane and listened to the whispery ping of sleet as it hit the glass. Her breath steamed the window; she couldn't see out of it and she couldn't see her reflection.

What was that funny animal with plates all over its body . . . she felt like that. Slow and lumbering, but safe underneath the armor. Oh—an armadillo. Poor Connor. He'd tried to pierce the armor with his sadness and his anger, but he couldn't. She wished he had been able to. She wished he had taken a knife and stripped away the scales that covered her from head to toe. Then maybe she could feel something.

She was surprised when he came back, even more so when he took her hand and led her back to bed. He made her sit down, and he sat beside her. She tried to pull her hand away—it felt strange, alien, in his—but he held on. He said, "Listen to me, Sophie. Are you listening?" She nodded. "Darling, I can't live like this anymore. It hurts too much. If I thought I could help you by staying, I would. But I'm only making it worse for you."

He bowed his head over her hand, and she noticed how glossy black his hair was. It reminded her of something, but she couldn't think what. "Are you going away?" she asked, trying to feel a connection with the sound of her own voice. "Are you leaving me?" That helped; those words made her feel something. Loneliness.

He looked up, and the bottomless sorrow in his eyes finally

wounded her. She touched his face, heartsick when she saw a tear spill down his cheek. "I thought we could make it," he said. "So much was against us, and I still believed we'd stay together. But it doesn't work anymore."

"No," she agreed, sighing, resting her cheek against his.

"I don't blame you for hating me. You've never said it, but I know the baby's dying was my fault."

"Oh, no. Oh, no, Con. I don't hate you. It wasn't your fault, I never thought that." He didn't answer. She found the energy to say, "It's just that I can't feel anything. I'm empty inside. My womb—my heart. Empty."

"Sophie, I'll stay if you want me to. Just say it. I'll stay."

She couldn't speak.

They were quiet for a long time. He took out his handkerchief, and she was careful not to look at him while he wiped his face. "It can be any way that suits you, Sophie. A divorce, a separation, whatever you want. I'll get a lawyer, make him draw up a legal paper that says Guelder is yours."

Some kind of new darkness was closing in on her, murkier, heavier than before. "Where will you go?"

"Somewhere." He shook his head. "I'll let you know. In case you need me."

She put her hand on her aching throat. "I'm so sorry. So sorry. I wish . . ."

"I wish . . ." he whispered back. Then he got up, and she watched him pull his old traveling case down from the top of the wardrobe and start to put his clothes in it. She kept trying to rouse herself, but she seemed to be paralyzed; she couldn't move from the bed, and she couldn't make herself say any of the words that might keep him.

In no time, he finished packing. He set his case by the door and came back to her. They both tried to smile. He put his hands on her shoulders, looking hard at her hair, her face. She could barely see him through the darkness that kept drifting between her and everything outside herself. When he kissed her, she felt a moment's warmth, and it was so sweet and shocking, she reached for his hands as they slid off her shoulders. But he straightened and backed away before she could touch him, and the urgency faded under the weight of her inertia.

"Good-bye," he whispered. "I love you."

"I love you, Connor." Would that keep him? No—but it made him smile before he turned from her and went away.

She listened to the sound of his footsteps growing fainter on the stairs, and then a silence, as if he were standing motionless in the hall. Quiet seconds ticked past, and then she heard it— the squeak of the front door opening, and the muffled click of it closing. Then nothing.

Nothing at all. Her clock had run down, and outside, the sleet had stopped falling. She could have been in a coffin, covered with earth—that's how quiet it was. She lay down on her back, legs hanging over the side of the bed, and listened to the slow, lifeless rhythm of her heartbeat. What was the difference between this and dying? Such a fine line. A vague alarm at the direction of her thoughts made her sit up, put her feet on the floor. She walked out into the hall, went to the top of the staircase. "Maris?" she called. "Maris, where are you?"

Presently the maid appeared in the hall below, holding a dirty cloth. "Here." She looked up expectantly. "Do you want something?"

Sophie hung on the stair post, empty-headed. "No."

"Sure? Want anything to eat?"

"What time is it?"

"About one. Do you want some soup?"

"No."

"The mister went out, did 'e? Will 'e be home for dinner?" She shook her head.

"Ma'am?"

"No. He won't be back."

"Oh."

They stared at each other, Maris's homely face creased with

concern. Sophie wanted to keep her somehow, didn't want her to go.

"Well, then. Got my polishin' t' do. 'Scuse me." She peered up at her worriedly.

*Talk to me, Maris, don't leave.* But she couldn't say the words, and Maris finally moved away, out of the line of her vision.

*I'll get dressed,* she thought. *Look at me. I'll have a bath, I'll fix my hair.* She went back to her bedroom, and by the time she got there her resolve had disintegrated. Her feet took her straight to the bed, her old friend. She got under the covers, shivering a little. The sky was clearing, the room brightening. If the sun came out, it would mock her: her mood matched the brown dreariness of the morning, spring at its most treacherous. Yesterday Maris had put a vase of wood sorrel and willow catkins in her room, and she'd made her take them away. Their fresh, light fragrance, almost too faint to notice, had sickened her.

Lying there, staring at the wall, she mused on how much grief felt like fear. She wasn't afraid—was she?—but that's what it felt like. She had a breathlessness in her chest; she kept yawning, swallowing, trying to focus her thoughts on everyday things. Why didn't she feel peaceful now, satisfied? She'd finally driven Connor away. Now she could be truly alone. Wasn't that what she wanted? This shivery strangeness would wear off soon, surely; it must be the novelty of solitude that was making her feel so peculiar.

Thank God for sleep. It was like a cover you could throw over the cage of a noisy, restless bird. She closed her eyes—and saw Connor's face. His tears. He was lucky because he could weep. She couldn't. You had to be alive inside to weep.

She dreamed of a funeral. Christy Morrell was there, but the churchyard was her mother's rose garden. It was nighttime. People she knew—William Holyoake, Miss Pine and Mrs. Thoroughgood, Tranter Fox—were gathered around an open grave, all of them silently crying. Sophie was there and not there, among the mourners sometimes, other times hovering above them in the air, a witness but not a participant. Whose funeral was it? She could smell the strong odor of the opened earth, dark and loamy. Christy took something out of the folds of his robe, a little velvet box, like a jewelry box. This moment went on forever, Christy taking the box out and holding it on the palm of his hand, extended over the grave. She felt a gentle melancholy, that was all, soft and almost soothing. Then Christy let the box slip through his fingers, and as it floated so slowly down into the deep black hole, it came to her that the little box was her baby's coffin. *Oh, no,* she cried, while someone's hands pulled her back from the grave's slippery edge. Her hair was caught on something behind her, something she couldn't see. Was it Birdie? She couldn't turn her head to look.

The mourners began to throw clods of dirt into the grave with their hands, and she screamed at them to *Stop, stop, you'll smother her.* But they couldn't hear her, and in no time there was no grave left, and nothing to mark where it had been; the smooth grass covered everything. Panic filled her. She was on her hands and knees, searching for the shape of the grave in the green, flawless grass, weeping, crying, *Help me,* while the mourners backed away from her, receded farther and farther. She saw Connor with them. *Don't go! Help me, Con!* But he couldn't see her because his eyes were blind and silver and swimming with tears. She tried to follow him, but he kept moving away; no matter how fast she went, she couldn't close the gap between them.

When she woke, she couldn't tell what was real. She had been crying in the dream, and she was crying now, painful, wrenching sobs that frightened her because the harrowing sound was so desperate. She hadn't been able to weep before, and now she couldn't stop. She cried for her daughter and her husband, and the loss of her own innocence—the childlike certainty that her life would be smooth and happy, free of darkness, one good thing after another. Tears choked her; she couldn't stop. Maris found her—held her—grew frantic with worry for her. Sophie wanted to tell her she didn't need help, that she was beyond consoling, but she couldn't speak. And her tears weren't the pitiful torment Maris thought they were. Even while the hard, aching sobs racked her, she could feel something settling, a tight knot inside loosening, untangling. Was the drought in her heart ending, were the ceaseless tears her salvation? She would grieve for her lost child until she died, but she was alive now, and in fleeting breaks in the darkness it was possible to imagine—not tomorrow, not soon, but someday—the dry desert in her soul blooming and flowering again.

The emotional storm left her limp. She fell into a dreamless sleep, and she didn't wake up until Maris came in with a cup of coffee and a message—that her uncle was downstairs and wanted to see her right away. "Why?" she asked groggily, feeling as if she'd been sleeping for years.

"I don't know, but he's riled up something turrible. Says he wants t' come up and talk *here*."

"Here?" She glanced down at her rumpled nightgown, ran a hand through the tangles in her hair. At least the room was tidy—Maris must have cleared away the broken dishes while she'd slept.

"You want to get dressed and come down, or should I just send 'im up?"

She took a swallow of hot coffee, trying to clear her head. "I don't care. Bring him up, I suppose. What could he want?"

Maris shrugged, handing Sophie her velvet night robe. "Better put this on," she advised, and Sophie thanked her absently, sticking her arms in the sleeves. "I've seen you lookin' better," she said frankly. "Want yer hairbrush?"

"No, just send him up, Maris. If he says it's important, it may be something about the mine."

While she waited, she got out of bed and put on her slippers. The curtains were closed, but the clock was running—Maris must have wound and reset it—and she saw that it was almost ten o'clock in the morning. Good Lord. She also saw, after a quick, depressing glance in the mirror, that she looked awful. No time to worry about that, though: two seconds later her uncle burst into the room, red-faced and windblown, and as upset as she'd ever seen him.

Her appearance stopped him in his tracks. "My God, Sophie! What's wrong with you?"

"Nothing's wrong—I just woke up. Tell me what's happened. Is it something at Guelder?"

He turned around to close the door. "Yes. You've been robbed."

"Robbed!"

"Your safe was burgled last night, and someone took the payroll money, about two hundred pounds. The thief knocked Andrewson unconscious, and no one found him until eight o'clock this morning when the cores changed."

"Oh, no. Is he hurt?"

"No, he's fine—he's the one who rode to my house an hour ago to tell me."

"Rode to your house? But—why didn't he come to me?"

Uncle Eustace smoothed his hand up and down the front of his waistcoat. For the first time, he hesitated. "Andrewson says . . ." He looked off past her shoulder. "Sophie, I'm sorry. Andrewson says the man who hit him was your husband."

She laughed. "That's ridiculous."

"I thought so, too," he said, nodding, looking slightly relieved because the worst was out. "But he won't budge. He swears it was Connor, and nobody can talk him out of it."

"But it couldn't have been."

"I'm afraid that's not all. Robert Croddy was with me when Andrewson, arrived—we were having a business meeting over breakfast."

"Oh, God . . ."

He nodded grimly. "I didn't know what Andrewson wanted—I told him he could speak in front of Robert. That was a mistake."

She went cold. "What has he done?"

"He wanted me to issue an arrest warrant immediately. I talked him out of that, told him there wasn't enough evidence yet. But I couldn't stop him from going straight off to Clive Knowlton's with the news."

"*What?*"

"Maris told me Connor's not here, wasn't here all night. Where is he?" She stared at him, her mind in chaos. "Tell me. Can't you see, we have to warn him. Croddy's out to ruin him, Sophie. Where is he?"

"He's gone."

"Gone?"

She reached for his arm, held onto the sleeve with desperate fingers. "Connor would never steal money, never, it's absurd! But—last night he—we—"

"What?"

"He left me. It wasn't his fault, we didn't argue, he just—left."

"Where did he go?"

"I don't know." Eustace began to swear, and she cut him off. "He might have gone to Tavistock. He has an office there, or rather Braithwaite does. It's on Tamar Street. He's stayed there—"

"I know it. I'll go there now. If he's not there, I'll go to Knowlton's and try to head Robert off." He pried her fingers away and gave her hand a squeeze. "Try not to worry." His eyes flickered over her doubtfully. "You know, you look terrible."

He was opening the door when she stopped him to ask, genuinely puzzled, "Why are you helping him? Isn't Connor's trouble a blessing for you? And your candidate?"

His fine brows drew together in disapproval. "That's irrelevant," he told her sternly. "It's the reverse of a blessing for my *family*."

Her throat closed up. She said, "Thank you, Uncle," but he couldn't have heard; he'd already turned away, and her voice didn't carry far.

After he left, she paced the room. Throwing open the curtains, she was surprised to see yesterday's dreariness had vanished in a flood of bright sunshine, birds singing, bees droning, squirrels rooting in the ivy. What day was it? Thursday? She had no idea what day of the month it was, none whatsoever. Pacing again, she tried to imagine Connor's reaction when he found out from her uncle that Robert Croddy was calling him a thief. Would he think she believed it? Oh, surely he wouldn't, surely he would know her better than that. The idea of him stealing money was laughable—but what if Knowlton believed it? Robert could be persuasive, and Connor's past could be made to sound disreputable. What if he were disgraced?

She hugged herself, shot through with anxiety. Her skin felt as if pins were pricking it everywhere "Maris!" No answer. She hurried out of the room and hollered down the stairs, "Maris!"

"Ma'am?" came a faint voice from the basement, over the sound of footsteps clumping up the stairs.

"I want a bath, right away, as quick as you can. Did Connor take the horse or the gig?"

Maris blinked at her. "What?"

"Did my husband take the pony gig last night when he left?"

"I don't—no, I'm sure 'e didn't, because Thomas was grumblin' and natterin' about Val this morning, how 'e'd rolled in something and needed brushed and whatnot, plus—"

"Tell Thomas to have the gig ready in forty minutes," she cut in. "Pick out something for me to wear while I bathe, and then I want you to help me with my hair."

The maid's eyes went so wide, Sophie could see the whites from twenty feet away. "Yes, ma'am," she exclaimed, pleased and excited. "Where you going?"

"Tavistock. To pay a call on Clive Knowlton."

She had to ask directions to his house. The narrow, two-story brick residence in the oldest section of the town wasn't what she was expecting, but after a second's reflection, she decided it suited him: a modest home for a modest man. The servant who opened the door was creaky, white-haired, and venerable; she didn't like having to bully him.

"But I must see him, it's urgent. He knows me. If you would just take my name up, I'm sure he'll receive me."

"I'm terribly sorry, madam, but Mr. Knowlton is in a meeting, and specifically asked that he not be disturbed."

"Is he with Robert Croddy? Is he? Please tell me."

Her urgency cut through his imperturbable veneer. "Mr. Croddy is among the gentlemen with whom Mr. Knowlton is meeting."

*Gentlemen.* Was her uncle here, too, then? And Connor? "I'm sorry, I must come in," she told the astonished butler, pressing forward until he had no decorous choice but to give way. "Where are they?"

"Madam, really, I insist—"

She could hear men's voices from the top of a dark flight of stairs straight ahead. Grabbing her skirts in one hand and the railing in the other, she started up, with the poor old butler hurrying behind.

All four men assembled in Clive Knowlton's small, simply furnished drawing room gaped in surprise when they saw her. "Sophie!" exclaimed her uncle, rising from a brocaded settee.

Connor came away from the window, alarm replacing the harsh stiffness that had been in his face. "Sophie, what's wrong? Are you all right?"

They touched hands for a second, only a light, reassuring clasp, but it warmed her to her bones. "I'm fine," she told him in a low, fervent murmur, then turned from him toward her host. He'd gotten up from his chair beside the cold brick hearth; she went to him, deliberately turning her back on Robert Croddy, who had also risen at her entrance, and offered Knowlton her hand. "I'm so terribly sorry," she said in an earnest rush, "I hope you'll forgive me, but I simply had to come. I'm afraid I was rude to your manservant when he wouldn't admit me, and I apologize—"

"Not at all, my dear lady," he said kindly, but his sad brown eyes missed nothing. "It's a pleasure to see you again. Won't you sit down? Wallace, bring Mrs. Pendarvis some tea, will you?"

"Oh, no, please don't trouble." She couldn't sit down; she was too wrought up. "There's no sense in pretending I've come on a social call. My uncle told me about the burglary last night at Guelder mine. May I assume that Mr. Croddy has come here to implicate my husband?"

They all began to answer at once, and she understood from the jumble of raised voices that Connor, Uncle Eustace, and Robert Croddy very much wanted her to leave. Not on their lives, she thought grimly, taking a seat on the edge of a straight-backed chair out of deference to her elderly host—if she didn't sit, he wouldn't.

"Mr. Croddy," Knowlton said, his famous voice, low and carrying, cutting through all the others, "has apprised me of a serious accusation against your husband, as well as certain other concerns he has. Concerns of an ethical nature, we might say, which may or may not have a bearing on Mr. Pendarvis's suitability for public office."

She could barely contain herself. "If Robert says my husband is a thief, that's absurd," she declared, "absolutely ridiculous. It's idiotic. Guelder belongs to him—why would he steal from his own mine? Anyway, if Connor were starving to death, he wouldn't take a shilling that didn't belong to him. There's no one more honest—" Croddy snorted, interrupting her. She hated the sight of him, but she made herself look at him to demand, "What else have you said? Well? What other slanders against Connor have you felt *morally obliged* to pass on to Mr. Knowlton?"

He folded his stocky arms. "Sophie, go home," he said pityingly.

She turned back to Knowlton. "Has he told you my husband secured employment at Guelder under false pretenses? It's true. He took his brother's name and worked as a tutman in the mine for two months. He did it to expose harsh working conditions that had existed at Guelder since my father leased it sixteen years ago."

"Sophie, don't," Connor said softly, and across the room her uncle ran a hand through his sleek silver hair and muttered inaudibly.

She ignored both of them. "Connor opened my eyes. Because of him, something is finally being done to make my miners' lot a little easier, a little more humane. It doesn't take much to change a job from unbearable to bearable—just common sense, some ingenuity, a *willingness* to change. Connor showed me that, and it's my fondest wish that the reforms I've initiated at Guelder will spread to other mines all over Devon—starting with Salem," she said pointedly, looking at her uncle. He crossed his legs and sat back, looking resigned.

"Bravo," said Robert, pretending to laugh indulgently. "That may be all well and good, but it's hardly the point."

She couldn't sit still; she jumped to her feet, motioning to Knowlton to keep his seat. "Did he tell you that Connor took a personal advantage of me? That's a lie." She could feel the heat of embarrassment seeping into her face, but she kept talking. "He never did anything I didn't want, or agree to, or ask of him first. I'm a grown woman, not a child, Mr. Knowlton. I was not used by my husband, and he did not marry me for my money, or to satisfy the property requirement so that he could stand for election in the House of Commons. The idea is repulsive and absurd, and it says more about Mr. Croddy that he would level such a charge than it does about my husband."

"I very much resent that," Robert said, voice shaking, face reddening. "This—this—*paragon* Mrs. Pendarvis is speaking of is the same violent brute who knocked me down in the street, with no provocation whatsoever!"

Knowlton looked shocked. "Is this true?"

Connor started to answer, but Sophie spoke up first. "It's true that he hit him. It's not true that he wasn't provoked. I had just told my husband . . . something about Robert." She hesitated, wondering how in the world to explain this.

Croddy took the dilemma out of her hands. "She must've told him I turned her down when she begged me to marry her," he announced, barely able to hide his triumph.

She didn't doubt that he'd been dying to reveal this sordid detail all along, and she'd just handed him the perfect opportunity. An instinct made her cross the room to Connor in three long strides and clasp his forearm in both hands. "Don't," she whispered. He was too angry to hear. She gave his arm a shake, claiming his full attention. "Connor, *don't*."

Behind her, her uncle roared, "What did you say?"

"It's true," Robert gloated. "This pillar of honesty got a child on Miss Sophie Deene before he was unmasked as an impostor and forced to leave town. That's the sort of man you would be endorsing, sir, if Mr. Pendarvis is allowed to sit on the bench in the Commons!"

"Damn you, sir," cried Eustace. "I'll challenge you for that!"

"You'll have to take your turn," Connor snarled. He was yanking at Sophie's clutching fingers, but she held on tight, blocking him from Robert with her body.

Clive Knowlton surged to his feet. "Mr. Croddy, I think it would be wise of you to leave now," he advised quietly, but once again the authority in his voice silenced everyone else. "These gentlemen appear to mean you a great deal of harm, and I must tell you in all candor that I would not lift a finger to stop them."

Robert paled, realizing he'd made a mistake. He made Knowlton a low, abject bow. "I beg your pardon, sir. Please understand, this is extremely distasteful to me; I would not have dreamed of compromising Mrs. Pendarvis unless—"

"Unless you saw a political advantage in it," Vanstone accused.

Croddy darted a worried glance at his old ally. The magnitude of his error was dawning on him before their eyes. He turned back to Knowlton, hands imploring, the picture of earnest entreaty. "Don't make any judgment in haste, that's all I ask. Keep in mind what you know of Connor Pendarvis—things no one here has disputed. Remember that he lied to Sophie and to the whole village of Wyckerley. He seduced her—"

"That's a lie," Sophie cried.

"—Betrayed and abandoned her, only married her because he saw gain in it for himself. I can personally attest to the fact that he's prone to violence; an eyewitness swears he's a thief. And that's not even taking into account his politics."

"Good day, Mr. Croddy."

"Sir, he's a Wesleyan socialist—radical—anarchist—" Robert shut up abruptly, as the futility of saying another word seemed to bear in on him all at once.

A few excruciating seconds passed. Just as he turned to go, Knowlton said, "I'm quite sure that nothing that's been said here today will be repeated. To anyone, by anyone. Am I correct in that assumption, Mr. Croddy? Because if I'm incorrect, the source of the repetition will be easy enough to identify. And while I'm only a former Commons man, and not a very important one at that, I still have a small degree of influence in certain circles. Particularly the local business world. I would not hesitate to use it against someone whose loose tongue did any harm to this lady. Are you following me, sir?"

Croddy's face was red as a beet. "Perfectly," he said through his teeth. He made a sharp, jerky bow, like a mechanical soldier, and stalked out of the room.

Sophie sagged a little, relieved beyond measure that he was gone, and that Connor hadn't hit him before he left. What she wanted to do more than anything was throw her arms around her husband and hold on for a long, long time. Instead she started to draw away, steeling herself to be dignified and proper for a little longer, until they could finally be alone. But he surprised her by cupping his hand on one side of her face and pressing his cheek to the other, and the light, intense embrace moved her so much, her eyes welled with tears. She heard her uncle's uncomfortable throat-clearing, but before they broke away she whispered, "I do love you," in Connor's ear. His eyes were hidden by his downcast lashes, but the soft smile on his lips told her everything was going to be all right now.

Mr. Knowlton had resumed his seat. He was lighting a cigar. Sophie tried to read his mood from his face, but he was a consummate diplomat: nothing showed that he didn't want to show.

Was he angry? Disgusted? He'd all but thrown Robert out of his house, but that didn't necessarily mean he found the present company very much more agreeable. "You've been silent for quite a while," he said ponderously, glancing at Connor from under his white eyebrows. "May I ask what you're thinking?"

Sophie thought he would set her away now, address his potential patron empty-handed, so to speak, because some might say a man who touched his wife in public was undignified or indecorous, or weak. But Connor kept her in a loose embrace, his hand on the curve of her waist, and answered, "I'm thinking it must be all the years you sat on the bench that have made you such a patient man, Mr. Knowlton. I'd have thrown the lot of us out by now if I were you and this were my home."

Knowlton made an enigmatic *hmph* and blew a smoke ring. "Anything else?"

"I'm thinking that some of the things Croddy said about me are true." Sophie started shaking her head. "And there are other things he didn't say—only because he doesn't know about them—that I'm not particularly proud of. I think I'm about as unlikely a candidate for Parliament as you're likely to find, sir. I haven't the nerve to ask you to endorse me, and frankly, I don't know why you would."

Sophie couldn't take another self-effacing word. "Well, *I* can think of—" she started to say, but Connor gave her a squeeze to keep her quiet.

"In spite of my inadequacies, though, I'll admit that I still want to serve in the Commons. In fact, I want it very much. But I'll also tell you this. If you decide you can't support me, Mr. Knowlton, for the rest of my life I'll look back on this day, this hour, and no matter what else happens it'll always be one of my happiest memories. Because this is the day I got my wife back." He smiled down into Sophie's shining eyes. "You could offer me the prime minister's job, sir, and in all honesty, it wouldn't hold a candle to that." Through tears she couldn't blink away, Sophie thought she saw a shadow of sorrow drift over Knowlton's still, thoughtful face. Connor must have seen it, too. His voice was low and gentle when he said, "We won't impose on you any longer. I want to say I'm grateful to you, sir, for your tolerance. And your kindness."

He was thinking of the promise of discretion Knowlton had forced out of Robert. Sophie murmured an echo of the sentiment, glancing away from Knowlton to her uncle, who was looking unusually subdued.

Knowlton stood up. "I'm against patronage," he said gruffly. "I don't want the responsibility of choosing my own successor. It ought to be in the hands of the electors, and if I choose you, Mr. Pendarvis, I'd expect you to work long and hard to make that process the law of the land."

"I would, sir," Connor answered in surprise.

"Not that I am choosing you," he added, puffing irritably on his cigar. "As far as I'm concerned Croddy's out, but his cronies will undoubtedly field someone else now. I hope he's a genius; I hope he's a saint. If he is, I'll pick him."

"Quite right, sir."

"Come to see me next week," he said unexpectedly. "Don't bring your handlers—come by yourself. I'll give you a meal. We'll talk."

"Thank you," Connor said, nonplussed.

"I think Croddy's probably right—you're too radical. But I'd like to find it out for myself. In any case, there's one thing on which I can agree with you right now. It isn't the power a man's wielded or the money he's made or the fame he's acquired that bring him contentment as he closes in on the end of his life. It's the ones he's loved. The ones who have loved him. Nothing else comes close to that. I didn't understand that bit of wisdom at your age. I'll admit, it's a point in your favor." Years fell away from his tired face when he smiled. "See that you don't lose sight of it."

"I never will," Connor vowed, and he wasn't smiling at all.

# XXII

They went to the office in Tamar Street, where Connor had spent the night, to retrieve the traveling case he'd left behind after Vanstone found him there and whisked him off to Knowlton's. "So this is where you've been going every day," Sophie said interestedly, standing in the center of the small, cluttered room and turning around in a circle. It was the most ordinary of offices, purely masculine and unornamented, but she surveyed it with great fascination. Indeed, all the way from Knowlton's house in the pony gig, she'd been eyeing the world around her as if she'd never seen it before, or not for a long, long time. She'd been sleeping. Now she was awake, and Connor gave her a soft hug, thanking God for the miracle of his wife.

"Oh, *bread*," she exclaimed, finding the remains of last night's supper on his desk half buried under a pile of scribbled pages. "How lovely. I'm starving."

"By all means, help yourself."

"Did you sleep on that?" she asked with her mouth full, pointing to the scruffy couch taking up space along the far wall.

"I did. Ian donated it when he found out I was spending nights here."

"Ugly, isn't it?"

"That's probably why his wife let him have it." She was removing piles of books and papers from the sofa, and the blanket he'd slept under last night. He watched her, perplexed, while she sat down at one end and patted the place beside her. "What are you doing?"

She sent him a blinding smile. "Getting ready to be properly kissed, I hope."

He dropped the shirt he'd been folding. His face must have looked funny, because she started to laugh before he could reach her. He laughed, too, for the sheer joy of touching her, his Sophie, and he swore out loud before he kissed her that he would never let her go again.

"Never," she promised, too, holding him close. "We'll be together for always, Con."

"Forever."

"And ever. No matter what."

They had made rash promises before—they'd never quarrel again, for example—but this one they would keep, he knew it. "Sophie, thank God you came back to me. Nothing mattered when I thought I'd lost you." He gestured to the cluttered room, the desk. "I didn't care about any of this, the election, Knowlton's approval. I'd have gone through the motions because of Ian and the others, but it wouldn't have meant anything. Even if I'd won—"

"You *will* win."

"—who could I have shared the victory with? It would've felt like nothing. Just the start of a long, hard job."

"I'm sorry about everything. I've been an *awful* wife—no, let me say this. Losing our baby was the worst thing that's ever happened to me, Con. I was in this *pit*, and I couldn't get out. I'm *glad* you left me, thank God you left me, because it woke me up! I'll never stop grieving for the child we lost, but I'm alive now and I can feel again, and I need you so much. I think *I've* been a child—I didn't know what husbands and wives should *be* to each other, or I forgot. You're my lover, Connor, and my best friend, and you always will be. Please tell me you forgive me for turning away from you. But I just—couldn't—"

"Sophie, Sophie." He couldn't stop kissing her, even though every word she said was like medicine for a sick man. "I'm so glad, sweetheart. God, I can't wait to get you home." Her face still bore the evidence of her tears, but to him she'd never looked so beautiful.

"I know," she whispered, "I can't either. It's been so long." Suddenly her eyes flew open. "But Con—why wait?"

The identical realization struck him at the same time. "Why wait?" he echoed, and it was as if they'd just invented the steam engine, or discovered a new route to the Indies.

"And to think I called this sofa ugly," Sophie said wonderingly, winding her arms around his neck and pulling him down. "Oh, I've missed you, missed you, missed you," she crooned, putting soft kisses on his cheeks for punctuation. "Hurry, let's hurry." She was wearing a little black jacket over a cream-colored shirtwaist, and he insinuated his hand between their bodies to slip tortoise-shell buttons out of the buttonholes, not hurrying, savoring the smiling curve of her lips against his. He slid the jacket off her shoulders and started on the blouse, and in no time at all he had her down to her skirt and corset. "Oh my, this is so wicked," she breathed, reclining against the sofa arm, playing with his hair. "Doing this here instead of at home, in our bed. Don't you think it's wicked?"

"Mmm. Decadent." The little snaps down the front of her corset weren't cooperating. "Come here," he ordered, making her lean toward him so he could untie the laces at the back. That was faster; the whole thing came off like a sexy straitjacket, and there she was, bare to the waist. He feasted his eyes on her full white breasts, so beautiful, murmuring, "Oh, Sophie, look at you." He made her lie back on a pillow he put against the sofa arm, so she would be comfortable while he took his pleasure with her, caressing her and making her sigh.

"I don't want to wait," she whispered.

"Shhh. Close your eyes."

"No, I want to watch you."

"Very contrary today. I'll make you close your eyes." And he bent to her and took one luscious nipple in his mouth, rasping his tongue against the tip, teasing it with dangerous little nips of his teeth. Her breathy, helpless little gasps excited him. He pulled away to look at her, her pouting lips and heavy-lidded eyes, cheeks pink and glowing with arousal. "I love the way you look right now. You're beautiful, Sophie."

"You are," she countered, trying to tug his shirt out of his trousers. "Would you still love me if I were ugly?"

"Yes," he said immediately. "But . . ."

"But . . . ?"

"It would've taken me longer to get to know you." He slid his hands under her knees and pulled her legs over his lap. "Now I've got you," he gloated. "Let me see your legs." She squealed when he threw skirts and petticoats up, half burying her, so he could look at her long thighs, neatly sheathed in white silk stockings. He hummed his enjoyment, watching her face while he tickled her very softly under her knee, and then the band of warm skin above the top of her stocking. She was holding her breath, wishing and waiting. When he pushed her legs apart a little, she gave a stifled gasp and then a groan of frustrated anticipation. He lifted one of her knees and pressed it out, and sleeked a hot, slow trail with his palm down the inside of her thigh to the center of her. Her eyes were squeezed shut, neck straining, waiting, waiting. *Touch me,* she begged him with her body. He thought of waiting until she said it with her tongue, but she was just too tempting. "Wanton woman," he whispered, and gave her what she wanted.

She cried out at the first light brush of his fingers, and he gentled his touch, caressing her slowly, deeply, gauging her response by her soft sighs and the wonderful expressions ghosting across her face. Oh, she was lovely, lovely, and she was all his. And he was thinking, *What did I do to deserve this?* when she clutched at his knee and slowly arched her back. "Con," she said in the merest whisper, and then she turned her cheek into the pillow. It took her fast and hard; he could feel the deep, deep shudders inside, undoing her. They released her with excruciating slowness and left her gasping; spent and wasted, she drooped over him like a wilted flower—and then all he wanted to do was give her the pleasure all over again.

She lay still, and the minutes slipped by peacefully in that limbo time, that delicious interval when lovemaking is both a memory and an imminence. He stroked her stomach, her ribs, the space between her breasts, amusing himself by debating which was softer, Sophie's skin or a satin pillow. The dreamy look in her eyes was clearing. When she sat up on her own power, he knew she'd come back to life.

"Why am I the only one half-naked around here?" she wondered, sliding her hands inside his waistcoat. He started to take off his jacket. "I'm doing this," she corrected, and he held his hands up, surrendering gladly. But he couldn't resist kissing her intent face while she went about her business, undoing his shirt buttons, unbuckling his belt. "What's this?" she mumbled, pulling on his clothes. He didn't pay any attention. "What *is* this?"

Too late, he saw what she'd found in the inside pocket of his jacket. He made an awkward grab for it, but she jerked away, sliding off his lap and scrambling to her feet.

"Connor—Connor—"

She couldn't talk. She held the small gray flannel bag, heavy with banknotes, at arm's length, her stormy eyes shifting from it to him, searching his face, frantic with confusion.

Connor sagged against the seedy old couch, dragging his hands from his knees to his thighs. He let his head fall back. Some kind of bitter laughter was welling up in him—but the taste was sour on the back of his tongue; he bit it back. He moved his sluggish gaze from the ceiling to Sophie, waiting for the ax to fall.

Instead, the bewilderment in her face slowly sharpened. He saw the truth in her eyes at the instant it hit her. "Jack. It was Jack." She looked at the bag of money in her hands, shaking her head, and the sad, resigned twist of her lips mirrored everything he was feeling. "It was Jack, wasn't it."

He could lie to protect him, just as he'd lied to Vanstone and Knowlton. But not to Sophie. Not now. "He came to the house yesterday. I told you—do you remember? He was drunk, sick. He said he was going away to die, and nothing I could say to him did any good. I had to let him go."

"Oh, Con." She came to him as he was getting up to go to her, and she put her bare arms around him and held tight.

"This morning he came here—I don't know how he found me—and told me what he'd done. He got the key to your desk drawer out of your purse in the hall yesterday—he knew you kept it there because he heard us talking about it once, months ago. He was going to take the money and run away, go somewhere to die in style, he said, and nobody he loved would have to take care of him or watch him fade away. This morning he was a wreck—ashamed, panicky. Hung over. He gave me the money, and I said I'd make it all right. Somehow. I told him to go home and stay out of trouble."

"Oh, God," Sophie breathed, resting her temple on his shoulder. "Connor, what should we do? We could put it back, but then . . ."

"Everyone would think you'd done it for me. They'd still think I stole it."

"I could say there never was a payroll . . . no, Jenks saw me counting it out on Tuesday. That won't work."

"Besides, Andrewson's still got a bump on his head. That can't be explained away."

"Jack really hit him? Hard?"

"Knocked him out cold."

"Oh, God." She put her cheek next to his. "Con, I'm so sorry. I mean for Jack, because he's so sick. I love him, too."

"I know you do." This was what he'd wanted and needed from her so badly yesterday. He took it now, forgiving her as she'd asked him to, and counting himself the luckiest of men. "Sophie, let me love you."

"Yes." She pressed against him, and they were heart to heart

338

at last, without secrets or pride. They lay down on the sagging sofa, and when they came together the sensation of merging was new, not quite like anything they'd felt before. They'd gone to some higher level, and it was scary and exciting to think that there would be other planes of intimacy after this, layer after layer, and it would never stop because there was no ending, no limit. Connor wanted this perfect time, this moment of aching, absolute rightness to last forever—but even as he thought it, he could feel his body starting to betray him, bent on another course entirely. "Sophie," he sighed, philosophical, and the last kiss he gave her blended wistfulness with anticipation. Surrendering to the inevitable, he took comfort in knowing that the elusive prize of oneness could be captured again, and again, and that they had a whole lifetime to strive for it.

They rode home slowly in the pony cart, dazed, aware that they were seeing the Devonshire spring for the first time but barely able to concentrate on it; they were still too wrapped up in one another. Tranter Fox riding a donkey between the two stone gateposts flanking the drive to Stone House was an arresting sight. Valentine turning in and Tranter's donkey coming out almost collided in the toll road.

"Whoa!" Tranter's worried face lit up when he saw them. "Praise the Lord, ee're 'ome! I been sended three times since noon t' tell you—there'm turrible trouble at Guelder!"

Sophie grabbed the seat on one side and Connor's thigh on the other, steadying herself while he wrestled with the reins, calming Val. "What's wrong?"

"Fire at the forty level. Nobody's sayin' who, but they think a man hung a lantern too close t' the scaffold beam, and it catched. Charles Oldene and his team was sinking a pit all the way down the south gallery and didn't see nor smell a thing till it were too late. Now they'm trapped."

Without a word, Connor turned the pony toward the mine and whipped him into a canter. Tranter jogged behind or alongside, shouting out the rest of the story, while Sophie held on, white-knuckled, to the jouncing cart and tried to control her fear. Fire had eaten away the support timbers at the entrance to the gallery, collapsing it under a ton of burned rubble and ore. The cave-in had stopped the fire by smothering it, but it had also walled up the winze through which fresh air pumped into the gallery. Miners had been working feverishly to haul away the fallen debris, but the danger of another collapse made the work slow and potentially deadly. In fact, half an hour ago Jenks had told them to stop, Tranter reported, until new timbers could be wedged in to protect them. Meanwhile, Oldene, Roy Donne, and Rollie Coachman were running out of breathable air. "Ee can 'ear 'em weakenin,' the tributers say. They'm layin' down flat where what's left is cooler, savin' up their strength. But every man knows, ma'am, it's likely the end of 'em."

Guelder mine swarmed with villagers; it looked as if half of Wyckerley had turned out to wait and pray for the three men trapped underground. The scraggly crowd parted to let the pony cart pass, and before Connor reached the mine office, Andrewson and Jenks burst out the door and rushed toward them. Sophie was struggling for composure, but memories of another disaster— three years ago, when Tranter had been trapped and they'd come so close to losing him—kept flashing through her mind.

Jenks reached for her hand and helped her down from the cart. "Sophie, thank God," he muttered. He never called her So-phie—she'd never seen his face so grim. She waited for him to tell her the worst, and when he didn't, she said, "Mr. Jenks, what's happening? Are they still trapped? Are you using mules to pull away the rubble? How many men do you have at the forty right now?"

He clawed at his black beard, avoiding her eyes to glance over her shoulder. "Come into the countinghouse. I've sommat to tell you and yer husband."

Oh, Jesus. They were dead, then, she knew it. Instinctively, she wheeled around toward Connor. Across Val's back, she saw his face turn paper-white, heard him gasp. "Connor? Con?" Swatting Jenks's hand away, she darted around the pony cart. "What?" she cried. "What is it?" Beside her, Andrewson backed away, head down.

She took Connor's hands—they were ice-cold. She saw her own panic reflected back in his eyes. "It's Jack," he said hoarsely. "Jack!"

"Andrewson says he went down. They needed a man to load buckets with attle and rock for the animals to haul out, and nobody would go. Because it's too dangerous, too close to the broken ceiling. Jack said he'd do it, and nobody stopped him!" He let go of her hands when she winced. Fear and anger hardened his face; he turned his stony profile toward the mine entrance. "I'm going down to get him."

"What?" Her first grab didn't stop him—the back of his coat slid right out of her hand. The second time, she grabbed his shoulder and pulled him back on his heels. "Connor—damn it—" He got away again. She had to run and stumble in front of him to block the way. "You can't go down—"

"Sophie, I have to."

"No!" When he shouldered past her, she seized his arm and held it. He kept moving, dragging her along, trying to pry her fingers away. "Damn it, Con, you can't go. It's my mine, and I'm telling you. Stop!"

He stopped. But only to take her by the biceps and give her a gentle shake. "I'm going. I'll be all right. I have to get him out."

"Fine, then I'm going with you." She turned away from the consternation in his face to shout, "Mr. Jenks! Bring me my hat and boots, I'm going down in the mine!"

"The hell you are," Connor growled, trying to turn her around by the arm. "Don't make me angry, Sophie, don't be a fool."

"I'm not the fool here. Will you listen to me? Or listen to Jenks—because you don't know what you're getting into, Con. Neither do I, and it's crazy to go down when you don't know if you can help or not or what the situation—"

He shut her up by pulling her into his arms for a fast, rib-cracking hug. "Sophie, you know I have to go. Jack's my brother."

He released her, and she started to cry. Was it right to let him go? Crazy? She couldn't decide, so she ran after him, and caught him at the top of the first ladder.

"Wait, Con, wear a helmet—go with Jenks, and Tranter, too—please, please, don't do anything stupid—"

A man popped up, soundless, onto the top platform of the newest extension of the man-machine. Under the grime, the whites of Bob Douthwaite's eyes gleamed like marbles. Another man, Hector Hardaway, came up after him. "They're out!" Bob yelled. Sophie, Connor, Jenks, Tranter, and a dozen others crowded around the two miners. "The Cornishman done it, loaded the buckets and cleared a way for 'em to scramble out. There ain't a scratch on 'em!"

Raucous cheers deafened her; Sophie saw Connor go close to Bob and shout a question in his face. She fought her way to them, in time to hear Douthwaite shout back, "No, he weren't hurt—there weren't a cave-in. But afterward, he collapsed—can't walk, can't get up—they're fixing to haul him to grass in the kibble bucket!"

The wait for Jack wasn't long, but it was intolerable. Dr. Hesselius had been at Guelder all morning, and he stood with Sophie and Connor at the mine entrance now. Christy Morrell was absent, gone to Exeter for a bishop's conference, but the Wesleyan preacher from Totnes lingered with the crowd, waiting to see if his services would be needed. The three trapped men had come up already, greeted with tears and embraces from their families and friends. The drama was over, but hardly anyone had gone home; they were waiting for the last man, the sickly hero they barely knew. Yesterday he'd stolen from them—the story was out; Jack had told Andrewson and the others what he'd done before he went down—and today he'd risked his life to save three of them. Sophie was aware of neighbors, friends, miners, gathered in quiet clusters across the muddy yard, voices subdued and their faces expectant. But she only had eyes for Connor, whose unbearable tension she shared like a twin, or as if invisible cable wires connected them, telegraphing thoughts and emotions instantly.

At last, over the low, rhythmic rumble of the steam pumps, she heard the creak of the bell crank as the huge winding machine began to turn. The great chain, thick as a tree limb, rattled slowly around and around the wooden wheel. After an eternity, the lip of the iron kibble appeared in the shaft and rose fast, its muddy, six-foot sides blocking her view of the occupants. Moody Donne scrambled out onto the bucket platform, and the other men in the kibble lifted Jack's limp, wasted body down into his arms.

They laid him on a blanket on the ground. Connor knelt on one side, holding his hand, while the doctor took his pulse and listened to his heart on the other. He was wide-awake, but his voice when he spoke didn't carry; Connor had to bend over him to hear. "Mucked up again," he said in a raspy whisper, trying to grin. "Can't seem t' do anything the right way."

"Shush, Jack."

"They were s'pose to bring me out feet first, Con. Not go through all this. Ha'n't got the strength for this."

Dr. Hesselius stood up. "Bring that wagon closer. I want four men to lift him, and I want more blankets."

Sophie asked softly, "Will you take him to the hospital in Tavistock?"

He shook his head. "There's no point, nothing I can do for him. Take him home, Sophie. Make him comfortable. That's all." His mournful eyes told her everything.

Sidony Timms had taken the doctor's place at Jack's side. Small and lovely, tears streaking down her cheeks, she held his hand in both of hers and told him how proud she was of him. "What a brave thing you did, Jack, truly. When you're well and strong, we'll have a celebration. Think of it—you might get a medal!" Her voice broke; she had to wipe her face with her sleeve.

Jack looked over her shoulder and crooked his finger, smiling weakly. Sophie hadn't noticed William Holyoake before; he was standing behind Sidony, and now he knelt down next to her. "Take good care of 'er," Jack croaked, still holding up his index finger. "She've chose the better man, but if I hear of any wicked treatment, I'll come back to haunt you, Mr. Holyoake."

William leaned in close. "I'll be as kind to 'er as you could wish, Mr. Pendarvis. I swear that." And he watched, still and patient, while Sidony put a soft, lingering kiss on Jack's gray cheek.

Connor helped them lift him into the wagon. "Drive it slowly," he ordered Tranter Fox, who was a good man with horses. "I'll ride in the back with him. Watch the ruts, Tranter, and go slow."

"Right you are," said the little miner, hopping onto the seat and gathering up the reins.

"You'll come in the pony cart, Sophie?"

She could feel his suffering, and the panic fluttering just below the surface calm. She touched his hand, whispering urgently, "He may not die, Con. He may not!"

"No, he can't die," he muttered against her hair, voice low and determined. "Hurry home, Sophie. I need you."

She watched him climb into the wagon and settle down next to his brother. Jack's eyes were closed now. On his other side, the Methodist preacher, Reverend Ewell, was bending over him, murmuring, a prayer book in his hand. Tranter jostled the reins, and the big workhorses started up, plodding out of the mine yard.

# XXIII

The theme of this year's Midsummer Day children's play was the same as last year's—Saint Peter at the Gate—but the production had been greatly expanded, chiefly by making it twice as long, and Sophie had to compose music for twelve of Miss Margaret Mareton's dramatic poems instead of only one. Directing from the wing—the wings being a shady, low-branching oak tree that partially shielded her from the audience—Sophie couldn't help thinking that these mini-operas were getting to be too much, and that Miss Mareton had over-reckoned her talents, not to mention the choir's.

Tommy Wooten had the coveted role of Saint Peter this year. The thrust of the plot was who he would let through Heaven's Gate (an impressive construction of papier-mâché, painted with whitewash to look "pearly") and who he would send down to the other place. Waiting to be judged, the children were queued up in pairs, boys and girls together. There wasn't much suspense; most of the dramatic tension had been dissipated by the costumes—dark colors for the sinners destined to be turned away, pastels for the lucky prospective angels. Saint Peter asked each heavenly arrival a few leading questions, a short song was sung, having to do with the good or bad life the child had led as the case might be, and Saint Peter made his judgment.

It was Birdie's turn at the Gates—she was the last. For weeks she'd been vacillating over whether she wanted to be a saint or a sinner, the choice resting entirely on whether she felt she looked better in a dark or light color. She had finally settled on midnight

345

blue, very becoming, but her prolonged indecision meant that instead of learning both parts—the Heaven- or Hell-bound knocker at the Gate—she had never really learned either. Sophie was nervous.

*Knock, knock, knock.* (The papier-mâché lacked that sharp resonance Miss Mareton was after, and so Jeddy Nineways' job, behind a colorful screen depicting Heaven, was to smack a piece of wood with a hammer, in approximate time with the knocker's fist beating on thin air.)

"Who's there?" said Saint Peter, holding the Gate in both hands and peering over the top.

"Florence." (The children had been allowed to name themselves, and Birdie's idol this year was Florence Nightingale.)

"Florence, did you lead a good life?"

"Yes."

Saint Peter looked confused, as well he might; the answer was supposed to be no. "What were you on earth?" he demanded.

"I was a work shirt."

Saint Peter shuffled his feet and darted a glance at Miss Mareton, who was "offstage" behind another oak tree. Sophie felt a grim satisfaction as she bit her lips, trying not to laugh: she'd told Margaret more than once that "work shirker" was too hard to pronounce, and Birdie ought to be allowed to say "lazybones."

"Did you always study your lessons?"

"No, I didn't."

"Did you make your bed every morning?"

"No, I didn't."

"Did you always keep your clothes neat and tidy?"

"Yes."

Saint Peter swallowed audibly. Apparently Birdie couldn't lie, even for art. "Did you take time to feed the hungry, help the needy, and clothe the people who didn't have any?" (Tommy was at an age, ten, when he found it excruciatingly embarrassing to say the word "naked.")

"Well, I always give my sister the rest of my sucker when I'm tired of it."

Saint Peter whispered something.

"No, I didn't," Birdie repeated dutifully.

"Then I cannot let you into the Kingdom of Heaven. You poor work shirker, you must go down to Hades."

This was Birdie's cue to turn around and sing. She turned— but stood silent, having forgotten her first word.

"Oh," Sophie sang softly. Hopefully.

Birdie's face cleared.

"Oh, I wish I'd been a better girl,
I wish I'd said my prayers.
I could've gone to Heaven now,
Right up those pearly stairs (gesturing).

"If I'd obeyed my mum and dad
And stayed away from evil,
I could've been with Jesus now,
Not roasting with the devil."

And so on, for two more verses. Miss Mareton's lyrics might not be inspiring, but they were always to the point. When she finished, Birdie couldn't refrain from bowing and curtseying to the onlookers, even though Miss Mareton had specifically forbidden these kinds of acknowledgments. Now all the players reassembled on either side of the Gate, right for the saints, left for the sinners, to sing the final song. Sophie came out of hiding to direct them, the final song being complicated and somewhat long. Then Saint Peter stepped forward with a last speech—short and didactic, Miss Mareton at her most direct—and the play was over.

Over the heads of the audience, whose applause struck Sophie as a mixture of relieved and amused, she saw Connor. He was laughing. He gave her a humorous salute with his hat, turned, and jogged back to his quoits match, which he had temporarily abandoned in order to watch her little choristers. His reaction tickled her; taking her bows with the children, she had to pretend she was laughing with pleasure at all the clapping and cheering, not her husband's silent drama review.

"That was charming," Rachel Verlaine told Sophie with a twinkle in her eye. "No, truly," she insisted—Sophie must have looked skeptical—"it was a delight. I can't wait until William's old enough to join your choir." They looked down at William, two months old, nothing but his face showing among the swaddling and blankets in his mother's arms.

Sophie thought he looked like his father; something about the curve of his lips, she thought, or the snooty arch of his little eyebrows. "Well, if he's going to be as musical as Lord Moreton, I can't wait either," she replied. "Heaven knows, we could use the talent." Sebastian was an accomplished pianist, she'd been surprised to discover. After a dinner party at Lynton Great Hall last week, he'd played for nearly an hour, beautifully and without a single page of music.

"William get down? Get down?" The yellow-haired toddler grabbing fistfuls of Rachel's skirt was Elizabeth Morrell—and here came her mother, out of breath from chasing her. The three women walked over to the leafy shade of the trees, where Rachel put William down on the soft grass, unwrapped him from his flannel bunting, and, under three pairs of watchful eyes, let Lizzy play with him.

"I broke down and bought your cousin's camera at the rummage sale, Sophie," said Anne, repinning her reddish hair, which had come down.

"So I heard. Did you get a bargain?"

"No, I did not. She wouldn't come down one penny, which I think was extremely crass of her."

"Well, it is for charity."

"Yes, but that's not the point. One *bargains* at a rummage sale, anyone knows that. Honoria's a skinflint, and I told her so."

Sophie and Rachel sent each other amused looks. Who would have thought Anne, of all people, would be tight with a shilling?

"But Lizzy's getting so big, I wanted to start making photographs of her before she's all grown up." She smiled at her daughter, who was kissing William's chubby cheeks and tickling him under his chin, making the baby gurgle. Sophie waited for the stab of pain that still pierced her occasionally when she wasn't on guard. But this time it didn't come.

The church bell struck two. "When are they going to dedicate the plaque, Sophie?" asked Rachel.

"Soon, I think." The town counsel had voted unanimously to erect a bronze plaque on the green to honor the bravery of Jack Pendarvis.

"Will Connor make the speech?"

"No, Uncle Eustace. He wanted to." She and Anne traded a significant glance. Her uncle's turnaround about Connor was a continuing source of wonder to them. He'd repudiated Robert Croddy and thrown his support, political and personal, to his nephew-in-law. Robert, desperate to reingratiate himself, had invited Honoria to the Navy Men's Ball, the social event of the season in Devonport. But Honoria had turned him down, showing unusually keen judgment when she'd called him, to his face, a "social-climbing son of a brewer."

"Look at the newlyweds," Rachel said softly, waving. Sophie and Anne turned to see Sidony and William Holyoake strolling across the green, arm in arm. William was the Verlaines' baby's namesake. "Don't they look happy?"

"Very," said Anne, smiling, waving.

Sophie smiled automatically. She was happy for William and Sidony—who wouldn't be?—but sadness for Jack tempered the gladness, and she thought it always would. They did look blissful together, though, and that was nothing but a good thing. They deserved it.

"Is it true they've moved into the old caretaker's cottage on the grounds?" asked Anne.

"Yes," said Rachel. "Sebastian had it repainted and fixed up for them. William's rooms in the house were too small for two."

"I suppose." Anne had a dreamy, wistful look in her gray eyes, and Sophie wondered what she was thinking.

Just then William the younger let out a squeal—Elizabeth had hugged him with too much exuberance. Before Rachel could pick him up to comfort him, her husband appeared out of nowhere and snatched up his son, crooning to him. Now Lizzy was wailing, too. Anne bent to console her, but just then Christy swooped down and picked up his daughter. Immediately both children stopped crying.

The fathers were sweaty and disheveled from their cricket match, which, Christy announced with undisguised elation, his side had won. Besides cricket, the two men had a love of horses in common, and Sophie enjoyed watching their unlikely friendship grow—the worldly, sophisticated earl and the simple country preacher. But those were only clichés: Christy wasn't really simple, and Sebastian Verlaine was nothing like the jaded "degenerate" some of the villagers had dubbed him not all that long ago. Right now they looked like ordinary proud papas, and smug ones at that, as if they saw no reason not to attribute their children's suddenly angelic behavior to themselves alone.

" 'Scuse me, Mrs. Pendarvis." Tranter Fox snatched off his cap, bowing to everyone like a miniature courtier. "Beg pardon fer intrudin' my nose in this important group."

"What is it, Tranter?"

"Ma'am, yer team 'ave won again, and are waitin' to bestow upon you the game quoit. Not least of all yer very own husband, our friend and new leader, so to say." Whom Tranter had taken to calling R. H., for Right Honorable.

Amid the laughter and congratulations, Sophie told her friends she would see them later, and went off with Tranter to claim her quoit.

The Guelder Hurlers wanted Connor to make the presentation speech, seeing as how he was a Member of Parliament now as well as a champion ring tosser. But he modestly declined, and insisted that Roy Donne, the team captain, do the honors.

"Mrs. Pendarvis, it gives me great pleasure to present—"

"And happiness," Tranter embellished. "Pleasure and happiness."

"It gives me great pleasure and happiness to present to you—"

"Fer the second year in a row."

Roy paused for a long beat, gathering himself. "For the second year in a row," he resumed slowly, "I'm pleased and happy to present to you this—"

"To you our beloved owner. Say that."

"Goddamn it, who's giving this speech?" cried the captain, and not a single man blamed him for cursing.

"Well, me, if ee can't do any better'n that," said Tranter, snatching up the iron ring and shouldering the beefy captain out of the way. "Mrs. Pendarvis, me and the rest o' the Hurlers take pride, pleasure, happiness, and delight in presenting to you, our beloved owner and leader, without who we'd be just a bunch o' tutmen and tributers looking fer work, which even if we found it wouldn't be as good as if you was the one in charge, you bein' the fairest and most evenhanded, so to say, of bosses which any miner could ask for—and miners ask fer plenty, for they'm a pesky lot in general, not given to takin' things as they come, you might—" Loud groaning all around brought him back to the point. "Anyways, here's yer quoit, ma'am, which we presents to you in all 'umbleness and gratefulness fer yer great goodness, beauty, and general perfectness. The Guelder Hurlers remain yer faithful servants in all things. Amen."

It was hard to keep a straight face when Connor was laughing out loud barely six feet away. Sophie kept her acceptance speech short, and didn't forget to wind it up with the part about free drinks at the George for the Hurlers and their friends—that always guaranteed a rousing cheer.

"Tranter has a new lady friend," Connor confided to her when the presentation was over. "Look."

"Oh, my word." She had to turn around and hide her face behind Connor's broad shoulder. "Rose? Rose from the George and Dragon?"

"He says they were made for each other."

Surreptitiously they watched the odd couple stroll off together, holding hands. Rose was pretty, but she was a big girl, no two ways about it. And Tranter—Tranter was almost a midget. From behind, they looked like a mother and her little boy.

"Did you know Jack had a fling with Rose last summer?" Connor said, taking Sophie's hand and starting to walk in the other direction.

"No! Jack did? What happened? Were they really fond of each other?"

"I suppose so, for a little while. Jack never stayed with one woman for long."

"But he loved Sidony," she said softly.

Conner squeezed her hand. "He did."

"I saw her today, with William."

"I did, too. They look right together. Happy."

She nodded. It was true, and it was a good thing. But it still made her sigh.

"Want a funnel cookie?" Connor asked to cheer her up.

She smiled. "You bought me funnel cookies last year—do you remember?"

"Of course. I remember everything about that day. You had on a yellow dress."

"And you had on a blue shirt with no collar. And suspenders."

He laughed, throwing his head back to the clear blue sky. "You gave all your funnel cookies to the ducks."

"I thought you were the handsomest man I'd ever seen."

"You were the prettiest girl in the world. Still are."

"You let me talk about my father."

"You let me kiss you in the churchyard."

They stopped walking. Sometimes the way he looked at her could make her toes curl. "I'd like to kiss you right now," she confessed in a whisper. "And that's not all."

His handsome cheeks pinkened faintly. He leaned over her, secretly stroking his thumb over the center of her palm. "What else?"

"Mm, better not tell you now."

"Tell me."

"You'd get too excited. No telling what you might do."

"Oh, please tell me."

She might have—she was considering it—when Jessica Carnock approached them from the direction of the church rectory and said it was time for the dedication ceremony. Conner made a comical grinding noise Sophie hoped Jessie couldn't hear, and then he charmed the older woman with what she was beginning to think of as his Parliament smile. He'd always had it, a quite beautiful smile, sweet and masculine at the same time. But now that he was a Member for Tavistock in the House of Commons, she'd begun to try to see him as strangers might. She tried to be objective, but it was hard to imagine anyone not finding her husband perfect. A man among men. Especially when she picked out his clothes for him.

"Does Jack need any help?" he asked Mrs. Carnock, strolling toward the crowd that had begun to assemble at the north end of the green. After the dedication, Jack's bronze plaque was going to be embedded in a large granite rock not far from the Maypole.

"No, I don't think so. Maris is with him," she added as she waved to Captain Carnock, who was already waiting for her with the other village notables—the mayor, the vicar and his wife, the lord and lady of the manor, most of the church vestry. Sophie's heart swelled with pride to think that she and Connor, especially Connor, had a rightful place among them, and she made a private vow that she would repay the blessings of God and good fortune by never taking the privilege for granted.

"Go on ahead, Sophie," Connor told her, hanging back. "Here they come from the rectory—I'll give Maris a hand."

"No, I'll wait for you."

Maris and Jack were crossing the High Street at a snail's pace. Jack looked gaunt but spiffy in a red necktie and a sober blue suit, and new shoes. He wasn't very steady on his feet yet—he held a cane in one hand and Maris's arm in the other—but at least he was walking. He'd spent all of May and half of June in bed, and since then he'd mostly gotten about in a wheelchair. But today was a special day, and Dr. Hesselius had said he could attend the ceremony in his honor on his own two feet if he stayed overnight in the village afterward, to avoid exhaustion, and the Morrells had promptly offered him the use of their guest room. Maris would stay overnight, too, of course—she'd become his shadow.

Sophie watched them together, smiling fondly, thinking they were at least as odd-looking as Tranter and Rose. Maris wasn't quite as tall as Jack, but she was at least twice as strong. Sophie had seen her pick him up in her arms with ease. She bathed and fed him, cajoled and entertained him. He could be crabby and she could be tart, but they had grown inseparable. Had Maris been in love with Jack all along? She was now, as anyone with eyes could see. As for him . . . Sophie couldn't be sure. He wasn't a man to lose his heart easily, and he was still afraid to make plans or look too far into the future. But Maris was working on him, slowly but steadily. And subtly. If she were a betting woman, Sophie would put her money on the nurse.

The villagers weren't supposed to applaud until after the ceremony, but as soon as they saw Jack shuffling toward them, they broke into spontaneous clapping. He kept his eyes down, kept walking, acknowledging it with nothing more than a blush. He had a rough, natural dignity Sophie was learning to respect, and not only because it reminded her of his brother's more polished version.

He took his place in the center of the semicircle of dignitaries, Connor on one side, Sophie's uncle on the other. The mayor cleared his throat, and silence fell.

"My friends, my neighbors. Over the years you've heard me give many speeches from this spot. Most of them ran on too long. This one will not, because what I have to say is very simple.

"We all know why we're here and who we've come to honor. Mr. Jack Pendarvis came among us a year ago. He was good-natured and good-hearted, and he made friends quickly. Then he went away. Many people missed him, but none of us knew then that he had the makings of greatness in him, or that three men would one day owe him their lives.

"On the twentieth of April, Jack Pendarvis showed his mettle. When no one else would go, he went down in Guelder mine, risking his very life to free Charles Oldene, Roy Donne, and Roland Coachman. Because of him, these men are here with us today. For this we are deeply grateful, even though two of the rescued men were instrumental in helping the Hurlers defeat the Salem Dragoons for the second year in a row."

Sophie's surprised laughter joined that of the others. Uncle Eustace hardly ever joked, and when he did the result was more often embarrassing than hilarious.

"Today we dedicate this plaque not only to Jack, but to the ideals of bravery, selflessness, and valor. Courage can come at unexpected times, from unexpected sources. We are more than fortunate that it came to Jack Pendarvis at the moment it did. We thank him today most humbly and most sincerely, and we honor him with this memorial in his name, which will remain in this spot long after the last of us is gone. Thank you, Jack. And God keep you."

Connor had been teasing Jack for a week about the speech he would be expected to make, and he'd scoffed every time, insisting his speech would be two words long: "Thank you." But when the cheers and applause died down, he stepped forward and said a little more than that. His gruff voice wouldn't carry far; to hear him, every man, woman, and child on the village green went absolutely quiet.

"Thank you, Mayor. And thank you fer leavin' out the bad part, which everyone here knows anyways, and which I'm still payin' for in my soul. What I done wasn't so much bravery as payback— but that's as may be. What I want to say today is thanks to all o' you, everyone who's been a friend and kind to me in the worst times. I been made to feel like I belong here, and that's worth more to me than even this dandy plaque. Which I expect I'll come t' look at about onct a day fer the next year or two. Anyways, thank you—I can't say it better than that, but I mean it in my heart. And don't ferget to vote fer my brother in the next general election."

Sophie saw a few tears mingled with the laughter in the cheering, appreciative crowd. People wanted to hug him or shake his hand, and she noticed the looks of dismay on their faces when they realized how frail he was. Connor found her in the throng and slipped his arm around her waist. His face was a study: she saw pride and deep emotion, and a shadow of the fear that had been haunting them for weeks. "He's all right, Con. He's going to be fine, I just know it."

"Yes." He nodded vehemently. "He is."

Jack joined them a few minutes later with Maris at his side. "Thank God that's over," he muttered, but there was no hiding the pleasure he'd taken in the proceedings, especially now that they were over. "I been offered drinks at the George by eight miners—and me not allowed so much as a thimbleful, mind—and dinner at the house o' six beautiful faymels, plus three different jobs, not a one o' which I'm able-bodied enough t' do."

"Yet," Sophie put in.

"Congratulations," said Connor. "I thought your speech was wonderful."

"Oh, did ee, now. Maybe speechifying runs in the fam'ly."

"I certainly hope so."

"Ha. Won't be long now, ee'll be standin' up in front o' them swells in the Commons, givin' 'em what for. Con, I'm proud as hell o' you."

"I'm proud of you, Jack."

They said it smilingly, but neither was joking. Misty-eyed, Sophie watched them embrace, and the gentleness with which Connor touched his brother gave her an ache in the chest.

Maris hid her emotion with gruffness. "Haven't you had enough blatherin' and backslappin' for one day, Mr. Big Hero?

Come along inside the vicarage now, it's time for a nap and yer medicine."

Jack said a few Cornish swear words not fit for ladies' ears. But he was tired; it showed in his face and the droop of his shoulders. They said good-bye, and that they'd see him tomorrow. Grumbling from habit, he let Maris lead him away.

The vivid blue sky lightened; the long day slowly drew to a close. Later there would be dancing around a bonfire for the grown-ups, a fireworks display for the children. But after Sophie finished helping Anne and the other vestry ladies clean up from the rummage sale, Connor caught her eye over the heads of a group of men with whom he was having a conversation about taxes, and a silent message passed between them: *Let's go home.*

He watched her wander over to the bridge and lean over the edge, waiting for him, looking at the ducks. She had on a pretty white frock, fresh as the summer day. She'd worn white the first day they'd met. Tall, slender as a reed, she was the essence of grace to him and she always would be. He made an excuse to his companions, keeping it vague, leaving them thinking he might return, and walked out to his wife.

Using him for a shield, so all of Wyckerley couldn't witness her unseemly display of affection, Sophie lifted his hands to her mouth and kissed the backs, slowly, dreamily. "Let's just walk away, Con. Good-byes take forever. No one will even notice we've gone."

He didn't argue. When Sophie had that look in her eye, tender and loving, wonderfully suggestive, there was nothing he wouldn't do to oblige her. They walked down the empty street past the deserted George, the First and Last Inn, Swan's smithy. The thatched, pastel cottages thinned and ended above the crossroads. To the right lay Plymouth, to the left Tavistock and the moor, and straight ahead, Lynton Great Hall. Turning left, north, they took hands and trod the narrow red lane, shady from the arching trees and fragrant hedgerows. Birds twittered in the underbrush and sang good nights across the paling sky. Honeysuckle perfumed the soft evening air, and they slowed their steps, beguiled by the sky, and the birds, and the perfection of the Devon twilight.

The road crested between a new-mown hayfield and the beginning of a dark pine brake. They stopped, turning around in unison to watch the sun drop behind the trees above Wyckerley. It was beautiful, they murmured to each other; everything was so beautiful.

"Will you work on your speech tonight?" Sophie wondered, leaning against him.

"I may." He'd won the by-election three weeks ago, and meant to go to London next month to take his seat. The House adjourned in August, which didn't leave much time for his maiden address. The Speaker might not recognize him at all, in which case he'd have to wait and worry about it until November.

"It must be nerve-racking, not knowing when you're going to address three or four hundred of your new colleagues for the first time. Aren't you nervous?"

"Nervous? No, no, certainly not. Scared to death."

"But you'll be wonderful, I know you will. I want to be there when you stand up to speak."

"I don't see how you can be, darling, unless you stay in London all summer."

"I know." She sighed. "At least I'll be there on your first day. Looking down at you from the Strangers' Gallery. Oh, God, Con, I'll be so proud of you! I hope I don't cry."

"I hope you don't laugh."

"Silly." She wound her arms around him. "You'll be magnificent. You'll change the world. England will never be the same."

He chuckled, but answered her seriously. "Reform comes so slowly. Tomorrow the queen's signing a bill into law that finally does away with the property qualification, Sophie. Do you know how long the Chartists have been fighting for that? More than thirty years."

"But change *should* come slowly, shouldn't it? Slowly and

thoughtfully. That's what makes our constitutional monarchy great."

"Spoken like a true Tory."

"Not in the least. I just don't think we should reform everything all at once."

"No danger of that. What I worry about is change coming so slowly, working men and women won't wait for it; they'll abandon the country and move to the cities to survive. And that would be a great shame."

She gazed out across the darkened landscape she knew and loved so well. "Yes, it would." Beyond the hay field, she could see pale, cottony clouds of steam puffing from Guelder's smokestacks; to the south, the black chimneys of Lynton Hall scored the sky; and to the west, the cross of All Saints Church towered like a blessing over the land. She slipped her arm in his. "Well, I'm determined to be a good parliamentary wife to you, Con, even when we don't agree on politics."

He smiled down at her. "That's nice to know."

"Repopulating the countryside, now, that's an important issue. I for one think it's a job that should begin at home."

How she loved the sound of his laughter. "Sophie, I adore you." They took hands and turned toward home, hurrying, eager to do their part for the country.

If you've fallen in love with Wyckerley, don't miss the other marvelous novels in Patricia Gaffney's beloved trilogy. Return to the place where enhancing romance and unexpected passions meet. . . .

# To Love and To Cherish

and

# To Have and To Hold

NAL TRADE PAPERBACKS
COMING IN SPRING 2003

Turn the page for a special early preview . . .

# To Love and To Cherish

EVEN ON HIS DEATHBED, Lord D'Aubrey was a hard man to love.

*God, give me patience and humility,* prayed Reverend Christian Morrell, who was in the business, as it were, of loving the unlovable. Leaning over the bed but not touching it—ill as he was, the elderly viscount still bristled when anyone except his doctor got too close—Christy asked his lordship if he would take the sacraments.

"Why? So I can go straight to heaven? Do you think I'm going to heaven, Vicar? Eh? Think I'm—" He ran out of breath; his parchment-colored face turned blue until he sucked in a wheezing gulp of air. By now he was too weak to cough; he kept swallowing until the spasm passed, then lay exhausted, hands limp on his sunken chest.

Christy sat down again in the high-backed chair he'd pulled as close to the bed as the old man would allow. *Dr. Hesselius ought to be here,* he couldn't help thinking. "Send for me if you need me, but I doubt that you will," he'd told Christy two hours ago, in this room. "He's not in any pain—they frequently aren't at this late stage. I doubt he'll live through the day. I've done all I can; old Edward's in your hands now, Reverend." Christy had nodded at that, gravely, calmly, as if the prospect didn't demoralize him.

In his own estimation, at least on good days, he was a reasonably effective clergyman, considering he was new at his calling and his best qualities were still only earnestness and perseverance. But he had numerous failings, and they had a perverse way of multiplying and combining at extreme times like this, when his deepest wish was to give comfort and consolation to the needy. Edward Verlaine offered a special challenge, and Christy despaired that he wasn't up to it.

Memories kept intruding on his best efforts to pray. In the sparsely furnished room, a dark, gilt-framed oil painting of Lord D'Aubrey's grandfather loomed conspicuously over the mantelpiece; a peculiar grayish blur under the haughty-looking ancestor's nose made Christy smile, albeit a bit grimly. He recalled the day, probably twenty years ago now, when he and Geoffrey, his best friend, had stolen into this room, giggling and shushing each other, giddy with nervous excitement. Christy hadn't really believed Geoffrey would do it, but he had: he'd stood on a chair and drawn a charcoal mustache on the scowling face of his great-grandfather. Faint traces still lingered, the charcoal having proven remarkably resistant to numerous efforts at removal. Christy wondered if Geoffrey still bore the marks from the thrashing his father had ordered for punishment—delivered by his steward, not himself, for even in his rages Edward Verlaine had kept his distance.

The words in Christy's Book of Common Prayer began to run together. He rolled his stiff shoulders, fighting off the sleepiness that kept dragging at him. He stood up and went to the window. Drawing back the curtain, he looked out past Lynton Great Hall's derelict courtyard toward the tall black spire of All Saints Church, half a mile away and all that could be seen from here of Wyckerley, the village where he'd grown up. It was April; the gentle, oak-covered hills were a brilliant yellow-green, and the Wyck, normally a placid little river within its steep-sided banks, churned down from Dartmoor with the force of a torrent. He and Geoffrey had fished in the Wyck year-round, ridden their ponies up and down every sunken red lane in the parish, left urgent messages for each other in a crevice of the gray stone monolith at the crossroads. They'd been all but inseparable for the first sixteen years of their lives—until Geoffrey had run away. In twelve years, Christy hadn't heard a word from him.

Until six days ago, when a note had come to the rectory. "Just tell me when the bastard croaks," Geoffrey had scribbled on the back of a tailor's bill—and that only after Christy had written repeatedly to the London address he'd finally gotten from Lord D'Aubrey's solicitor. "How the hell are you?" he'd scrawled in a postscript. "You're joking, aren't you? A *minister*? ?"

Christy wasn't surprised that his new vocation seemed like a joke to Geoffrey, considering all the times that, as boys, they'd made fun of Christy's gentle, pious father. "Old Vicar," the villagers called Magnus Morrell now, although he'd been dead for four years; and Christy, inevitably, was "New Vicar." Stories of Geoffrey's wild, decadent life in London and other worldly fleshpots were hard to reconcile with competing and almost equally incredible rumors that he was a mercenary soldier, ready to take up arms for any cause that paid enough money for his services. Christy had stopped missing him—even the deepest wound heals in time—but he'd never stopped wondering what had become of him.

A noise from the bed made him start. The viscount's face, yellow with jaundice, had turned on the pillow; he was glaring at him. "You." It came out an accusing croak. "Don't want you. Where's your father?"

"My father's dead, sir," he reminded him gently, leaning over the bed.

Recollection took the anger out of the old man's hard black eyes, but a truly ghastly smile curled at the corners of his mouth. "Then I'll see him soon enough, won't I?"

Christy fumbled with his prayer book, reconsidered, and laid it aside. He hated the pain he felt at this moment, and the inadequacy, and the trivial sound of all the things that came into his mind to say. He felt like a child again—like the boy who had grown up terrified of this dying wreck of a man, hating him on principle because Geoffrey, his best friend, had hated him.

He bent closer, into the old man's line of vision. "Would you like to pray?"

Out of habit, the viscount's eyes narrowed with contempt. A moment passed. He turned his face away. "You pray," he exhaled on a feeble sigh.

Christy opened his book to the Psalms. "The Lord is my shepherd," he began, prosaically enough; "I shall not want. He maketh me to lie down in green pastures; he leadeth me beside the still waters. He restoreth my soul—' "

"Not that one. Before that."

"The—"

"The twenty-second." His eyes closed in exhaustion, but the bloodless lips curved again, sardonic. "Read it, Parson," he rasped when Christy hesitated.

He scanned the seldom-read psalm in dismay. "My God, my God, why hast thou forsaken me? Why art thou so far from helping me, and from the words of my roaring?' " He read the prayer in a low voice, but it wasn't possible to soften the desperate message. "They cried unto thee, and were delivered; they trusted in thee, and were not confounded. But I am a worm, and no man; a reproach of men, and despised of the people. All they that see me laugh me to scorn . . .' "

A sound silenced him; he looked up. Edward's eyes were closed, his jaws clamped in a grimace; but, for all his efforts, tears trickled through his papery lids. Christy reached for one of his hands and held it tightly, while the viscount's weeping turned into weak, desolate cursing. The words became garbled as he grew more agitated. He gave Christy's wrist a feeble yank. "Do it," he muttered. "Do it, damn you."

He stared at him, baffled. "I don't—"

*"Absolve me."*

Christy looked down at the fierce, spidery grip the old man had on his hand. "Almighty God," he prayed quickly, "who desireth not the death of a sinner, but rather that he may turn from his wickedness and live, hath given power to his ministers to declare and pronounce to his people the absolution of their sins. Edward, do you truly and earnestly repent of your sins?"

"I do," he grated through his teeth, eyes closed.

"Are you in love and charity with your neighbors—"

"Yes, yes."

"And—will you lead a new life, following the commandments of God and walking from henceforth in his holy ways?"

"Yes!"

"Go in peace, then. Your sins are forgiven."

The viscount peered up at him in panicky disbelief.

"They're forgiven," Christy repeated, insistent. "The God who made you loves you. Believe it."

"If I could . . ."

"You can. Take it inside your heart and be at peace."

"Peace." His hand loosened and fell away, but he continued to gaze up with pleading eyes. All the hopes of his life had narrowed and funneled into this one hope; that he was loved, and that he was forgiven. Christy was learning that at the end it was all anyone wanted.

"My lord," he asked, "will you take the sacraments?"

A minute went by, and then the old man nodded.

Christy prepared the bread and the wine quickly, using the bedside table for an altar, reciting the words of the ritual in a voice loud enough for Edward to hear. He was to ill to swallow more than a tiny morsel of the Host, and he could only wet his lips on the edge of the chalice. Afterward, he lay utterly still, the flutter of the wilted lace on his nightshirt the only indication that he still breathed.

Time ticked past in the dim box of a room; the lamp wick began to sputter, and Christy rose to turn it higher. A choking sound from the bed made him turn back quickly.

Edward was trying to sit up on his elbows. "Help me . . . help . . . oh, God, I hate it . . . I'm afraid of the dark . . ." Christy put his arm around his thin shoulders, propping him up. "Geoffrey?" He stared straight ahead, unblinking. "Geoffrey?"

"Yes," Christy lied without hesitation. "Yes, Father, it's Geoffrey."

"My boy." His smile was rapturous, a little smug. "I knew you'd come." His head bobbed once and fell on his left shoulder; a long, ragged sigh rattled up from his chest, but he was already dead.

Christy held him in his arms a little longer before laying his slack torso back on the bed and gently closing his eyes. "Go in peace," he murmured, "for the Lord has put away all your sins." The unmistakable aspect of death had already seeped into the viscount's corpse; his soul was gone. Christy administered the last sacrament, the anointing of the body with oil, taking a melancholy comfort in the solemn rite. When he finished, he sank to his knees by the bed to pray, hands folded, his forehead pressed against the side of the mattress.

That was how Geoffrey found him.

Christy hadn't heard footsteps but something, maybe a change in the air, made him lift his head and look toward the doorway to the hall. A tall, dark-haired man stood in the threshold. Sallow skin, sunken cheeks, black, burning eyes in hollow sockets—for one grotesque moment, Christy thought it was Edward, returned from the dead in the semblance of his youth. But a second later, a flesh-and-blood woman materialized behind the man's shoulder, and Christy realized he wasn't seeing ghosts. He got to his feet in haste.

He met Geoffrey in the middle of the room. He would have embraced him, but Geoffrey held out his hand and they shook instead, clapping each other on the back. "My God, it's true," Geoffrey cried, his voice sounding shockingly loud after the long silence. "You've gone and become a priest!"

"As you see." His gladness gave way to concern as he took in his oldest friend's profoundly altered appearance. At sixteen, Geoffrey had been a strapping, muscular youth; when they'd wrestled together, they'd almost always fought to a draw, and on the rare occasions when Christy had won, it was only because he was taller. Now Geoffrey looked as if a well-placed blow from a child could knock him down. But his charming, wolfish grin hadn't changed, and Christy found himself smiling back, wanting to laugh with him in spite of the somber circumstances of this meeting. "Geoffrey, thank God you've come. Your father—"

"Is he dead?" He moved around him to the bedside without waiting for an answer. "Oh, my, yes," he said softly, staring down at the still corpse. "He's dead, all right, no question about that."

Christy stayed where he was, to give Geoffrey a little time to himself. The woman in the doorway hadn't moved. She was slim, tall, dressed sedately in a dark brown traveling costume; the veiled brim of her hat cast a shadow over her face. He glanced at her curiously, but she didn't speak.

Geoffrey had his back to the room; Christy tried to read his emotion from the set of his shoulders, but the rigid posture was unrevealing. After another minute, he crossed to the bed to stand beside him, and together they gazed down at Edward's lifeless face. "He didn't suffer at the end," Christy said quietly. "It was a peaceful death."

"Was it? He looks ghastly, doesn't he? What was wrong with him, anyway?"

"A disease of the liver."

"Liver, eh?" There was no hint of sorrow in his frowning, narrow-eyed countenance; rather, Christy had the unnerving impression that he was scrutinizing the body to assure himself it was really dead.

"He asked for your before he died."

Geoffrey looked up at that, incredulous, then burst into high, hearty laughter. "Oh, that's good. That's very good!"

Dismayed, Christy looked away. The woman had come farther into the room; in the shadowy lamplight, her eyes glowed an odd silver-gray color. He couldn't read the expression in them, but the set of her wide, straight mouth was ironic.

"I think he was sorry at he end," he tried again. "For everything. I believe he felt remorse in his heart for—" This time Geoffrey cut him off with a crude, appallingly vulgar oath that made Christy blush. The woman arched one dark brow at him; he'd have said she was mocking him, but there was no playfulness in her face.

Then Geoffrey flashed his charming smile, and the anger in his eyes disappeared as if it had never been. He spun away from the bed and draped his arm across Christy's shoulders, giving him a rough, affectionate squeeze. "How've you been, you ruddy old sod? You look . . ." He stood back and made a show of examining him, head to toe. "Christ, you *still* look like an archangel!" He ruffled Christy's blond hair, laughing, and under his breath Christy caught the unmistakable odor of alcohol. He stiffened involuntarily. All the things he could have said about Geoffrey's appearance seemed either tactless or hurtful, so he didn't answer.

"Come on, let's get out of here," Geoffrey urged, guiding him toward the door. Christy resisted, and Geoffrey stopped short, adjacent to the silent, motionless woman. "Oh—sorry, darling, forgot about you there. This is Christian Morrell, an old chum from my halcyon youth. Christy, meet my wife, Anne. Anne, Christy. Christy, Anne. Shake hands, why don't you? That's it! Now let's all go have a drink."

"How do you do, Reverend Morrell," murmured Anne Verlaine, unsmiling, ignoring her husband's facetiousness.

Christy struggled to hide his surprise. Rumors about Geoffrey were always rife in Wyckerley, had been since he'd run away at sixteen and never returned. About four years ago Christy had heard that he'd married the daughter of an artist, a painter; but the next rumor had him off fighting the Burmese in Pegu, and there was no more talk of a wife. As a consequence, Christy had assumed that the marriage was just another in the colorful catalog of stories about the village's prodigal son that might not be true but never failed to entertain the natives.

"Mrs. Verlaine," he greeted her, taking the cool, firm hand she held out to him. She was younger than he'd thought at first, probably not even twenty-five. Her accent was English, but there was something distinctly foreign about her; something in her dress, he thought, or the penetrating directness of her gaze.

"No, no, it's not Mrs. Verlaine anymore, is it? It's Lady D'Aubrey! How does it feel to be a viscountess, darling? Frankly I can't wait for someone to call me 'my lord.' Come on, we must go and drink to Father's demise. It took him long enough, but better late than never, what?" Geoffrey's arm around his wife's waist looked steely; she resisted for only a moment, then let him lead her out of the room. Christy had no choice but to follow.

# To Have and To Hold

"But it is too rude of you, Bastian! How can you send me away like this? Don't you like Lili anymore?"

"I adore you," Sebastian Verlaine avowed, prying away the grip of his mistress's tiny white hand, clamped to his thigh like a nutcracker. Through the carriage window, he watched the chimneys of Lynton Great Hall, his dubious inheritance, recede behind a screen of ancient oak trees. He couldn't help liking the look of his new house. But it was hard to sustain admiration for its rough granite grandeur when he thought of everything that was broken, peeling, crumbling, smoking, or leaking, and how much even rudimentary repairs were going to cost him.

"And have we not had a nice time? Did we not play lovely games in your new *baignoire*? Eh? Bastian, listen to me!"

"It was paradise, my sweet," he answered automatically, kissing her fingers. They smelled of perfume and sex, an essence he wasn't capable of appreciating just now, at least not in any way that required virility. Enough occasionally was enough, and four days and nights in the intimate company of Lili Duchamps was, as the lady herself would put it, *plus qu'il n'en faut*—more than enough.

"*Oui, paradis,*" she agreed, insinuating her index finger between his lips and tapping his teeth with her fingernail. "Put off your silly men's business and come to London with me. We have never made love on a train, *oui*?"

"Not with each other," he conceded after a second's thought. He bit down on her finger hard enough to make her snatch it away and glare at him. It would have been amusing to say, "You're beautiful when you're angry," but it wouldn't have been true.

"Oh, you are cruel! To send me off all alone to—to— *Plymouth*—" she made it sound like *Antarctica*— "and make me ride on the train to London all by myself—*c'est barbare, c'est vil!*"

"But you *came* by yourself," he pointed out reasonably, "and now you just have to do everything in reverse." Past her lavishly styled, champagne-colored hair, he watched the quaint parade of thatched-roof cottages glide by as the carriage bumped and rumbled up Wyckerley's cobblestoned High Street. The cottages were charming, he supposed, with their fat dormers, profuse gardens, and pastel fronts; but his aesthetic appreciation was tempered by the thought that his own tenants probably lived in half of them. Then they weren't so charming. Then, like the manor house, they were just a lot of old buildings that needed his money and attention.

"But *why* can you not come with me? Why? Ooh, I hate you for this!" She drew back her hand, but he grabbed it before she could strike him. By now he knew her shallow tempers; she rarely caught him off guard anymore. "Take care," he said in the soft, menacing tone with which he'd originally seduced her; the fact that it still worked was one reason their affair was growing stale. "Do not try my patience, *ma chère*, or I'll have to punish you."

The lurid flare of excitement in her eyes made him laugh— spoiling the mood. "Oh!" she cried, thumping him on the chest with her fist. "Beast! Cad! Ungrateful bitch!"

"No, darling, that's *you*," he corrected, holding her hands still in her lap. Lili's English wasn't fluent, and sometimes she called him the things her own spurned lovers called her. "Now, kiss me and say good-bye. Justice is waiting for me."

"Who? Oh, your silly court business." Suddenly her peevish scowl lifted. "I know—Bastian, I will come with you and watch!"

"No, you will not." The good souls of Wyckerley already worried that their new viscount was a degenerate; one look at Lili and their worst fears would be confirmed. He wanted to save them from that, or at least delay the awful truth a little longer.

"*Mais oui*! I want to see you in your black robes and your *perruque*, sending poor criminals to the *guillotine*."

"Ah, darling, what charming blood lust." He leaned across the carriage seat, intending to retrieve his walking stick. Lili intercepted the move by seizing his hand and pressing it to her powdered white bosom, inhaling to inflate it to the maximum—a needless augmentation of an already prodigious endowment. In fact, Lili's bust was what had first attracted Sebastian, four months ago at the Théâtre de la Porte, where she'd made her debut in *Faust* as the living statue of la Belle Hélenè—a good role for her because it didn't require her to speak. Despite her reputation as one of the most heartless of the *grandes horizontales*, she'd proven an easy conquest: one intimate supper at Tortoni's, absinthe afterward at the Café des Variétés, and then the *coup de grâce*, a pair of diamond eardrops in the bottom of a bottle of Pontet-Canet—*et voilá*, they were disporting themselves on the black satin sheets in her gaudy rue Frochot apartment. She'd been his mistress ever since, but she wouldn't be for much longer. They both knew it—how could they not? They were professionals, he as keeper, she as kept; they knew how to recognize the first stirrings of ennui before it could blossom into full-fledged contempt.

With a little shimmy, Lili got her left breast into the center of his palm; he felt the nipple harden into a warm little peak. She uncovered her teeth in a carnivorous smile and slipped one of her knees over his.

The carriage had just stopped at the entrance to Wyckerley's exceedingly modest town hall, or "moot hall" as they still called it, inside of which two magistrates and who knew how many poor criminals were waiting for him to help dispense justice in the petty session. Pedestrians were passing on the street, staring openly at the new D'Aubrey brougham, while above, the coachman waited patiently for his lordship to alight. Satisfying Lili didn't take long, Sebastian knew from experience, and sending her away happy would be the better part of discretion. But the logistics, not to mention a disinterest that might be temporary but was nevertheless profound, defeated him. With a sigh, he gave her luscious breast a soft farewell squeeze and withdrew his hand.

Predictably, her eyes flashed with anger—"eyes like multifaceted marcasite, their soft glance more stimulating than a caress," according to a so-called critic in one of the Paris theater revues. Not so predictably, her dainty little hand drew back and slapped him hard across the cheek; he barely caught her wrist before she could do it again. *"Pourceau,"* she spat, her long-nailed fingers curving into claws. *"Bâtard.* I loathe you." But the lascivious look was back, and it grew heavier, lewder, the harder he squeezed the bones in her wrist. All at once the carnal gleam in her eyes irritated him. They'd played this game too often, and now he was mildly repelled, not aroused by it.

She must have seen his disgust; when he pushed her away she made no protest, and except for one brief, longing look at his cane, she seemed to be through with violence. *"Au revoir,* then," she said airily, pulling up her low bodice, patting her hair, every inch the insouciant *coquotte* once more. "Darling, how do you say *'je m'embête'* in English?"

" *'I'm bored,'* " he answered fervently.

*"Exactement.* So I will leave you to your so *bourgeois* business affairs. When you are next in London, you must do me a great favor, Bastian. *S'il vous plaît,* do not come to see me."

*"Enchanté,"* he murmured, privately amazed that she was letting him off this easily. The Comte de Turenne had been foolish enough to break off his liaison with Lili while dining at the Maison D'Or, where she'd retaliated by dumping a plate of Rhine carp *à la Chambord* in his lap.

He opened the door and sprang down to the pavement, breathing deeply of the unperfumed air. "John will take you to the posting inn where the Plymouth mail coach stops, Lili. I'd let you have my carriage, but then, how would I get home?" He gave a Gallic shrug, enjoying the tightening of her carmine lips. "You'll be fine," he said more kindly. "John will wait with you and see that you're safely ensconced and on your way." He reached into the inside pocket of his frock coat and withdrew a jeweler's box. He flipped it to her in a quick underhand lob she couldn't have been expecting. But with the dexterity of a cricket ace, she threw her hand up and caught it—*chunk*. Like lead to a magnet, Sebastian analogized; or a lure to a great, hungry bass. "I wish you well," he said in French. Less truthfully he added, "I treasure our time together. You may be sure I'll never forget you."

Mollified by the gift more than the words, she lifted her chin and her theatrical eyebrows in what she no doubt intended to be a regal look; he could imagine her practicing it in front of one of the dozen or so mirrors in her boudoir. "Good-bye, Bastian. You are a terrible man, I do not know why I put out with you."

He grinned. "That's put *up* with me, darling—although your way is closer to the mark." She was softening, she was all but ready to forgive him. To forestall her, he swept off his hat and made a low, fatuous bow. *"Adieu, m'amour.* Be happy. My heart goes with you." Before she could respond, he slammed the door, sent John a discreetly urgent look, and backed away to the curb, keeping his hand on his breast as if overcome with feeling. The carriage jerked away, and he had a last glimpse of her scowling face, cheeks just beginning to flush with anger as she realized he was mocking her—for whatever else Lili might be, she wasn't stupid. But it scarcely mattered now, and all he could feel as he watched the coach turn the corner and disappear was relief.